Praise for *Coal Creek*

'Told in sinewy, taciturn prose, *Coal Creek* is a brilliantly realised character piece.'

— *The Herald* (Glasgow)

'[Miller's] most recent novel, *Coal Creek*, may well be his finest work. It is an astonishing story of love caught up in a savage injustice . . . the novel triumphs through the evocation of the bush as an intimidating wonder ready to test all comers.'

— Eileen Battersby, *Irish Times*

'Alex Miller's *Coal Creek* is a triumph. If ever there were an example of a novelist simultaneously commanding yet somehow at the mercy of a character's voice, this is it.'

— Tim Winton, *The Australian*, Best Books of 2013

'Miller has been a master of visceral description from as long ago as the first novel he published . . . What might also be considered are the likenesses, more than ever apparent, between his career and that of Patrick White. Each draws deeply on his youthful experience working in the outback. Each writes of the making of art. They are alike adept at acrid comedies of manners.'

— *Weekend Australian*

'It's difficult to shake off the sense that in *Coal Creek* Miller has struck a kind of grace note in a literary career already lauded for a certain touch of resonant genius. For *Coal Creek* is that rare, mystifyingly powerful novel that lodges itself, unbidden, deep in the human marrow . . . Miller brings a rare empathy and melodic power to this tale which is, at one level, a timeless tale of friendship and love, betrayal and injustice. At another it is like a ballad to country – timeless, evocative, and unforgettable.'

— *West Australian*

Praise for *Autumn Laing*

'. . . in many respects Miller's best yet . . . a penetrating and moving examination of long-dead dreams and the ravages of growing old.'

— *Times Literary Supplement*

'A beautiful book.'

— *Irish Times*

'Such riches. All of Alex Miller's wisdom and experience—of art, of women and what drives them, of writing, of men and their ambitions—and every mirage and undulation of the Australian landscape are here, transmuted into rare and radiant fiction. An indispensable novel.'

— *Australian Book Review*

'That Alex Miller in a seemingly effortless fashion is able to gouge out the innermost recesses of the artistic soul in his latest novel, *Autumn Laing*, speaks volumes about the command he has of his craft and the insights that a lifetime of wrestling with his own creative impulses has brought. Miller has invested this story of art and passion with his own touch of genius and it is, without question, a triumph of a novel.'

— *Canberra Times, Panorama*

'Miller has fun with his cast of characters and humour, while black, ripples through the narrative, leavening Autumn's more corrosive judgements and insights. Miller engages so fully with his female characters that divisions between the sexes seem to melt away and all stand culpable, vulnerable, human on equal ground. Miller is also adept at taking abstract concepts—about art or society—and securing them in the convincing form of his complex, unpredictable characters and their vivid interior monologues.'

— *The Monthly*

'Few writers have Miller's ability to create tension of this depth out of old timbers such as guilt, jealousy, selfishness, betrayal, passion and vision. *Autumn Laing* is more than just beautifully crafted. It is inhabited by characters whose reality challenges our own.'

— *Saturday Age, Life & Style*

Praise for *Lovesong*

'With *Lovesong*, one of our finest novelists has written perhaps his finest book . . . *Lovesong* explores, with compassionate attentiveness, the essential solitariness of people. Miller's prose is plain, lucid, yet full of plangent resonance.'

— The Age

'Miller's brilliant, moving novel captures exactly that sense of a story-built life—wonderful and terrifying in equal measure, stirring and abysmal, a world in which both heaven and earth remain present, yet stubbornly out of reach.'

— Sunday Age

'*Lovesong* is a limpid and elegant study of the psychology of love and intimacy. The characterisation is captivating and the framing metafictional narrative skilfully constructed.'

— Australian Book Review

'. . . a ravishing, psychologically compelling work from one of our best . . .'

— Courier Mail

'. . . another triumph: lyrical, soothing and compelling. Miller enriches human fragility with literary beauty . . .'

— Newcastle Herald

'The intertwining stories are told with gentleness, some humour, some tragedy and much sweetness. Miller is that rare writer who engages the intellect and the emotions simultaneously, with a creeping effect.'

— Bookseller & Publisher

'With exceptional skill, Miller records the ebb and flow of emotion . . . *Lovesong* is a poignant tale of infidelity; but it is more than that. It is a manifesto for the novel, a tribute to the human rite of fiction with the novelist officiating.'

— Australian Literary Review

Praise for *Landscape of Farewell*

'The latest novel by the Australian master, so admired by other writers, and a work of subtle genius.'

— Sebastian Barry

'*Landscape of Farewell* is a triumph.'

— Hilary McPhee

'Alex Miller is a wonderful writer, one that Australia has been keeping secret from the rest of us for too long.'

— John Banville

'*Landscape of Farewell* has a rare level of wisdom and profundity. Few writers since Joseph Conrad have had so fine an appreciation of the equivocations of the individual conscience and their relationship to the long processes of history . . . [It is] a very human story, passionately told.'

— *Australian Book Review*

'As readers of his previous novels—*The Ancestor Game, Prochownik's Dream, Journey to the Stone Country*—will know, Miller is keenly interested in inner lives. *Landscape of Farewell* continues his own quest, and in doing so, speaks to his reader at the deepest of levels. He juggles philosophical balls adroitly in prose pitched to an emotional perfection. Every action, every comma, is loaded with meaning. As one expects from the best fiction, the novel transforms the reader's own inner life. Twice winner of the Miles Franklin Award, it is only a matter of time before Miller wins a Nobel. No Australian has written at this pitch since Patrick White. Indeed, some critics are comparing him with Joseph Conrad.'

— *Daily News,* New Zealand

Praise for *Prochownik's Dream*

'Assured and intense . . . truly gripping . . . This is a thoroughly engrossing piece of writing about the process of making art, a revelatory transformation in fact.'

— *Australian Bookseller & Publisher*

'With this searing, honest and exhilarating study of the inner life of an artist, Alex Miller has created another masterpiece.'

— *Good Reading*

'*Prochownik's Dream* is an absorbing and satisfying novel, distinguished by Miller's enviable ability to evoke the appearance and texture of paintings in the often unyielding medium of words.'

— Andrew Riemer, *Sydney Morning Herald*

'Miller is a master storyteller.'

— *The Monthly*

'A beautiful novel of ideas which never eclipse the characters.'

— *The Age*

Praise for *Journey to the Stone Country*

'The most impressive and satisfying novel of recent years. It gave me all the kinds of pleasure a reader can hope for.'

— Tim Winton

'A terrific tale of love and redemption that captivates from the first line.'

— Nicholas Shakespeare, author of *The Dancer Upstairs*

'Miller's fiction has a mystifying power that is always far more than the sum of its parts . . . his footsteps—softly, deftly, steadily—take you places you may not have been, and their sound resonates for a long time.'

— Andrea Stretton, *Sydney Morning Herald*

Praise for *Conditions of Faith*

'This is an amazing book. The reader can't help but offer up a prayerful thank you: Thank you, God, that human beings still have the audacity to write like this.'

— *Washington Post*

'I think we shall see few finer or richer novels this year . . . a singular achievement.'

— Andrew Riemer, *Australian Book Review*

'A truly significant addition to our literature.'

— *The Australian*

'My private acid test of a literary work is whether, having read it, it lingers in my mind afterward. *Conditions of Faith* fulfils that criterion; I am still thinking about Emily.'

— Colleen McCulloch

Praise for *The Sitters*

'Like Patrick White, Miller uses the painter to portray the ambivalence of art and the artist. In *The Sitters* is the brooding genius of light. Its presence is made manifest in Miller's supple, painterly prose which layers words into textured moments.'

— Simon Hughes, *Sunday Age*

Praise for *The Ancestor Game*

'A wonderful novel of stunning intricacy and great beauty.'

— Michael Ondaatje

'Extraordinary fictional portraits of China and Australia.'

—*New York Times Book Review*

'A major new novel of grand design and rich texture, a vast canvas of time and space, its gaze outward yet its vision intimate and intellectually abundant.'

— *The Age*

Praise for *The Tivington Nott*

'*The Tivington Nott* abounds in symbols to stir the subconscious. It is a rich study of place, both elegant and urgent.'

— *The Age*

'An extraordinarily gripping novel.'

— *Melbourne Times*

'Altogether brilliant. This man knows his hunting country.'

—*Somerset County Gazette*

'In a virtuoso exhibition, Miller's control never once falters.'

— *Canberra Times*

Also by Alex Miller

ALEX MILLER

THE PASSAGE OF LOVE

ALLEN&UNWIN

First published in Australia in 2017 by Allen & Unwin
First published in Great Britain in 2018 by Allen & Unwin

Allen & Unwin
c/o Atlantic Books
Ormond House
26–27 Boswell Street
London WC1N 3JZ

Phone: 020 7269 1610
Fax: 020 7430 0916
Email: UK@allenandunwin.com
Web: www.allenandunwin.com/uk

A CIP catalogue record for this book is available from the British Library.

Trade paperback ISBN 978 1 76063 066 9
Ebook ISBN 978 1 76063 825 2

Text design by Sandy Cull
Set in 12/20 pt Granjon by Bookhouse, Sydney
Printed in Great Britain by Bell and Bain Ltd, Glasgow

10 9 8 7 6 5 4 3 2 1

For Stephanie

PART ONE

1
—

When I drove the twenty kilometres from my home to the prison it was a soft cloudless afternoon such as we often enjoy here before the summer heat arrives. Once I'd left the last houses of the town behind, the road wound through the low hills of the box-ironbark forest. The original native timber of the forest trees was harvested in the nineteenth century to fuel the steam engines of the goldmines that then flourished in the area. In the more than one hundred years since it was felled, the forest has regrown into a modified version of its native form. Each stump of what was once a single tree now supports several trunks, giving the impression of a uniform age to the trees, as if the forest had always been there just as I was seeing it that afternoon, timeless and undisturbed. But for some time, for years, after the tree-fellers left, there must have been a disheartening expanse of bare stumps. It was this image that remained with me as I drove on.

The road emerged from the forest and passed through the old township of Maldon. The modest mid-Victorian buildings on either side of the main street remain much as they were at the time the forest was felled. When goldmining ceased in the early part of the twentieth century, the town, like the forest, was more or less abandoned. Two or three kilometres beyond the town I crested a hill and a view of extensive grasslands opened out in front of me. The treeless savannah was interrupted here and there by the bold forms of rounded hills topped with enormous granite boulders. From a distance these grey, lichen-adorned boulders looked like shaggy prehistoric beasts at rest, the progress of their journey arrested by some mysterious instinct.

A large green sign advertised the prison. I didn't want to arrive before the scheduled time of my talk, so I didn't drive into the prison grounds yet but parked in the shade on the side of the road. I could see the prison through the roadside trees: a cluster of new buildings, low and neat, painted a pale shade of green. Until I was invited to speak to the members of the prison book club, I'd thought young male offenders were held there, as in the dreaded borstals of my childhood in London. Among us school-boys the borstal had a fearsome reputation as a place where brutal older boys and vicious guards would tyrannise us. The idea of the place terrified us. The boys from among our number whose rebellious natures attracted the attention of the authorities and who were sent to borstal, we knew to be lost to us and to the small compass of our lives forever. I had no memory of any boy ever returning. I suppose they did return, or some of them surely did. Others, their temperament of rebellion confirmed by the brutality of the experience, no doubt moved on to prisons for adult men.

We knew from an early age that the forces of the law were not for our protection but for the protection of property. And as we and our parents possessed no property that needed protecting, the only times we saw the police in our neighbourhood streets were when they came to arrest one of our fathers, usually on suspicion of stealing someone else's property that they, the police, had failed to protect. The friendly English bobby was not a feature of our Council estate.

In 1963, when I was a student at the University of Melbourne and was reading the English Romantics and the humanist educators of the Italian Renaissance, the borstal came to my attention once again. Though it was not prescribed reading in any of my courses, it was the Irish writer Brendan Behan's novel *Borstal Boy* that left the strongest impression on me during my second year at Melbourne. In Behan's book, the borstal of my childhood fears was vividly brought to life. The Irish-Catholic connection with Behan was real for my mother, but I never heard her invoke it against her love of England, which she required us to respect. As a boy I knew that my mother's immediate forebears, and therefore my own, lay in unmarked graves in the yard of the ruined Catholic church at Donoughmore in Kilkenny, and while neither I nor the friends of my childhood ever thought of becoming traitors to the country of our birth, when I read Behan's book in 1963 I nevertheless saw that in an important respect he had spoken for the subject conditions of my own caste in England, as well as for those of his people in Ireland. Behan's description of the English doctor before whom he was required to stand naked when he was first admitted to the prison was a reminder to me of those men who were placed in authority over us as children and whose contempt we endured every day. 'He was a dark man,' Behan wrote of this prison doctor, 'not very old, and very hard in an English way that tries to be dignified and a member of a master race that would burn a black man alive.'

It was these memories of my childhood, ghosts of the old shame of knowing myself despised by those in authority over me, that came unbidden into my mind as I sat in the car looking down the hill at the prison buildings. It still troubled me that I had never quite rid myself of these early insecurities. They were faded, to be sure, like tattoos on the arms of old men, but they still possessed the power to unsettle me.

Over to the left of the prison buildings the open grasslands fell away from the crest of the hill into a distant haze. On the far horizon I could just make out the bold forms of Mount Moorookyle, Mount Buninyong, and maybe even as far as Mount Warrenheip, the remains of the volcanic forces that had shaped this land. The grandeur of the setting rendered the prison buildings temporary and out of place.

It was time to go. I drove on and turned in at the prison entrance. I parked in the shade of an old peppermint gum and took from the seat beside me the copy of my book that we were to discuss. I got out and walked across to what looked like the main building. There were no signs or directions. When I checked my watch I saw it was a quarter past four. I was still a few minutes early. The count of prisoners, I'd been told, was taken at ten past four. I was expected at the reception area at twenty minutes past four. My talk with the members of the book club was scheduled to begin at four-thirty. The woman who'd invited me had been precise about these times—she'd bolded them in her email.

As I walked across the deserted car park towards the principal building I was impressed by the blank face presented by the prison to the outside world. There was no bell or handle to the door, but before I could knock it was opened by a woman in her fifties, slim and fit-looking, wearing a crisp summery dress. She looked as if she got up every morning at five and went for a ten-kilometre run along the country roads. Her teeth were even and white. She offered me her hand. 'Hi, I'm Jill.' Her grip was cool and firm, her manner not hurried exactly, but businesslike. 'You found us okay then?'

'Hi, Jill. You're pretty conspicuous out here.'

'Isn't it a lovely setting?' She might have been proud of the position of her own home. She stood to one side and I stepped past her through the door. Before closing the door she took a quick look out into the car park, as if she wanted to make certain there was no one with me.

A telephone on the desk behind the counter was making a soft burring sound, like a repeated shudder. She ignored it.

I followed her along a short passage which opened into a space much like a seminar room at one of the new universities. Four tables were arranged into a hollow square, with four chairs behind each of three of the tables, and one chair in the middle of the table at the front of the room. Copies of my back titles lay spread out fanwise on the front table. My books looked vulnerable lying there, something forlorn about this collection of prison library books with their protective plastic coverings—my life's work! I was sure the opinions of the prisoners were going to be more challenging than the opinions of my regular book-club readers and I was feeling a little anxious.

Through a single narrow strip of window high on the wall facing me across the meeting room the rugged contours of the granite hills were softened in the hazy afternoon sunlight. The land had never looked so lonely or so poignantly beautiful to me as it did through that window just then. This place, obviously, wasn't the brutal borstal of my childhood fears, but it was still a prison. The feeling of being enclosed and contained was palpable.

A woman of around forty was sitting at the end table facing us. She was making notes in an exercise book, an open copy of my last novel lying on the table beside her. She didn't look up when we came in but paused to consult the novel, placing her finger on a line of the open page before returning her attention to the exercise book and writing something. Her dark brown hair was cut fashionably short and caught the light as she moved. She was wearing a fresh white blouse with short sleeves, her bare arms evenly tanned. She looked like an attractive middle-class woman. She did not look like my idea of a prisoner, and I did not feel any of that shame at brandishing one's freedom before the eyes of the captive that Henri de Monfreid speaks of so eloquently in his book *La Croisière du Haschich*.

Jill introduced me to the note-taking woman. She stood up and offered me her hand confidently and looked directly into my eyes. 'I've prepared some questions for you, Mr Crofts.' She was very serious and might almost have been about to interview me for a job.

I said, 'Please call me Robert.'

She continued to hold my gaze. I was aware of being assessed, in a way that implied the expectation of something substantial from our meeting. She evidently wished to let me know she was well prepared for her encounter with the author of the book she'd just read. Her name had vanished from my mind the moment Jill uttered it and I regretted not making a conscious note of it.

More women were coming into the room behind us through the door Jill and I had entered by. Jill introduced the women to me one by one and I shook their hands—their names flitting through my mind one after the other like bats whizzing into the night sky from the mouth of a cave. They talked with each other in low voices as they found places for themselves to sit. Once settled, they looked at me with interest. There were eleven of them. Jill took the instructor's chair at the front table, making our number thirteen in total. Every seat was taken.

Four of the women were Asian, three Chinese and the fourth Japanese. Two of the Chinese women sat close together at the table directly across from me, the older of the two frowning at me as if she didn't know what to expect from the meeting. When I smiled at her, she looked away and shifted closer to her friend. The Japanese woman sat alone. The third Chinese woman sat immediately to my right, the sleeve of her t-shirt touching my shoulder. The Japanese woman's features had the closed serenity of a character from Murasaki's *Tale of Genji*. She might have been the author of Ise's line, *In longing my soul has ventured forth alone*. She gave an impression of being disconnected from the others—an errant spirit from a time long past to which I would never gain access or understanding. Her beauty and her exemplary solitariness. What had all these normal-looking women done to end up in here?

In choosing to sit midway along the table facing the only window, I'd claimed a view of the stony hills. Gnarled and twisted yellow box trees of great age rose from the crevices between the grey humps of the granite boulders. I spotted a pair of wedge-tailed eagles riding the thermals above the nearest hill. No sound from the world outside found its way into the room with us. Mesmerised by the slowly circling pair of eagles above the grey boulders, I realised I'd become momentarily disengaged from what was going on in the room.

The chatter had stopped. It was very quiet. They were waiting.

Jill was holding herself erect, her shoulders back, both hands spread above the table in front of her—the readiness position of a woman with a tight schedule to meet. She had a typed sheet of paper and a copy of my latest book on the table between her hands.

When she saw she had my attention she picked up the sheet of paper and began to read what turned out to be a long and rather elaborate introduction of me and my writing. I recognised some of it from an old publicity blurb. She didn't refer to the women in the room as prisoners, but spoke of them as *the women*—just as she had avoided the word prison when I arrived and had referred to it as *the facility.*

I spoke about how the idea for the book had come to me, and then made some general remarks about my approach to writing. I'd been speaking for some time and had paused with the intention of further developing my remarks when the note-taking woman cleared her throat and shifted in her seat.

I looked at her. Everyone looked at her. She said, 'I'm nearing the end of a seven-year sentence, Mr Crofts. I've read all your novels. And I've noticed the mothers in your books all have something in common.' She was nervous, the colour risen to her cheeks. She looked sad and beautiful. I was moved by her plight.

Was she going to tell me I didn't understand mothers? Her eyes were red with emotion and she had trouble holding my gaze. Her fingers fidgeted with the corners of the pages of her notebook. The other women were watching her, silent and expectant.

'What sort of thing in common?' I said.

The note-taking woman placed her hand on the book and looked down at it. 'The narrator's deceased mother is an important presence in this story.' She looked up at me. 'Wouldn't you say?'

'Yes, for sure.' She wanted me to take her seriously.

'You could even say,' she went on, 'the narrator's dead mother is the guiding spirit of the whole story.'

'Morally, I suppose she is.'

She frowned at the book. 'It's almost as if he's writing his story to explain himself to his mother. That's what I thought.' She looked at the other women, either hoping for their support or offering them the chance to say something. None of them spoke. She turned to me. 'I thought he was explaining himself to his mother as a way of explaining himself to himself. Is that right?'

I said, 'There's no right or wrong about it really, is there? It's up to you. We all read our own story, don't we?'

'I've noticed this presence of absent mothers in several of your books.' She paused, her gaze steady now on mine. 'The presence of absent mothers.' She left it at that for a moment. 'It's a theme in your work, wouldn't you say?'

I was astonished. I'd never been aware of writing about absent mothers. A strange thing happened to me when she said this. My earliest childhood memory came into my mind. This old half-buried memory had always haunted me, a kind of background tremor I could never quite rid myself of. I'd thought of talking to a psychologist about it but never had. Unsettling feelings of guilt and shame were associated with this memory. I didn't like thinking about it.

The note-taking woman was waiting for me. I wasn't sure what to say.

'So can you say something to us about the theme of the absent mother in your books?' She glanced at Jill, as if she was checking that it was okay for her to persist with this line. Jill was watching me and didn't say anything.

I caught the faint scream of the eagles.

The note-taking woman, I supposed, must be an absent mother herself. No critic or reader I knew of had ever mentioned absent mothers as a theme in my work. But when I thought about it, as I now did, I saw they were there sure enough. In those books lying on the table in front of Jill there were bad mothers, mothers who gave away their children, absent mothers whose moral influence guided the behaviour of characters throughout their adult years, dead mothers, and no doubt others I couldn't think of just then. All enshrined in that pile of shabby prison library books. Secretly I loved them all. I was wishing I could remember the note-taking woman's name. I smiled at her. She didn't smile back at me. 'I find what you say very interesting. I mean, I've never thought about absent mothers in my books. But you're right. Now you mention it, I see there are several of them.'

She nodded and took a breath, as if she'd been holding her breath in case I denied her claim or was offended by it. 'I'm sorry, Mr Crofts. Perhaps I shouldn't have said anything about it.'

'No! Don't be sorry. Please. It's true. I'm glad you did say something.' I was impressed. 'I'm grateful to you for pointing it out to me. It takes readers like you to tell us what we've really been up to.'

A small uncertain smile of satisfaction crept into her eyes and I began to see that there was a fine tortured grace in her disciplined reserve. She surely knew something I would never know. Her emotions knew it. The hidden pain I would never be called on to endure. The anguish of a mother separated from her children. I was moved by her courage in speaking up and wanted to tell her so. And I also wanted to tell her about my earliest memory. To confess it to her. She'd made a vital connection for me, and I wanted to share my thoughts about it with her. What might she see in this memory that I hadn't seen? She was the perfect reader for my absent mothers. 'I'm really grateful. I hope you believe me.'

She gave me a lovely warm smile and looked down at the table, colour coming into her cheeks again.

With the flat of her left hand she covered the book lying open in front of her on the table—she might have been going to swear an oath on it. 'It's in at least four of them.' Her voice was quiet, controlled, her tone confiding, speaking to me now of something intimate to both our lives, something that could cause pain and distress but also wonderment, something hidden and durable beneath the flickering surface of our daily living. 'If you include the influence of the dead grandmother in your book about your Queensland friends, that would make it five, wouldn't it?'

'Probably. I believe you. You've obviously thought a lot more about it than I have. I'd like to tell you something that might help explain it. I'm reminded by what you say of my earliest childhood memory. You've seen a connection between my writing and this memory that I've never been aware of. I've never spoken about this memory to anyone, because when I think of it I feel ashamed for my father and what he was forced to do. When I was eighteen months old I was taken by him to a home for children and left there for a week while my mother went into hospital and gave birth to my younger sister.'

I waited. But she said nothing. She was watching me closely, anxious with anticipation of what I was about to reveal—the secret emotions of an abandoned child the very thing she most feared and over which she must have agonised every night of her seven years of imprisoned life, her children growing up without her.

'I've only got a broken memory of that event. Nothing's really clear to me. It's just three fragments. They've stayed with me. When you mentioned absent mothers in my books, this memory came vividly into my mind at once. It's something that must have happened to lots of children in those days, I suppose. While that week lasted, at eighteen months of age I must have been convinced I'd lost my mother forever.'

She put her hand up to her face and wiped at her eyes. When she spoke, it was in little more than a whisper. I had to lean towards her to catch her words. 'And you still believe your mother betrayed you?'

I realised what I'd done. 'God, no! No! Definitely not.' But my denial was too late. 'I've never thought of it like that,' I said. 'I loved my mother. I still love her. I thought it must have been my own fault, not my mother's.'

Neither of us said anything. I hadn't realised what I was saying. We sat looking into each other's eyes. We might have been alone in that quiet room. How many children had she been forced to abandon when she came to the prison? What had happened to them? Was there a father at home with them? Or had they gone to foster homes? Were they old enough to have some understanding that it had not been their mother's wish to desert them? Or did they believe, as she dreaded they would, that they had been abandoned and betrayed by her? Or even worse, in its way, did they think—as I'd thought—that they must have done something to deserve their abandonment? Surely I'd just confirmed her worst fear. Convinced her that her children would always feel abandoned and betrayed, for the rest of their lives, guilty for their own part in it, their memory of the event held deep in a secret place of shame.

What crime could it have been, I wondered, that had landed this woman here for seven years? I couldn't imagine her committing the sort of crime that would earn her seven years in prison. I thought of my own children and their happy childhoods, grown now to adulthood, the pair of them, without wounds from their pasts to deal with. I realised then that it wasn't seven years this woman was serving. She was serving a life sentence. She was never going to recover those seven lost years. The loss of those precious years was going to stay with her and with her children till the end of their days, and she knew it, and I'd confirmed her fear of this very consequence. I'd been thoughtlessly honest with her. I had to say something. 'I greatly admire your courage,' I said, and felt awkward saying it, conscious that my words were useless to her. I wished I could have addressed her by her name.

She reached up and pushed back her hair with her fingers and she looked at the other women, as if she wished to challenge their silence and their private thoughts, some of them surely absent mothers themselves. Then she closed her notebook and placed it carefully on top of my novel and she folded her hands on the table and looked at me, her emotions once again under control. 'One of your characters says somewhere, I forget where, that a lifetime isn't long enough for him to ever forget what has happened to him.' She paused. 'Do you think I'll ever forget this thing that has happened to me?'

My first impulse was to reassure her that it would all pass and be forgotten one day. But I knew she would see through that lie at once and despise me for it. 'I haven't even forgotten that week I spent in the children's home, have I? And that was nothing compared to what's happened to you. How can we ever forget these things?'

'It's not nothing that happened to you, Mr Crofts. Because of what happened to you, your books have helped me to understand what I've done.'

Jill tapped the table sharply with her biro. 'Perhaps someone else would like to ask our author a question?' When no one spoke she looked at me and smiled, her even white teeth twinkling at me. 'Perhaps I can ask a question. Can you tell us something about the book you're working on at the moment? Some of the women are writing books.'

'I'm not working on a new book.' My life's work was lying on the table in front of Jill. That was it. I was tempted to tell her, It's over. I'm done. There it is in front of you. I smiled. I had my own crisis to manage. I turned to the note-taking woman and stood up. I offered her my hand. She stood and took my hand in hers. I said, 'Good luck.'

She held my gaze. 'Thank you,' she whispered.

Walking across to my car from the prison, I heard the eagles scream. I stood and looked up into the sky. But I couldn't see them against the dazzle of the evening sky. I stood gazing upwards, listening to the melancholy of their cries—it was as if they called for something lost and unattainable, to a companion of the past. I was seeing my stricken friend, the absent mother locked in the prison behind me. I had always taken my liberty for granted and had done so little with it. I looked hard for the eagles but couldn't find them. Ever since my arrival in Australia on my own as a boy of sixteen, the cry of the eagle had signified my passionate sense of freedom. If I'd ever thought to say what I believed to be the soul of the Australian bush, I would have said, the cry of the eagle. I first heard that strange, lost cry of those great birds when I was working as a stockman on a remote cattle station in the Central Highlands of Queensland. I sat on my horse alone among the wild stone escarpments of that country and watched enthralled as a pair of wedge-tailed eagles soared into the sky above the forest, their pinions locked, circling above me in a slow dance; higher and higher they went, until I could no longer make them out, their screams audible long after they had disappeared from my sight. And then the silence and the distance closing over me, until there was just the creak of my saddle as my horse shifted its weight under me, the two of us more eerily alone in that place than we had been before the eagles' cries.

When I drove out of the prison car park I was so distracted by what had happened that instead of turning to the right, towards the junction with the main road that would have taken me back to town, I turned left. I'd been driving for some minutes before I realised I was on a road that was unknown to me and I was going the wrong way. I kept going. I was glad to be going the wrong way. The strangeness of it was a relief. Sometimes the wrong way is the right way.

I was driving at a dangerously high speed, the narrow strip of broken and neglected bitumen dancing about in the uncertain evening light. I had no idea where it was leading me, except that it was taking me further away from the town and from my home. I was exhilarated by the speed and the danger and by my anger and the wild scheming in my head of ways I might find to meet the note-taking woman again on her own so that she and I could continue the friendship we had begun. I knew such a meeting was impossible. But still I schemed. Ridiculous and stupid.

The massive trunks of grand old yellow box trees flashed by close to the verges on either side of the car. At this speed I had only to swerve from my line by a fraction and I would collect one of these giants and meet my certain death. I didn't mind the thought of death. Mine was the indifference to death of the drunk or the despairing lover. I wasn't in love and I wasn't drunk, but there was that kind of reeling in my head that we know in both these states. Now, right at this minute, along this unknown road, in the grip of this strange youthful madness, it might be just the right time for me to go. Why not? Death might even be my best option. It wasn't the first time I'd thought of it. Perhaps there really was no way forward for me from here. Perhaps I really was finished and just had to find the courage to admit it. The observant note-taking woman in the prison had neatly removed my fictional mask and laid it to one side and placed herself close to me. I wanted to see her again. In a strange and contradictory way, she had given me hope. I pushed the accelerator pedal hard to the floor.

As I crested a low rise, the glare of the sun burst into my eyes and I caught a flash of something red ahead of me. A fox was lying curled up in the centre of the road, so still and so perfect it might have fallen asleep there. The fox's coat had a coppery sheen in the last of the sunlight. It looked to be in the fullness of its vigour; I would not have been surprised to see it jump up and run away. But it was dead. It was all over for the fox. It was lying there alone in the open where it had sought the final companionship of its own warmth at the moment of its solitary death. I slowed to a walking pace and eased the car around the body. It had evidently been struck such a mortal blow that it had been unable to crawl to the side and take cover among the tangle of undergrowth under the box trees. I stopped the car and got out and picked up the body and carried it into the cover at the side of the road and placed it carefully on the ground. And I wept, for the fox, for its beauty, for the woman in prison, and for my own doom. I got back in the car and sat a while till I had recovered and then I drove on at a sedate pace.

I continued along the unfamiliar road well after darkness had enfolded the landscape. I saw no other cars. Eventually I stopped in the middle of the road. It was no good going on forever. Against the blackness of the night the massive scarred trunks of the great trees were thrown into sharp relief by my trembling headlights. I sat there for a long time in the perfect stillness of the night, looking at the trees and thinking about the note-taking woman in her fresh white blouse, her fingernails bitten to the quick, her eyes reddened with emotion as she spoke to me of her terrible fears. I'd almost shared with her my precious three shards of memory of the children's home. With her I would have broken the silence of that old taboo that had lain on me and on my family all my life. I sat in the car gazing through the windscreen at the ancient trees and I told my memories to the fantasy of her presence. It was a way of keeping alive for myself something of the intimacy between us, becoming for her the voice of one of her abandoned children.

'I'm riding in a taxi with my father through the streets of London,' I said, telling my story aloud. 'I'm gripped by a vivid excitement that's edged with an uncomprehending anxiety. It's a fine summer day. My nose is pressed against the shuddering window of the cab, London's crowded streets and views of parks whizzing past outside, inside the exotic smell of the leather seats and the intimately reassuring aroma of my father's pipe tobacco. The view of London's streets that sunny day has remained with me as an ideal of what London should look like. It's a view I've never quite managed to recover, though sometimes in Hyde Park on a summer day I've sensed the magic of its presence fleetingly, like a half-remembered dream. Although this first fragment is not an unhappy memory, its atmosphere is nevertheless touched with the foreboding that sometimes enters into even our most innocent dreams. I remember the ride in the taxi with a strange clarity that hasn't faded with the passing of the years. I suppose it is the mystery of the journey's purpose that accounts for my sense of foreboding—I seem to know in my infant soul that some ill is to befall me at the end of the taxi ride.

'The second fragment is colourless. A large woman is standing at the top of a short flight of grey stone steps looking down at me. I'm being led up the steps by my father and am holding tightly to his hand. I feel the firm grip of my father's hand in mine—he will *never* let me go! The woman at the top of the stairs is wearing a black apron over a long grey dress that reaches to her ankles. She is foreshortened and made even more imposing and heavy than she would have been if we'd been approaching on a level with her. And of course I'm small and my angle is even closer to the ground than that of a grown-up. I've no memory of my father letting go of my hand. Just the looming figure of the woman waiting for me at the top of the steps. My mother, in contrast to this massive grey woman, was small and of slight build and often described herself to us as a little mother sparrow. As we go up the steps towards this woman I'm overwhelmed by such a powerful conviction of my guilt that my emotions are brought to a frozen standstill. What terrible crime am I guilty of that has driven my loving father to hand me over to this fearful person? The memory is shrouded in a hopeless feeling of shame and a helpless desire for redemption and forgiveness. Such feelings make no sense to me as an adult, but they persist all the same in their association with this memory.

'In the third, and final, fragment I'm being punished for the crime against my parents that has made it necessary for them to abandon me. My face is being pushed against the shiny green tiles of a wall in a long corridor that ends in distant blackness. The unnerving sound of my child's screams fills the air. It is a fragment of terror. I've no other memories of the children's home beyond the shiny green tiles of the wall and my helpless screams. Green tiles have always held a morbid fascination for me. I included a single row of shiny green tiles in my bathroom when I had it renovated some years ago. When I was inspecting his work one morning, the tiler pointed out to me that he'd made a mistake and had set one of the wall tiles crookedly. He said he would correct it. I told him to leave it as it was. "I like to see some little sign of error in things," I said. Standing naked under the shower in the morning, there is a peculiar satisfaction for me in seeing that crooked green tile. I alone know the meaning of its skew. But I cannot say what that meaning is. It is simply meaning. Seeing the crooked green tile gratifies me.'

I fell silent. I reversed the car and turned around and drove slowly back along the road I'd come by.

I hadn't been working on a new book since my last book had come out, now more than two years ago. Till then, for more than thirty years, whenever I finished a book, I'd always had another book waiting to be written. I'd been struggling for some time to come to terms with this. The will to write, the need, the desire to do it yet again, they weren't there anymore—I was the forest of stumps, a dispiriting expanse of emptiness.

2

——

On the Thursday after my visit to the prison I was in upstate New York to deliver a lecture at Vassar College. The weather was unusually warm for October and I decided to stay on in Manhattan for a couple of weeks. I rented an apartment on the Upper East Side and put my life on hold. I told myself I needed a break. And I did need a break. But it was more than that. I was being a coward. At home I would have to confront the fact that I didn't possess the will or the desire to go on writing. New York's parks and museums were the perfect distraction, and for two weeks I looked at pictures and at dogs and children playing in the park, and was careful to read only books that I was confident would not unsettle me.

The day before I was due to fly home, I was sitting in the sun on one of the benches overlooking the East River, my back to Carl Schurz Park, reading John Berger's collection of essays *About Looking*. I walked to the park and spent an hour there reading and daydreaming most afternoons—practising being an old man in the final years of his decline. I was getting quite good at convincing myself I'd paid my dues and had no further challenges or respon-sibilities to meet. Contemplating death a little way ahead of me was quite a pleasant thing to do, and I smiled at the thought of it as I watched a young boy floating by on his skateboard—there goes the future. I have no part to play in it. Smile, old man! Just smile.

The park was only two blocks from my apartment and was filled with children and idlers like myself. I liked to watch the dogs in the small dogs' playground and the children and their parents in the small children's playground. The big children's playground was mostly given over to boys shooting for the basket, and the big dogs' playground was generally given over to arse-sniffing by the biggest dogs and cowering from the not-so-big dogs. I was only half attending to my reading and was pleasantly aware of the warmth of the sun and the yelling of children and the occasional stately passage up the river of a cargo boat when it registered with me that I'd read something of interest on the previous page.

It was as if a standby light blinked in my sleeping brain, reminding me that death had not yet taken full possession of me. I turned back the page and found the passage. It was in Berger's essay on the Turkish artist Seker Ahmet Pasa's painting *Woodcutter in the Forest*. 'The novel, as Georg Lukács pointed out in his *Theory of the Novel*, was born of a yearning for what now lay beyond the horizon.' Here it was! *A yearning for what now lay beyond the horizon*. A startling reminder to me that it was the empty horizon in a photograph of the Australian outback that had inspired my first great boyhood dream and resulted in my flight from the dreary post-war streets of South London to the limitless expanses of the great Australian outback. The joy of the openness to all possibilities of the empty horizon, after the enclosed stupor of working-class South London after the war. I was sixteen then and consumed with a need to get to the promised land of the outback. That I did get there, and that it was as I had dreamed it would be, seemed then to be a miracle.

Something of that sense of a miracle touched me now through Lukács's words: *A yearning for what now lay beyond the horizon.* Not only a yearning for the outback, then, as I'd always thought it to be, but also that other yearning which had inspired my life as a writer. Were the two of them the same impulse after all and not, as I had always thought them to be, distinct and hostile to one another? Were the bush and the city, two antagonists in me whose differences I'd been unable to reconcile, two parts of one whole life? Lukács had made this precious link for me. It was a gift, and although I'd never read his book, sitting on the bench reading his words over again and savouring their meaning, I knew the warm emotion of being in the presence of an old friend, a friend whom I'd not seen for more than half a century and whom I'd long ago thought dead. So he still lives! That was my thought, my feeling. So *I* still live! I knew at once that I must ask myself the one great unasked question of my life: what was it that I had found over the horizon line of nothingness? Was it, in the end, grace or damnation? And did I have the courage to confront the truth of it?

I felt grateful to Berger for touching me lightly on the shoulder and waking me from my dream of death; for reminding me I was embraced within a circle of kindred spirits; for rekindling in me a yearning to reach for something.

I closed his book, got up from the bench and headed for my regular diner. I sat in the booth I'd occupied for breakfast and my evening meal every day for the past fortnight and ordered a beer and the meatloaf with mushroom gravy. While waiting for my meal to arrive I took my notebook out of my satchel and began to write. I didn't hesitate. I knew where to begin. Not at the beginning—I had no hand in my beginnings—but at what I had long understood to have been the bottom. For it did not occur to the young man I was then that he was in possession of his liberty, the greatest thing known to humankind, possessed only by a privileged few. The young Robert Crofts took his liberty as much for granted as he did his youth. Was the woman in the prison right when she said, 'I thought he was explaining himself to his mother as a way of explaining himself to himself'?

And so, after a long and anguished silence, I began to write again, sitting there in that diner in Manhattan.

3

After three years in the vast hinterland of the Australian north working alongside the legendary black ringers, Robert Crofts quit his job. When the camp broke up at the end of that mustering season he collected his cheque from the manager and headed for the coast and the city of Townsville. It was over. He was twenty-one and his great and beautiful dream had come to an end. He had not expected the dream to lose its hold, and for the first time in his life a great emptiness was in him. In despair, he wrote a line in pencil on a toilet wall in Townsville: *The desert took my soul.*

From Townsville he drifted south, until he arrived in Melbourne, thousands of miles from the Gulf of Carpentaria, where he'd set out, and another world entirely. He had no money, no friends, no family and no connections in Melbourne. He had stopped drifting because he had run out of money and had also run out of Australia. He was at the bottom. There was no further down to go.

He slept the first night wrapped in his swag on a bench in the Malvern railway station, close to where his last lift had dropped him off. He was woken early in the morning by the rattling and screeching of the first suburban trains coming through. He sat up and looked around. His lift had dropped him in the dark and Robert had no idea where he was. The platform was teeming with city people going to work. There was a newspaper in the bin next to his bench. He reached for it and sat wrapped in his old grey blanket and wearing his sheepskin coat and he read the Rooms to Let columns. He set the paper aside on the bench and got up and took a drink of water at the tap on the platform. He gave his face a going-over and dried himself on the sleeve of his jacket. He went back to the bench and tied his things with the bull strap as he always did and he said good morning to the station attendant and showed him the paper and asked for directions to the nearest of the three rooms he'd circled with his pencil.

The station attendant took him out to the gate and he pointed. 'Go on up here till you get to Dandenong Road. You can't miss it, son. She's got double tram tracks running down the centre of her with trees along each side. Alma Road and the house you want is just along to the right.'

Robert thanked him and headed off along the busy street.

He kept the newspaper folded so he could check the address of the house. The streets were full of people and every so often he asked for new directions in case he'd taken a wrong turn. He kept his sheepskin jacket on, but he didn't put on his hat with Frankie's fancy plaited band around the crown, as he did not wish to be stared at. The hat he carried in the same hand as the newspaper. The swag he had swung over his shoulder and he held it by the strap. The sun was shining and the morning chill soon wore off and he was sweating in his jacket, but he kept it on for the comfort it gave him of a close and familiar thing, the smell almost the smell of home.

He stood on the footpath in front of the broken gate for some time looking along the driveway at the house. He was checking for signs of dogs before venturing in. The place looked to be abandoned, the garden overgrown with weeds and half-dead shrubs, the foliage wilting and dry, the iron gate swung half off its hinges. It was a mansion out of a story book, old and grey and rundown, with elaborate cast-iron balconies and a tall square tower. The glass was broken in one of the tall downstairs windows, the gap boarded up with a length of ply, stained and warped from exposure to the weather, newspaper stuffed in along the warps to keep out the rain. He went along the drive and rang the bell. The deep porch stank of cat's piss. No one came to the door, so he rang the bell again.

The door was opened by a fat woman in her mid-fifties. She was short and square, her red hair—the grey growing out along the roots—hooked up in an untidy pile on top of her head and held more or less in place by an elaborate arrangement of combs and pins. The sleeves of her blouse were rolled above her elbows. Her breasts were massive, straining the material of her blouse out the sides of her apron. Robert was glad to see the woman's apron was clean. His mother had always kept her aprons fresh.

The woman said, 'So what are you staring at?' Her accent was Irish.

He apologised for staring and said, 'I've come for the room. I haven't got the money for the first week's rent, but I'll pay you as soon as I get a job.'

'You will, will you?' Her thick fleshy lips pushed out, her fat cheeks glowing, tiny rivers of veins like worms crawling under the skin of her nose and her cheeks. Her eyes had a shrewd judging look in them as she examined his clothes and his swag. She said, 'You think I haven't heard that one before? Are you going to introduce yourself or do I have to guess who I'm talking to?'

'I'm Robert Crofts,' he said.

'Well, Robert Crofts, are you coming in or are you going to stand there gawping all day?'

He followed her along the dark hall and past the stairs and into a back kitchen. She told him to wash himself at the sink. He set his swag and his hat down behind the door and took off his sheepskin and hung it over the back of a chair and he gave his face and hands a good soaping and dried himself with the piece of damp towel that was hanging there on a rail beside the sink. The faint smell of gas and the white stone sink with little cracks running all around gave him the feeling he had returned to something familiar, a place he'd known or dreamed about a long time ago, and here it was again.

While he was eating the eggs and bacon and the two slices of toast and drinking the black tea, the Irish woman sat across the table from him smoking a cigarette and studying him, not saying anything, her elbows on the pale scrubbed wood, her thick fingers playing with the cigarette packet and the brass lighter she had, swapping them back and forth from one hand to the other, as if it was a nervous habit she had got into to help her think. She kept the cigarette in her mouth, giving it a puff every now and then, screwing up her eyes against the sting of the smoke but not taking the cigarette out from between her lips. She turned aside to blow the ash off the end.

He finished eating and thanked her and set his plate to one side. She leaned across the table and offered him a cigarette from the packet then lit it for him with the brass lighter. She stood up, leaning her fat hands on the table and grunting, butted the remains of her cigarette in the sink and lit a fresh one. 'Come on!'

She went ahead of him up the stairs, sighing and wheezing. She paused to breathe then opened the door to a room off the first-floor landing. They went in and stood. It was a big room, the air stale and musty, as if it had been closed up and unoccupied for some time. A narrow single bed was pushed against the wall in the far corner over by the window. An upright wardrobe with a mirror door stood along the wall next to the bed, the mirror door swung open. At the end of the bed there stood an easy chair with frayed red upholstery. It looked like a cat had been using it for a scratching post. Beside the chair was a small dark wood table, on it a brass ashtray and an empty milk bottle holding a withered hydrangea. The only other piece of furniture was a straight-backed chair against the far wall over to the right, like a child that has been told to stand in the corner and wait to be forgiven.

Robert and the woman went over and stood by the window and looked down into the garden. Below them a disused tennis court surrounded by a copsing of English elms. The early summer leaves of the elms catching the sun, pale and green and not in their full strength yet, the sunlight shining through them. A memory stirred in Robert of the stone barn on the farm in Somerset where he'd worked before leaving England. They had wintered the bullocks in the old barn, the gypsies setting their camp there in the autumn. A pair of giant elm trees growing out of the hedge by the barn. Trees two hundred years old. A pair of owls nesting in one of their hollows. And the winter morning when Robert went down to feed and bed the bullocks, those two great trees lying on the ground, the sky empty where they had stood, the bank and the hedge torn up where their roots had ripped out of the ground. There had been no wind or storm that night to bring those trees down. They had come down for no reason that he could see and he was greatly impressed. He remembers his thoughts then, spoken aloud in the solitary silence of the trees: 'Those trees came down because it was their time.' Big powerful trees like that in their prime, felled by something unearthly and beyond him. He was moved by the sight of them lying in their silence. He went up to them and touched their shattered branches with a feeling of concern and trespass. After he had fed the bullocks, he explored among the freshly exposed red loam where the bank of the hedge had been torn up, opened to the light of day by that wound for the first time since those trees began to grow there. He found a heavy coin and when he rubbed it clean he saw it was gold and was minted in the time of William and Mary. How long had it lain in the dark soil under the elms, waiting to return into the light? He pictured to himself the horseman who had lost it; in his imagination he saw the gold piece glint as it fell from the man's purse while he was looking away, distracted by a shout from the barn. Robert could have gone on with that story if he'd bothered to. It was a beginning. A little offering he had not taken up. The mystery of the people lying lightly covered in that country, scattered and broken and lost to the present day, just below the surface of things. He had felt it, their presence, and had loved the feeling that his own history was mingled briefly with the secret life of that ancient place. Would anyone ever know he had passed that way?

He'd not seen an elm tree since he left England before his seventeenth birthday. At the sight of the copse in the Irish woman's garden he felt a touch of nostalgia for the farm and for those magical innocent days of riding second horse to the hunting farmer, old Master Warren, days which had passed in a kind of dream for him. And the thought came into his mind, as he stood beside the Irish woman at the window looking down on the elm copse, that death might come to him as it had come to those two elms by the Norman barn. And it seemed to him to be a terrible possibility that he might exist to no purpose.

When the Irish woman spoke, he was off with these thoughts and he jumped at the sound of her voice.

'And will this suit your majesty?' she said.

Without thinking at all, but wanting to please her, he said, 'It's wonderful.'

She snorted. 'Wonderful, is it?' She looked at him, considering. 'You're an odd one.' She shook out another cigarette from the packet. He took it and thanked her.

'You'll be all right up here, son,' she said. 'The bathroom's down the hall. There's plenty of hot water. Don't be afraid to use it.' At the door she turned around. 'Breakfast's from six till eight.'

After the door closed behind her he took off his boots, got the ashtray from the table and lay down on the bed. He held the ashtray against his stomach and smoked the second cigarette. The last time he had slept in a real bed was in the stockmen's quarters on Augustus Downs station, far away in the Gulf of Carpentaria. He thought about Frankie and their last camp, when the muster was over and they were back at the homestead and separated, him in the men's quarters and Frankie out in the family camp with the women and children. The day before Robert flew out to the coast, the two friends met up by the river on neutral ground. They sat side by side high up on the bank, smoking and looking over the waterhole. There was a sign of the coming wet season in the air. They could smell the gidgee trees, which they called stinking wattle, as the leaves gave off a stink like a septic tank when there was humidity in the air. They kept still and quiet, the two of them sitting on the high bank, waiting until the freshwater crocs came creeping out of the water again to sun themselves. When the crocs had arranged themselves on the far bank—there must have been a couple of hundred of them—Frankie threw the stone he held ready in his hand. When the stone hit the water the crocs were gone in a furious flash of threshing and tumbling, panicked to get into the seething water. The smell coming up to the young men, the stale animal stink of the stagnant water at the end of the dry, the crocs swarming with hardly room to move around and nowhere to get away to from each other. Hundreds of them crowded up together and shitting in that green sludge of the dying river.

Frankie said, 'So what are you going to do now, old mate?'

Robert did not answer his friend at once.

Frankie picked up another stone and lobbed it into the water.

Robert said, 'Well, I'll go to Townsville and see what's happening out there on the coast.' He felt guilty saying it. Frankie could not offer to go with him and he could not invite him to, even if they had both wished for it. Frankie resented not having the freedom of a white man. The two of them had talked about it often. Frankie and the other black stockmen were on their own tribal country out there. They were the kings of the Leichhardt River, but they had no birth certificates and could not travel without a permit from the police, and they were not able to get a permit from the police but only some sarcastic response if they ever asked for one. Robert was paid four pounds ten shillings a day while the black stockmen were not paid anything for their work. Frankie had told him their pay was supposed to be held in trust for them at a rate of four pounds ten shillings a week. 'We never see it,' he said. He turned aside and spat. He was bitter. Frankie and the other young men felt the humiliation of it keenly, but the older men said nothing about it. Robert had known nothing of how things stood with them and was shocked to learn these things from his friend. In his ignorance, he had believed that in Australia everyone was free to come and go as they chose. To learn that this was not so troubled him and made him thoughtful. 'Maybe you could just ignore the rules and come out to the coast with me anyway.'

They were two young men of the same age and Frankie was as interested to know Robert's story as Robert was to know his. Frankie said, 'I would like to go and see England for myself one day.' His resentment and anger burned inside him that he was not free to make such a journey. Robert was silent. It was a fearful thing to think Frankie was not a free man and he feared that with the passage of time his friend would become a man of anger and hatred. The hate was already there, the helpless bitterness of it.

The moment was awkward for them both and they were silent for some time. Robert had seen the way Frankie looked at the eagle and the wild dog and how he admired the solitariness of those creatures, and he saw something of himself in Frankie and had learned to love his friend and to admire him. They sat in the burning silence together up on the river bank, each knowing they would never meet again once Robert caught that plane out to the coast.

It was at this moment, and without a word, that Frankie took off his hat and passed it to Robert. Robert took off his own hat and handed it to Frankie. Neither spoke. Their hats were to them as a badge is to a soldier, or a flag. Frankie's hat had a fine plaited band around the crown. Robert had watched him make it one time at a lunch camp. They were sitting in the thin shade of some red ash trees and Frankie had his legs stuck out in front of him and he worked the fine grasses and creepers he'd been plucking from the bushes they rode past during the morning, making a nice little collection for the hatband he had in mind. He was like a scrub bird collecting for its nest. He knew just what to take and he took things Robert did not even see. Robert admired the plaited hatband and Frankie showed him how it was done. They had laughed together at the clumsy results of Robert's efforts.

Robert lay a while longer on the bed thinking of that life he had left behind and wondering what lay ahead of him. He butted the last of the landlady's second cigarette and got up off the bed. He set his swag on the bed and undid the strap and laid everything out. It was all he owned lying there on that boarding house bed. There was nothing else, except the saddle and gear that he'd needed out in the cattle camps. He had given his saddle to Frankie. Seeing those few things lying on the bed, he knew he would never be going back to Frankie's country. It was done. He did not know why. But knew himself to be more alone in that boarding house room in Melbourne just then than he had ever been before in his entire life. He was there to no purpose that he could see.

There was a brass hook behind the door. He hung his leggings and spurs and Frankie's hat on the hook. As he was putting up Frankie's hat he held it to his face and sniffed the inside of it. They were both there, the deep smell of their sweat mingled together, Frankie's dry and sharp with a touch of cinnamon, Robert's own a little sweeter to his idea of it. He smiled thinking of it and how the distinctive smell of their sweat was something they got so used to they stopped being aware of it.

He hung up the hat and went back to the bed and unfolded the two spare shirts and another pair of moleskins. The red paisley silk scarf his mother gave him the day he left home. He shook it out and held it up against the light from the window. It was a sudden gift which she brought out of her bag at St Pancras station as they were about to embrace for the last time. She didn't speak but handed it to him. There was in that scarf still something of his parting from his mother. He set it beside his sewing gear, the needles and awls and hole punches for working leather and repairing the gear, the scarred ball of hard wax and the bobbin of twine. He could feel these things in his hands and was not ready to toss them out just yet. His clothes were stiff with dirt and sweat and when he shook the moleskins out he smelled the camp and the cooking fire and the horses.

He wondered then if having his freedom was such a great thing after all. Maybe he would have been better off bound as Frankie was bound, to his piece of country and his people. Frankie might not be free and equal before the law as he was, but he belonged in a way Robert knew he never could belong. Standing there in that musty old room, thinking these thoughts and looking at his things laid out on the bed, Robert felt as if the purpose of his life had come to an end. There was a nervous alertness in him, a tension that made him pause at the sound of a door closing downstairs, then a man's voice calling, the sound of hurried footsteps on the stairs. Maybe this disturbance was meant for him. Maybe there would be a message from someone. But the silence fell again.

The wardrobe had a narrow hanging space and two drawers. When he swung the door he saw himself in the mirror, his hair long and all over the place, his cheeks unshaved, his eyes reddened with a startled look in them. He had not realised how beaten down he was looking and was surprised now that the Irish woman had not turned him away from her door. The inside of the wardrobe gave off the smell of some old familiar place or thing that he could not name, a smell from childhood with the mystery of adults in it. It was too remote to pin a particular image to. He folded the paisley scarf and set it in the top drawer and thought of his mother giving it to him on the platform at St Pancras station. It struck him for the first time that it had been a strange gift from her, and he wondered what she had been thinking as she handed it to him that day. He had never worn it. It had always seemed too fine a thing to wear and he did not understand his mother's meaning in giving it to him, unless she had imagined her son looking like John Wayne in the Australian wild west of her imagination. So it had kept something of the question that lay between the two of them, mother and son, and was to lie between them till her death. And then on into the bigger silence after her death. That silk scarf a talisman concerning some meaning or duty he did not see but would no doubt come to see one day. That was how he thought of it. A portent of something that was yet to unfold in his life. He laid his palm on it. The silk was warm to his touch. Silk, keeping its own warmth.

He left everything else out to be washed.

He slid the drawer back in and closed the wardrobe door and he walked across to the window. The wardrobe shook behind him, the floor uneven and the boards loose, the mirror door swinging open again. He struggled with the window and managed to get it up a few inches before it stuck again. The roar of the city rushed in and a small breeze carried the leafy smell of the garden into the room, a smell laced with exhaust fumes. He leaned down and looked through the narrow opening. A smart little green car was parked on the gravel at the far edge of the elm copse.

4

——

Two older men were seated at the kitchen table eating eggs and bacon and drinking tea when he went down in the morning. It was not the Irish woman but another woman, darker and more silent, who was in the kitchen. The men greeted him and he told them he was looking for work. They said they had just come off the night shift on the bottle line at the Abbotsford Brewery and he was welcome to go in with them that evening and the foreman would be sure to put him on. 'The night shift always has places for starters,' one of them said and they both laughed.

That night he went to the brewery with the men. The foreman had a clipboard and shouted his questions at Robert above the rattling and grinding of the returned bottle line. Robert yelled back his name and the foreman pointed to the line and told him to get over to it. Robert stood shoulder to shoulder with other men on a raised platform receiving the crates of empty bottles. They set the bottles upside down onto the constantly moving conveyor belt that carried them into the washing plant. Standing there plucking the empty bottles six or eight at a time from the crates and flicking them upside down onto the line had a knack to it. Robert mastered this trick in an hour and after that it was nothing but repetition hour after hour throughout the night without a pause or change in the pace of it.

Carlton & United brewery trucks were backed up to the unloading ramp, their trays stacked high with thousands of crates of empty bottles. Work went on at an urgent pace, as if there was a terrible hurry to get it done. The machine set the pace. As soon as one truck was emptied another truck backed in and took its place. When the unloading fell behind, there was a bank-up and the foreman and drivers started yelling and swearing at each other. The empty bottles of one night shift were identical to the empty bottles of the previous night and might well have been exactly the same bottles going round and round in an endless circle from the brewery to the bottle shops and drinkers in the city and back to the line again to be washed and refilled with beer.

The same bottles night after night. Millions of them.

Robert stood at his station on the line all through the long nights, the dark and the clatter and the warm stench of fermenting beer from the great vats and the shouts of the men and the hurrying demand of the ever-advancing line. He was half stupefied with it by the time the shift ended in the grey dawn and he was released from the grip of the machine.

In the chill early hours of the morning on the sixth night he stepped down from the line and walked away. He said nothing, just collected his jacket and the cash owed him. He walked out into the night past the waiting trucks with their loads of empties and went on through the dark streets with a feeling of lightness and liberation. Then the thought came to him that as a boy he had made the leap and claimed his freedom; now here he was, out of work and living with a bunch of single men who had no plans for their lives but simply to exist from week to week on their pay packets, their minds lit up by the chance of backing a winner once in a while. And as he walked those dark streets he saw that he was to be counted among men such as these. The weight of it stirred in him like an old curse come back to life.

He kept walking till he came to the bank of a river. He stood looking down at the black surge of water and he wondered how long it would take to drown. A man walking his dog along the river path said good morning and Robert came out of his despair and said good morning back to the man. He walked on and thought then of his mother and father and their belief in him. In foreseeing the leap he must make to liberate himself, it had never been his aim to betray or to forswear his origins, but to transcend the poverty of his situation and to seek a grander destiny for himself elsewhere. When it came to the point, the boys at school who had claimed to share his dream had fallen silent and had accepted their fate, like the men in the boarding house. He was on his own again.

He walked back to the boarding house and had a shower and put on a clean shirt. Then he walked into the city and called in at the government employment office. They sent him to the Myer store. He stood in line and waited. Standing in that line he knew himself to be among the people living at the margins of society in this city and he had no answer to the question of how he was to move from those margins to a place where his life might have a more noble purpose. He knew no one he could speak to about what was in his mind. He was glad of one thing only: that Frankie had not been free to follow his lead and suffer this humiliation.

He was given a job as a probationary day cleaner on the confectionary floor and was sent to the cleaners' room to see the foreman and to get a uniform. The job was weekdays and Saturday mornings. Sweeping the floor. That was it.

He went in next morning and opened his locker and changed into his uniform and he picked up his broom for the day and he pushed that broom around and told the people, 'Mind the broom, please,' and they got out of his way. That's all it was.

➤

On Saturday afternoon he went into the grandly proportioned room on the ground floor of the boarding house and had a look around. It must have been one of the principal reception rooms in earlier times, reserved now for the single men as a common room. There were old armchairs and couches and several tables. The place stank of stale beer and tobacco and men's sweat. Four men were sitting up at a table drinking beer and playing cards. The races were on the radio, the voice of the race caller competing with the noise from a black-and-white television set propped on a pile of old encyclopaedias in front of a black marble fireplace.

Robert said good day and the men nodded and greeted him and went on with their game. The two men from the bottle line weren't there. He went over to one of the tall French doors with elegant arched fanlights. Beyond the glass was a broad verandah with tessellated paving. The small coloured tiles of the paving were broken and lifted in places by damp and tree roots. Lofty decorative iron columns ended in elaborate arched cast-iron work, supporting a second-storey verandah above, making of the lower verandah a covered promenade. Guests must once have felt invited to step out on spring evenings to take the air. Standing at the window looking out onto the verandah, Robert saw it as a place for romantic meetings between well-dressed ladies and gentlemen.

From where he was standing he could see the neglected garden with its elm copse over to the right beyond the broken tiles of the verandah. From this low angle he might have been looking into a leafy forest. It was a European view and unlike anything he'd seen on the great cattle stations of the north. He turned around from the window and watched the men playing cards. His fear of their fate hung on him like a smell.

➤

He swept the floor each day. He was like a man with a disease, the thing progressing step by step inside him. Sweeping that floor strewn with lolly wrappers and other rubbish that people had discarded. He existed inside his bulb of silence. Pushing that wide broom around he knew, with a deep intuition of its approach, that something final and bad was going to come out of his anger and frustration and that he would not have the power to oppose it. Wide awake at midnight in his narrow bed in the corner of his room, the band around his head tightened its grip. Wide awake, he lay waiting for the crack in his skull that would bring this thing to its end.

He was walking down Swanston Street to catch his regular tram back to the boarding house when he could go no further. The crowds of people hurrying home to make the most of the weekend pushed past him. He had been standing there for some time when he saw he was in front of the window of an art supplier's shop. He must have walked past that shop every day since he started working at Myer but had never noticed it before. He stood now looking in at the lovingly arranged display of pencils and paper and paints and sketching pads and all the other wonderful things that were familiar to him from his childhood painting days with his father. After his father returned home from the war he took Robert out into the Kentish countryside every weekend. Father and son spent their summer days and evenings drawing and painting together. They spoke very little to each other during those times, and never of the war. They spoke only of art. Their love for each other then was perfect, a harmony between them they had never known before and were never to know again. Robert stood looking in the window of the art shop thinking back over those days with his dad, and he wondered why he had never tried to make another drawing ever again after he left home.

He went into the shop. He knew what to ask for. He watched the man behind the counter wrap the sticks of ochre pastel and half-dozen sticks of charcoal and the sketching pad and the two 110B pencils. Watching the man wrap the things with care in brown paper and tie them into a small package with string, Robert saw how the man's respect for the task spoke of his love of these things, and Robert felt touched by the fine world of that respect for things that he had shared with his father. The man handed Robert the package and smiled at him. He said, 'Good luck, son.' Robert would have liked to shake the man's hand but the man did not offer it and Robert was too shy to offer his own.

In his room back at the boarding house Robert rescued the solitary hard-backed chair from its isolation in the far corner and he sat at the low table in front of the window. With the ochre pastels he began to frame a drawing on the first sheet of the sketching pad. An hour went by, silent except for the light hissing of the pastel against the grain of the paper. He was working up an image of a naked man, building the muscular figure up layer on layer with the ochre pastel against a charcoal background that grew darker and more dense towards the base of the picture, until at the very bottom it was so dark it resembled a swirling black mist rising from below and obscuring the man's lower legs and feet. The red ochre man was fighting down this dark threat rising up to engulf him. Robert was lost in the task.

He worked without pausing all through that afternoon and on into the night, shaping and reshaping and rubbing out and shaping again, finding details and moments in the drawing that surprised and excited him. His energy for the work was vast. He was happy. He was free again. He even forgot to smoke.

That night he slept scarcely more than a couple of hours. He rose before the dawn on Sunday and started on the drawing again. He forgot about everything else but the drawing of the fighting man that was materialising under his hands. From time to time he stood back from the table and walked about the room and remembered to smoke a cigarette and he looked out the window at the light of the morning on the elm leaves. Then he was pulled back into his drawing and he looked down at it and saw with excitement how much might still be done to fully realise its presence on the page. The naked figure emerging on the sheet of paper was half turned away from the viewer. His right fist and right leg were raised threateningly, the hairless globe of his skull catching a highlight from some hidden source of illumination as he bent forward, gazing down at the black mist below him, his cock and balls tight and firm as if carved from red stone.

He worked on through Sunday afternoon. He longed to give to his figure the power and poise it possessed for him in his imagination. As the hours went by the drawing became overworked in complex tones of terracotta, the movement and tension of muscles revealed with the ochre stumps and the pads of Robert's fingers, as he had seen his father do. Eventually the repeated rubbing and scrubbing back produced a luminous patina on the surface of the heavy paper, lending the drawing an illusion of age and substance and depth that delighted and gratified him.

Then, so suddenly he was shaken by the abruptness of it, there was no more to be done. It was over. He stood staring at the drawing, his heartbeat thick in his throat. His throat was so dry and sore he couldn't swallow. The drawing looked like something that had always existed. It did not look like something he had made. He asked myself how he could have made it. Rendered in the glowing subdued redness of his inner fury, the naked man stood alone against the darkness and fought for his life. It possessed the appearance of something that had survived the wear and tear of the ages, a drawing long forgotten, battered, neglected, retrieved from the deepest layer of memory. A chance survival from some other place. Robert was moved and couldn't believe it was the work of his own hands.

He examined the pads of his fingers, as if he would see in their grainy lines the source of his inspiration. He knew, with a deep intuitive self-assurance, that if he ever again attempted to do something like this drawing, the attempt would fail. The drawing was unique. He knew it. He touched it with the tips of his fingers. Perhaps he would send it to his father. He needed someone to admire it. He wanted to know it made sense to someone else so that he could believe in its reality himself. If someone asked him, why did you do it? he would have nothing to say to them. And yet he was proud of having done it.

His shirt was rank with stale sweat. He took it off and dropped it on the floor and went down the passage to the bathroom and had a shower. When he got back to his room he didn't look at the drawing but put on a clean shirt and went out and walked to the Greek cafe on Glenferrie Road and sat in a booth. His stomach was aching with hunger. He ordered a T-bone steak with eggs and chips and slices of white bread and butter. While he was eating he was seeing the sketching pad lying open on the table by the window of his room.

He was at the cash register paying his bill and buying cigarettes when a woman got up from one of the booths on the other side of the cafe and came over and stood beside him. He felt her looking at him and he turned to meet her amused gaze.

'So you're not going to say g'day?' she said, her tone edged with a defensive sarcasm.

There was something familiar about her. 'Sorry,' he said. 'I didn't recognise you.'

She laughed. 'You wouldn't have a clue, would you?'

'I've only ever seen you wearing those overalls with your hair in that bandeau, or whatever it is.' She usually came in to clean the cleaners' change room at the Myer store when he was leaving, pushing her cart and collecting the rubbish. She only came in Monday to Wednesday. She was a good few years older than him and he'd never taken much notice of her. Today she was wearing a pale green dress open at the throat with a wide leather belt and a short brown jacket. He said, 'You look very different with your hair like that.'

She said, 'So what are you doing here?'

'I live just across the road. What are you doing here yourself?'

'This is what you do on your weekends? Come in here all on your own?'

'I've been drawing all weekend.'

'So you're secretly an artist. I knew you'd be up to something. I know a lot of artists.'

'I'm not an artist.'

'You spend your weekends drawing. Who does that except artists?'

'Only this weekend,' he said.

'Would you like to show me your drawings? I know something about art.'

'I've only done one drawing.' He was imagining her in his room looking at his fighting man. 'You're on your own too,' he said.

She laughed. 'It's a lonely world.'

People were beginning to crowd the cash register area and Robert and the woman moved away towards the door. 'It's just one picture,' he said. 'It's nothing.' The idea of her in his room admiring his drawing excited him.

She considered him. 'How about you let me decide that? Or is it a secret? For your eyes only.' She laughed and snapped open her bag and took out her cigarettes. She shook a cigarette out of the packet and offered it. He took the cigarette and she lit it with a lighter. They stood smoking and looking at each other. Her smile was self-mocking, or was maybe mocking him. He wasn't sure. The situation seemed to amuse her. In a moment she would be gone. 'If you're really interested, I suppose you could have a look.'

'So let's go,' she said.

He caught then a sense of her nervousness and it made him nervous too.

She said, 'How many cleaners do I know who spend their weekends drawing?'

He opened the door for her. 'I live just up the road here.'

They went out of the cafe and walked back to the boarding house. As they were crossing the broad stretch of Dandenong Road she put her arm through his, her hip and shoulder touching him lightly. Her confidence confused and excited him. He had been alone so long he hardly knew how to behave. He said, 'Are you married?'

She laughed and squeezed his arm. 'What a question.'

'Are you?'

'We're separated.'

'So it didn't work out between you?'

'For God's sake, who wants to talk about that shit?' There was a warning in her voice.

He wondered if she had children. He didn't ask.

They turned in at the broken gate and walked up the drive. He was worried the landlady might object to his inviting a woman into the house. He opened the front door with his key. There was no one in the hall. The noise of the television in the lounge room. He was nervous and clumsy and bumped against her as they started up the stairs. He whispered an apology and she laughed, their shoulders touching again. They went up the stairs and he opened the door to his room and stepped aside to let her go in first. He went in after her and closed the door. He stood watching her, his room charged with anxiety and hope.

She walked over to the table and looked at the drawing lying there in the open sketchbook. He did not know what was expected of him and was ashamed of his ignorance. He had never been alone with a grown woman in a bedroom. Maybe she really had only come to his room to see his drawing. How was he to know? Should he just walk over there and take her in his arms and kiss her? Get it over with? Do the manly thing? One girl of nineteen in Taunton. That was it. They'd made love in the doorway of her house, awkward, terrified, clumsy, both more than half drunk, her weeping afterwards with fear. The entire history of his love life in that darkened doorway one rainy night.

She turned and looked at him. 'You're an intense bugger, aren't you?'

'Intense? Am I? I don't really know. Why do you say that?' He moved away from the door and went over to the desk and stood next to her.

She turned to him and put her hand on his upper arm. 'How old are you?'

'Twenty-two. How old are you?'

She let go of his arm. 'Your drawing's very good,' she said. 'It's you.'

'I suppose so.' He reached and touched the drawing with his fingers. Her admiration pleased him. He looked at her and met her eyes, wondering about her. He might give her the drawing. Her eyes were grey. She seemed to be relaxed, calm, sure of what she was doing. She said, 'You should come and meet the crowd at the Swanston Family Hotel. You'll meet artists like yourself there. We're all struggling after something.'

'So you think the drawing's okay?' Her approval touched something vital and hungry in him and he needed to hear her tell him again that his drawing was good. 'What do you mean, that it's me?' The ease with which she had touched him. He longed to feel the certainty of that confident connection himself.

They stood side by side looking down at the red ochre man in his nakedness. She reached and ran the tips of her fingers lightly over its surface, just as he had done a moment before, as if his gesture had given her permission. The drawing's heavily worked surface inviting touch.

'The fighting man,' she said thoughtfully. 'His fury and his helpless anger.' She looked at him. 'That's you, isn't it?' She held his gaze, her own eyes filled with longing and understanding and sadness and many other things he could not and never would fathom. 'All this energy,' she said. 'And the strength. And no idea what to do with it.' She paused. 'I've watched you at work.'

He couldn't take his eyes from the pulse of the artery in her neck. He dared himself to feel her warm blood pulsing under his fingers, or under his lips, the lightest kiss there, her blood speaking to him of his own blood.

She said, 'You're ambitious. But you don't know what for. I suppose you stood in front of that mirror in the nude posing for yourself?'

They stood looking at each other, the tension in him so great he forgot to breathe. 'I just did it out of my head.' His voice was hoarse, his heart pounding.

She smiled and reached to touch his lips with her forefinger. 'My God, you have such deep lustrous brown eyes.'

The light brush of her finger across his lips sent an electric pulse into his groin. A fierce shiver of anticipation shot through him. He was trembling.

She put a hand to his cheek. 'You're cold.' Her voice little more than a whisper. She took him by the hand and walked him to his narrow bed in the corner. At the side of the bed she turned to him and they kissed, her full warm body pressing against him. His uncertainty vanished, banished by a powerful wave of lust. They took off their clothes and lay down on the bed together. She lay on her back beneath him and looked into his eyes, then she took him inside her and she sobbed and cried out, her eyes closed, her white arms stretched out above her head as if reaching for something to hold on to, to save herself, and she cried out again and again.

He opened his eyes. She was looking at him. Her eyes with tiny flecks of green and blue scattered among the grey. She took his hand and kissed his fingers. 'Thank you.' There were tears in her eyes. 'I'm old.'

He laughed. 'Don't cry!'

'Women cry,' she said. 'I'm happy.'

'You're perfect. You're not old. I've never made love with a real woman before.'

They lay close up together in the narrow bed. A door slammed downstairs and a man's voice called.

He whispered, 'I don't know your name.'

'Do you want to know my name?' she whispered back.

'Do you want to know mine?'

'Wendy,' she said.

'Robert.'

She murmured, 'Hello, Robert.'

'Hi, Wendy. I've never been this happy.'

She snuggled against him and he held her close. Neither spoke for some time. Then she eased back from him and said, 'You must have done other drawings. You know how to draw. How did you learn?'

'My dad taught me when I was a boy.' He kissed the pulse in her neck, touching the beating artery so lightly with his lips it felt like the struggles of a tiny trapped insect.

She put her hand down between his legs and held him with a sudden strong grip. 'You've still got your lovely erection.' She laughed softly. 'What are you going to do with it?'

They made love again, gentle and slow this time. She whispered, 'Stay inside me!'

5

——

Her voice close to his ear woke him. 'Get me a cigarette. There are some in my bag.' He opened his eyes. She smiled at him. 'I haven't had an orgasm as good as that for years!'

He said, 'I've never had one like that.' He lightly caressed her lips, her nose with the tips of his fingers. Then he leaned over the side of the bed and found her cigarettes. He lit two and placed one between her lips. He wanted to tell her he was in love with her, but he held back. He rested on his elbow and looked down at her, admiring her. Gently he caressed her nipples.

She blew smoke at him. 'You're an idiot. I must seem so old to you.'

'You mustn't keep saying that. There's nothing old about you. You're beautiful. I like you being older than me. You should be proud of your beauty.' He placed his hand on her belly. 'I love you! I want to know everything about you.'

She pushed his hand away and sat up. 'You mustn't fall in love with me! Promise me!'

The room was almost dark. She was silhouetted against the pale rectangle of the window. 'It's too late,' he said. 'I'm already in love with you. You've worked your magic spell on me. Lie down again. I need to feel you beside me.'

She stood up and stepped across him and off the bed. She picked up her underpants and pulled them on.

'I'm sorry,' he said. 'I shouldn't have said that.'

She said, 'I had true love. It stinks. True love is a bucket of shit.'

The harshness of her tone shocked him. He was shocked by this sudden turn. He watched her putting her clothes on. She turned and looked down at him. He said, 'I shan't say it again. I promise. I can't help how I feel.'

'You're a loner,' she said. 'Face it.' She buttoned the front of her dress.

'So what if I am? What's that supposed to mean?'

'You don't need love.'

'Everyone needs love.'

'That's crap!'

'You sound bitter about it.'

She was sitting on the side of the bed putting her stockings on.

'Anyway, how do you know I'm a loner?' He was longing for the good feeling between them to come back but had no idea what he had to do to retrieve it.

Wendy stood up then bent forward, took her hair in both hands and dragged it forward over her face. She stood ruffling her hands through the thick mass of her dark hair. Then she straightened and pulled her hair back hard. She turned and looked down at him. 'There's no need to go all quiet and hurt. Okay? I like you. I like your drawing. We can be friends and lovers, can't we?' She picked her cigarette off the bed end and took a drag. 'There's a wine bar off Glenferrie Road. We can get a drink there. There's no need to go all sad and gloomy. We had great sex. We don't need to spoil it by making a big deal of it. Sex is great. Love stinks. Get over it.'

6

——

They went out and turned into a small side street off Glenferrie Road. It was little more than an alleyway. He followed her down the steps. There were no lights. She knocked on a door. It was opened by a tall thin man with red hair and bright red lips wearing a large blue and yellow silk bow tie and a striped silk shirt. He stood examining them in the soft golden light of the interior. 'Hello, darling, who's your beau?' He kissed Wendy on the cheek and shook Robert's hand. 'I'm Nigel.' He bent and looked closely at Robert. 'It's lovely to meet you, Robert. Any mate of our Wendy's is always welcome.' He made a wide flourishing gesture with his right arm. 'Sit anywhere.' Nigel bestowed upon Robert a grave and gentle smile, then he closed the door on the night and the outside world.

A man was sitting on a stool on a raised platform in front of a curtain, playing a saxophone, the sound soft and intimate, drifting on the smoky air, almost going into a silence. There was a murmuring of talk from the people in the booths. When Wendy and Robert came in, one or two of the people looked across and waved to Wendy. A large woman stood beside the saxophonist, her eyes closed, swaying to the music, one chubby hand resting lightly on the saxophonist's shoulder. She was wearing a blue floor-length silk dress cut very low. He was wearing a white open-necked shirt and slacks and was leaning over his gleaming instrument as if he was telling it a secret, his long blond hair falling in a curtain either side of his face.

There were several tables in the centre of the room and three booths along each side, their curved seating upholstered in worn red plush. There were people in each of the booths. The five tables in the centre of the floor were unoccupied. Wendy walked to the back of the room and pulled out one of the tub chairs at the last table by the wall. An amateurish mural in bright pinks and blues and greens on the wall behind her, naked boy and girl nymphs bathing in a mountain stream, unlikely-looking willows hanging over them.

Nigel came over and Wendy asked Robert what he would drink. She said, 'It's mine.'

He said, 'I'll have what you're having.'

She ordered two martinis.

Nigel served the vermouth and gin in small Y-shaped glasses, and left them to it.

They lit cigarettes and sipped their drinks. Robert looked around with interest. 'Your secret haunt,' he said.

'I love it here.' She leaned back, crossed her legs and took a sip of her drink, looking at him through the drift of smoke from her cigarette. 'So tell me about yourself.'

'There's not much to tell.'

'Tell me anyway.'

He sat looking at her for a while, saying nothing, admiring her. 'You just saved my life.'

'Don't start that shit again. Tell me your story.'

He was thinking that she looked tired around the eyes, older, more thoughtful, more elusive, remote, as if she had drawn back away from their too-sudden intimacy into her own place. He was deeply enchanted by her and wanted to reassure her. He said, 'So what do you do when you're not working at Myer?'

She said, 'I work for a socialist workers' newspaper, writing, editing, designing, distributing it around the factories and work-places, having meetings, raising funds. We do everything ourselves.' She drank the last of her martini and set the glass on the table.

'Is the money any good?'

She regarded him narrowly. 'We don't do it for money. Now it's your turn.'

As the night wore on, the tables in the middle of the room filled up with people and the big woman with her hand on the saxophonist's shoulder started singing, a low, crooning, throaty accompaniment to the mellow, interior voice of the sax, the two of them weaving in and out of each other like playful lovers in a dream of their own. Wendy and Robert talked and smoked their cigarettes and drank several martinis.

He told her his life story, from the Blitz in London to his arrival in Melbourne. She didn't interrupt but watched him. When he fell silent she said nothing for a long time but sat looking at him. Then she said, 'So what you've lost your boyhood dream?' Her voice was just a little slurry, tiredness and an edge of impatience in her tone. 'We all lose our youthful dreams. We need to. It's like losing our virginity. That stuff's useless to us. We have to take ourselves seriously sooner or later. Youthful dreams confuse us if we don't let them go.' She signalled to Nigel and he brought over two fresh martinis and set them on the table. She said, 'It's time you faced up to yourself. You say you've got nothing and no idea what to do with your life. I say you've got everything and it's time you started paying your dues.' She lifted herself in her seat, picked up her drink and took a sip and gave a heavy sigh. 'Everyone has to pay his dues sooner or later. It's your job now to write about your time up north with Frankie and his people.' She pointed her finger at him. 'That's your duty. It's the least you can do for him, and for the rest of us.'

'You think so?'

'I know so.'

'I'm not a writer.'

She mimicked his voice, giving it a whiny edge. 'I'm not an artist! I'm not a writer! You're a writer if you *write*! It's that simple. I'm a writer when I write for our paper and I'm a cleaner when I'm cleaning at Myer. They taught you how to write at school, didn't they? It's disgusting that people like Frankie and his mob have to put up with that shit from us! It's the middle of the twentieth century, for God's sake. No one down here knows about it. I didn't know about it. You say there's nothing to be done. That's bullshit. You can do something to help your friends up there. It's what you should be doing now instead of sitting around moaning about losing your stupid dreams. It's what you owe your friend.' She regarded him with a look of contempt. 'It's time to stop moaning, Mr Robert Crofts, and to do something serious for others. Write the story you just told me. Make people sit up and take notice. Tell them the way it really is. Give them the facts. Okay? Our paper will publish it.' She sculled her drink then sat back. 'Do it! I'll love you for it if you do.'

'Promise?'

'I'd be happy to edit your writing for you. We'll work it up. I'll see to it the story gets published.' She uncrossed her legs and gathered herself. 'I'm whacked! I'm going home to bed.'

'Come home with me,' he said.

'Your bed's too small. Anyway, I have to feed the cat.' She stood up. 'Some of us have responsibilities.' She laughed. It was not a happy laugh.

They got up and said goodnight to Nigel. Robert followed her out of the wine bar and up the dark stairs. Outside on the street it was quiet, the night air cool. An empty tram was rattling slowly towards them along Glenferrie Road. Two men arm in arm greeted

Wendy and went down the steps and knocked on the door. Wendy ran for the tram and jumped on board. Robert stood watching her. He was expecting her to turn at the last minute and give him a wave, but she didn't. He stood watching the tram, swaying and clattering, until it went out of sight down the hill. He had a deep feeling of emptiness.

He turned and walked back towards Dandenong Road and the boarding house. He let himself into his room and lay face down on the rumpled bedsheets without undressing and he breathed in the smell of her body and her sweat and their wonderful sex.

7

—

On Monday after work he waited around in the change room but Wendy didn't turn up. He'd been thinking about her all day, wondering how she was going to greet him when he saw her coming in wearing her bandeau and her overalls, pushing her rubbish cart. He sat on the bench smoking a cigarette, waiting for her. But she didn't come. It was after six by the time he left. On the way down Swanston Street to catch his tram home he went into the art supplies shop. He bought a lined exercise book and a fountain pen, and when he got home he sat at the table by the window overlooking the elm copse and he started writing the story he'd told her about Frankie and his mob. She had said, *I will love you for it.*

Two hours later he gave up. He knew the story by heart. He had lived it. Telling Wendy had been a pleasure. He didn't have to make anything up. So why was it so difficult to make it come alive on the page? When he'd sat down to write he had assumed he would just put the story down more or less word for word as he'd told it to her. He sat at the table smoking another cigarette and staring out at the elms, wondering why it was that Frankie's story resisted him now. There had been an enchantment in telling Wendy the story of himself and Frankie, a secret sexual pleasure between the two of them, thinking of her naked and hidden away in his bed with him, their bodies touching, the after-ache of sex in his loins, Nigel's gin and the saxophone working their little tricks in his head. There was no magic in trying to write it.

He tore out the pages in the exercise book that were filled with his writing and screwed them up and chucked them on the floor. Then he leaned over the fresh clean page and with care in a neat hand he wrote at the top of the page: *Speak to me of my blood*. He knew what he meant. The phrase was in his head and it had to be said. It was like the graffito he'd written in pencil on the wall of the pub toilet in Townsville. A thought he could not share with anyone else. *Why do I live?* he wrote underneath the first phrase. Then, *What is the purpose of my life?* He sat back and looked at the three phrases, all written in his best handwriting. The first phrase was the most satisfying. The others had meaning but were less so. Reading the first phrase he experienced the surprising feeling that with the simple act of setting it down he had established a place from which to reach out beyond the mysterious thing itself. Not an answer or a starting point, but a place. He could not see why this was so, but as he carefully inscribed these thoughts in the pages of his notebook, he had the feeling he was not writing to himself, but was writing to someone who was even more real than he was. Someone; a nameless identity who understood him as precisely as he understood himself. He wrote: *My first self. My inner self. The one who does not have to try to be real but who is real just by being there.* There was an exhilarating satisfaction for him in this unexpected sense of an intimate communication with himself that he'd not felt while he was struggling to write the story of Frankie and his mob.

He sat looking at the neatly inscribed phrases on the new page of the notebook. What intrigued him was the question of how he was to bridge the gap between this real self and the person who struggled to write the story of his friendship with Frankie. It obviously wasn't simply a matter of setting down the facts. The confused struggle to be real and to exist decently and with some purpose. The serene certainty of this inner self. How was he to bridge the gap between these two senses of himself? He leaned forward and wrote beneath the last phrase: *You're ambitious. But you don't know what for.* Was he ambitious? He'd never associated any of his feelings with the idea of ambition.

Then, with his softly smooth new fountain pen, which he had begun to love, he wrote, giving to each phrase its own private blue line in the exercise book, *His fury and his helpless anger.* Her admiration for his drawing thrilled him. Her beautiful woman's body naked beside him in his bed, warm and close and trusting, her desire for him. He should have run after her and jumped on the tram and insisted on going home with her. He wrote, and it was as if he wrote a sacred text that only he would ever understand or decipher, *The fighting man.* Her voice in the phrase. 'All this energy. And the strength.' His own strength. He said aloud, 'I love you, Wendy.' What was her surname? She was married. Divorced. Did she have children? How old was she? Where did she live? Alone with her cat?

He was confident the notebook would accept any thought or idea he cared to put to it, no matter how intimate or how deeply concealed. He thought of his mother, when they were alone during the war, and she was sitting in the window smoking a cigarette some rainy afternoon, taking a break from the chores and reflecting on her life, as she used to do, telling him stories of her hopes when she was a young woman at the convent in Chantilly before she returned to England and met his father. If she were here she would read these phrases and smile and touch his hair. 'My difficult child.' And she would turn away and look out into the street, reminded of herself and her regrets.

It was very late and he was tired but he was reluctant to close the notebook and go to bed. He wrote one last phrase: *The close acquaintance of my soul*. He heard himself speak the phrase aloud, his voice in the hollow throat of the empty room.

8

———

He sat on the bench in the middle of the locker room at Myer on Tuesday after work, smoking a cigarette and waiting for her, his elbows on his knees, staring between his legs at the floor. He had decided to try writing about his friendship with Frankie as if it was a letter to Wendy. Even just thinking this, he could hear the phrases flowing smoothly in his head, the story unfolding of its own volition. He was smiling at the thought of just listening to the voice of the story and writing it down.

The door to the passage swung open and Wendy came into the change room. She was wearing her brown and yellow bandeau and her pale brown Myer-issue overalls with the yellow embroidered M on the breast, pushing her cart with its brooms and mops and bags. He stood up, a huge wave of relief and love sweeping through him. 'God, you're so bloody beautiful!' he said, and he stepped across and took her in his arms and kissed her.

When he paused to breathe, she said in a small, teasing voice, 'So you still want to know me, then?'

He dared not tell her he loved her in case it angered her, so he said the second thing that came into his head, which was just as true: 'You smell wonderful.' He had liked her smell from the beginning. She didn't wear perfume, but when he was close to her she had a lovely warm womanly smell that made him feel deeply good. He did love her. He would keep it a secret. Friends and lovers, she'd said. He would be content. She snuggled close to him in his arms and he held her tightly against him, the starched, cheap material of her overalls under his hand. There were obviously multiples of this woman. She might run away any minute and jump on another tram. He might never see her again. She might elude him forever. Now she was in his arms. He said, 'You're a mystery and an inspiration to me.'

She laughed and freed herself from his embrace. 'Well, you won't mind giving me a hand to clean up this room then, will you?'

He grabbed one of the canvas bags and went around the change room emptying the ashtrays and picking up the bottles and papers and cigarette butts the cleaners had left lying around. When they were done he left her and went out into the street and waited till she came out wearing her dress and Cuban heels, her thick dark mass of hair flowing around her shoulders. She kissed him and put her arm in his and they walked down Swanston Street side by side and got on his tram. On the tram they sat close together and kept looking at each other and smiling. He leaned close and kissed her. 'You are even more beautiful than I remember you.'

The landlady was coming down the stairs as they were going up. She nodded to Wendy and said good evening to Robert and they went on up to his room and the landlady went on down to her kitchen. When he had closed the door to the room, Wendy turned to him and they embraced, their hunger for each other urgent. They laughed and grabbed hold of each other wildly, moaning and swaying around, kissing and nearly losing their balance, their hands going everywhere, bumping into the door, then staggering over to the bed and struggling out of their clothes.

It was dark when he woke, the cool vertical of the window leaking a weak illumination into the room. He was lying on his back. She lay with her arm and one leg over him, her face nuzzled into his chest. He folded his arms around her and kissed her neck. 'I do love you,' he whispered. She murmured and rolled away to lie beside him. He sat up on his elbow and looked down at her. She was laughing softly to herself. 'What's so funny?'

'I'm happy,' she said. She reached and ran her finger lightly across his lips. 'You make me feel like a girl again. I'd almost forgotten it could be like this.'

He could see the pale rectangle of the window reflected deep in her eyes.

They kissed then lay beside each other in the silence. The sounds of the house, the screeching tram wheels going around the corner into Glenferrie Road, were sounds from another world, her sweet breath in his face.

She said, 'Did you start writing Frankie's story?'

'I'm writing it for you,' he said.

'Can I read it?'

'Not yet. I'm imagining you living thousands of miles away in another country waiting anxiously to hear from me. It's my letter to you from the outback.'

'So where am I?' she said.

'You're in the country where your people came from originally.'

'And where is that?'

'It's over there, somewhere. It's dark and cold in the winter. It doesn't have a name. You're waiting for the postman to bring you my letter. You look out of your window every day and watch for him coming down the road on his bicycle. Your mother worries about you.'

She was silent a while, then she said, 'You're such a romantic. Your mother must have waited in England for a letter like that from you after you came out here as a boy.'

He leaned over the side of the bed and felt in his trouser pockets for his cigarettes. He lit a cigarette and handed it to her. She had a puff then handed it back. He lay on his back and looked at the pale window. He said, 'Can you see the clouds going by? They're lit up underneath by the lights of the city.'

Wendy said, 'I've been offered a job with the union. It's part-time. I'll still be able to work with the paper.'

'Are you saying you'll be quitting Myer?' He had a nasty feeling she was going to tell him this was goodbye.

She took the cigarette from between his lips and had another puff then set it between his lips again. 'I'm finishing up next week. I've done this job for long enough anyway.' She sounded relaxed about it.

'Will we still see each other?' He was afraid of her answer.

She put her hand on his thigh, the touch of her fingers sending an electric pulse into his balls. 'Of course we'll see each other. We're friends now.'

Friends and lovers, he thought.

'And, anyway, I want to read your Frankie story when it's done. It's important. You'll need help to get it published.'

'You scared the shit out of me there for a minute.'

She sat up and leaned over him and kissed him on the mouth, her breasts pressing against his chest. She sat back. 'Let's go and have a meal at the Greek cafe. I'm hungry.'

'So you didn't mind me saying I love you just now?'

'Just don't make a habit of it.' She kissed him again, her breath smoky. 'Okay?' She put her finger to his lips and pressed it hard. 'I mean it. I'm not going down that track with you or with anyone else ever again.' Then she said, 'True love is a bucket of shit, believe me.'

'That bad, eh?'

'Yeah.'

'You taught me something about myself,' he said.

'It's what friends do. It always takes someone else to tell us the truth about who we are.'

9

——

He was sitting at the table in his room, his fountain pen in his left hand, a new exercise book open in front of him. He was writing his long letter to Wendy, the woman who waited for him on the other side of the world, the woman he loved and longed to be with all the time. Writing to her was a way of being with her. And with himself. While he was writing he never asked himself what his life might be, or what the meaning of it all really was. When he was writing his letter to his lover he did not doubt the meaning of his life. He had found that the more he dwelled on those days in the Gulf with Frankie the more detail he was able to recover. The detail of their lives, which he thought he had forgotten, was still there; as he wrote, so it opened out to him. He was deep into a memory of Frankie and himself dogging a wild micky when there was a sharp knock on his door. He stopped writing and sat looking straight ahead out the window into the night. The knock came again. He heard the door open and swung around in his seat.

A man looked around the door and smiled at him. 'Sorry,' the man said. 'I saw your light under the door.' He came into the room. 'I hope I'm not interrupting anything.'

Robert said angrily, 'Do you always barge into people's rooms like this? You want to watch yourself, mate.' Robert had seen him driving in the little green car. He was not one of the workers but was always smartly dressed in a suit and tie, as he was now. A man in his mid-thirties. Smooth.

'Sorry!' the man said, but he didn't turn around and go out again. He walked over and stood close beside Robert, a broad smile on his face as if he thought he was sure to be made welcome. His confidence irritated Robert.

The man held out his hand. 'John Morris,' he said. 'I've seen you about.'

Robert didn't stand. He reached over and shook John Morris's hand. The skin was dry and crinkly, as if it had a fine plastic covering over the bones. He was over six feet, taller than Robert by a couple of inches. His teeth were astonishingly white and perfectly even. He had the smile of a movie star. Robert thought of Rock Hudson, only leaner. His face was tanned, his skin smooth, his features sharp and cleanly made, his hair thick and dark and glossy, swept back from his broad forehead. Robert caught a faint whiff of cologne. John Morris was wearing a white shirt and tie and a greenish tweed suit. Very smart, the whole outfit.

'Meg's always talking about you,' he said, 'so I thought I'd come and see for myself.'

'Who's Meg?' Robert said.

John Morris leaned over the table and looked at the exercise book. 'Meg's our landlady. So what are you writing? Can I have a look?'

He didn't wait for Robert's permission but picked up the exercise book and started reading. Robert watched him. He was thinking of snatching the book out of the man's hands and telling him to get the fuck out of his room and to mind his own fucking business. What held him back from doing this was a queer little desire in him for this man's approval. Instead of kicking the man out, Robert said nothing, but sat there glumly watching the intruder reading the words that were meant only for the eyes of the woman he loved.

There were times in Robert's life when he felt nothing but contempt for himself. This was one of them. He lit a cigarette and sucked the smoke deep into his lungs. What disgusted him in particular was that he was seeing in John Morris the same authority he had known in his teachers. An educated man of the middle class, someone who knew what was what. Robert believed in his Frankie story. He thought it was just as good as his fighting man, or maybe even better, and he wanted to have this opinion confirmed by John Morris. The work, he might be about to say, of a naturally gifted writer. Something like that. Robert smoked his cigarette and crossed his legs and looked up at John Morris, waiting for the verdict. And he saw that John Morris was reading with concentrated care, turning each page slowly and frowning through his horn-rimmed glasses. Downstairs a woman's voice was raised in anger and then a door slammed. Robert knew there were a number of boarders in the house he'd never met, people who had rooms on the other side, close to the drive, where painting and repairs had been carried out.

John Morris closed the exercise book and set it down on the table beside Robert's hand and he looked down at Robert. 'Well,' he said, measuring Robert with his gaze, not particularly friendly now but not altogether unfriendly either, examining his new find.

Robert said, 'Well what?'

'Don't get upset.' John Morris laughed, his even white teeth flashing. 'Well, you've had an interesting life.'

Robert butted his cigarette in the ashtray and looked out at the night. The leaves on the elms shining in the light from the window, the distant sound of traffic, not a breath of wind. Robert turned around and looked at Frankie's hat and his spurs and leather leggings, blackened and stained and smelling of the sweat of horses, hanging on the brass hook behind the bedroom door like the skin of some old carcass. That life he had known with the legendary stockmen on the great plains of the Gulf Country. He and Frankie hadn't needed many words. In Frankie's company, silence had its own way of delivering their thoughts. It was his silence that Frankie shared. Robert looked up at John Morris standing there beside him, standing far too close for comfort, his expression serious, thoughtful, pondering something. A man who would perish alone in the Gulf. A man who would have no chance of making any headway in those boundless grasslands. Frankie and his mob were contemptuous of the kind of man John Morris was and they made no secret of it. A useless poor bastard, that was how they would describe him. He would need rescuing. He would not stand alone for longer than a day. And yet Robert knew that just then this man was more powerful than the superior race of men who had stood with him in the Gulf, and this knowledge made him sorrowful. Morris's eyes were grey and pale and the look in them made Robert uneasy with feelings of a deep inadequacy to ever prosper in the same world as the world in which John Morris prospered. He was powerful. His presence. What he stood for here. The privilege of education, money, success. His substance in the life of the city. His authority. Part of Robert hated him.

Robert said, 'So what do you do for a living?'

'I'm a lecturer in the economics department at Melbourne University.' John Morris smiled down at him. 'Before that I was a high school teacher. I haven't had an interesting life the way you have.'

Robert said, 'It sounds okay to me.'

'If you want to be a writer,' John Morris said, 'you'll have to go to the university and learn something about the history of your culture. You'll have to read the great literature.'

'I didn't say I wanted to be a writer.'

'But you *do*,' he said vehemently, impatient with Robert's denial. 'Those guys downstairs aren't sweating over their writing in the evening. *You* are. Don't look so down about it, for God's sake. You might not enjoy the university but you'll meet people like yourself there. One or two, if you're lucky. And maybe get one or two good teachers who'll inspire you.' He gestured dismissively at the exercise book on the table. 'You'll soon improve on that. You might even make something readable of it. It's basically a good story. You just need to learn how to write. And you will. I'm sure of it. You've made a start on your own. That's important. You've got ambition.'

Robert didn't say anything. This man's recommendation that he go to the university sounded like Wendy's recommendation that he go to the Swanston Family Hotel and meet her artistic friends. A place to meet your own kind, she had said. Loners. Robert doubted it. What were they doing drinking in a mob if they were loners? At least this John Morris character hadn't said he was a loner. John Morris stood there looking down at Robert, and when Robert didn't say anything, John Morris said, 'There are coaching colleges in the city. Taylor's is the best of them. You should enrol there for your university entrance exams.'

Robert said, 'I'm not bright enough for the university.' What he really meant was that in his mind the word 'university' stood for Oxford and Cambridge, a world of birth and privilege as far removed from the world of the Council estate where he'd grown up as it was possible to be; a world he knew to be insulated against the entry of people like himself. Secretly, of course, his inner self knew very well he was intelligent enough to go to the university. In that place where things touched his soul, where the sources of his self-esteem were guarded, his confidence in his intelligence was pure and unlimited.

'That's bullshit, and I think you know it,' John Morris said, his confidence washing around him like a tide of excessive goodwill. 'You're as intelligent as any of my students. And you've made a start on your own! You wouldn't have done that if you'd thought you weren't up to it. You've got a bit of catching up to do, Robert, that's all. You'll benefit at once from being guided in your reading and writing by people who know their subjects. On your own you'll flounder helplessly and get frustrated. Or, God forbid, you'll become one of those self-taught fools who think they know better.' John Morris placed a hand on Robert's shoulder and leaned down; Robert flinched when he caught a whiff of the other man's sour breath. 'We all need the help of other people,' John Morris said confidingly, his lips uncomfortably close to Robert's face. 'None of us does it alone. None of us!' John Morris straightened and took a step away, then swung back, as if the energy of his conviction moved him. 'Just do it!'

The idea of the university was remote and exotic, something Robert had never even dreamed about. But there it was, a glimmer of possibility in this man's words. He looked up and met John Morris's gaze. Despite his visceral dislike of John Morris, Robert trusted his judgement. There was no doubt about it: loathsome and condescending as he was, he was nevertheless authentic. Robert said, 'Have you done any writing yourself?'

'I've published three books. All economics, I'm afraid. I'm working on a fourth.'

'What's it about, the one you're working on?' Robert was thinking that if he were to go to the university he would no longer have to stand in line with the helpless people on the margins and might step across that line from ignorance and poverty and become a fully real person. He might even become a writer who would tell the world about Frankie and his mob and the disgusting way they were being treated by people who thought themselves civilised and superior. Robert looked at his exercise book and he knew the power of that truth wasn't in what he'd written. John Morris was right. He knew that. It hurt to know it. But still he knew it.

'Well, it's actually about my first love,' John Morris said. 'Which is probably why it's going so slowly. I'm writing a double history of Venice and Sydney. They're both great cities on the water. They have a lot in common.'

'And it's not going so well?'

'Slowly,' John Morris said and laughed. He was relaxed now and he stepped back and looked around the room. 'So that's your stuff there?' He was looking at Robert's gear hanging on the back of the door. 'Mind if I have a look?' Again he didn't wait for the okay from Robert but walked over to the door and took Frankie's hat off the hook.

Robert watched John Morris with a mixture of disgust and disbelief as he put Frankie's hat on his head and walked across and looked at his reflection in the mirror door of the wardrobe, putting his head on one side, adopting a pose. 'The Marlboro Man,'

John Morris said, and he looked around at Robert and laughed, delighted with himself, ready to be admired.

'Keep it,' Robert said coldly, a snarl in his voice. He hated himself for saying it, but he said it all the same, then he repeated it for good measure, pressing the blade into his own flesh. 'Keep it!' It wasn't an offer but an order.

John Morris whipped the hat off at once and looked at it as if it had burned his head. 'No, no. Don't be silly. You can't give me your hat. I'm sure it's precious to you.'

Robert scraped his chair back and stood up so he was facing John Morris. Slowly, articulating each word separately so as not to lose control, he said, 'I told you to keep it.'

John Morris stood with the hat in his hands, helpless suddenly.

'It's yours.' Contempt, self-loathing, anger, the sinister presence of violence in Robert's voice. His heart beating fast, shortening his breathing, a thickening in his chest.

'Don't be silly.' John Morris spoke gently, softly, almost pleading, cowed now, afraid and at a loss for his confidence. 'You don't have to give it to me. It means far too much to you, I can see that.'

Robert stepped up to him and John Morris stepped away, the backs of his legs coming up against the edge of the bed. 'Take the fucking hat!' Robert said. His father's old post-war rage rising in him. He heard it; it rose in him and he was dismayed. But there wasn't anything he could do to stop the fury coming out of him at the sight of this man with Frankie's hat. That was it for him. John Morris playing at cowboys, mixing the smell of his sweat with Frankie's sacred smell. There was no way now for Robert to take back the hat without knowing himself defeated by this miserable situation. There was no reason in him about it, just a terrible disorder and fury. His father's antique values. That's what this was, according to which Frankie's hat now belonged to John Morris, a precious thing enriched by the faltering story Robert had written about it, the story John Morris had read and discarded. Something of the predator in his presence in the room. Robert felt pillaged by him. The violence of it surging in him as he watched John Morris turn around and place the hat gingerly on the bed. He straightened and stepped away from the bed. 'You must keep it,' he said, moving away from Robert, fear in his eyes.

Robert picked up the hat and thrust it at him, crushing the crown against John Morris's chest, dislodging Frankie's plaited band, John Morris's back colliding with the mirror door of the wardrobe. Robert grabbed him and spun him around and pushed him hard, driving him towards the door. 'Fuck off,' he yelled. 'I gave it to you! It's fucking yours, you cunt!' He was choking on his fury now. 'Just fuck off!' If John Morris resisted, Robert knew he would smash him. He might even kill him. His heart was pounding. He couldn't get enough air into his lungs. He was set to go off. Sweat breaking out between his shoulder blades. He pushed John Morris out the door and slammed it shut, then he leaned against the door breathing hard, an image in his head of John Morris's terror.

When Robert had recovered his breath he straightened up and lit a cigarette and went over and sat on the bed. He held his hands out in front of him and watched them trembling. He was afraid he might become his father. He was seeing his dad sitting in his armchair by the coal fire reading the poems of Robert Burns that evening soon after he was home from the front, the sound of Robert's mother in the kitchen preparing the evening meal, the hiss and creak of the coals. And his father looking up from his book and asking in the menacing voice that commanded his father at times then, 'Are you going to clean up the mess you've made?' What had Robert been doing, sitting at the table in the centre of the room? Drawing or writing? Crumpled balls of paper lying on the floor. There was nothing unreasonable in his father's question. Just that tone of voice. Robert got up off his chair and collected the pieces of paper and took them out through the kitchen to the dustbin on the back balcony. His mother reached and touched his arm as he went past her, warning him, cautioning him, her beautiful black eyes on him, the faint smell of her, her divine mother smell, the smell of love. He came back into the front room and stood by his father and looked into the fire. His father was reading Burns again—his poet hero whose name he had given to his son. But everything had changed. The clock on the sideboard ticked. Then the question: 'Have you finished cleaning up?' His father's voice quiet, the menace in the peculiar rhythm of its silence, its waiting moment, the step between each word. 'I've done it,' Robert said, a dumbness settling in him. And his father looked up from his book of poems and stared at him. Robert met his gaze. Father and son looking at each other in the terrible silence, from the kitchen the cautious click of a plate set down carefully on the stone sink by the mother, her anxiety in that small sound, a door closing in the flat below, Mrs Snee coming home from the pub. 'What about that piece under the sofa by your feet?' His father's voice from a long way off now. Robert said nothing, his eyes fixed now on the red coals of the fire, committed to the playing out of the ritual. There was no way back. What was it that prevented him from picking up that last piece of paper and taking it out and putting it in the dustbin with the others? Why was he unable to obey his father on this one small point? Why was he unable to speak? Was he determined to bring it on? Did he sense, in some awful way, that he must offer his father his chance to express the fury that was devouring him? Who else would offer his father this terrible freedom? 'Come here!' his father said quietly. And in his eyes the control was failing him now. He closed his precious book and set it aside on the table next to his chair. That book, his old Burns, a first Glasgow edition, quarter calf and deeply worn from several lifetimes of loving use. It had belonged to his own grandfather and his father, and was probably picked up for a song in a second-hand bookshop in Glasgow by the grandfather in the first place, a book already old even then, a thing from the eighteenth century, loved, cherished, its lamentations ringing out for all men to hear. Its spine broken. Its endpapers detached. A book of verse. The songs of his father's people. The war was over. Robert almost a man in his own eyes; his father, going back to the front from a twenty-four-hour leave, instructing him: 'Look after your mother and sister. You're the man in charge now.' He stood between his father's knees, gripped by his father's thighs, and father and son looked into each other's eyes. 'Are you going to answer me?' his father said. The clock ticked. His father struck him on the cheek with the flat of his hand. Robert regained his balance after the blow and waited and was ready for it when he was struck again, harder this time, his father adjusting his shoulders to get the force of the swing into it, more fierce now, more brutal. His father had boxed in his regiment and knew how to strike a blow. Robert saw the tears in his father's eyes. Before he could regain his balance his father struck him again, and then again, and again, the frenzy taking him, depriving him of his breath, his sobs tearing at his throat. Robert didn't cry out. He rode each blow as it came. He made no sound. At last his mother came in from the kitchen and took Robert's arm and dragged him away from the furious beating. She took him into his bedroom and sat him on the bed and she wiped the blood from his face with her handkerchief and hugged him to her chest and she wept, holding his head to her breast, the smell of his mother's hair. 'He doesn't mean it, darling,' she sobbed. 'It's the war.' She didn't have to tell him that. He knew his father didn't mean it. He knew, without knowing, that his father's suffering, his despair, was beyond him and he loved his father to distraction and was glad he could take the beating from him. Knowing silence to be the only response to the murder and horror of it. And Robert was proud to join his father in his pain, father and son locked in a loss of belief in the race of beings to which they belonged. Robert knew even then there was nothing to be said. They were like dead men. He knew, as a boy, that language was not up to it but was for lesser things than these dark horrors.

—➤—

His violent reaction to John Morris frightened Robert and he lay in bed wide awake for hours worrying about his future. He feared that loss of control and hated to know that such a force was in him, waiting to be provoked by the likes of John Morris. But he owed John Morris something for acknowledging his intelligence. That meant something to him and he was encouraged. For, more than anything else, Robert dreaded that he might come to share in the pointless existence of the men downstairs in the common room. The chance of such a fate haunted him.

10

———

By morning he had decided to take the challenge of his life in the city seriously. The first thing he did when he got out of bed was to put his exercise book in the bottom of the wardrobe. He wanted to tell Wendy about his decision at once but it was only Friday and he wouldn't be seeing her until Tuesday. She had become strict about rationing their meetings and insisted on keeping them to once a week. 'We'll stay hungry for each other,' she said. 'We won't be tempted to start nagging.' He wanted to see her every day and to share his thoughts and ideas with her, but he didn't push it. He saw that his demand for a greater commitment only made her uneasy. There were other things going on in her life. She kept them to herself, but he could sense her preoccupation with them.

At lunchtime he went to Taylor's Coaching College and asked them if he could enrol in the course for university entrance studies. They gave him an English test and told him he should begin at a lower grade and work his way up from there year by year. The woman was motherly and encouraging. 'I can catch up in the year.

I know I can,' he said. 'Give me the chance, will you?' She shook her head and touched his arm and let him enrol. 'You wouldn't be the first,' she said.

On the way back to work he stopped off at Hall's Book Store in Bourke Street. He handed the reading list to the young man behind the counter. Buying the books, Robert knew he was making the connection real. There would be no going back from here. He watched with a feeling of anxious excitement as the young man pulled the volumes from the shelves and set them on the counter in front of him. Robert took the first book in his hands and opened it. The heavy green cloth-bound volume of Carlton J.H. Hayes' *Modern Europe to 1870*. There was an ornate woodcut frontispiece of the emperor Maximilian Augustus. Standing at the counter in the bookstore looking at that old woodcut, it seemed to Robert to be an enchanted emblem of all that was desirable and mysterious in his own future. For the first time in his life he believed he could be part of such things and have a place among them. Something serious and grown-up, Wendy had said. Well, that's what he was doing. Walking back to Myer with his bag of books he was happy.

He was almost an hour late. The foreman was standing in the passage outside the locker room, his arms folded over his gut, smoking a cigarette, waiting to give him a telling-off. Robert felt invulnerable to him and in no mood to accept the humiliation the foreman was ready to dish out. So he got in first. 'I'll pick up my pay and get out of your way,' Robert said.

The foreman said, 'Now, look here, Robert, there's no need for that.'

Robert gave the foreman a smile and shook his fat hand and wished him luck and he went to the office and picked up what was owing to him. There were plenty of other desperadoes lined up ready to take his place with the broom on the lolly floor. He was done with it. He walked out into the street feeling like a free man again for the first time since he'd arrived in the city. He was himself. And the sun was shining.

At the employment agency the clerk took a look at his new status as a student enrolled for university matriculation and asked him why he didn't join the state public service. He was put on as a temporary clerical assistant grade four in the Department of Immigration. The offices were on the corner of Spring Street. Grade four was not four grades from the bottom, but was the bottom. He was to begin work on Monday. He had a weekend of reading to himself. Before he caught the tram home he bought a new pair of grey slacks and a brown jacket and two white shirts and a brick-red woollen tie and a pair of black brogues, and he bought a soft leather briefcase for his textbooks and notepads.

11

On Monday morning he started work at a desk in a vast open office on the ground floor of the green-tiled Commonwealth Offices in Spring Street. He was stamping his daily quota of Form 40s between the hours of nine and five, and reading history and literature the rest of the time. The grade four clerical assistants were a collection of driftwood from all over the world. People like himself. Debris. Out of touch with the mainstream, hanging between failure and hope, migrants and refugees, would-be poets and misunderstood geniuses, actors and female impersonators. Loners with dreams. They were all there, temporary till the good times came along. They recognised each other at once and might have had their status tattooed on their foreheads. Each one had a story. They were all doing their private work at their desks besides attending to the tedious routine clerical work. Reading alone in his room at night, attending the evening classes and daydreaming about Wendy, these were Robert's precious realities.

On Tuesday he didn't go home first after work but went straight to the Greek cafe. It was a hot day with a wild gusty north wind ripping between the buildings, dust and grit in the air, the tram wheels screaming on the rails with an extra pitch of distress as they dragged themselves around the corner from St Kilda Road into Glenferrie Road, people nervous and tense and in a hurry to get to where they were going, giving that extra push to things, looking around at each other, irritated. Since Wendy had started working for the union three days a week, the Greek cafe had become their regular meeting place. They usually ate a meal at the cafe then went back to his room and made love and talked. Later they went down to Nigel's wine bar for a drink. She asked him a couple more times to go to the Swanston Family Hotel and meet her friends, and when he didn't go she stopped asking. There was a stubborn hold-out in him about this and he did not try to reason it away.

She was sitting in their regular booth. He saw her before he went through the door of the cafe. He felt a thrill of excitement, he always did, seeing this beautiful woman who was more than half a mystery sitting there waiting for him. Today he was a little self-conscious and nervous about how she was going to react to his new outfit. She could be moody and was always fiercely independent. He was careful with her.

There had been a midweek meeting at the Caulfield track and the cafe was crowded and noisy and full of smoke and heat. Two men from the boarding house were sitting in the booth behind Wendy. Robert nodded to them and they nodded back. Wendy was reading. She was always reading. Usually pamphlets or free news sheets about workers and their conditions, making notes and rearranging things. He didn't know if maybe she and her comrades had a revolution in mind, but it would not have surprised him if they had. Today she was looking alone and vulnerable and his heart went out to her and he wanted to protect her from life and harm and disappointments. She was wearing a yellow sleeveless summer dress and was looking older and more lovely than ever.

He leaned down and she lifted her face to him and they kissed. The touch of her soft lips sent a pulse of lightning into his groin. She shifted across and he sat beside her. 'I've got some great news,' he said. He set his satchel of books on the table. She was looking at him with that critical air she sometimes put on, looking from him to the books as he pulled them from his satchel, her own reading set aside.

The waitress came over and they both ordered steak and chips with tea.

Wendy said, 'So you've joined them?' She gave an ironic kind of laugh that Robert didn't much like the sound of, her critical gaze giving his new clothes the once-over.

'Joined who?' he said.

She was looking tired and maybe saddened by something that had happened and which he was pretty sure she wasn't going to tell him about. Her air of sadness and irritation made her more intensely beautiful—a dangerously elusive kind of beauty that belonged more to her other world than it did to his world.

She tapped the ash from her cigarette into the tin ashtray on the table. 'So did you finish writing Frankie's story?'

'I went on with it,' he said. 'But it's no good.' He was nervous and was rushing her with his news but he pressed ahead anyway.

'How would you know whether it's any good or not?' she said, leaning her elbow on the table and blowing smoke into the air.

'Well, it just isn't any good,' he said. 'That's how I know.'

'First drafts are never any good. Any idiot could have told you that. It's just laying the thing out at that stage.'

'You're not talking to a halfwit,' he said. He was offended by the way she seemed prepared to take out her mood on him.

This brought a smile to her eyes. She was gripping the elbow that was resting on the table with her other hand and holding the cigarette close to her lips. 'So you're going to tell me you burned it.' She laughed and took a drag on her cigarette. 'You're about to develop the disease of artistic entitlement. I can see it coming in that red tie of yours.'

'We have to wear a tie in the office.'

'So we're in an office now? Is that your news?'

'I've started night school,' he said. 'I'm going to go to the university when I qualify. The English test is in five months. I reckon I can do it.' He had wanted to share his confidence with her but he could feel it going off the track. He needed her to believe in his plan.

She smoked her cigarette, not looking at him now, gazing around at the people in the cafe as if his news was nothing to her. 'So you're a student, not a writer.' She tapped her cigarette in the ashtray and looked sideways at him.

'I'll write Frankie's story with more power, the way it deserves to be written, when I've got a better education,' he said.

'Writers write.' She was dismissing all other possibilities, dismissing him and his plan. That was the way he heard it. 'Singers sing,' she said. 'Painters paint. You either do it or you don't do it.'

The waitress arrived and laid their plates of steak and chips in front of them. Wendy looked at her. 'We need a new one of these.' She held up the tomato sauce bottle. The neck of the bottle was thick with a black goo of dried tomato sauce. The girl, who was maybe seventeen, said, 'There's plenty in that one.' Wendy gave her a mean kind of smile that more or less indicated she thought the girl was a fuckwit. 'It's got a snotty nose, darling. Do you want to give it a wipe for us?'

When the waitress had gone, Robert said, 'She'll probably spit in it.'

Wendy was eating chips from her plate. She looked around at the other diners. 'I hate these places.'

The waitress did not return with the tomato sauce bottle.

He cut a piece from his steak and forked it into his mouth. 'It's best to be polite to waitresses,' he said. 'And what's the matter with you, anyway?'

'You're just like the rest of them.'

He looked at her. 'What is this shit?'

'You're going to betray your class and become just another one of *them*.'

'That's fucking bullshit. Whatever else I might become, I'll always be who I am.' His stomach was churning with the way this was going.

'You sure of that?' She pushed her plate away and lit a cigarette.

The waitress came over and set down their thick china cups of tea and a new sauce bottle. Robert thanked her. Wendy gave her a wink. The girl made a contemptuous noise and swung away.

They sat in silence. The place was in uproar. Everyone yelling over the top of everyone else. Out the window he could see a big black cloud rearing up from the direction of the bay. He was filled with dismay. He looked at Wendy. She looked like someone's mother. He could see it in her, this older woman with a long history of strife and anxiety, some weirdo giving her a hard time. Sorrow of some kind. Responsibilities. He put his hand on hers and she looked at it as if something had settled on her hand. 'I love you,' he said. 'You know that.' He tried a smile, but he knew he wasn't going to be able to lighten the feeling between them.

She gave him a sidelong look and said nothing.

'I'm making a new start in life,' he said. 'Like you said, it's time for me to get serious. I'm doing the grown-up thing. I'm grateful to you.' There was something not quite right about the tone in which he delivered this but he couldn't fix it.

She said, 'Don't do this, Robert.' She took her hand back, reached for her bag and put her reading matter into it.

'So which part of what I'm doing are you talking about?' he said.

'All of it.' She drank the last of her tea and wiped her lips with a paper napkin. 'I don't like it. I've been there before. The nagging has begun. We're into discord. It's not your fault and it's not my fault. It's the way it is.'

'So what's his name?' The jealousy hit him low down in his guts. A wave of nausea going through him. He took a swig of tepid tea.

She said, 'This one's my shout. Can I get out, please?'

He said, 'You're not leaving.'

'I'm leaving,' she said, and she was no longer Wendy his lover but was someone else. He slid out and stood up and stepped to one side. She got up and picked up her bag and stepped out of the booth. 'Thanks for everything, Robert.'

He said, 'For Christ's sake, give me a fucking chance. Let's at least give it a minute. Please!'

She paused, standing there looking at him. 'When something's not working you're a fool to stick with it. The signs are not good.' She touched his cheek gently. 'Take it easy, eh? I'll see you around.'

He watched her walk over to the cash register and pay. And he watched her go out the door into the street where the southerly buster was making the plane trees sway and thrash. He saw her yellow dress blowing around her and he saw her hunch up against the hard wind and the sudden slap of rain. And he didn't follow her. When she was gone he slid into the booth and sat down again. He told himself she would come back.

He finished his tea and smoked a cigarette, then he put his cigarettes in the side pocket of his new brown jacket and he put his books back in his smart new leather satchel and he got up. He was angry and confused. One of the men in the booth behind him said something and both men laughed. Robert stopped and looked down at them. The skinny one said, 'It's not working. The signs are not good.' They both cracked up. The other one said, 'So, it's kaputi with the sheila, eh, mate?' A couple of other people at nearby tables were enjoying a laugh with them.

Robert stood by the booth looking down at the two men from the boarding house. A good half-minute ticked slowly away. He could snatch the hair of the skinny one and smash his face into the table top. Bang! Bang! Bang! Sudden and fierce. Smash their skulls together and thrash the pair of them till they pissed themselves. He just stood by their table looking down into the shifty eyes of the skinny one, watching him blinking and wavering and glancing around for support, the fear coming into his eyes. The cafe had gone quiet. People were watching, hoping for a bit of action. But Robert was thinking of the Springsure rodeo the year Ronnie Doorman beat the whitefellas and became Australian saddle bronc champion. When Ronnie was walking back to the chutes after his winning ride on Nobody's Darling, someone on the rails shouted a racist taunt at him and the crowd laughed. Ronnie did not look aside or adjust his stride but kept walking as if he had heard nothing, and when he reached the chutes the crowd cheered. Robert had admired Ronnie that day and still admired him for the simple dignity of his powerful response. He smiled now at Shifty Eyes and said, 'Yeah, kaputi. Like you, mate.' And he turned and walked out of the cafe into the rain.

It was bucketing down, splashing up out of the gutter and running across the footpath, the cars going by with their headlights on. He walked through the downpour to the boarding house, getting soaked to the skin. He said to himself, She knows where to find me. But he knew that Wendy wasn't going to be coming around looking for him.

12

———

He loved the solitude of the long nights alone in his room working on his books. He kept his window open, the air of the warm nights filling his room, and when a cool southerly change came through from the bay there was always the faint distant smell of the sea. The uninhabited mustiness of his room had been replaced by the smells of his own life, his cigarettes, his books, his own sweat, and the night air. For a long time he thought often of Wendy and daydreamed he was making love to her. And on Tuesdays after work he went to the Greek cafe for his dinner and ate his meal alone, the chance in his mind, vague and formless, but a chance all the same, that Wendy would walk into the cafe and come over to his booth and kiss him and sit beside him once again. He knew this was never going to happen, but the idea of it spiced his Tuesday evenings and whenever the cafe door opened he could not resist looking up to see who was coming in.

Each weekday morning he carried his leather satchel into work at the Commonwealth Offices and as soon as he'd finished his quota of Form 40s for the day he worked on his essays and assignments and read his textbooks and studied Italian irregular verbs. A language other than English was compulsory for an arts degree and they had suggested Italian to him at Taylor's. He got on well with the Italian teacher, who was a young man from Egypt with red hair, and enjoyed hearing the foreign words on his own tongue. Robert was a ready mimic and soon developed a good rounded accent, something the tight-lipped Australian students had a problem with.

His English and Italian teachers let him know they were expecting something special from him. He felt himself acknowledged by them and was grateful to them and confirmed in the dream he was determined to realise. He now knew who the Emperor Maximilian was, that grim-featured man in the broad hat whose antique portrait adorned the front of *Modern Europe to 1870*. Modern, as with many other terms whose meanings he'd once taken for granted, had acquired a new uncertainty for him, its meaning seemingly a matter of opinion and argument. There was no place for Australia in the idea of Europe. Not for Hayes, anyway. Arguing about those old certainties with his teachers and listening to the opinions of his classmates, many of whom were migrants like himself, excited him and made him feel he was among like-minded people. Vienna and Hungary and the Hapsburg Empire were unfolding in front of him. He knew this was his one chance to draw even and was nervously energised by the challenge he had undertaken.

He spent all his spare cash in the second-hand bookshops along Swanston Street, buying the original sources from which his class extracts had been selected when he could find them, and began to accumulate a small library, which he arranged on a plank raised up on bricks beside his desk. Excerpts weren't enough for him. He wanted the whole story. He wanted to experience the intimacy of the old days and to share the thoughts of the people. Details fascinated him. He wanted to see the people drinking their wine and fighting and making love. Excerpts were like being allowed to take a peek through a keyhole at a fascinating landscape. He was hungry to see the whole landscape at ground level, as if he was present in it himself. Although the book wasn't on the English syllabus, he consumed David Magarshack's translation of Tolstoy's *War and Peace* in one lost weekend. When he finally dragged himself away from his studies and went to bed in the early hours of each morning, he found it hard to get to sleep. As soon as he closed his eyes he thought of something he wanted to check and he got up again and consulted his books and began making notes and was soon absorbed in the work and forgot to go back to bed until noises in the house warned him the day was beginning. The year was racing by and there was never enough time to read everything he wanted to read before an essay or other assignment fell due.

Outside in the wild garden below his window the elm copse was looking grey and tired after the heat of summer. He was due to sit the English competence test in a week and was hunched over the second-hand desk he'd bought, working on a précis of an extract he'd been given from Francis Bacon's *Of the Proficience and Advancement of Learning.* He had been reading far more widely than the set texts and his history essay on the question of the eastern borders of the Hapsburg Empire was already overdue. He was eager to be done with the précis and return to the wondrous place names—Karelia, Ingria, Estonia, Livonia—and the powerful men and their astonishing ambitions to rule their worlds.

He was absorbed in his work when he became aware that someone had been tapping on his door for some time. When the tapping came again, a little louder, a little more insistent now, he got up to open the door. John Morris was standing there. He stepped back a pace and raised his palms, as if he would ward Robert off. His manner was reserved and careful. 'I'm sorry if I'm disturbing you,' he said. He was being very formal.

'It's all right,' Robert said. 'You're not disturbing me.'

'Oh, I'm sure I am,' John Morris said, as if the effort to address Robert civilly wearied him.

They stood there looking at each other, neither speaking, then John Morris laughed uncomfortably. 'God knows why, and don't ask me, but a friend of mine wants to meet you. She's probably quite as mad and as dangerous as you are.'

Robert said, 'I'm sorry for the way I behaved that time.'

'No you're not. But it doesn't matter.' John Morris looked Robert steadily in the eye for some time. The sound of the television downstairs in the common room. 'You were quite menacing,' he said, an edge of malice and hurt in his tone. 'I was a bit pushy, but I don't think I deserved that.'

'Neither do I,' Robert said. 'Which is why I just apologised to you.'

'You did. It was handsome of you.' John Morris said, 'So, would you like to meet this friend of mine or not? You don't have to. I'm going away. I've been appointed to a lectureship at King's College in London.'

'I was born and grew up in London,' said Robert.

'You don't have an accent.'

'I can do one if you'd like to hear it.'

'I'm quite sure you can.'

It was hard to say why exactly, but despite his smart blue and grey rugby top and his pale slacks and his expensive Italian sandals and his job at a London university, John Morris looked to Robert just then to be forlorn standing there on the landing outside his room. Robert felt strangely moved by the man. There was something infinitely lonely about him. 'All right,' he said. 'I'll come and meet your friend.' Perhaps accepting John Morris's invitation seemed to him at that moment to be the least he could do to make up in some way for his earlier cruelty. For that was how he saw it now: he had been cruelly and unnecessarily brutal. He was also curious about this friend of John Morris's who had expressed a wish to meet him.

He said, 'I took your advice and enrolled for the university entrance exams.'

'Good for you,' John Morris said.

'I'm grateful to you for that.'

'Oh, you don't need to be grateful to me. Anyone could have told you that you needed to get a decent education.' John Morris considered him. 'Meg was right: you are an odd bastard, aren't you?'

'And you?' Robert said. 'Are you an odd bastard too?'

'That's a good one.' John Morris looked at Robert levelly. 'Have you realised I'm homosexual?'

'It did vaguely occur to me, I suppose.'

'And is it this that worries you about me?'

'Nothing worries me about you,' Robert said. 'I don't care what you are, so long as you realise I'm not a homosexual. Have you realised that?'

John Morris laughed. 'I suppose I have,' he said. 'What a pity. But never mind.'

Robert let John Morris wait on the landing while he fetched his jacket.

They drove out along the bayside in John Morris's smart green car, the wide blue waters of the bay over to their right dotted with white sailing boats, black and red cargo boats anchored far out, waiting to come into the port. The tight cluster of the inner city falling behind them. John Morris stopped at a traffic light to let a bunch of people cross over to the beach side of the road. Women and children wearing swimming togs and clutching towels and baskets and plastic floaters and cricket bats and other stuff.

Robert could feel John Morris looking sideways at him. John Morris said, 'So apart from studying, what else have you been up to?'

'You've got the green,' Robert said, and John Morris put the car into gear and moved off.

They went along in silence for a while, then John Morris said, 'I haven't seen you with your girlfriend for a while. What happened there? To be honest, I thought she was a bit old for you.'

'Nothing happened that's any of your business,' Robert said.

John Morris laughed and began whistling a tune from *My Fair Lady*. He whistled brilliantly, touching all the notes accurately. It was a little virtuoso display. He turned off Beach Road and drove a couple of blocks before going down one of the suburban streets. The street was empty. No cars and no people. Big brick houses along both sides with mature European trees in their gardens. He pulled up and switched off the motor and they sat in the warm silence of the little car. 'I should tell you,' John Morris said, 'Lena's father died two months ago. She and her dad were very close.'

'That's tough,' Robert said and wished he could have thought of something better to say.

'I've known Keith ever since I came to Melbourne from the country to go to university. He was a kind and thoughtful man. He loved the outback and often went off on long trips into the hinterland of Queensland and the north. You two would have had a lot to talk about.'

Robert took out his cigarettes. He held the packet out to John Morris, who took a cigarette and thanked him. Robert lit it for him then lit his own. There was a little moment of intimacy between them. They smoked and looked along the vacant street ahead of them.

John Morris said, 'It's a pity you couldn't have met him. He would have helped you find your way in Melbourne.'

They sat smoking their cigarettes.

Robert said, 'What did he do? Your friend's father.'

'Keith was a journalist. One of our best.'

'A writer then?'

'A writer and an accomplished watercolourist. You should get Lena to show you his drawings.' John Morris sat there looking along the street, taking small puffs on the cigarette, as if he was sipping a drink. 'You'll like her mother. She was terrified Lena was going to marry *me*.' He laughed, a full-throated bellow of amusement at the idea.

'So was it sudden,' Robert said, 'or were they expecting him to die?'

'It was dreadful. It went on and on. Lena and her dad used to go horseriding together. He was a good horseman, so people said. I wouldn't know. They say she is too. Last summer Keith was injured in a fall and had to take time off work. He never really got better.' John Morris butted his cigarette in the ashtray. 'I suppose we'd better go in and meet them.' He opened his door and stepped out of the car.

They walked up the path through the front garden. Flat greyish-green weeds growing up between the crazy pavers. The grass on the lawn dry, the shrubs sad and droopy, everything in need of water and attention. Nothing flourishing. A blackbird, the female, flew across the path in front of them, diving at full speed into the forlorn shrubbery, sounding its chittering alarm. The big brick house in its solid privacy. He had never been inside such a house. He and John Morris stood side by side in the cool darkness of the porch and John Morris rang the bell. There was the sound of someone playing the piano. 'It's a Schubert impromptu,' John Morris said.

The piano stopped abruptly and a few seconds later the front door was opened by a young woman. She didn't greet John Morris. She didn't even look at him, but stood looking at Robert. He had the queer feeling she was expecting to know him. Behind her in the unlit hall the pale face of a tall grandfather clock seemed to be watching them, through an inner door the gleam of polished wood on a piano.

'Thank you for coming,' she said. She looked at John Morris then. 'John said you probably wouldn't come.'

She had dark brown eyes with faint half-circles of purplish shadow, her hair also dark brown, glossy and short, sweeping around her cheek in a sensuous curve. Her face was broad, a strong and slightly square jaw. She was wearing a pale linen blouse open at the neck and a grey cotton skirt with a narrow belt. He saw her as a well-groomed middle-class young woman he would have admired in the street or on the tram but would never have spoken to.

Usually people smile when they meet someone for the first time. Lena Soren didn't smile. Standing at the door in the deep shadow of the porch, Robert's attention was held by the peculiar steadiness of her gaze, the white face of the clock watching from the shadows. It was as if she expected something from him, was waiting for a response or some kind of recognition, a sign from him. Her steady scrutiny and her composed beauty made him feel inadequate and uncomfortable and he didn't know how to react to her. He couldn't imagine there was anything about him that would interest such a woman. What could she possibly be expecting from him?

13

The following Sunday morning, Lena Soren called him at the boarding house. He was surprised to hear from her. Nothing that had passed between them during the visit with John Morris had led him to expect that he'd ever hear from her again. She said her mother would like to meet him and could he come to lunch? 'We're having roast lamb, as usual. Don't be late. Come early. Sorry for the short notice. Decisions aren't that easy in this house at the moment.'

He hung up the phone and said aloud, 'She's beautiful and rich and educated and her mother wants me to come to lunch! So go on then, Robert Crofts! Get off your arse and go.'

He went into the city and caught the train to Red Bluff. When he got to the house, Lena answered the door at once. She surprised him by taking his hand, as if they already had an understanding. 'Come and meet Mum.'

She led him down the dark hall and through into the kitchen at the back of the house. It was a small room with a low ceiling, most of the space taken up by a dining nook and a walk-in pantry.

A radio was playing classical music. Lena's mother was standing at the table of the dining nook shelling peas into a colander. She was short and roly-poly with a bun of grey hair and was wearing a blue and white cross-stitched apron over a flowered cotton dress. When Lena brought Robert into the kitchen, she wiped her hands on her apron, backs first then fronts, and offered her hand to him. 'I'm sorry about my apron, Robert. It's very nice of you to come and see us. Lena tells me you're going to start an arts degree next year?'

'If they'll have me,' he said.

'Oh, I'm pretty sure they'll have you. Don't you think so, Lena?'

Lena said, 'We're going for a swim, Mum.'

'All right, darling. You won't be too long, will you? The potatoes are in the oven.'

He followed Lena out into the hall. 'I haven't brought any togs,' he said. In fact he hadn't owned a pair of swimming togs since he was at school and swimming in the freezing public baths was a compulsory weekly torture.

'You can wear Dad's.' She went along the hall and into a room and came out holding a floppy old pair of black Speedos.

Robert looked at the togs. 'Maybe we could give the swim a miss this time?'

'You'll be glad once you're in the water.'

He knew he wouldn't be glad once he was in the water. Just thinking about being in the water made him shiver.

They went out the front door and walked along the street together. He said, 'We're going to need towels, aren't we?' The day was cloudy and there was a chilly breeze blowing in off the bay. She said cheerfully, 'There are plenty of towels in the bathing box.' He said, 'Why did you tell John you wanted to meet me? I don't get it.'

She laughed and stopped on the footpath, turning to face him. 'What don't you get? That I like you and want to see you?' She took his arm and they walked on. 'I'm sick of young doctors and lawyers and architects and their endless table talk about their stupid ambitions. They're all the same. When John told me a wild cowboy who had threatened to kill him had come to live in the boarding house, well, I had to have a look, didn't I?' She was laughing. 'Did you really threaten to kill him? How were you going to do it? Strangle him? I've often felt like strangling John.'

'He was exaggerating,' Robert said.

'But did you threaten him? I want to know.'

'He probably felt a bit threatened. I wasn't sure what I was going to do. I was angry. Can we leave it at that?'

They went on together, arm in arm. Her confidence in claiming him astonished him. He wasn't quite sure how to interpret it.

'I had to get out of that house,' she said. 'It's like a morgue since Dad died. I could see how uncomfortable you were last week. What did you think of my mother?'

'I liked her,' he said. He'd been relieved to find Mrs Soren wasn't someone who was going to condescend to him. 'She's homely.'

'Everyone likes her,' Lena said, dismissing his opinion of her mother. 'She's not as homely as she looks.'

'But *I* don't like everybody,' he said.

They crossed Beach Road and went down a steep earthen ramp through thick tea-tree and came out onto the sand at the bottom. A row of brightly painted sheds faced the beach and backed onto the tea-tree. A man was throwing a stick into the water and a dog was swimming out and retrieving it. Apart from these two the beach was deserted. Lena unlocked the door of a blue-and-white-striped bathing box. 'We can leave our stuff in here,' she said.

He stepped into the confined space of the bathing box with her. Piles of towels and cricket bats and stumps and various other stuff lay around in a general clutter. 'Dad was always threatening to sort all this stuff out. It's been stacking up in here since Erik and I were kids.' She took off her blouse and stepped out of her skirt and kicked off her sandals. She was already wearing a black one-piece swimsuit. Elegant and expensive. Her perfect skin with its light summer tan glowing in the half-light. She stepped past him, giving him a quick smile, touching her hand lightly to his chest. 'I'll wait for you.' She went outside and stood on the sand.

He took a couple of deep breaths and unzipped his pants. He was white as a maggot. He took his clothes off and pulled on her dad's old black Speedos. He had half an erection and it showed. Her dead father's togs clung to him. He wondered if they'd been washed since her old man last wore them. When she saw him coming out of the box, she headed for the sea at a run. He sprinted down the sand after her, the chill of the air on his bare skin, his lifelong dread of the sea.

There were no waves, just a listless slapping where the water met the sand, the cold onshore breeze ruffling the surface like a threat. The man and the dog had gone. There was no one else about. The bay looked grey and steely. He was sure it was concealing something sinister. Lena was up to her waist when she dived and began swimming without looking back to see if he was following her. He stood hesitating at the water's edge, watching her. She might have been on her own, a solitary swimmer heading for some place she had in her mind.

He walked into the sea and swam as fast as he could, which was not very fast. He wasn't able to catch up with her. She was sliding away from him through the water like a black seal, her effortless overarm. He was a thrasher, like a hooked fish in its death struggle. The harder he tried for speed the more seawater went down his throat. Swimming in the sea had always been for him a case of doing his best not to drown. She was heading out towards the rusting hulk of a ship. A couple of times he thought he saw a shadow moving through the water towards him. Lena had disappeared around the bulkhead of the dead ship.

He was on his own now, the little wavelets slapping into his face. He was out of breath and had to take a break. He stopped thrashing and floated on his back. Lying out there on his own, looking up at the low clouds, he could see himself from above, a bluish corpse drifting out to sea, Keith Soren's Speedos billowing around his arse and his shrunken dick, his balls tight as wood knots with the cold and his fear. He was certain he was shark bait. He was wishing he had the courage to turn around and head back to the shore. But he was too proud, or too weak, to give up. It was not his intention to be humiliated by Lena Soren, the rich, educated, beautiful young woman who had hooked him onto her line for whatever reason she had in her mind. He would probably rather have drowned. He turned over onto his front and pushed on. Eventually he made it around the bullnose of the old hulk and began to swim along its outer side. The beach and the coloured bathing boxes were now hidden from him. There was nothing between him and the horizon. To his left the sheer cliff of the half-sunken ship's rusty side towered above him, smooth and red, offering no chance of a handhold. He took in another mouthful of water and choked and flopped around for a couple of despairing minutes.

By the time he'd got himself around the far end of the ship and made it back to the shore, he was coughing seawater and close to exhaustion. He stood bent over on the sand, recovering, his hands on his knees. When he straightened up he saw Lena sitting on the step of the bathing box robed in a white towel, her tanned legs crossed at the ankles. She was smoking one of his cigarettes, watching him. He might have been a stranger who'd happened onto the beach and caught her attention. He walked up the sand and stood above her. She sat there like an Italian film star, the white towel loosely around her shoulders, the cigarette smouldering between her fingers, the fullness of her tanned breasts in soft shadow. She looked up at him and smiled. She moved over and he sat next to her on the step. He was still breathing hard. She offered him the cigarette. He was too wretched to smoke and waved it away. 'You win,' he said.

'Are you okay?' She put her hand on his bare shoulder. 'You're freezing!' She got up and took his hand. 'You'd better get dried off. I didn't realise you were in trouble. Honestly.'

If she hadn't said 'honestly' like that, he probably would have believed her. But when she felt the need to add the word, he knew at once she was secretly enjoying his defeat and discomfort. He got up and went ahead of her into the bathing box. She closed the door and leaned her back against it. He turned away and stripped off the clinging black things that were gripping his arse like the cold hand of her dead father. He picked up a towel from the pile and began drying himself. He was shivering. When he turned around she was still standing there against the door looking at him. He saw suddenly where she was going to take this. She stepped forward and stripped off her black costume in one long movement. When she straightened from stepping out of it she was blushing, her eyes bright and glittery with determination and excitement, something fierce in her. The pale untanned shape of her costume on her naked body made her skin look private and exposed.

She held herself for his inspection. 'Well?' she said tightly. 'What do you think?'

He was transfixed. Her aggressive manner confused him. 'I think you're beautiful,' he said helplessly. Did she do this with every man who came down for a swim with her? Or was this special for him? He dropped the towel and she looked at his nakedness. He stepped up to her and took her in his arms, the heat of her skin against his chilled flesh, a shiver of adrenaline shooting through his thighs as their bodies touched, her salty lips on his. They lay clasped together on the towels, a strange, almost panic-stricken plea in her eyes. She cried out as he entered her, her fingers digging painfully into his back. Her cries sounded despairing and hopeless, something so strange and unsettling in her fierceness he was shocked by it. There was nothing in her of Wendy's confident pleasure.

Afterwards he held her in his arms and covered them both with the towels. He felt as if he held a stranger in his arms. The screaming of gulls outside. Her dark eyes fixed on him, glittering in the half-light of the bathing box. She stroked his hair and his forehead with her long fingers. 'I could have drowned you,' she said softly, a kind of wonderment in her voice, as if she was seeing his bloated corpse out there in the sinister gleam of the sea, his backside clad in her dead father's horrible black Speedos, a small black bump on the steely water. He didn't know what to think of her. 'I've never met anyone like you,' he said.

➤

He sat at the table in the dining room across from Lena and watched Mrs Soren slicing the meat from the leg of lamb. She would have had to have been blind and stupid to be unaware of the intensity they carried with them into the sombre stillness of the house. They had walked back from the beach, Lena holding his arm tightly, and when they turned the corner into her street she had stopped and kissed him. 'I'm not going to let you go,' she said. 'I hope you know that.'

'I think maybe I do,' he said. 'You're not normal. Do you know that?'

'I'm glad *you* know it.'

He felt as if he didn't know her at all.

They ate the Sunday roast in silence. The click and scrape of cutlery on china. The sedate order of things. The stillness. The long table with the eight dining chairs, five of them empty. Lena extending her feet under the table and touching him. She kept looking across at him, trying to make him laugh. He glanced at Mrs Soren.

'Please help yourself to more potatoes, Robert,' she said.

Lena said, 'Yes, Robert. Don't be shy.' She laughed.

He reached and forked another roast potato onto his plate.

Mrs Soren said into the stiff silence, 'Are you a believer, Robert?'

'A believer in what?' he said.

Lena laughed. 'Mum wants to know if you're a Christian.'

'Well, I was baptised,' he said. 'I'm not sure why. We never went to church. My mother and father were married in a registry office. My sister and I went to Sunday school a couple of times, just to see what was going on there. And we sang hymns at school assembly. I can still remember them.' He looked at Mrs Soren and smiled. 'We don't forget those sorts of things, do we?'

She was in her sixties. Her face round and pinkly flushed. She was shorter than Lena, but he could see something of Lena in her broad features. She didn't match his idea of a rich woman. There was nothing haughty about her. She didn't seem to be out to prove anything to him. He could imagine her being more at home in a cottage in the country than in this big house with its lush green fitted carpets and strange mixture of spare modernist furnishings and old-fashioned dark oak pieces. No clutter. Not a book spine out of alignment in the deep shelves either side of the fireplace. His father would not have been interested in the two oil paintings that hung on the walls, one above the fireplace in the dining room and another, its twin, above the fireplace in the sitting room, both beach scenes, a red cliff and a sweep of yellow sand with two figures and a dog beneath a blue sky.

Mrs Soren said, 'You mean you haven't forgotten the hymns you sang at school? Or was it something else you meant?'

'I meant everything we learn when we're children,' he said. 'It becomes part of us the way things never really become part of us later on, when we're grown up.'

Mrs Soren had finished eating. She set her knife and fork side by side, handles perfectly aligned, like the spines of the books in the shelves behind her. He thought of her being obedient still in old age to the rules her mother had taught her. She dabbed her lips with her napkin. Then she turned to him and looked at him steadily for several long seconds without speaking. He was chewing a last mouthful of roast lamb. She waited for him to finish. He thought she might be going to tell him—politely, in an honest upright sort of way, even generously—that, regrettably, it was time for him to leave.

She said, 'It's just Lena and me now, Robert.' She paused, allowing a moment for the significance of her statement to establish itself with him.

Lena said, 'Oh, Mum. Don't, please!'

'Three months ago we were a family,' Mrs Soren went on, still holding his gaze. She had blue eyes, pale and clear, and he saw how they had reddened slightly now, tears glistening in the corners. 'A year ago Keith and my son, Erik, were both here.' She was making an effort to control her emotions. 'We were a family of four. Now it is just the two of us. Erik's working in London. He never writes.'

Lena reached over and laid her hand on her mother's hand. 'It's all right, Mum.'

Robert murmured, 'I'm very sorry for your loss.'

'I'm not trying to impress you with my loss,' Mrs Soren said. She was impatient with herself and dabbed at her eyes with her handkerchief. 'I just want you to know, if Lena and I sometimes seem . . .' She searched about but couldn't think of a word that would do. 'We're struggling. That's all I meant.'

Was she asking him if he was a man who could be relied on to do the right thing by her daughter in her vulnerable state?

'I just wanted you to know our situation. Lena has probably told you she's in her first year as a social worker at Prince Henry's

Hospital. Our lives are not what they were this time last year. We are dealing with a great many changes.' She held his gaze. 'It is a difficult time for us. I hope you do understand. Lena and I both need time to adjust to what has happened.' She stood up abruptly and began to gather their plates. Lena got up and took the plates from her. 'Sit down, Mum. I'll get the sweets. Talk to Robert.'

There was a sudden rumbling and thumping out in the driveway. The glass in a narrow window above the built-in bookcase next to the fireplace trembled. Mrs Soren sat down, her hand going to her mouth. She was looking at Lena. In a dismayed voice, as if she was expecting to be told off by her daughter, she said, 'George has brought the blocks. I forgot to cancel him!'

Lena said, 'It's not the end of the world, Mum. It's just fire-wood.' She turned to Robert. 'It's our regular winter wood supply. Dad always organised it for the autumn. Dad liked to be prepared.'

They all went out and stood in the driveway and looked at the impressive pile of red gum blocks. The blocks were giving off the smell of fresh-sawn wood. The delivery man was roaring off down the road in his truck, an old green Fargo, leaving a smell of half-burned diesel fumes in the air.

As if she was talking about a terrible catastrophe for which there was no remedy, Mrs Soren said, 'I won't be able to get the Renault out! I'll need it in the morning.'

Lena said, 'Robert will stack it.' She looked at him. 'Won't you?'

'I'd love to do it,' he said. 'Have you got a wheelbarrow?'

Lena's mother said, 'We can't possibly expect you to do this. I'll get George to come back. He'll put the wood in the shed on Monday. He won't mind. I'll get a taxi in the morning.'

Lena said, 'Mum means she'd be very happy for you to do it. Come on, I'll show you where Dad keeps his barrow.'

Robert looked at Mrs Soren and smiled. 'It's okay. Really.'

'Thank you,' she said.

He felt sorry for her. He wanted to help her.

Lena said, 'He's a cowboy, Mum. Stacking wood is nothing to him.'

Mrs Soren touched his arm. He thought she was going to cry but she held it back. 'Thank you,' she said again, and she turned and walked back down the drive to the front.

Robert and Lena clambered over the pile of wood blocks and went into the back garden through the side gate. A weatherboard shed was built onto the back of the brick garage. The door of the shed was held closed with an old-fashioned iron hasp. Lena lifted the hasp and opened the door. They went into the dark interior. She turned around and they kissed. 'Alone in the garden shed with my cowboy lover,' she said.

He held her away from him. 'You know what a cowboy is on the cattle stations up north? He's a no-hoper who milks the station cows and cleans out their shit and does odd jobs around the place. He's not what you think. I was a ringer, not a cowboy.'

'Don't spoil the story!' she said dismissively. 'You're my cowboy.' She looked at him seriously. 'I was amazed at Mum talking to you about Dad. She never admits she's hurting. She keeps it locked up inside. She tells her sisters and brother she's fine and refuses their help. She likes you.' She took his hand and they stood looking at the remains of last winter's firewood. Her hand was warm and soft in his, like a tiny trusting kitten he had once held. There was the sound of the back door opening followed by a short silence, then her mother's anxious call, 'Are you there, Lena? Don't forget you haven't done any practice yet.'

Lena said quietly, 'Yes, Mum. I'm in the shed and Robert is insisting on having sex with me again.' She closed her eyes and called in an innocent girlish voice, 'Coming, Mum.' To Robert she said, 'I'd better go and do my practice before she has a fit.' Her expression became serious. 'She's a textbook study, isn't she? Honest, upright and credulous. She's in a cage and she'd like me to be content to stay in the cage with her.' She let go of his hand and went out into the garden. A moment later he heard the back door close.

He took her father's wheelbarrow around to the woodpile in the drive and chucked the blocks of red gum into it. He wheeled the loaded barrow through the side gate and into the back garden and he stacked the blocks in the shed. It felt good to be on his own doing something physical. He paid a lot of attention to the way he built the stack. There was no electric light in the shed but there was an old-fashioned hurricane lamp of the kind they had used in the cow byre on Warren's farm on dark winter mornings. He lit the lamp and it filled the shed with a soft yellow light, the old familiar smell of lighting kerosene filling the air with a feeling of intimacy and work. He enjoyed building the wood stack, keeping the walls straight and tying in the corners the way brick walls are tied in. When he'd finished carting and stacking the blocks he decided to split some of them, as there were only a few pieces of split wood left and Mrs Soren would need to split more herself when the cold weather came. He could imagine her doing it, swinging the axe and thinking of her dead husband, tears running down her rosy cheeks. She was a relief to him. He had seen that she was a woman without the pretensions of the middle class. It was easy for him to like her. The barrier he had expected wasn't there.

The late afternoon was quiet and still, just the smack of his axe driving into the wood and the distant barking of someone's lonely dog. He disdained the use of the heavy splitter Keith had left beside the block. He knew just how to catch the grain at the right angle to open up the tight-bound red gum blocks. In his old life it was a skill that had been taken for granted among all useful men and women. Lena's dad's axe was correctly ground and had kept its edge. His tools were clean and arranged in order against the wall, axes and saws and rakes and spades and forks and hoes. They were all there: a bench with a vice and files and the other familiar paraphernalia that every useful man requires. Robert had only glimpsed the inside of Keith Soren's study when Lena was showing him around the house and he was curious to give the room a closer inspection. Mrs Soren couldn't bear to go in there herself and kept the door closed. Lena had only half opened the door; 'Dad's study.' Robert's glimpse had been enough to give him the impression that it was where the real clutter of their lives was hoarded. A desk covered in papers and open books, piles of papers and books on the floor, photos and drawings on the walls, journals and newspapers stacked in corners.

When Mrs Soren spoke from the doorway of the shed he jumped. 'You've done enough,' she said. 'We're going to have a cup of tea.'

He realised she must have been standing there watching him in silence for some time. He set the edge of the blade into the chopping block as he'd found it, and straightened up. His body was glowing.

'You've stacked it just the way Keith did,' she said. She stepped into the shed and stood beside him, admiring the neat wall of blocks. 'I think Keith used to resent having to take it down again and burn it in the winter.' She looked at Robert and waited for him to respond.

He said, 'His tools are all in good nick.'

They stood together in the mellow light of the kerosene lamp looking at the neatly ordered interior of her dead husband's shed. Robert said, 'Were your people from the country?'

'Oh no,' she said. 'We're all Melbourne. Keith's grandparents came from Sweden.' She considered him. 'You must have met with hardships and loneliness coming out here on your own as a boy, not knowing anybody and being so young.'

'I've never thought of it like that,' he said. 'I was lucky. I met good people. And I enjoyed my work.'

A sound in the woodpile, a settling of the blocks, a shifting in the back of the shed, as if a rat or a possum had decided it was time to leave.

'Your mother must miss you,' she said. 'I hope you write to her often.' She waited a moment, and when he didn't respond she said carefully, 'Did you leave home for a reason?'

'I needed to get out on my own and have an adventure. That's all. I'm lucky my parents gave me their blessing.'

He opened the lamp and blew out the flame. They left the shed. Mrs Soren snapped shut the hasp on the door and they went across into the house. Lena was playing the piano. Mrs Soren turned to him in the hall. 'You'll have to get used to Lena's moods. It's nothing to do with you. I've put a fresh towel in the blue room for you if you'd like to have a shower.' She took him up to the front of the house and opened the last door. 'We always called it the blue room. We had it painted blue when we bought the house just after we were married.'

They stood looking in at the bedroom. It was large and comfortably furnished, soft grey-blue carpet and a great bow window like the one he'd noticed in the sitting room, a double bed with a blue flowered cover, lamps on the side tables. There was an air of emptiness about the room, as if the door was seldom opened onto the stillness of its silent interior. Mrs Soren went off to make the tea.

The bathroom was next door to the blue room. Shiny green tiles, green toilet, green bath. He was drying himself when he heard angry voices. He stood and listened, but couldn't make out what was being said. When he went out, Mrs Soren was sitting on the bench in the kitchen alcove, the teapot and the milk and sugar and three cups and saucers on the table in front of her. There was a plate of Anzac biscuits. He surprised her and she looked up at him quickly as he came into the kitchen. He saw in her eyes the exposed wound of her grief, the brutal pain of her loss. He thought then that the life that was left to her to live must seem to her to be too short for the wound she had suffered to ever heal.

Their eyes met. His heart went out to her, but he didn't have the words for it. When he was a small child he and his sister used to gaze into each other's eyes and eventually one of them would ask the question of the other: So what is it really like to be you? And they knew, even then as little children, that they could never know the answer to this question and they felt the terrible reality of their solitariness. It was a frightening game to play and so they played it often, sitting on the bunk in the air-raid shelter, the whistling bombs screaming down and the guns blazing away from the rail yards, gazing into each other's eyes in the candlelight, the ground heaving when a bomb exploded.

Going down the street later to the train station, Lena took his arm and pressed herself against his side. 'I don't want you to go. Can't you just stay with us?'

He said, 'What was the row with your mum about?'

'It wasn't about you. Don't worry, she likes you. She thinks I don't focus properly with my piano practice. It's stupid. We could easily kill each other about it. She's always dreamed I'd become a famous concert pianist one day. Don't worry; it sounds worse than it is. We've been screaming at each other since I was five.'

They waited together on the station platform, her arm firmly in his, her shoulder pressed against him.

When the train was pulling away and he looked out the window for a last wave, she was standing there alone on the platform in her neat white blouse and skirt, and she seemed to him in that moment to be vulnerable and even afraid. There was something like a confusion of anger and anxiety in her eyes. He wanted to go back and reassure her.

He sat watching the backyards flicking by. He had been overwhelmed by the way she had claimed him. He was glad to be away from the heavy gloom of her mother's house. He closed his eyes and a vivid image of Lena's perfect skin and lovely breasts came into his mind, the salty taste of seawater on her lips in the bathing box, the intense, intimate taste of her on his tongue.

14

It was a revelation for him to learn that it was the French Revolution which had introduced into Europe the idea of equality and the rights of ordinary people. Before then, throughout the entire history of the human race it seemed, the rights of ordinary working people had never been formally expressed or codified or even thought about seriously. That the French had decided everyone, including the poor, should be equal before the law was apparently a completely new idea at the time. He decided at once that this event marked the beginning of modern times. For Robert, the question of what was and what was not modern was settled. He decided he would read everything that had been written by the Enlightenment thinkers.

It was after midnight. He was reading. There was a soft knock on his door. He got up and went over to open the door. John Morris was standing there. He was wearing a black coat with a striped scarf and a suit and tie. He was dishevelled and flushed in the face. He said, 'I thought I'd drop in and say goodbye. I'm going to London in the morning.'

'Looks like it was a good party,' Robert said. 'You'd better come in.'

'I won't stay,' John Morris said. 'I just didn't want to leave without saying goodbye to the odd bloke who lives in this room.' He walked over and sat on the chair at Robert's desk. He picked up the book Robert had been reading. It was Voltaire's satire *Candide*, which was set for the English syllabus. He set the book down and looked up as Robert crossed the room towards him. 'You haven't got a cigarette, have you? I've run out.'

Robert said, 'There's some on the desk in front of you. Help yourself.' He went over to the wardrobe and took out one of the bottles of beer he kept there, tall brown bottles from the Abbotsford Brewery, a fine burr-line around the widest part of the bottle's shoulders, etched by the vibrations of the bottle line. He opened the bottle and passed it to John. John thanked him and said, 'Good luck!' He drank deeply, then wiped his mouth and gave a low belch and handed the bottle back to Robert. Robert caught a whiff of stale whisky breath from him, a touch of his own father's late-night breath.

Robert lifted the bottle in a salute. 'I hope London works out for you.'

John said, 'My dad's got cancer.' He sat looking at his hands. 'I'll probably never see him again.' He looked up at Robert and Robert saw that he was moved. 'I was never sure if he knew or not,' John said. 'This time I decided he did know and had accepted it. Which I knew would have been difficult for him. When I was leaving we stood out on the verandah and we hugged each other as we always do. I love my dad. I stepped off the verandah and was about to get into my car when he called out, "Have you got a woman yet, son?" I was so fucking angry I yelled back, "I'm a fucking homosexual, Dad. Get fucking used to it."'

Robert waited. John said no more.

John got out his handkerchief and blew his nose. 'Sorry.'

Robert tried to imagine telling his dad he was a homosexual, but he couldn't make the leap.

John said, 'Why didn't I leave him with his dream of his son intact? I yelled it at him and drove away. And that's that, isn't it? What difference does it fucking make? The truth can be a load of shit sometimes.'

They passed the bottle a couple of times in silence.

'So how's it going with Lena?' John said.

'We saw each other last week. It was pretty intense. I haven't heard from her since.'

'People get ideas,' John said, and he laughed. 'We expect things, we believe in them, and then they don't work out. And we realise we're not in control.' He squinted at Robert through the smoke of his cigarette. 'We imagine we're in control?'

Their eyes met. John gave Robert a small ironic smile. 'I'm pissed. I'd better go before I say something I'll regret in the morning. You're a fucking attractive man, Robert Crofts. There, I'll regret that in the morning. You scared the shit out of me that day. I'm not scared of you now. You couldn't scare me now if you tried. I'd fight back. Okay? Do you understand that?' He laughed. 'I might decide to take a swing at you. So watch yourself.'

Robert said, 'Things could easily have gone the wrong way for me without your encouragement.'

They both stood up. Robert held out his hand and John took it. 'I have a lot to thank you for,' Robert said.

John kept hold of Robert's hand when Robert would have let go. 'We don't need to thank each other,' John said. He swayed towards Robert and let go of his hand. 'You're on your way! You'll travel. It's in you.' He waved his arm and took an unsteady step back. 'You may not always thank me for introducing you to Lena Soren. She's a troubled girl. Like a lot of us. It won't be straightforward.'

Robert said, 'Maybe the best people are always troubled.'

'I like that,' John said and he repeated it: 'Maybe the best people are always troubled.' He went over and opened the door.

Robert said, 'I'll see you around then.'

John looked back at him. 'No you won't.' He went out and pulled the door closed behind him.

15

Before he left the boarding house for the office on Wednesday morning, the landlady called Robert to the phone. He went down to the hallway and picked up the receiver. It was Lena. She said, 'Meet me after work at Prince Henry's. I'll wait for you. Just ask at the front desk for the social work department. We're in the basement. I have to go now.'

He went to the main entrance of the hospital on St Kilda Road and was directed to a side door in an adjoining street. He found the swing doors that had been described to him—wide enough to admit a corpse on a trolley. And there she was, at roughly the halfway point of a long subterranean corridor. The tiled walls gleaming dully, the lighting jaundiced and pale. She was a figure in a white dustcoat, hands in pockets, talking to a young man who was standing in front of her, his shoulders hunched. When Robert got closer she turned and looked at him. She said something to the young man and touched him on the shoulder. The young man turned and sloped off, going deeper into that endless corridor which was lit by a series of dull greenish strip lights set in the ceiling. There was a smell, cold, metallic and chemical. Lena in her white coat, a professional woman in that place. Institutional settings like this had always made Robert anxious. There was a steady humming noise which seemed to be coming from the weighty fabric of the building, somewhere deeper.

She waited for him to reach her. 'Come into my office,' she said. He followed her into a small office with no window. She closed the door and embraced him quickly, their lips meeting for an instant, then she stepped away and moved behind the desk. She sat in the shiny blue office chair and picked up a file that was lying open on the desk. 'I just need to get this done while it's fresh in my mind,' she said. 'I won't be a minute. We can go for a walk in the botanic gardens.' She took a fountain pen from the pocket of her white coat and began writing in the open file. Robert sat in the straight-backed chair that faced her across the desk. He said, 'The patient's chair.' She frowned at the file and went on writing. The humming sound from the depths seemed to grow more insistent.

He said, 'I was interviewed by a lady almoner when I was a kid.'

She didn't look up. 'We're not lady almoners these days.'

'It's just a name change,' he said. He found himself wanting to speak up for the child he had once been. 'Everything else is the same. You still think you can help that dero you were talking to just now. I can tell you, he can't be helped. Is it him you're writing about?'

She looked up at him, her pen poised over the file. 'We do help people. They need our help. They depend on us. And, yes, I'm writing up his case notes.'

'You can't help people who don't know how to help themselves,' he said. 'It's like holding someone up in the water who can't swim. The minute you let them go they thrash about and drown.'

'Please!' she said. 'We're a team here. You can't possibly understand what we do. You don't know anything about our work. Just let me get this done. We'll go for a walk.'

'I know more about it than you think,' he said. He didn't really want to persist with this line, as he could see it was annoying her, but he felt compelled to have his say. 'I've known plenty of people like that guy you were talking to. You think they want to change. But they just want to go on being who they are, the same way you want to go on being who you are. They're hooked on the feeling of sinking the way your mob is hooked on the feeling of rising.'

She said calmly, 'My mob? Let me finish my notes, please.'

He sat for a while, saying nothing. He wondered if the chemical smell was something to do with the mortuary. Her office and the hallway had no windows. 'This is a creepy place to work,' he said. She didn't respond. 'The smell of despair,' he said. 'I don't know how you stand it. A parade of tragic human beings going through your door every day.' She went on writing in the file. 'How can you understand them or their lives? You don't know anything about their world.' He watched her sitting there across the desk from him writing in the file, wearing that white coat, separating herself from them. He said, 'You're a figure of authority to those people. There's no way I could work in here, even for a day.'

She looked up and said brightly, 'It's just as well, then, that you don't have to, isn't it?' She went back to her writing.

He watched her. His world and her world had never touched, except across the almoner's desk when he was a kid. He felt too uneasy and troubled to stay quiet. He stood up. 'I need a smoke,' he said. 'I'll wait for you outside.'

She looked up and smiled. 'All right. I shan't be long. Is it sunny out?'

He stood looking at her. She said, 'What's wrong?'

He was thinking: You and me, this is not going to work out. 'Yes,' he said.

Outside he sat on a low yellow brick wall on the side street and smoked a cigarette and watched the traffic and the people going home. He was feeling lonely. Suppose he were to get up and just walk away? And when she called, tell her to forget it. It's over. You and your Red Bluff house and your mother make me feel lonely. Seeing her in that gloomy office wearing her white coat, confidently making judgements about the life of someone whose intimate realities she couldn't possibly know anything about. He didn't know how he was going to deal with it. He had never felt lonely with Wendy. Not this kind of lonely. He and Wendy knew each other's worlds. How was Lena ever going to understand how someone could reach a point of disconnection so complete that they would have to sleep on a bench in a railway station?

He felt a touch on his arm and he turned and looked up into her eyes. 'Hi,' she said. She sat on the wall beside him and snuggled up close against him. She laid her head on his shoulder. 'It's been a horrible day.'

He put his arm around her and held her. When he looked he saw her eyes were closed. The trams screeched around the corner from St Kilda Road and the people on the street hurried past and the traffic waited till the tram passengers were out of the way then sped up, the air filling with blue smoke and the smell of exhaust fumes. She roused herself. 'Let's go to the park before the sun goes off the grass.' They got up and walked arm in arm to the lights and waited, then crossed the road to the King's Domain.

They walked deep into the park and sat side by side under an oak tree, their backs to the rough bark, their legs sticking out in front of them. She said, 'I told some friends of mine about you. They want to meet you. They're my best friends. She was my German teacher at school. They've invited us to dinner.'

He pointed and said, 'Look at those hawthorns over there. When I have a house of my own I'll grow a hawthorn hedge.'

'*Wer jetzt kein Haus hat, baut sich keines mehr,*' she said. She reached and took his chin in her hand and made him look at her. 'I really want you to meet them, Robert. Birte has saved me from myself a number of times. And I know you'll like Martin. Say you'll come! Please?'

He laughed at the earnest entreaty of her expression. He kissed her on the lips then drew back and looked at her. 'You can make yourself appear helpless and vulnerable when you want to. Do you know that?' He touched the smoothness of her cheek with the back of his hand. 'Of course you know it. And maybe you do also know just how disconnected it's possible for people to become. I'll come and have dinner with your friends. But just please have a look at those hawthorns before the sun goes off them.' The leaves of the hawthorns were a lovely soft russet in the late-afternoon light. 'They remind me of the hedges in Somerset when I was a boy.'

She leaned against him. 'They're beautiful. One day we'll go to England together and you can show me the farm where you worked.'

'Your hair,' he said. 'It smells familiar. It smells like home.'

She held herself against him, her arms around him, her head on his chest. 'I can hear your heart. Just think, it's beating only a couple of inches from my ear!'

He felt the soft weight of her against him, the rise and fall of her breathing, and a deep contentment came over him. He watched the last of the sunlight through the gold of the hawthorns, the slow leaching of the colours, vivid a moment then throwing off a gleam of brightness, then dying, the furthest tree on the near horizon already a grey silhouette. 'What were you quoting?' he asked her.

'*Whoever has no house now, will never have one*. Rilke—Birte's second favourite poet.'

They lay together in the stillness, the sun gone off the hawthorns, the roar of the city.

16

——

Home again and glad to be sitting at my desk looking out the window at the familiar view of our garden. Blackbirds nest every year in the enormous Albertine rose which has grown over the skeleton of an apricot tree that was dead long before my wife and I came to live in this town. The Albertine has exceptionally vicious thorns and even the most determined cats never get far into its labyrinth before being forced to retreat in pain and frustration. Except for the coldest months of winter the blackbirds ignore the seasons and renew their nest all year round in the deepest tangle of the rose. I am watching them now busily feeding newly hatched chicks, their beaks bristling with spiders and caterpillars and the occasional pink worm, flying back and forth repeatedly across the garden and diving straight into the rose at high speed. I've been sitting here watching the birds for a long time, wondering how the note-taking woman is getting on. It's less than a month since I met her. It feels as if it's much longer. Almost as if she's always been part of my story. Her impressive courage, the challenge of the intelligence shining from her eyes as she held my gaze and asked me her serious questions, my answers crucial to her wellbeing.

I get up from my desk and go out to the kitchen and make a pot of coffee. The house is quiet and empty. Our old cat, Gus, is asleep in the sun on the mat by the back door. I carry my coffee back into the study and close the door and sit at my desk. For some reason my eye searches out Thomas Mann's *Doctor Faustus*. The book has been on my shelves for decades, following me around from house to house, never finding itself among the hundreds of books I've discarded or given away over the years. My copy of Mann's great novel reminds me of my friendship with Martin Bloch and the evening we first met. At the end of that first evening with them, as Lena and I were leaving, Martin took down from his shelves this copy of Mann's novel and presented it to me. *Doctor Faustus* is, without doubt, one of the most demanding and complex novels in all of modern literature and takes for granted in its readers a familiarity with the German culture of its time. There were dozens of books on Martin's shelves that he might have given me instead of that one. In those days I had no understanding of the issues that Mann dealt with in *Faustus*. Despite this, the book shaped my earliest ideas of the kind of novelist I hoped to become. Mann's *Faustus* stood like a beacon at the starting line of my writing life.

Hearing from Lena that my ambition was to become a novelist, Martin let me know at once the kind of novel he admired when he gave me *Doctor Faustus*. It was typical of him that he wasted no words on this during the evening, making almost no contribution to the passionate discussion that was carried on about literature and its values, mainly by his wife, Dr Birte Bloch, and by Lena. It was not until we were leaving that he disclosed his thoughts by handing me the book. He said something like, 'I should like to know what you think of Mann's *Faustus*. Perhaps you can call on me when you've read it.' As I took the book from his hands I felt that he was acknowledging my intelligence and placing his trust in me. Martin's gift of the book has remained with me, along with his question. My response to that question is still unfolding.

I go over to the bookshelves and take down the old volume. I blow the dust from the top edge and open it. I bring the open book close to my face and close my eyes and breathe. And there it is! A trace, but unmistakeable still: the wonderful smell of Martin and Birte's sitting room, a faint composition of pale Scandinavian furniture, the perfume of fresh flowers and the aroma of good cooking. And books, of course. The smell of the cultivated lives of those two.

I pick up my coffee and take the book to the armchair under the window and begin to read. Rereading Mann's novel after more than fifty years I am surprised that I managed then to read it from cover to cover. Perhaps it was Mann's discussions of complicated guilt-ridden sex that kept my interest alive. Sin, good and evil, the war, theology, pages and pages of philosophy, the beautiful and the ugly, and love. Lots of tortured love. It is all there, mostly in the form of intellectual discussions between young men, with scarcely any action to sustain it, but enthralling. And music, of course, the deep tones of music in the lives of the narrator and his subject throbbing through every page—the sound of the mind of the writer.

I am soon absorbed, my memories of those days accompanying me as I read. It is surely the enrichment of my intimate memories of Martin and Birte that lends to this second reading of *Doctor Faustus* an intensity that it couldn't have possessed for me if I'd come to it now in my last years for the first time. I am conscious of reading something that belongs to my own history. Having become a part of history myself, I am deeply glad to recognise myself within the pages of this great book.

17

On that chilly autumn Sunday evening, Lena took young Robert's arm as they walked up the garden path towards the lighted windows of Birte and Martin Bloch's house. It was a solid old bluestone villa from the Victorian period, set well back from its quiet Caulfield street, just off Alma Road and only a few minutes from Robert's boarding house. Well-tended lawns on both sides of the path, the closely clipped grass bordered by dark masses of old rhododendron bushes, a single rose climbing around one of the ornate cast-iron verandah columns, a soft yellow light from the porch lamp.

Lena was cradling a bunch of flowering eucalyptus in the crook of her arm. Robert had climbed the stepladder earlier clutching her dad's secateurs and snipped the flowering branches from the great gum tree that hung over her mother's garden from the garden next door. 'Birte loves to be given flowers,' Lena said, pointing to a branch for him to cut. Before setting out from Red Bluff for Birte and Martin's in Mrs Soren's mustard Renault, which Lena drove with a careless disregard for their lives and for traffic lights and other cars, they had both downed two glasses of sherry. He was surprised by the slightly panicky wildness in her. He told her to slow down before she killed them both. She laughed and ran the next set of lights, her foot on the accelerator. He said, 'That was pretty bloody stupid.' She said, 'Don't be so bloody stuffy.' But she did slow down and drove the rest of the way more carefully. She had something to prove—to herself about herself, no doubt, and perhaps to the world.

As they walked up the path to the Blochs' house he sensed Lena's need for his reassurance in the firmness of her grip on his arm. She'd had an asthma attack on Thursday night and had been too exhausted to go to work on Friday. She was still looking pale and washed out, the circles under her eyes darker. Her asthma attack had been violent and frightening to witness. She sat in one of the armchairs in the front sitting room at Red Bluff, wheezing horribly, getting only a thin seepage of air into her lungs, gripping his hands, her mouth distorted, fear in her eyes. He could do nothing to relieve her distress. Remembering Thursday night now he pressed her to his side and leaned down and kissed her on the lips. 'I love you!' he said. He said it to reassure her.

'I don't know why you do,' she said.

She rang the bell and turned to him and smiled. 'Are you nervous?'

'Not really.' This wasn't true. He was concerned about the impression he was going to make on Lena's cultivated Europeans, as she'd called them.

Lena laughed and squeezed his arm. 'Maybe you should be nervous. Birte has never approved of any of my boyfriends.' Her voice was still throaty from Thursday night's struggle.

He said, 'So how many boyfriends have you had?'

'Dozens,' she said lightly and rang the bell again.

A woman's voice, with a thick foreign accent, shouted impatiently from inside, 'All right! All right! I'm coming!'

The woman who opened the door was in her middle fifties. She stepped towards Lena with a dragging limp and embraced her. The old woman and the young woman stood hugging each other for a long time. Robert saw that this was not the light social greeting of two friends but was the embrace of people who are emotionally close and in need of one another. It was a loving embrace. When they moved apart and turned to face him they were holding hands. Lena's colour was up and she looked restored, the light from the porch lamp in her eyes. She was holding the bunch of flowering gum erect, like an Olympic torch.

'So this is your cowboy?' Birte said. She didn't offer to shake hands with Robert but inspected him openly and in a manner that might have seemed rude in someone else, but with her seemed natural. She let go of Lena's hand and stepped up to him. She astonished him then by pinching his cheeks between her thumb and forefinger, while peering closely into his face through the strong lenses of her oversized glasses with their great black frames. She laughed and stepped away from him. 'But he's beautiful!'

He smoothed his palms down over his cheeks and laughed at the eccentricity of her behaviour. There was such a confident intimacy in her pleasure at meeting him that he felt pleasure himself. He knew at once that this extraordinary woman approved of him. He was moved and delighted.

She took hold of Lena's hand again and the two of them went ahead of him into the generous hall. 'Close the door, Robert,' Birte called back over her shoulder, as if she and he had been familiars for years. He followed them into a wide, high-ceilinged room. The appearance was of comfort—shelves of books, pictures on the walls, indoor plants flourishing, the floor of pale polished timber, richly patterned Persian rugs scattered about.

'Martin!' Birte called out in a loud aggrieved voice as she went through the door. 'Stand up so Robert can see you! Why are you sitting in the corner like that?' Her voice rose to a high pitch of astonishment towards the end of her question, as if she could scarcely believe what she was witnessing.

The man who stood up and came forward to meet Robert hadn't really been sitting in the corner at all, and Robert couldn't see that there was anything for Birte to be so dramatic about. But it was true that the man whom she had addressed as Martin did manage to give the sense of not really being there, or that he would rather have been elsewhere, or might like to have been invisible, if only any of these things had been possible. He had evidently been reading and when he stood up had set his book, still open, face down on the chair with his glasses on top of it, marking his place so that he could pick the book up again and go on reading as soon as he had the chance to do so. He was of medium height and slight build, his thin greying hair brushed straight back off his broad forehead, the skin tight and pale. He was wearing a white shirt and a brown tie under a grey tweed jacket, and darker grey slacks. He gave an impression of physical frailty, which Robert was to learn was false, and of a sensitivity of an extreme kind, almost as if he was vibrating in response to his surroundings, shrinking from the coarser elements while tentatively advancing towards those things that appealed to him. There was something elusive and haunted about him. Robert was immediately attracted to him.

Martin looked into Robert's eyes with a direct enquiring candour that was engaging rather than disconcerting, and when he took Robert's hand in his he inclined his head slightly, acknowledging something. The odd formality of this inclination of his head, almost the beginning of a bow, made him seem reserved and in possession of an inner calm that would not be breached by this encounter. Like Birte, he was in his mid-fifties, the age of Robert's father. And like Robert's father, the skin of his forehead and his cheeks was smooth and without any sign of wrinkles. His grip when he took Robert's hand was light and seemed to signify a touching of hands, a meeting, rather than the competitive encounter Robert was used to from men. His voice was quiet and unhurried, the volume falling off towards the end of his sentences, so that it was difficult to catch the last few words, and Robert found himself leaning towards him to hear. Martin's accent was not as pronounced as his wife's. After exchanging a brief greeting, Martin turned to Lena and they embraced warmly. 'Oh, Martin,' she said with feeling, 'it's so good to see you.' Robert saw that Martin was a man who appreciated her beauty.

Birte brandished the unwieldy bunch of flowering gum branches that Lena had presented her with and buried her face in them. She sniffed and announced loudly in a dramatic tone of shock and affront, as if she'd been stung, 'Martin! Martin! They have no smell!'

Martin shrugged and murmured, 'So? They're beautiful. What do you expect, smell as well as beauty?' He shot Robert a quick look, a mischievous smile in his eyes.

Lena said, 'Well, they do have a sort of smell. Especially if you go out into the garden in the evening or the early morning, then you can smell the blossom.'

'It's evening now!' Birte said, stating the fact. 'Flowers should have a smell. These don't have a smell.' She thrust them at Martin. 'If you like them so much, put them in that ugly black jug Peta and Leonard gave us.' She turned away and, gripping the arm of the sofa, eased herself down onto the cushions, grimacing and making small anguished sounds of pain, stretching her left leg out in front of her while glaring at it as if it was wilfully determined to torment her. 'And bring the vermouth,' she shouted. 'And some ice! And turn the oven down to three.'

She turned to Lena and said something in German. Lena sat beside her and answered her in German. Lena sounded so

completely German that Robert laughed at the sudden transformation. He sat in the vacant easy chair opposite them, facing
Martin's chair with the book and glasses on it. On a low table
between them were two blue glass bowls filled to overflowing
with peanuts and cashews, and in the centre of the table a large
blue and white Chinese plate with an arrangement of smoked
oysters on cracker biscuits. The oysters were the dark meaty colour
and texture of the Danish bog man. Robert tried one, chewing
it thoughtfully before swallowing it. He decided it tasted much
nicer than it looked. A heavy glass ashtray on the edge of the
table closest to the chair with Martin's book and glasses on it was
crammed with crushed cigarette butts. Beside the ashtray was a
packet of Peter Stuyvesant, a brass lighter, and a glass with what
looked like the remains of whisky in it—the faint familiar smell
of whisky, always in the air after Robert's father got home from
work. Whisky and Digger Shag tobacco. The smell of the old
front room of his childhood home.

Although Lena and Birte were talking in German, Birte
holding Lena's hand in her lap, Robert didn't feel ignored by them
or shut out. Sitting there in the easy chair smoking a cigarette,
comfortably aware of Lena and Birte catching up, he looked around
the room while he waited for Martin to come back. On both sides
of the fireplace, which had been converted to gas, there were
bookshelves filled with a jumble of books. Opposite the fireplace
on the far side of the room, between the two tall windows, leafy
pot plants stood in large green ceramic jars. The fine material

of the curtains moved slightly, affected by a draft, the movement catching his eye and making it seem as if someone was about to come into the room from the darkness of the front garden. There were three pictures on the walls. A traditional Chinese watercolour above the fireplace, a delicate picture of flowers and a bird, its beak open, trilling. On the wall facing him was a coloured reproduction of one of Picasso's clowns in a blue outfit. The picture that most intrigued him was a black and white drawing or etching, he wasn't sure which it was. It was a head-and-shoulders portrait of an old woman facing the viewer, her head inclined slightly forward. She was shielding the expression in her eyes with the spread fingers of one hand across her forehead, the large bony hand strongly modelled and casting her right eye and the right side of her face partly into deep shadow. The half-concealed expression in the old woman's eyes was one of sorrow or despair, or perhaps it was the fatigue of old age. The look in her eyes seemed to him to say, *My feelings are private and are not to be shared.* And yet there it was, the sitter's inner sorrow displayed and withheld at the same time. Robert got up and went over and looked closely at the picture and its ambiguous enticement: *Don't look at me! See my sorrow!* His father would have admired it.

From behind him, Martin said, 'So you like our picture?'

Robert turned around. Martin was holding a tray with a bottle of dry vermouth, an ice bucket and four glasses on it. He set the tray down among the bowls of nuts and the plate of smoked oysters on the low table.

'I like it very much,' Robert said. His father would have said there was great tenderness in the drawing. Tenderness was one of his father's most frequently used words after he returned from the front. His father's wounds were raw and fresh then, in his mind as well as in his body. He was unable to express tenderness himself and was often moved to tears of shame when he met it in others. The clenched emotion of the picture, the refusal to directly expose her feelings, also made Robert think of his own struggle with the image of the fighting man. He could easily imagine a man like Martin being as deeply fatigued or as affected by sorrow as the old woman in the picture.

Martin said, 'It's one of her last self-portraits. Käthe Kollwitz did many self-portraits. She mirrored the tragedy of her times through her self-portraits. This one is unfinished.' He stood looking at it and Robert turned and looked at it with him. That the artist had not finished this last self-portrait made it even more expressive of loss and sorrow, the empty space, untouched by the pencil or the burin, a space in which something had remained private and closed from view. His father would have pointed out to him that the empty space was the picture's most poignant statement. Robert said, 'It's beautiful. Did you know her?'

Birte said, 'We didn't know her. But you are right, it is beautiful. She was one of Germany's greatest artists. She used art for good, not evil.' She looked at Martin. 'So, are we going to have a drink or not?'

Martin gave an expressive little shrug of his shoulders and murmured, 'So, who uses art for evil?' He served Birte and Lena with a glass of the vermouth each, two blocks of ice in each glass. Then he turned to Robert and asked if he would prefer a glass of beer, or perhaps a whisky?

Robert said, 'Thank you. I'd like vermouth.' He watched Martin serving the drinks. There was an almost abstract poise in the way he carried out the small tasks, taking ice blocks from the bowl with the tongs and releasing them into the glass with a light clink, each one separate and real, the glint of the stainless steel as he turned the tongs in his hand. He made it all seem intensely present in a way Robert knew himself to be incapable of, as if he would remember forever these small movements of Martin's hands—long after he had forgotten what had been said, he would see Martin preparing the drinks. He thought to himself that an artist would make a delicate etching of the moment, and he would stand and look at the etching a hundred years later and know the moment just as it had been. He despaired of ever being able to make his own actions as real as Martin's. Everything Robert did seemed to him to be an amateurish attempt at reality compared to the grace and poise of this man. There was no simple explanation for any of it. I would fail, he thought, if I tried to be like him. Martin poured a drink for himself and picked up his glasses and the book from the chair and sat down.

They all leaned forward and clinked their glasses and wished each other good health. Martin reached for his cigarettes and shook one from the packet and lit it with the brass lighter. 'When she was old,' he said, 'and had lost her husband and her son, she used to dream that she was dead.' He paused to draw on his cigarette and looked at Robert. 'At first she liked her dream of being dead, then after a while she began to find the dream of death boring.' He smiled. It was a moment before Robert realised Martin was talking about Käthe Kollwitz.

Birte said, 'Art and literature can serve the cause of evil, Martin. You know very well they can. Just as they can serve the cause of good. Young people must be taught history and be trained in the art of criticism so that they can recognise evil when they come across it in art and literature and will not be so easily fooled by it. Young people want to believe in what is most passionate and so they are vulnerable to the passionate lies of demented demagogues. At universities they give students only the works admired by the professors. But literature is not so one-sided as they like to make out. I can't understand why you ask me who uses art for evil. I'm not deaf, you know. It's stupid to speak like that, even to yourself. Art has often been used for evil. We expect good writing to have a good effect on the young, but we don't warn them against the impassioned ravings of the demagogues and the demented.'

Birte was not speaking casually. She sounded seriously upset and determined to give the matter a full and passionate response. She reached for her drink and took a large sip, frowning at the glass as if she might decide to criticise the way it was looking at her.

Martin said quietly, 'There are plenty of good books. We don't have to read rubbish.' He said this in such a subdued voice that it seemed to Robert to come as an aside from a conversation they'd had with each other many times in the past. But Birte was right: the possibility of evil in literature had never occurred to him, and no teacher had ever drawn his attention to the possibility of it, but had only ever urged him to read and to read more.

Birte said, 'How can we expect young people to recognise evil in works of literature when they come across it if we hide it from them and don't teach them about it? It's what the Victorians did with sex. And everybody forgot how to enjoy sex and started looking at pornography in secret instead, feeling ashamed of themselves for even thinking about it. Even today modern art is still under their ban. The male erection is never celebrated. Have you noticed that? When did you last see the male erection in a work of art? The last people to celebrate the male erection were the Romans. If the influence of literature and art is really as important as we say it is, then the young must be educated about the difference between propaganda and the real thing. We can only do this by making them familiar with both. The young are seduced by passion.' She reached for her leg and shifted it with both hands and groaned, then she reached for her glass. It was empty.

Lena said, 'So why didn't you teach us about evil literature at school?'

Birte made an explosive sound and cried out, 'But I did! You think it's that simple? At the Methodist Ladies' College? It would take a revolution. I'm talking about what we *should* do, not about what we can do freely in this prudish climate in Victoria. The school governors would sack me if I put that kind of thing on the syllabus. But you remember, we *talked* about everything. I didn't leave you girls in the dark. I let you know such things could be found and were worth talking about and reading. I made you curious to go in search of them yourselves. I used to say, *Close the door or Miss Curling will hear us.*' She laughed. 'Remember?'

Martin sipped his drink and smoked his cigarette. He looked comfortable and relaxed.

Birte said, 'Those of us who have witnessed evil have a moral duty to teach the new generation to recognise it.' She held her empty glass towards Martin. 'Martin! Are we going to be allowed to have more than one drink before dinner?' Without pausing she went on, 'Evil is not so easy to see when it's masked by the banner of art and literature. Evil can creep up on us, and before we know it we are in bed with it and enjoying it.' She turned to Robert, the thought evidently flashing across her mind like the shadow of a bird and startling her. 'So tell me, Robert, what is it you want to write *about*? Lena has told us you want to be a writer.' She thrust the question at him so abruptly he was completely thrown.

'Well,' he said, trying to think of something worth writing about and managing to think of nothing at all, his mind a perfect expanse of nothing. There was something he wanted to write about, but what was it?

Birte was staring at him, as if she was expecting an interesting revelation from him.

'I don't know,' he said at last. Right at that moment he could think of nothing it might ever be possible for him or for anyone else to ever write about. 'I don't know,' he repeated emptily, echoing the hollowness inside. He felt doomed. Stupid. Empty. Certain he was never to shine for these people. Martin would be sure to think him a fool.

'You don't *know*?' Birte almost screamed. She appealed to Martin and Lena as if they were a crowd. 'A writer must have something to say! You can't be a writer if you have nothing to say. Imagine Goethe having nothing to say!'

Martin handed her a fresh drink and said quietly, setting his words out with care, so that even Birte paused to listen to him, 'Robert didn't say he has nothing to say, Birte.' He looked at her steadily.

'So?' she said.

'He said he didn't know what he has to say.'

Birte said dismissively, 'Ach, it's the same thing.' She appealed to Lena. 'We have to know what we want to say, don't we, or how can we say it?'

To Robert this seemed reasonable enough. Logical and clear. But he knew in his heart that it couldn't possibly be true. But he didn't know how to say it couldn't be true. He could think of no way of challenging Birte.

Martin said, 'No, it isn't the same thing. Not knowing what we have to say and having nothing to say are not the same thing. We find out what we have to say when we attempt to say it. We think we want to say one thing, then in the attempt to say it we find there is a deeper and clearer truth waiting for us just below the surface of our first thought. And this comes as a delightful surprise to us. The thing we wish to say is never just as we thought it would be. And we are either delighted by this discovery, if we are not fanatics out to prove our own prejudices, or, if we are, then we are dismayed and we reject our own truth.' He turned and looked at Robert. 'When Robert writes, then he will begin to know what he has to say. And then you will have an answer to your question, Birte. The poet is taken by surprise by the poem. You will be able to make up your own mind what Robert has to say when you read what he has said. Unless we intend to write polemic, it is important for us to begin by not knowing what we are going to say when we are faced with the necessity of having to say something.'

Birte said, 'So, is he writing poetry? I thought he wanted to be a novelist. They're not the same thing.'

Martin said, again with a quiet sense of belief and amusement, 'How do you know they are not the same thing?' He grinned at Robert. He was enjoying himself.

Robert was thinking of Frankie and his failed attempt to write the story of their friendship, but he felt he had missed his cue and it was too late to bring this up. He was imagining Birte asking

Lena, 'So what is it about him that attracts you apart from his good looks?' What would Lena say to that?

Later that evening, in the middle of delivering a long and rambling soliloquy, and in the same panic-stricken voice in which she'd said the flowers had no smell, Birte fell silent abruptly and turned to Martin and appealed to him dramatically. 'Martin! Martin! I've forgotten what I was going to say!' It was as if she had been deprived of air, a woman thrown into the deep and drowning. The effect of her panic-stricken appeal was startling. The sudden cessation of her monologue. The awful silence, until Martin suggested quietly, 'Well, why don't you say something else?'

Robert caught a glimpse of a hidden world lying between these two, a chasm that could open at any moment and swallow them, a world that was troubling and dark and threatening and which lay just below the surface of ordinary things. The comedy of Martin's response to Birte's panicky appeal to him for help was eclipsed by this sense of a real threat to Birte if she were to fall into the gulf of silence. Talk, it seemed, was a necessary haven for Birte, just as silence was for Martin. They were a pair. Silence was obviously a place behind the lines for Martin, behind the lines of social engagement, a refuge where he felt safe—tell them nothing! While Birte could be safe, it seemed, only so long as silence did not open beneath her and swallow her. They were both vulnerable. Robert saw it in her panic. And perhaps he understood something of the love Lena had for Birte. And something, too, of Lena's own vulnerability, her own inclination to panic, the terror in her eyes when she was at the mercy of the asthma attack. And he saw how for Lena, the company of these friends liberated her from the threat of an airless confinement in her own life at home with her mother. He saw all this in the instant when Birte turned to Martin and pleaded with him to re-join the broken ends of her thought. She might have cried out, Save me!

It was after midnight when Lena and Robert got up to leave. They had returned by then from the dining room at the rear of the house to the front room for coffee. As they were going out the door into the hall, Martin turned back into the room and took down Thomas Mann's *Doctor Faustus* from the shelves and handed the book to Robert.

'You might find this interesting,' he said. 'I should like to know what you think of Mann's *Faustus*. Perhaps you can call on me when you've read it.'

Robert took the book from Martin's hand and thanked him. He knew it was not only the gift of a book, but was an invitation to friendship and an expression of trust. Martin smiled with quiet pleasure.

Birte glanced at the book and made an irritated noise. 'You're giving him Thomas Mann to read?' She looked at Robert. 'You should know that Mann accused Martin and other German intellectuals of failing to resist Hitler. And Mann did it from the safety of America, while Martin and his comrades remained in Germany and were hunted down and tortured and murdered by those people. Mann knew nothing of the heroic resistance of people like Martin!

Nothing!' She turned to Martin. 'Robert can't read a book like that without knowing something about its author.'

Martin sounded angry when he said, 'That's far too simple, Birte!' He was clearly annoyed with Birte for spoiling the simplicity of the moment. 'Mann was a sceptic,' he said. There was a fierceness in him that they'd had no hint of during the evening. As he raised his voice his German accent became more pronounced. 'Why do you have to talk about that now?'

Birte looked crestfallen. Clearly Martin could be a match for her when aroused. She reached for Lena's arm and drew the younger woman to her side. 'So,' she said, 'are we going to have a row just as Lena and Robert are leaving us?'

Martin glared at her. Robert thought he was going to say something more, but he let it go. Birte might have scratched a sharp object across Martin's skin. The pain in his angry outburst had seemed to frighten her.

18

———

Robert was already imagining returning to the house after he had read the book and sitting in the front room talking about Thomas Mann and great literature with Martin. The gift of the book reassured him that Martin expected something good and decent from him, something intelligent and worth his while. Robert wanted to begin reading the book at once.

Lena unlocked her mother's car and stood by the door, waiting for him. The Renault's duco gleaming under a fine silvering of dew. Robert stood on the passenger side of the car opposite her, examining the dust jacket of the book under the streetlight. *Thomas Mann* in white letters across the top against a blue background. *Doctor Faustus* in green lettering underneath the author's name. At the bottom a suggestive subtitle: *The life of the German composer ADRIAN LEVERKÜHN as told by a friend*. A dark portrait of a stern-looking man gazed out from within the blue background of the cover, a likeness masked by the bold lettering of the title and the author's name, staring at the viewer, as if he could be reached only with a great effort, the round black eyes demanding. So was this figure 'the friend' of the subtitle or the author himself? Robert turned the book over and looked at the back cover. Under the heading *The works of Thomas Mann* there was a list of his published books. Robert counted them. Fourteen titles. He ran his fingers over the name of the publisher, Secker & Warburg. The magic of the book in his hands. The promise of it. Everything it meant to him. Mann had evidently been a grand, serious writer of vast accomplishment. And Martin was confident he, Robert, would understand him. With this book in his hands, and the promise of friendship with Martin, Robert's ambition to be a writer had acquired a new seriousness. As he stood there under the streetlight gazing at the book, he conceived an obligation to live up to Martin's expectations. The challenge was far greater than he had imagined. And far more worthwhile. It would not be reached easily. The glaring portrait of Thomas Mann, half concealed within the cover of his book, made that clear.

Lena said, 'Are you coming?'

He opened the book and read the first couple of lines: *I wish to state quite definitely that it is by no means out of any wish to bring my own personality into the foreground . . .*

Lena stepped around to his side of the car and caught him by the arm. 'Are we going?'

He closed the book and met her angry gaze and he said, 'I can't wait to read it.'

'Are you coming with me, or not?'

He said, 'Well, actually, I might walk back to the boarding house. It's just up Alma Road here. It'll only take me ten minutes.' He would have the whole night to himself. He could read undisturbed.

He might have slapped her.

'What are you saying? You can't abandon me! You've got to come home with me! Mum expects you to bring me home.' She clutched his arm. 'I'm not going home without you, if that's what you think. You must think I'm bloody stupid.'

He said, 'Hey, hey. Settle down. It's no big deal. We'll see each other tomorrow after you finish work. Anyway, I need to pick up a clean shirt.'

'That's fucking crap! You're a rotten liar.' She didn't let go of his arm, but steadied herself, focusing her suspicions. 'If I thought you were going to meet up with that woman—Wendy, or whatever her stupid name was—I'd kill you.' She was coldly serious. 'You really must think I'm an idiot.'

'Well now you *are* being bloody stupid,' he said. 'I haven't given her a thought for ages.' This wasn't true. He often thought of Wendy.

Lena made up her mind. 'I'm coming with you,' she said. 'Get in the car!'

As she drove at speed up Alma Road he was half dreading they'd find Wendy waiting for him when they got to the boarding house, one of those weirdly unlikely coincidences when people's lives collide with a shock and their direction is changed forever. Lena drove straight down the driveway and around to the back of the house, kicking up the gravel. He thought she was going to take out the back fence. The little Renault's wheels locked up and they slid to a crunching stop, his foot braced against an imaginary brake pedal. She got out and slammed her door. They walked back along the path between the dark laurels. Neither spoke.

They went in and up the stairs. He unlocked the door to his room and stepped aside to let Lena go in ahead of him. He closed the door quietly. She stood in the room looking around. 'You're lucky she's not here,' she said. She went over to the desk and riffled through his papers. Then she went across to the wardrobe and stood looking in at his clothes.

He was waiting by the door, watching her. She opened one of the small drawers in the wardrobe and lifted out the only thing in the drawer: the paisley scarf his mother had given him the day he left home for Australia. She held the square of scarf up by a corner, as if it offended her to touch it. She turned and faced him. 'So, what's this?' She was certain she'd found something.

He said, 'What does it look like?'

'Why have I never seen it before?'

'It's been in that drawer since the day I arrived here.'

'Is it hers? Did she give it to you?'

He went across and set Martin's book on his desk. He adjusted it so that it sat exactly in the centre of the desk in front of his chair, ready to be opened and read the moment he was alone. He turned to Lena. 'My mother gave it to me the day I left home.'

She looked at the scarf again. 'So why have I never seen it?'

'Because I've never worn it. Can you imagine me wearing it?' He watched her struggling with her jealousy and distrust, her need to expose his infidelity, her need to do something with her anger, to find something to attack.

He said, 'You can have it. It would look smart tucked in around the collar of your coat.' Even though she'd found no evidence that Wendy had been in his room, no treasured memento of past occasions with his lover, nothing at all to justify her suspicions, he saw that Lena wasn't going to give up being angry with him. She needed her anger and was determined to justify it. She held the scarf up, then she let it drop onto the end of his disordered bed, its silken folds opening and almost floating before lying still. He thought of a wounded bird that makes a last feeble attempt to fly.

She walked over to the desk and stood looking down at Mann's novel. She opened the book in the middle and read a couple of lines aloud in a half-mocking voice. '"Vale," *he said, "and may God be with you, Leverkühn.—The parting blessing comes from my heart."'* She closed the book and went over and looked out the window. 'You won't like it,' she said. 'You won't understand it.'

'Have you read it?'

She was wearing a black dress with a string of pearls and a short grey jacket. She looked very smart and sexy and middle class and out of place in the shabby room. Her anger made her beautiful and sad and elusive. That strange unsettling feeling she gave him sometimes, a feeling of being alone while in her presence.

'You'll find Mann heavy going,' she said.

He didn't say anything. He was determined not to respond.

She said, 'I'm going home.' She didn't move or turn around.

They'd made love that morning at the Red Bluff house while her mother was at church. All day they had been close and calm with each other. Watching her standing there at the window now he was aware of the fragility of their relationship. The mystery of her interior life, undisclosed to him. Was he just as much a mystery to her? He lit a cigarette and went over to the wardrobe and reached into the bottom and pulled out a bottle of beer. He called over to her, 'You want a beer?'

She turned around and looked at him. He thought how sad and beautiful and lonely she looked in that moment of turning away from gazing into the night garden.

He held up the bottle. 'Come and have a drink.'

'Do you really never see her?'

'Never,' he said. He opened the bottle and took a long swig of the warm beer then held the bottle out to her at arm's length. He might have added truthfully that he would have liked to see Wendy again. Without trust, it was obvious there could be nothing good and calm between him and Lena. Other things: a form of madness, anger, lust and anger. Dangerous stuff. He didn't want that.

She came over and sat beside him on the edge of the bed. 'I don't know what to think of you sometimes,' she said.

He handed her the bottle. She took a long drink and gave a belch then handed it back to him. 'It's easy for you,' she said. 'You know what you want.'

He was astonished to hear this from her. 'Easy for me?' he said. 'And you? You've already got everything you want.'

She considered him for a long moment. 'So what do I want? I don't know what I want. I only know what is expected of me. No one expects anything of you. You've got your ambition and you've got your freedom. No one cares what you do. You do whatever you like and you know what it is you want to do with your life. You've found a cause for yourself. That's what I want. Something I can dream about, the way you dream about writing your books.'

It was true. He did know what he wanted. He wanted to get a decent education and to become a novelist. It might not be easy, but that's what he wanted. He hadn't seen it her way at all. The question of how he was to understand people troubled him. He was afraid he might not have enough empathy or insight into the lives of others to ever be a good novelist.

She said, 'I envy anybody who knows what they want from life.' She was silent a while. 'The day John brought you round to meet me I saw it at once.'

'You saw what?'

'I saw that you were free.' She took the bottle from him and drank. She grimaced and handed it back. 'I shouldn't have come here tonight. I should have let you go when you said you wanted to. I've never stayed out all night before, except with the girls, when it's been arranged. Do you believe that? And I'm spoiling the night for you. I don't know why I have to be so awful.'

He put his arms around her and held her. She relaxed against him.

'You're not being awful. You're right. It is easy for me. I do know what I want.'

After a while she said, 'Can I stay the night in your bed? Will you hold me?'

He had a sudden disturbing thought then of her father and how she must miss him. He forced himself to ignore the thought. He got up and turned off the light. They undressed and with a helpless kind of awkwardness they got into his narrow bed. He pulled the covers up and they turned to each other and embraced. He whispered, 'Why are you holding your breath?'

'Do you mind if we don't make love?' she said, her voice small, contrite, helpless—the frightened little girl, suddenly, needing the comfort of her father's arms.

They lay together in the quiet hours of the great house. He was astonished to realise she had gone to sleep almost at once. The faint light from the window cast a soft glow across her cheek, her eyelashes perfectly formed, the impossible smoothness of her skin, the intimate warmth of her voluptuous nakedness against him. She opened her eyes and looked at him. 'I was dreaming,' she said. She asked, 'Why did you leave the outback?'

'I was wrong about what I wanted from life. It was only a boyhood dream. I learned that even the most exotic place soon becomes normal and routine once you're living in the reality of it.'

'You got bored?'

'Sickened by some things. Bored by the routine. The same thing every day.'

'And did you decide then to become a writer?'

'I panicked and left. I had no idea what I was going to do. I'd lost my dream. It was a shock. The idea of being a writer came more slowly.'

'And you're not afraid you might get sick of being a writer? That it might also just become a daily routine?'

'I don't know. It seems like the most difficult thing it would be possible for me to do. I can't imagine a routine.'

They lay quietly side by side. After a while she whispered, 'Make love to me.'

Robert woke to the sound of the men from the night shift coming into the room next door, the long night and the clamour of the bottle line in their exhausted voices. His room was filled with the grey light of dawn.

Lena was awake and was watching him.

He said, 'I was dreaming I was rowing a boat across the biggest of the three Keston Ponds. I used to go fishing there with my dad. We threw our lines in and then did our drawings and watercolours while we waited for a fish to bite. There was supposed to be a giant pike in the pond, the king of the pond terrorising the other fish and eating the frogs. We always searched the weeds for him but I never saw him. In my dream a thickening tangle of water weeds was holding the boat back and I was struggling to move it towards the shore. The oars were far too long and unwieldy and the harder I tried to move the boat forward the more thickly the weeds clung to it and held it back. I despaired of ever being strong enough to beat the grip of the weeds.' He turned to her. 'What do you suppose it means?'

She touched his forehead lightly with her fingertips. Her face was close to his, her eyes dark and shining in the grey light, her full soft lips without a trace of lipstick, her hair sprung into wild ruffles around her head. She didn't say anything and he closed his eyes again. His throat was dry and he needed to piss. He thought of getting up and going to the bathroom down the passage and getting a drink of water.

She said, 'What would you do if we found out I was pregnant?'

He opened his eyes.

'I might be,' she said. 'Mightn't I?'

The idea of a child made him feel doomed. He said cautiously, 'Do you want a child?'

She didn't say anything for quite a while. Then she said, 'I suppose if I was actually pregnant I would want to have the baby. But if I'm not pregnant, I don't want one.' She got up on her elbow and looked down at him. 'Would you desert me?'

He said, 'I don't think there's any chance of that. But I've never been tested on that one. So who knows?'

She said, 'Seriously! Tell me. If I'm pregnant, will you desert me?'

'Are you pregnant?'

'Probably not, but you never know.'

He leaned over and kissed her on the lips. 'I'll stay with you, whatever happens.'

'Mum said you were the reliable type.' She laughed. 'I told her I didn't want a reliable type, that's why I went for a cowboy.'

'This cowboy needs to take a piss,' he said. He got out of bed and pulled on his trousers and went along the passage to the bathroom. One of the night shift boys was having a shower. He called out a greeting after pissing. Robert went back to his room and took off his trousers and climbed back into the bed.

She snuggled in close against him. 'I have to go and face Mum.'

'I'll come with you,' he said.

Lena drove the Renault through the early-morning streets. The day was clear and windless. The waters of the Bay flat and still, lying like a sheet of silvery glass to the horizon, a string of cargo ships and low tankers lined up waiting to get into the port. He suddenly remembered *Doctor Faustus* sitting on his desk waiting for him. It was hard to believe he'd forgotten all about it.

'Yes, Mum,' Lena said. 'Robert and I slept together last night.'

Mrs Soren was calm, her blue eyes flinty, her manner determined, no longer the comfortable little woman in the country cottage. The three of them were standing in the sitting room, she facing the bow window, Lena and Robert a step inside the double glass doors to the hall, facing her. Mrs Soren had standards.

Indeed, principles. She got straight to the point. 'I've been expecting this from you two. You'll get engaged at once. I shall put the announcement in Saturday's *Age*. Lena will have her grandmother's engagement ring. I'll set a date for the wedding with Dr Eady.' She regarded them both steadily. There were to be no negotiations.

Lena said, 'Mum, I'm twenty-two! You can't force us to get married.'

Mrs Soren said, 'Yes, I know you are, darling. I can't stop you from leaving home with Robert if that's what you want to do. But will any of us be happy if you do that?' She paused. 'I don't think so. Do you? You're talking about the kind of unhappiness that tears families apart. Your father would have wept to hear you suggest it.' Tears sprang to her eyes at the mention of Lena's father.

Lena said, 'Of course that's not what I want, Mum.' She stepped forward and embraced her mother. Mrs Soren closed her eyes, resisting Lena for a moment, then she relented and hugged her daughter to her.

Robert stood there watching them. He didn't feel any hostility towards himself from Mrs Soren. She didn't seem to bear him or Lena any ill will, but apparently felt compelled to issue them with her ultimatum all the same. She was like an officer who gives an order he doesn't agree with for the sake of the greater discipline of his caste. Robert felt that Mrs Soren was prepared to be as tough on herself as she was on her daughter and on him. She would rather risk losing Lena than disobey her conscience. He had never before met anyone capable of this kind of thing. And he began to see her as a representative of an inflexible social order that was foreign to him and to his experience and upbringing. He had been prepared to meet her anger and had had an apology ready. He hadn't expected this.

Lena and her mother were standing facing him, their arms linked. If he turned around and left the house, that would be the end of it. The thought flitted across his mind and was gone. Lena was taller than Mrs Soren by half a head. The two of them were close, they understood each other, they knew what to expect from each other. He saw that they were looking out at him from within their own place, and he knew it was a place whose values he did not understand and probably didn't share. The cage of Lena's un-freedom, her divided self. Mother and daughter might have problems with each other, but that was another matter. For now it was him they were waiting for; waiting for him to say his piece, waiting for him to affirm his honourable intentions. He was nervous. He wanted a cigarette. He wasn't sure he could handle the situation well. He said, 'Look, Mrs Soren, I don't mean any harm by this, but I really don't think marriage is the right way for me and Lena to go.'

'I know that, Robert,' she said calmly. 'I know how you feel about it. But there's no other way.' She gave him a chilly smile. 'You can live here and you can use Keith's study. I know you like his room. It can be yours.'

He looked at Lena and knew the whole setup was wrong. He said, 'You can't just dismiss my views like that, Mrs Soren. That's not on. Okay?' Her lack of respect for his views hurt him and angered him. She was sweeping his feelings aside as if they were irrelevant. He had met such responses as a child. He wanted to tell Mrs Soren she was not his superior. There are no superiors here. This is not England.

She sensed the fierceness in him, and knew the danger of it for her daughter, and she smiled and reached for his hand and said, 'Well, why don't we all sit down and talk about it over a cup of tea, Robert. There's no point in our opposing each other, is there? Come along!'

He went. Unwilling and resentful. Burning inside. But he went.

19

———

I'm watching through the study window as my wife cuts winter roses and sprigs of pink blossom from the leucoxylon, which she will arrange later in the grey stoneware vase in the sunroom. To watch her out there in the autumn day cutting flowers is a joy for me, and I am reminded that the beauty of our lives cannot last forever. The apple tree has finally lost its leaves. Our apple tree is one of the last trees in our garden to lose its leaves in autumn and one of the last to get them in the spring. Only the hedge of red hawthorns along the back boundary that I planted our first winter here is slower than the apple tree and still has a rusty flecking of autumn.

My wife straightens up and looks over her shoulder, as if she has felt me watching her. The pattern of my leaf piles on the lawn reminds me of the pattern of dung mounds in the arable fields I made in spring after the cows had been turned out to pasture from their wintering in the byre. In winter the ground was white and hard, the turnips frozen in the iron earth, the sky a solemn unrelenting grey. Here in winter the grass is always green. Gus is lying with his front paws on one of the leaf piles, watching my wife, a dapple of branch shadow cast over him from the bare tree. I see in him an old gentleman reclining on a chaise longue, the shadow of his spectacles on the end of his nose.

20

———

Mrs Soren's notice of the engagement of her daughter to Robert Crofts appeared in *The Age* and Robert moved in with them at the Red Bluff house. He'd managed to pass his three subjects and was admitted to an arts degree. They were married on a Saturday morning in the Sandringham Presbyterian Church at the end of second term. A light rain was falling and a cold wind blowing in off the Bay. Lena wore a simple tailored white dress and Robert wore a new dark grey three-piece single-breasted suit. Mrs Soren's friend the Reverend Dr Frank Eady—her partner in violin and piano duets in the sitting room of the Red Bluff house, an old friend of her husband's and her spiritual adviser—performed the ceremony. Lena and Robert looked into each other's eyes and swore with due solemnity to uphold the traditional vows: honour, obey, protect, forsake all others. All that.

Robert approached the church ceremony cynically, even though in the back of his mind the word *vow* troubled him. Making a vow wasn't just promising in the ordinary way of things. It was surely something bigger than that. It was a word he'd never had to deal with and had probably never used. A concept foreign to his way of thinking. Something rare and potent about it that he believed in as part of the bargain. When the moment came to commit himself he was moved. The emotion caught him off guard, the sudden tension in his chest, the tightening in his throat. It wasn't the church or any sense of religion or the rules of middle-class behaviour, but something far more powerful. It was the knowledge that he was changing himself. He was afraid he might also be losing himself.

There were half a dozen of Lena's old girlfriends from school and their husbands, and two of her colleagues from the hospital. And there were Mrs Soren's two sisters and their husbands and her brother, the patriarch of the clan. And, of course, Martin and Birte were there, standing beside Lena's piano teacher, Leonard Kohner, and his wife Peta. And Mrs Soren herself. Mrs Soren's brother, the patriarch Ralph—an anxious thickset man, a millionaire many times over with no children and a tall film-star-style wife with sparkling eyes and golden hair—gave Lena away.

During the service and at the reception afterwards Robert found himself being welcomed by these people. They were pleased to see him coming over to their side. They were all smiles and congratulations. All of them, without exception. Unreserved. Glad to have him. A new recruit. He was caught by the force of their combined decency and enthusiasm and he responded with genuine feeling to Dr Eady's portentous question, 'Do you, Robert Crofts, take this woman, Lena Soren, to be your lawful wedded wife?'

Or whatever the precise words were. The vow. He made it. He gave his solemn word.

And when Lena looked into his eyes, what he saw was not the happiness of a bride, but a kind of sorrow, a longing and a melancholy that lay deep within her, as if the person she really was, her own person, that secret person not displayed in the portrait but left blank, would be required to fight its way to the surface from the suffocating confinement of this other existence. He saw that he did not know her. And he understood in that moment that the passage of love was not to be known any more than was the passage of death. And as he looked into her eyes there in the church, the congregation listening to the vow that was coming out of him, he was remembering her swimming freely ahead of him through the cold grey sea that day when they made love in the bathing box, heading out confidently and alone towards the rusting hulk of the sunken ship. And he saw that she was still far ahead of him, seeing something deeper than he was seeing, something older, something more adult and more mature and more lonely, lured out by it, leading him to a place he would never have gone to alone. And he knew he had been right all along, and that marriage was not the way for the two of them. But all the same he said it, he responded as he was expected to respond, 'I do,' and was obedient to everyone's expectations that day, and to Dr Eady's portentous question.

Lena, he understood, but too late, had expected more from her wild cowboy lover than obedience to the stifling rules of her caste. Maybe she had even expected to be rescued by him from the confinement of her solitude. To ride behind his saddle into the sunset of a romantic and mysterious freedom. He didn't know. How could he know? He was still young. She hadn't joined him. That was what he did know. He had joined her. And perhaps she was disappointed. The force of his reality had capitulated to the force of her reality. It was real, this moment, for both of them; it was a revelation and a disavowal of their freedom. And it was more powerfully real than he had foreseen. He placed the plain gold band on her finger, sliding it next to her grandmother's sparkling diamond. Her hands were beautiful, her fingers long and smooth and flexible, full of expression and music and the secret sadness of her heart.

And of course there were none of his friends from his past life in the church to witness it that day, none of his own family and no one from his school. The only friend who came into his mind that day was Frankie. He saw Frankie look at him and nod and know him. And he looked back at Frankie with gratitude and knew he was a man who had known how to love properly, and that to know this is not given to everyone. He knew Frankie understood and would not mock him for it.

That afternoon at Mrs Soren's Red Bluff house the guests shone, their eyes brighter than usual, a golden mist in the crowded rooms while they drank French champagne and laughed and clasped each other's hands, some even clutching Robert to them in a sudden excess of goodwill, embracing him and taking him to their hearts.

Welcome! Welcome! Welcome, Robert! And they drank more French champagne and laughed and raised their glasses and Lena and he kissed and he made a surprising speech that was met with cheers and applause and more laughter. Mrs Soren stood beside him and held his hand while she said her few modest words in reply, and then she turned to him and put her arms around him and hugged him close to her for everyone to witness that she and he were friends, and there were tears in her eyes. And by then Robert was drunk. And Dr Eady played his violin and Leonard Kohner played a joyful dance on Lena's upright Rönisch.

And Robert did not yet see that he was no longer as free as he had been.

He thought he had joined them. They thought he had too. What did any of them know?

Lena and Robert spent that night in a grand suite at the Windsor Hotel, paid for, like everything else, including his new suit, by her mother. And in the morning they drove to Point Lonsdale in the little yellow Renault. They stayed a week in a darkly panelled boarding house where a gong was sounded at dinnertime. And every day they swam together in the ocean and made love in the dunes. The sea was cold and thunderous and the wind from the south was colder than the ocean, and Robert learned during that week to enjoy the first chilling plunge and the blows of the surf. When the week was over they returned to the house at Red Bluff to begin their life with Mrs Soren in Lena's old family home.

The blue room was theirs. He was at the university most days and Lena had moved across town to the alcoholism and drug dependence unit at St Vincent's Hospital, where she was already more than half in love with one of the doctors. In the evenings he chopped wood in the shed and lit the fire in the sitting room. Mrs Soren sat in one of the armchairs and knitted and he sat across from her and read. He read everything. Day and night. He was desperate to catch up. Nothing on the English reading list escaped him. He read far out beyond the reading lists supplied to him by his history tutors. He wanted not simply to catch up but to overtake and ride on ahead and scout the clean country. And he made Keith's study his own. It was the one room in the house where the clutter of their lives had gathered and been stored, piles of books and periodicals on the floor. Even a saddle and a pair of riding boots. Drawings and photos on the walls. Half-finished articles and old newspapers. And the green *Roget's Thesaurus* his mother and father had sent to him with their loving wish that he achieve his new ambition. *This will help you, son. All our love, your mother and father.* And three kisses.

While Lena practised Chopin's Prelude No. 24 at the Rönisch, Mrs Soren and Robert held their breath and hoped she would get through it without slamming the lid of the piano and storming out of the room.

Mrs Soren was eager to know what he thought of the possibility of an afterlife. 'So, Robert, tell me, do you ever wonder if there is really life after death? Do you think about it sometimes?'

He stared into the red gum fire. 'I think death is death,' he said. He was seeing the bodies of their neighbours when the doodle bug blasted their home to pieces and the firemen dragged them out onto the grass, their bodies smoking, the arm of Mrs Ezzard raised, still moving, attempting a signal for help. As a child then he protected himself from the horror by believing those burnt carcasses had nothing to do with the living people he had known: kindly Mr and Mrs Ezzard, their neighbours. It was the ugly difference of death that haunted him. And so he turned to Mrs Soren and, without thinking too much about it, said, 'The idea of an afterlife seems to me to be a way of trying to avoid accepting the finality of death.'

She looked down at her knitting and said nothing.

21

———

It was late afternoon, a Wednesday, when Robert had no lectures or tutorials. He and Martin were sitting together in the front room of Martin and Birte's house. They had been talking earlier about Arthur Koestler's *Darkness at Noon*, and the collection of essays by disillusioned communists of Martin's generation, *The God That Failed*, both of which Martin had given to Robert some weeks earlier. They sat in a companionable silence now and might have been waiting either for the conversation to regenerate itself or for the sense of an end to Robert's visit to arise. The day outside was rapidly fading and the shadows in the room had deepened. The books on the shelves, the three pictures, the dark gloss of the leaves on the pot plants by the windows, they had all receded into the shadows. Robert felt it was time for him to leave, but he was reluctant to break the spell of their communion in the silence, the smoke of their cigarettes drifting towards the ceiling, the empty white china bowls on the low table between them, the remains of the chilled yoghurt and cucumber refreshment Martin always provided on these afternoons, the crumbled remains of dry biscuit on the small white side dish.

Martin leaned forward and lit a fresh cigarette from the smouldering butt of the one he had been smoking. 'Yes. You are right,' he said, as if Robert had only just spoken. 'All that is true. But in 1933, not much more than a hundred years after your wonderful French civil code was introduced, when I was a young man and still believed the Nazis could be defeated, Joseph Goebbels was cheered like a modern pop star in the Berlin Sportpalast by a vast crowd of ordinary people from the suburbs when he declared the rights of man to have been abolished. So, it was all words. Goebbels had judged the mood of the people correctly. It was now a time for evil, a time for demagogues and dictators. The people didn't care about the rights of man and had long ago forgotten the enthusiasms of the French Revolution.'

Martin fell silent again, his cigarette held delicately between his thumb and forefinger, the cork tip almost touching his lips. He seemed to be waiting for something, the sallow skin tight across his broad forehead like the membrane of a mask, his grey eyes alight and keen with his thought, reflecting tiny points of light from the windows opposite.

'Two weeks after Goebbels' speech I was arrested in Breslau by the Gestapo.' He said this quietly. 'People who say such a rule of terror can never happen again are wrong. Evil has its time.' He shifted in his chair and looked directly at Robert. 'Torture is a life sentence.' He watched Robert, his eyes narrowed against the smoke, watching for his reaction, for a sign from him that he understood.

'I was your age, a year or two older,' Martin said. 'It was not the physical pain that broke me. I was beaten senseless many times. There is a limit to the amount of pain the human nervous system can register before it is overloaded and is shocked into numbness. While the nightly beatings lasted I existed in a toxic limbo between nightmare and waking. It was not the beatings that broke me; it was when I came to understand that my torturer was my brother. That was when I lost my belief in our human project.'

They sat in the ringing silence. Martin had never before spoken to Robert about his own personal history. Robert felt rebuked for his naive attitude to the French Revolution. Martin's astonishing confession had made him feel as if something was frozen inside him, as if he had heard a scream and then the silence again, and was waiting. Neither of them spoke. Martin's features were a pale oval among the shadows, the glint of his eyes fixed on Robert. He said, 'Do you want to know what I did? After I was deported from Germany because of my Polish birth I joined the resistance. My cover was to pose as a union organiser and delegate to the provinces. I travelled throughout Upper Silesia looking for men in the union movement who could be trusted to form secret cells in our movement. Everything rested on my judgement of their character. My task was to assess the steadiness of a young man's resolve and his ability to inspire and to lead others. My task was nothing less than to see into the souls of these young men.' He paused and drew on his cigarette, allowing the silence to open between them again, the lighted end of his cigarette glowing then fading. The cello moaning in the room across the hall. Martin went on then, speaking so softly Robert had to lean towards him to catch his words.

'And seeing into their souls, to see into my own soul.' Martin flicked the ash from his cigarette towards the ashtray. 'I sat with those young men in their barrack rooms and in factory yards, or in the backrooms of taverns where they were known. I was one of them. I was as impressed as you are by history. We were all young men. For the first half-hour or so we talked of our official union business and of how I might support them from Breslau. I have often tried to remember, but without success, how I judged my moment to disclose that the true purpose of my visit was not the affairs of the union but to recruit them into a resistance movement against the National Socialists. Once that purpose was even hinted at, there was no going back. As soon as I mentioned my membership of the group, I placed my life in the hands of the young man I was talking to, a young man I scarcely knew and whom I was usually meeting for only the first or second time.' Martin stopped speaking and looked at Robert. He might have been trying to decide if this was the moment for him to disclose his true purpose in befriending Robert.

'When I entrusted a young man with my true purpose, it was always a moment of great emotion for both of us.' He waited, staring now into the unlit gas fire. 'Our thoughts raced and our pulses quickened. It was the moment when the stranger became my executioner or my comrade. It was always a shock, to both of us. We at once assumed with each other an entirely artificial coldness, knowing that now we must defend ourselves from the contagion of emotion. Few were able to disguise their fear. I watched for that fear and saw it cross their features before they had a chance to mask it. And they knew I had seen it. When I told him what I expected of him, the young man was flattered to have been chosen, and terrified of the consequences. If he had a wife and child he was also terrified for his family. Some had dreamed of being entrusted with just such a mission. For these the weight of responsibility darkened their eyes and aged their features in an instant. They were no longer the person they had been a moment before. I had trusted them with my life, and had asked for their life to be entrusted to me in return.'

Martin stood up and walked over to the curtained windows. He pulled the curtain aside and stood looking out into the darkening garden where the rhododendrons were like a black forest. Without turning back into the room he said, 'In those days we had no way of knowing who was operating with the Gestapo. The Gestapo itself was a new organisation. I could have been setting a trap. Some of the young people I recruited had long dreaded a call such as mine, and had also believed it to be their right and their destiny to receive such a call. These young men, the ones who had dreamed dreams of themselves, accepted their new role gravely and in silence. They were the ones who knew in their hearts that they would not turn back, no matter what. They had passed through a gate, and the gate had closed behind them, and at once they knew themselves to be more alone than they had ever been before in their lives. They no longer belonged to the easygoing world of family life and work but had entered into the deep conspiratorial world of the resistance. To leave and seek safety abroad was no longer an option for them.' Martin paused. 'There was a kind of purity in our situation at that moment that was beautiful and which was also wholly unnatural.'

He turned from the window and looked at Robert. For Robert he was a dark silhouette, the figure of a stranger at the window.

'In the silence that followed my disclosure, I saw that the young man asked himself if he would be able to withstand torture or if he would crack and betray his comrades. Everyone asked himself this question and none knew the answer to it. The question haunted them. They didn't really know yet what torture entailed: the final humiliation of one individual by another individual. Few of these young men—and there were a few women too—few of them were so fortunate as to never discover the answer to this question. We had informants within the Gestapo, but generally once one of our members was arrested they went into the silence alone and we heard no more of them.'

Martin came back and sat down in his chair again. He leaned forward and carefully butted his half-smoked cigarette in the ashtray. Then, with great deliberation, he lit another one, as if the first one had become distasteful to him. He drew deeply on the cigarette.

'Our strategy was flawed,' he said. 'We believed it was imperative for us to build a national network of cells among the workers, who would then align themselves with our movement. It was our dream to unite the working class and the intellectuals in a common resistance against the National Socialists. For this strategy to work the ring of secrecy had to remain inviolate. Maintaining complete secrecy is a human problem, not an intellectual one, and of course we failed at it. When the ring of secrecy was broken in one place, the Gestapo swept through town after town arresting everyone connected to our group, and our carefully constructed network was destroyed. Most of us who survived the purge began again, and slowly the ring was rebuilt and sealed once again, until it was again broken.'

Martin sat very still for a long time, his cigarette forgotten between his fingers, gazing emptily into the shadows of the room. 'Because of our mistaken strategy,' he said, 'most of those young men and women were murdered.' He turned to Robert. 'Our resistance was futile. We should have fled.'

In the silence that followed Martin's confession, Robert was imagining the vast shadowland of Martin's past standing behind him. He knew now that for his friend that dark past, and his feelings of futility, remained an unfinished story within him. He looked at Martin and he couldn't think of anything to say that would do justice to his feelings for the older man, his gratitude that Martin had entrusted him with such a confession.

Martin said, 'I've kept you late. Lena will be wondering where you've got to.'

Both men stood, facing each other, neither speaking. Then suddenly they embraced.

22

____

Driving home to Red Bluff through the evening traffic, Robert was thinking of Martin for the first time as a man wounded in his soul, like his own father; both of them men who'd somehow survived the very worst. For himself, the unimaginable. He parked the Renault in the garage and went around to the front porch and let himself in. Lena was practising the piano. She stopped playing when he came through the front door. There was the smell of cooking. Mrs Soren did everything for them. She was happy. They were her purpose. Lena came out into the hall. 'How was Martin?' she said.

'Fine. Birte sends her love.'

They went down the hall and into her old bedroom, which they were using as a private sitting room these days. She'd had his red chalk drawing of the fighting man mounted and framed and had hung it on the wall above her writing table, where her books and papers were spread about. An open notebook, her writing forward-leaning, small and neat. He began to read her notes. She reached past him and closed the notebook and said, in a slightly annoyed voice, 'I can't understand why you don't just start writing.'

He stood looking at her in amazement. She had the frowning, troubled expression that he had come to know whenever she was in the mood for a fight.

She held the notebook and sat down at the desk. 'I don't know why you think you need to do all this study,' she said. 'You should be writing your stories.'

He said, 'I can't believe you're saying this. You know I'm not ready to write yet.'

She looked up at him. 'I've always thought you'd just start writing your stories. If you really want to write, you should be doing it, shouldn't you? You've got the time.'

'Your mother wouldn't be very impressed if I got distracted from my degree at this stage.'

'I hope you're not doing it for Mum, for God's sake.' She rolled her eyes.

'You do exactly what she wants,' he said.

'She's my mother, not yours.'

They stared at each other. He said truthfully, 'I might write Martin's story one day. He should be recognised.'

She snorted. 'What nonsense. You'd have to learn German.'

'And I might just do that.' He felt indignant at her attack on him. 'Why do you do this sort of thing? I don't know where you're coming from sometimes.'

She opened her notebook and sat looking at it. In an abstracted voice, she said, 'Maybe you're not really going to be a writer after all.'

He said, 'Fuck you! I'll go and talk to your mother.'

She looked up at him and smiled. She seemed to be delighted that she was having an effect on him. 'When we first met I thought you were exciting. I wondered what was going to happen. You were the only really free person I'd ever met. I thought you were going to be unpredictable. I thought of you as my cowboy.' She gave a short laugh and kept looking at him.

He said, 'So I've disappointed you.'

She said quietly, 'I expected you to go on being you.'

'I am being me.'

'No you're not.' She picked up her pen and began writing in the notebook.

He stood looking down at the back of her head. He said again quietly, 'Fuck you!'

'You're trying to turn yourself into one of us,' she said. She didn't look up.

He grabbed her shoulder and roughly turned her towards him. She smiled at him. His heart was thumping. He let go of her shoulder. 'I'm just trying to become educated,' he said. 'I can't just flick a fucking switch. I'll never be one of your lot.'

She turned back to her notebook and went on writing.

Mrs Soren called from the kitchen, 'Dinner's on the table, you two.'

Lena closed her notebook and stood up. 'I love it when you're angry,' she said. 'Did you think of hitting me then?'

He said, 'I thought of killing you.'

23

Lena's breathing was reduced to the tiniest gasps. She was already wheezing when she got home from work. It was the middle of winter, the weather grey and raw. Robert heard a cry and went out into the sitting room. She lay on the couch like a broken bird, sipping water, her eyes filled with panic, begging him for his help. Mrs Soren came into the room white with fear. 'I've called the ambulance,' she said.

He was sitting on the couch beside Lena, holding her hand. 'Shouldn't we call the doctor?'

'She needs the ambulance.'

The ambulance men gave her oxygen but it didn't help; the oxygen mask even seemed to suffocate her. Robert went in the ambulance with her to St Vincent's, where she was known. The instant she saw the doctor walking towards her along the corridor her breathing eased. It was like magic. The throttling grip on her throat relaxed the moment the doctor took her hand in his, the colour flowing back into her bleached skin, her eyes filling with tears of gratitude and love. She gripped the doctor's hand and thanked him. She called him David and he leaned down and kissed her forehead. The doctor went along with the trolley, holding her hand, and Robert brought up the rear. He felt useless.

That night he dreamed he was wearing his leggings and boots and spurs. He couldn't find his horse. He woke in the night thinking of his old room and smelled the mustiness of disuse, the damp under the peeling wallpaper, heard the elm copse swaying in the breeze out the window. The scene of his struggle with the fighting man and his lovemaking with Wendy, and those first months of his life as a student. The narrow bed in the corner. The mood of those days vivid in him as he lay there in bed beside Lena in the blue room. He felt as if he had left behind him something precious. Had abandoned it without thinking. And he felt again the quality of the freedom he'd forfeited. It seemed to him as he lay in bed thinking of these things, the possums dancing in the roof cavity above, that if he really wanted to he could pick up his old life again. Find once again that troubled freedom he had known without knowing it.

24

It was August. Robert was in his third year. He came home from the university that afternoon and from the hall saw the Reverend Dr Eady sitting on the couch in the front room, holding a cup and saucer. He turned and looked at Robert. Lena was sitting opposite him, a tea tray on the table between them. They both looked at Robert as he came into the room.

Lena said in a matter-of-fact voice, 'She's dead.' That was all. And she smiled. It was the secretive smile of a child who has misbehaved. She might have said, It's over! It's finished! She didn't want to hear his condolences.

Robert had never experienced grief before. The thought of Mrs Soren dead. She'd had a massive stroke while shelling peas into the colander at the kitchen table, Mozart on the radio. She had died instantly. It did not seem possible. Robert said, 'Sorry.' He was weeping. He went out to the blue room and sat on the bed and wept. He was still sitting there when, a few minutes later, he heard their voices and then the sound of the front door closing.

Lena came in and stood by the open door. He looked up at her. She said, 'I'm fucking free!'

He stood up. The fierceness of it went through him like a knife; the exultation, her pain, the shock. She bent double and laughed hysterically, her weird laughter ringing through the empty house.

He said, 'You're crazy!'

'Yes!' she said. 'I suppose I am. She's gone!'

➤

In the weeks after Mrs Soren's funeral, Robert and Lena lived in the strange emptiness of the house as if they were waiting for her to come back and things to return to normal. They were like squatters; a feeling of intense impermanence, a sense of trespass and disquiet. Mrs Soren had done everything for them: shopping, cooking, washing their clothes, ironing, cleaning the house. Neither Lena nor Robert took over. They let things slide. Clothes lay on the floor of the bedroom, dirty dishes were piled in the sink, the fridge was empty. The vacuum cleaner never came out of its cupboard.

He was getting the wood in for the fire one cool October evening when he looked in through the side window and saw Lena dancing in the sitting room, her skirt whirling out around her, her bare legs and bare arms, her mouth open, an ecstatic expression on her face, her wildly erotic dance. She had never looked so beautiful or more solitary to him. He ached with lust for her. He didn't know what was going on. Without her mother's boundaries, Lena seemed no longer to know who she was.

Later that night he was in Keith's study, struggling with his medieval history essay, which had something to do with the twelfth-century philosopher and theologian Peter Abelard. The house was deeply silent when he was startled by the sense that someone was standing in the open doorway to the hall.

He looked up. 'Jesus!' he said. 'What the fuck are you doing?'

Lena was naked. She was pressing her palms to the sides of her face and massaging her lower jaw with her thumbs, staring at him as if something awful had happened that she could barely dare to tell him about.

'What is it?' he said.

She went on massaging her lower jaw. 'Do you think my face is getting fatter?' she said.

He laughed. 'How can your face get fat? You know you're gorgeous.'

She continued to stand there holding her face. 'Just tell me the truth.' There were tears in her eyes. She turned and walked away. He jumped up and ran after her along the hall. 'Hey!' he said, taking her in his arms. 'It's all right. Nothing's wrong.'

She began to sob, her body shuddering. She was like a child. He was bewildered. Was she really crying because she thought her face was getting fat? It was absurd. 'Your strong jaw is one of your most striking and attractive features.' Lena's face was a pleasure to look at. Her thoughts and emotions were always active in her features, shadows of delight or anxiety or dreaming, the pleasure of her secrets like light and shade passing over her. Lena's features were never blank. She was a beautiful woman, whose deepest thoughts and fears were never shared, but were nevertheless visible in the quality of her presence. She gave him the impression of moving within her own complicated and elaborate place. He thought of it as her city of the mind.

She eventually stopped crying. 'I'm being a nuisance,' she said, snuffling and wiping at her nose with the back of her hand. 'You have to get that essay done. I'm just mucking things up for you.'

He gave her his handkerchief. She looked at it. 'Is it clean?'

'Probably not,' he said. They both laughed.

She blew her nose a couple of times and handed it back.

He said, 'You can keep it.'

She said, 'I'm cold.'

He led her along the hall to the blue room and she climbed back into bed and pulled the clothes up under her chin. She stared at him. 'What are we going to do?' She sounded helpless and slightly panicky.

'About what?' he said. 'Everything's going along just fine, isn't it? I'll get the vacuum out tomorrow and we can go to the market together and stock up. And, truly, your face isn't getting fat.'

It was as if she hadn't heard him. 'I'm never going to be relaxed enough about music to play just for pleasure, and I'm never going to be good enough to play the way Leonard expects me to play.'

'Maybe it's time you gave up the piano then. It seems to make you anxious, more than anything.'

She was silent a while then she said, 'Have you ever really thought about Mum and Dad's bedroom?'

He waited.

'Just that double bed out there in the sleep-out. A small chest of drawers and that awful old wardrobe. No pictures. No chair. No mirror. Their smell. Their lives were terrible. Terrible! We're stuck now.'

'What do you mean, stuck?'

She took her hand out from under the covers and took hold of his hand. She turned it over and looked at his palm, as if she thought she might find the answer there. 'I'm not being fair to you. We can't sort out another person's life for them.' She looked up at him and smiled. Her eyes were reddened and still teary. 'I'm sorry I made a fuss. I'm all right now.' She ran her fingers up his arm and held his bicep. 'You've got lovely arms. You've been a real workman. You've done real things. Dad would have liked you.' She smiled. 'Really. I'm all right. You must get back to your essay. Go on! It's just that their lives were so narrow. And now they're gone and there's nothing. Just that barren room down the back of the house and the smell. It was really all over for them so quickly. Nothing happened.'

'There are your dad's drawings and his notebooks,' he said. He tucked the covers in around her chin.

'Mum was so inflexible. God, I can hardly bear to think of her.' She looked at him. 'I don't know what I want from life. But I don't want what they had. I'm terrified I'll finish up just like her despite everything. I loved her. But I hated her.' She said with sudden fierceness, 'I just won't let myself become stuck!'

He said, 'You'll work it out over time. Don't put so much pressure on yourself.'

She said, 'Oh, fuck off, for Christ's sake! Go and do your fucking essay.'

He got up. She reminded him of his own desperate need as a boy to make the leap and escape the narrowness of his situation.

'I'm sorry!' she cried out as he was going out the door. 'I just can't bear it!'

He went over to the bed and got undressed and put out the light and climbed in beside her. He held her in his arms. He thought of the time she stayed overnight with him in his room at the boarding house, the way she had needed to be held and reassured, almost as if he was her dad and she was a little girl again. There, there, everything's going to be all right. Wipe your tears and I'll read you a story.

She said, 'I feel as if I haven't got any time. It makes me breathless.'

25

He had done the shopping and was digging over the garden patch where the lettuces had been in the summer. He thought maybe if he made an effort to get the house and garden back into some kind of order she might begin to feel more secure and settled. It wasn't clear whether she was suffering grief from the death of her mother or sheer bewilderment from some other hidden cause.

She came out and stood watching him. When he straightened she said, 'Have you got a cigarette?' She went over to him and he gave her a cigarette and lit it for her. 'It's going to be good when you've done that,' she said, and she turned and went back inside the house.

He caught the elusive scent of the flowering gum. He went back to work, digging over the plot. Would her inner world and his own become joined one day? Or would they always remain strangers to each other in some deep way?

A blackbird was finding worms in the dug-over ground. Morris Aplin, the labourer on Warren's farm, had taught him the correct way to dig a garden bed. The blackbird was not afraid of him.

The following Thursday Lena called him at home from the hospital and asked him to meet her at lunchtime in the Exhibition Gardens, next to St Vincent's Hospital.

He saw her before he got off the tram. She was sitting on a park bench, her back to the street, facing the big fountain in the park. Her shoulders were hunched over and it looked like she was reading a book held on her lap. She was just like any young professional woman having a bite of lunch on her own in the park.

She looked up and watched him coming along the path towards her. He waved but she didn't wave back. He had the feeling she was watching him from another place. When he reached her she held out both her hands to him. He took her hands in his and leaned down and kissed her. He sat on the bench beside her. She put her arm through his and cuddled up close against his side. 'Thanks for coming,' she said, and she rested her head on his shoulder. It was a lovely sunny day, a huge shade tree spreading its branches above them, the cascade of the fountain catching the sun. The clatter of the trams and the roar of the traffic accelerating along Nicholson Street behind them.

She lifted her head from his shoulder and straightened her hair. She was looking drawn and tired around the eyes. She had been trying to lose weight. He'd repeatedly tried to reassure her that she was perfect as she was. He said, 'Did you eat a proper lunch?'

She smiled. 'What is this? Did I eat a proper lunch? You sound like Mum. Next thing you'll be asking me if I'm warm enough.' She laughed.

'You're looking a bit strained, that's all.'

'I know how to eat,' she said, her tone a touch sardonic. 'And yes, I probably do look a bit strained. I need a break.' She looked at him, unsmiling now, and put her hand on his arm. A tram was squealing past when she said something he didn't catch and he leaned closer and asked her to repeat it. 'I've enrolled in a course of Italian language and culture,' she said, and paused. 'It's at the university for foreigners in Perugia.'

'You're going to Italy? A break from what? From us? From me?'

'Of course not from us. I need a break from work. From routine. You said yourself you left the outback because the life there became routine. Well, I need to try myself out too. Don't get upset. It's not that strange. Lots of people do it. Helen Armitage—you've met her—she did it. And other people. There are lots of Australians studying in Perugia.' She shifted a little away from him. 'Please don't make a fuss,' she said.

'You speak German and French. You don't know any Italian.'

She gave him a funny lopsided smile. The smile more than half convinced him she wasn't telling him the real reason why she was going. 'You can come over after your exams and we can spend Christmas there together. You'll be able to practise your Italian.'

'This is bullshit.' He imagined himself abandoned in her house while she played some game in Italy. 'Are you serious?'

She touched his cheek with her fingers. 'It's all right. Don't worry about anything. I know what I'm doing. You can come over after your finals and we can even spend some time in England. I can meet your family. It's a sensible plan.'

'It's a stupid plan,' he said. 'You're deserting me. Wait till after I've done my finals, then we can both go and spend the long vacation there together.'

'You're carrying on as if I'm doing something weird. You're just not used to people travelling and doing things and being out in the world. Working-class people don't do that kind of thing. But we do.'

'This is pure crap! *We*? Your own lot? What are you saying? What am I? Ask Martin. He's the one who understands race and class. The only one I've met so far.' He was thoroughly pissed off.

'I did try talking to you,' she said calmly. She was looking away over towards the fountain. A man was taking a photograph of a woman. The woman was posing for him. 'You just didn't show any understanding at all of what I was trying to say so I went ahead on my own.' She took his hand in hers. 'Don't be angry. I've deposited enough in our joint savings account for you to buy your airfare when you're ready to come over.' She smiled. 'We'll be able to speak Italian together.'

'You've tricked me,' he said. 'You're leaving. You can't do it.'

'And you can't stop me from doing it. I've hardly spent a minute outside Melbourne. You're being selfish and unfair.'

How strangely cool about it all she was. Living in her private world of ideas and plans. 'Postpone it till we can go together,' he said. 'That's all I'm asking you to do. I'm not asking you to give it up.'

She stood up. 'I've got to get back to work.'

He sat looking at her.

'I've got to go, really. There are people waiting for me.'

'Deros?' he said.

He got up and they walked back to the hospital together, arm in arm, just as if it was a routine day in their ordinary lives. He hated her for what she was doing and the sneaky way she was doing it. At the hospital entrance she turned to him. 'I'm going by boat! Did I tell you that? It's a cargo boat! It's going to be my first real adventure.' She laughed and kissed him on the cheek then turned and went into the hospital. He stood there for a long time.

26

Her boat left from North Wharf. They were loading it with timber. The air was full of the smell of fresh-sawn hardwood. There were six other passengers. Three couples. All older. Her cabin was tiny. The passages on the ship stank of marine oil and black grease. Seamen walked about whistling. They looked like an insolent lot to Robert. He felt sick and abandoned to see her boat cast off and leave the wharf. He stood looking until the tugs turned it around and began hauling it out towards the Bay as if it was a great dead whale. He could still see her white handkerchief. She was showing him how faithful she was, semaphoring her trust in him. He had never seen her so happy as when she stood looking down at him from the deck.

He drove home through Port Melbourne to the beach, turned left at Beach Road and headed for Red Bluff and the bayside suburbs. The water of the Bay was still and cold and grey, the red and black cargo ships all looking just like one another. He pulled into a beach car park and watched the only boat that was heading out towards the open sea.

When he got back to the house he stood in the hallway listening. The grandfather clock was tock-tocking. He went down the hall to the kitchen and made scrambled eggs and toast and a cup of tea and he sat in the alcove and ate his meal and drank two cups of tea.

The weeks became months and he heard nothing from Lena. He kept the house as clean as Mrs Soren had kept it and he looked after the garden and put in his order for meat with Mr Creedy, the butcher, once a week. He paid the electricity and the gas bills from their joint savings account and he found where Mrs Soren kept her spare bags for the vacuum cleaner. He kept the Red Bluff home of the Sorens in good order, as if he was taking care of it till the day when it could all start up and be normal again. He was so busy with this and his studies it took him a while to realise he was waiting for things to return to the way they had been. Once he started thinking like that he began to suspect that maybe the change was a permanent one after all and he'd missed his cue. Which opened up an enormous question for him. Had he been left behind not only by Lena, but by the subtle change that was supposed to have been a sign to him? Was that it? Here he was taking on a poor copy of their old way of life while they all went off on a new tack. Dying and running away. Father and son first, then mother, and now the daughter. Leaving it to him. Trusting him to take care of it. Which was exactly what he was doing. Their bidding. That's what it began to feel like when he was out in the garden weeding the vegetables. He would stop and look up and half expect to see Mrs Soren watching him approvingly from the back door.

There were eerie days and nights when his solitude was a burden and Mrs Soren's ghost was no company for him. And there were calm days and nights when he was productive and content and for hours at a time even preferred his solitude to having company. But always in his mind there was Lena and his anxiety about where she was and what was happening to her and why she hadn't written to him. He sent off several letters to the Università per Stranieri at Perugia, one written in Italian and corrected by his old teacher. But he received no acknowledgement. Nothing. Not a word. It began to feel as if she had cut her ties and gone out into the world and would never be seen again.

Lying awake at night in their big bed in the blue room he developed elaborate and horrible fantasies about her fate—scenes of rape and torture on board that ship, her corpse being thrown overboard by the insolent sailors. His need to know something, anything at all, one way or the other, crawled in his head all day and all night. For brief hours he would be distracted and forget her, then remember with a sudden leap of the heart. Sitting alone in Keith's study poring over his books one night he heard himself yell into the silence, 'So where the fuck are you?!' There were times when he was a little unhinged and stood at the window looking out into that deserted street, the front garden, the telegraph pole. The nothing of the suburban. And he did not have the courage to go out and face it.

27

Robert was sitting with Martin in the silence when the door to the hall opened and Birte looked in. The cautious way she opened the door and peered around it into the room, she might have been checking to see if Martin and Robert were still there or had left hours ago. She stood in the doorway looking at them. 'It's all right, Martin; don't look at me like that,' she said. 'I'm not going to interrupt you.' She was carrying a sheaf of typed manuscript. 'I want to give Robert my brother's lecture on Thomas Mann before he goes home. And I want to show him our card from Lena.' She opened the door wider and said to Robert, 'So she's in Florence, falling in love with art. I didn't know Lena was interested in art. She wasn't interested in art at school. Why didn't she go to Germany?' She waved an impatient hand at Martin again. 'It's all right, Martin, I just want to hear from Robert what Lena is doing. I know you're never going to ask him.' She fully opened the door and the light from the hall fell across Martin. 'She tells us nothing on the card.' Birte's voice had taken on a plaintive, puzzled tone, as if she felt hard done by for only getting such a skimpy bit of news from Lena.

Robert said, 'I've heard nothing from her.'

'What are you saying? We have heard from her but you haven't? Why haven't you heard from her?'

The two empty bowls in which Martin had earlier served his usual mid-afternoon offering of cool yoghurt and sliced cucumber sat on the low table, glowing whitely in the light from the hall.

Birte said with irritation, 'Why don't you put on the light, Martin? You look like lovers sitting in here in the dark. Robert didn't hear from Lena, Martin!' She stamped her good foot. 'Did you hear what he said?'

Martin murmured, 'There's no need to shout, Birte.'

'She sends us a postcard and she doesn't send one to Robert. Why is this? I don't understand. Tell me, what is the reason for it, Martin?' It was a peremptory demand. She wanted an answer.

The end of Martin's cigarette glowed then faded. He lifted his shoulders but said nothing.

Robert said, 'Is there an address on the card?'

'I'll get it!' Birte hobbled off down the hall without giving him the copy of her brother's lecture on Mann. Martin and Robert sat and waited. A moment later there was the sound of Birte coming back, her injured leg going thump-drag-thump, her voice complaining of the pain as if it were an infuriating companion.

Robert got up and went out into the hall. She handed him the postcard and watched him read it under the hall light. The first thing that struck him was that either this was not Lena's handwriting or her neat handwriting had altered dramatically, had escaped from its sedate order and gone wild. He stared at the card for a long time before the freely looping scrawl began to make some sense to him. Her writing looked more like a flurried impression of storm clouds than a series of words.

Dearest Birte and Martin,
I've seen the magic of drawing and can't wait to do it myself. I'm ashamed now that I've never really looked at your Käthe Kollwitz.
My love and hugs to you both,
Lena xxx

Robert turned the card over and looked at the picture. It was a free pen-and-wash drawing in which the carelessly applied blobs and stains of brown ink made suggestive sense. A group of figures huddled together beside a broken tree, battered by a violent storm of wind, the arm of one figure flung upwards as if to shield them from the wild swirl of lines in the sky above them, lines that might have been a dragon or a devil falling on them, a fierce mythical bird of prey. The artist was Pier Francesco Mola. The title of the drawing was *The Expulsion*. It was so free it might have been modern but the date was the early seventeenth century. So Lena had been fascinated by the wild energy of the disordered blobs and scrawls? The drawing's simplicity was deceptive and Robert could imagine her looking at this picture and seeing herself flinging ink and random lines onto a sheet of white paper, her emotions transmuted into visible signs, an action of exuberant freedom. He turned the card over and read the message again. *My love and hugs to you both.* No reference to him.

He looked up from the card.

'Why doesn't she write to you?' Birte asked in a small voice. 'Martin and I are worried about you. You don't look well. Martin tells me to mind my own business, but you and Lena are my business. Is there nothing you can tell me?'

He looked at the card in his hand. 'Her dad used to draw,' he said. It was the slimmest of threads, scarcely a thread at all, but it was all he could think of. There was no address and no date. He imagined her out there alone, writing the card while sitting at a cafe table in a sunlit square in Florence, then getting up and posting it, drifting in her freedom without ties or responsibilities, no fixed address, no dates or times tethering her hours. No marriage vows. No duties. No mother to remind her of her responsibilities. Out of the cage, free to move around at will. Free to dance in the limitless space of her liberty, a stranger abroad, a foreigner, an outsider, terrifying and compelling, glimpsing the possibility of a goal, a reason for being there, a reason for living. To draw meaning and purpose out of the helpless chaos of her inner life. Or was she just sleeping around? It made him feel sick to think about it.

He wanted to keep the card. As long as he held it the connection was there with Lena, meandering impulsively in the dangerous airs and alleyways of Lorenzo de Medici's cruelly exotic Florence, her excitement and fear, the danger of her situation, unguarded and alone, without the cover of language, seduced by the mysterious beauty of Mola's masterful drawing. He knew Florence second-hand from the set texts for Renaissance studies, Ferdinand Schevill's history of the city and Machiavelli's *Florentine History*. He had no sense of Florence as a modern city. For Robert, Florence had held its breath since the sixteenth century. Her postcard was precious.

Birte was looking at it. She shrugged and said, 'You can keep the card if you like.'

He could see she also wanted to keep it. He handed it to her and she took it from him.

'She'll write to me sometime,' he said. 'I'll let you know when I hear from her.' But he knew now that he was not going to hear from Lena. If he wanted to see her again he would have to go and look for her. He would have to demonstrate his commitment. To show his unassuageable desire to be with her. *Whoever has no house now, will never have one. Whoever is alone will stay alone.* Suddenly her love of Rilke's obscure phrases, which she'd translated for him, made sense to him. But did he have an unassuageable desire to be with her? He wasn't sure. Perhaps that was how she wanted it to be. Their marriage merely part of the old regime of obedience to her mother. Their vows no longer binding, emptied of meaning by death. Perhaps she was embarked on a new dream. A dream without the dragging weight of family. A dream that had once been his own dream.

Birte and Robert stood in the hall under the light looking at each other. For once Birte didn't say anything. There were tears in her eyes. She stepped forward and put her arms around him and held him firmly against her. Then she released him abruptly and turned and stumped off down the hall, forgetting to give him her brother's lecture. He watched her lurching along. Despite her position of authority at Lena's old school, where she was the deputy head and had great influence with 'the girls', she seemed to him to be a tragic figure from the past, a lonely survivor doing her best to give life its due of seriousness, keeping her curiosity hard at work, pursuing culture as fiercely as she knew how. He admired her courage and he loved her. That was her real heroism: her persistence. Impatient always with Martin's despair. She had told them one evening that her mother had locked her in the henhouse in the back garden all night when she was a child. To cure her, she said, of a phobia of birds and feathers. He thought of her that night in the henhouse, a vulnerable little girl, intelligent and intensely sensitive, locked in terrifying solitude among the troubled fowls—like a sign of the coming nightmare that was going to engulf her and her family and her entire people, her beautiful Europe destroyed in a blizzard of hatred and murder. Birte was never going to give up. They had not beaten her. She was defiant. A bit crazy, definitely a bit crazy, but heroically defiant.

He watched her till she went in through the kitchen door at the far end of the hall. When he heard the door close behind her he turned around and went back into the sitting room. He was glad Lena had written to her. It would have hurt Birte deeply if she'd heard nothing from Lena. For him it was not hurt but puzzlement and something else. His life lay ahead of him. It was his own to do with as he chose. His love for Lena was real, but he didn't know that it was necessary. For Birte, friendship was the essential, the remains of the sacred in a broken world that was never going to be fixed ever again. She would make the best of it.

Martin was lighting a fresh cigarette when Robert returned. Martin's hand trembling, his features illuminated by the shivering flame of the lighter. He was a portrait study by his hero Käthe Kollwitz. He snapped shut the cap of the lighter, snuffing the flame, and sat back in his chair and drew on the cigarette, the smoke drifting around his head. Robert closed the door and sat down.

When Robert was leaving later, Martin went out with him to where he had parked Mrs Soren's car in the street. Usually Martin said goodnight to him at the front door. The street was silent. They stood beside the car.

Martin said, 'So will you go and look for her?'

'I have a feeling she doesn't want me to find her.'

'But you want to find her,' Martin said.

'I don't have an address.'

'It's not so easy to cover our tracks from someone who is determined to find us,' Martin said. 'Especially if we don't want to be found, we always leave a trace.'

They looked at each other. Martin had been on the run from the Gestapo. He had crossed Poland and Russia and half of China to reach Shanghai and freedom. 'Being careful to cover our tracks makes us stand out from the people around us who are going about their daily lives openly.' He lit a cigarette. He looked younger when he smoked. He smiled at Robert, who saw that he was enjoying the situation. 'It's not so easy to go unnoticed by the waiter in the cafe or by the tobacconist or the paper seller when you are afraid someone might recognise you. They remember you. The nervous one. In a hurry to get away. A stranger they have never seen before. Even on the finest spring days you choose a table inside the cafe without a view of the street. You sit facing the rear, perhaps with a view in a mirror. And when you leave you do not respond to the banter of the waiter but get up and go quickly. Once in the street you hurry away. The waiter stands at the door to the cafe and watches you, and he knows. Waiters are the best sources of information for the police. They go straight to the waiters.

'A young Australian woman of Lena's description, recently arrived in Florence or Perugia, with not a word of Italian. Believe me, she will stand out. There will be people who will remember having seen her. And you have a photo, and you speak some Italian. Believe me, you can find Lena even if she doesn't want you to find her. And she knows this, Robert.'

He gazed steadily into Robert's eyes, and Robert was imagining himself to be one of the young men whom Martin had recruited to his resistance group. He said, 'You are very persuasive.'

Martin smiled. 'And you are not reluctant to be persuaded. I don't believe for one moment Lena doesn't want you to find her. That she doesn't write to you is her challenge to you. You know her. You know the games she plays with all of us, and you most of all. After she first met you, she talked to us of nothing else but you. She recognised in you the same resolve and possibility Birte and I both see in you. She saw that you were one of us. We have known Lena since she was a young girl, since she first came to this house and began studying the piano with Leonard and he accepted her as a gifted student. And then, of course, Birte became her German teacher at school. Believe me, Lena has always been setting puzzles for her friends to solve. She is a puzzle to herself. She always has been. That is the real Lena we all know; the Lena who woke up one day at the centre of a puzzling game and who set about solving the puzzle and finding her way out to freedom.'

The two men embraced and said goodnight. Robert continued to stand by the car watching Martin walk back along the street and turn in at his gate. He watched until Martin reached his front door, which had remained open to the night, the light streaming across the garden. At the door Martin turned and lifted his hand, his inevitable cigarette between his fingers describing an arc, like a distant flashlight waving to attract attention. He called out, 'Robert! Birte and I would like it very much if you find her.' He went in and closed the door. Robert got into the car and started the motor.

He turned the car and drove to where their short street met Alma Road and he turned left and drove on towards the Bay. So Martin was telling him it was not just for himself that he should go and find Lena, but was for the friendship. For the four of them. Where else would he find such friends? You are one of us, Martin had said. They were the most precious words Robert had ever heard. As he drove along the familiar streets, Robert knew that Martin had set him a challenge.

His finals were three weeks off. He didn't for a moment consider abandoning his degree. If he sat his exams, then he would at least be guaranteed a pass. And with any luck Lena and he would be back in Melbourne before March and the commencement of his fourth year. Martin had decided the question for him. He had reassured him that he was part of a circle of kindred spirits. He said aloud, 'After my exams I'll close up the house, give the key to Dr Eady and go and look for her.'

PART TWO

28

———

During a calm windless night, and without a sound, the great spread of the Albertine rose grappled to the ground the dead limbs of the apricot tree which had long been its reliable support, as if this had always been the Albertine's purpose, and now at last its purpose had been achieved. When I walked into my study that morning, it was shocking and strangely exciting to see them lying there together in a final thorny embrace, like exhausted lovers, the great tangled rose and the old dead tree, its black limbs spread like the silent cry of the crucifix. I saw in it something beautiful. I saw tragedy in it. I was enthralled and stood gazing at the changed scene from my window for a long time. Gus, my old cat, was out there nervously inspecting the scene.

Since we first came here to live I've waited each spring with innocent anticipation to enjoy from my study window the Albertine's vivid display of fragrant blooms. So naturally I felt a sharp pang of guilt at the satisfaction it gave me to see that the rose's massive root had been cleanly snapped at the base—the glistening stump looked as if a beheading axe had sliced it through at a single confident stroke. It was done for. There was no doubt about that. It was finished. There was a brutal finality to its end that excited in me a disconcerting elation and I let myself believe for a moment that a vandal with violent envy in his heart had sneaked into the garden during the night and destroyed my rosebush. I even felt a kind of kinship with this vicious stranger. Standing there looking out at that scene of destruction from my study window, it was as if I'd been waiting for it to happen and could now say to myself with relief, So there! You see? It is done! It was at this moment that I believe I understood something of Lena's shocking anguished cry in response to her mother's sudden death, 'I'm fucking free!'

➤

When Robert closed the front door of the Sorens' Red Bluff house behind him that warm summer afternoon, it had the sound of finality in it for him and he knew, with an unchallengeable intuition, that he would never return to the house.

It was raining the morning he landed in Rome, the low sky dark and wintry in an old European way that made him think of his childhood in England. He caught the train north to Florence.

That afternoon the sky over Florence was a clear cold blue, the air chill and windless. He bought some postcards at the railway station and walked to the Piazza del Duomo. There it was, the great green and white front of the cathedral topped by Brunelleschi's astonishing cupola, shining in the cold light, unchanged from the photograph in his copy of Ferdinand Schevill's *Medieval and Renaissance Florence*. A familiar sight. He felt welcomed. He went into a cafe on the piazza, intending to question the waiter. He ordered spaghetti with meatballs and a coffee and sat in the window sipping his coffee and smoking a cigarette while he waited for his meal to be brought to him. He looked across the square to Giotto's bell tower and watched the throng of people coming and going. Every young woman looked to him, for a heart-stopping moment, like Lena walking towards him, smiling, eager to tell him all about her adventures.

The waiter set his meal on the table in front of him. Robert thanked him and asked for red wine. His simple Italian seemed to be working perfectly. When he'd finished the meal he wrote a short message on one of the postcards he'd bought earlier at the railway station.

> Dear Martin and Birte,
> I am here in Florence. I have a feeling she is not far away. I will write again when I have found her. I hope you are both well. Don't worry too much about her. Now that I am here I feel sure she is fine.
> With my love to you both,
> Robert

When the waiter came to take his plate Robert showed him the photo of Lena and asked him if he had seen her. The waiter took the photo in his hands and studied it for some time. 'She is very beautiful,' he said gravely. 'If I had seen her I would remember her for the rest of my life.'

He handed the photo back to Robert. Robert asked him about a place to stay for a couple of nights. The waiter drew a map with his pen on a corner of the paper table cover, tore it off and handed it to him. 'Signora Cafarella. She will take good care of you while you search Florence for your wife.' He wished Robert luck. 'If I see your wife, I will call Signora Cafarella and tell her.'

Robert ordered a second coffee and lit a second cigarette. He was feeling cheerful and optimistic. His view of the bell tower and the Duomo seemed to him the most promising sight he had ever seen. He knew their history. They were even more impressive than he'd imagined them to be. He was feeling generous and left a good tip for the waiter and thanked him for his kindness. The waiter went with him to the door and opened it for him and stood to one side. 'Show your photograph to Signora Cafarella. She will know who to ask.' The waiter didn't smile. This was a serious matter.

Robert followed the waiter's map. It led him up a gentle hill to a narrow street off Via San Gallo. A woman of around thirty-five greeted him at the door of the pensione. She was unsmiling and businesslike and clearly considered the job of receptionist beneath her dignity. The pensione was a warren of small rooms at the top of a dark stairway. Robert told her he would stay for two or three days and showed her the photo of Lena. She barely glanced at the photo and said in English, 'I know nothing about such things. You must ask my mother.'

That night Signora Cafarella, a large woman in her middle sixties, dished up salt cod with pan-fried potatoes. The room in which they ate was without windows. The stale air reeked of wine and cooking and men's sweaty socks and strong tobacco. There were four other boarders, all men. No one spoke a word of English. Their Italian was difficult for Robert to follow. He showed Signora Cafarella the photo of Lena. She said a great deal and passed the photo around among her other boarders, who also said a great deal. Robert understood none of it, but he got the impression they were sympathetic and would do their best to help him.

He was glad to get to bed. The rough red wine and his lack of sleep, together with the effort of speaking in Italian, had given him a fierce headache. He lay on his back on the small single bed and smoked a last cigarette for the day. His mind was too busy with thoughts for him to sleep. The last time he had eaten salt cod was when his mother had cooked it for him during the Blitz. He had never thought of salt cod as something anyone would choose to eat if they had a choice.

The next morning he walked down Via San Gallo to the Piazza del Duomo and took up his station at the table in the window of the cafe where he'd eaten the previous afternoon. It was a position that commanded a wide view of the piazza. It was a different waiter, an older man. Robert ordered a coffee and showed the waiter the photo. The waiter gave it a quick glance and handed it back without a word. Sooner or later, Robert was certain, he was going to see her. Surely every visitor to Florence crosses the Piazza del Duomo? But of course, if Lena was still in Florence, then she might have been there already for several months and would by now have settled into some kind of routine and wouldn't be out looking at the tourist sights every day.

That evening he walked back along Via San Gallo and climbed the stairs to Signora Cafarella's pensione and ate a dish of pasta. No one had any news for him. He went to bed and began reading for the second time Arthur Koestler's novel *Darkness at Noon*. He had snatched the book up at the last minute as he was leaving the house. It was the story of a man alone in his cell, a man who feels no enmity towards his gaoler but accepts his condition as part of some greater plan, over which neither he nor his gaoler has any influence. Reading Koestler, the cheerful optimism Robert felt on his first day in Florence soon evaporated. Quite often during the day he had no idea what people had said to him in reply to his questions and he was feeling dismayed that his Italian was so weak after all. The air in his tiny room was heavy with the smell of stale humanity and he felt he could quite understand the fatalistic state of mind of the doomed prisoner in Koestler's novel.

He was woken in the early hours by a nightmare. He didn't witness the events directly himself but was told about them by someone else and had to form his own picture of them, which made them more believable and more horrible. Lena, his anonymous informant told him in a voice of great authority, had been hit by a train and her corpse buried under great slabs of granite that could not be moved. The granite slabs were covered in grey lichen, so

Robert's informant said, and had not been disturbed for hundreds of years. Robert lay awake in the dark for a long time, the horror of the dream clinging to his mind. A man was snoring heavily next door, great heaving shudders that vibrated the thin substance of the wall. It was the sound of a man being tormented. Robert knew he wasn't going to find Lena in Florence.

In the morning he went to the station and caught the train to Perugia. He checked in to the first pensione he saw, then asked directions to the university for foreigners. The day was cold and it had been raining earlier, the cobbles still glistening. He was soon lost among a maze of narrow streets, each one of which looked just like all the others. He had been walking for half an hour when he emerged from a side street into an open square, a fountain spilling water at its centre.

She was sitting on the wide stone steps in front of a large building on the other side of the piazza. She was hugging her knees, her head resting on her arms, her hair tucked untidily into a knitted beanie. He couldn't see her face but he knew it was Lena. He walked towards her across the square. His heart was beating quickly. He was nervous. A woman coming down the steps looked at Lena as she walked past her. The woman must have said something to Lena, as Lena lifted her head and looked at the woman. He saw that Lena's feet were bare, her shoes lying on the step below her, as if she had kicked them off carelessly. They were scuffed and dirty. A plastic bag and a small case that was not familiar to him were on the step beside her. The grey overcoat she was wearing was obviously a man's cast-off. She looked like a bag woman, someone who might live under a bridge, one of her patients from the hospital, a member of that lost community.

He went up the steps and sat beside her. He was shocked by her appearance. 'How did you manage to become a scrawny bag lady in four months? Jesus, Lena! You look fucking terrible. What have you done to yourself?'

Her smile was the slow tired smile of someone who was exhausted, a woman at the end of her strength. She had a sketching pad between her feet and had been drawing. A pencil lay on the pad. She didn't seem surprised to see him.

She laid her hand on his. 'I knew you'd find me. I've been waiting for you.'

When he didn't say anything, she said, 'I'm glad you came.'

He could smell the staleness coming off her.

She said, 'Do I disgust you?'

He shook his head. 'I don't know what to say.'

'Don't worry,' she said. 'Give me your hand.'

He helped her to her feet. He could feel the bones of her back under his fingers.

In a matter-of-fact voice, as if it was neither here nor there, she said, 'I'm pregnant.' They stood on the stone steps in that ancient Italian town looking at each other, neither of them speaking. He said at last, 'I don't know how to talk to you. This is not you. Pregnant? You're sure?'

She touched her belly. She looked down at herself. 'You can leave me here if you want to.' She looked at him. 'It might be better in the long run.'

Her grey eyes were ringed by fatigue, her skin unwashed, her forehead tight and wrinkled. 'You're a stranger,' he said.

She said quietly, a touch of sorrow or regret in her voice, 'I suppose you and I have always been strangers.'

He said, 'We'll go to England and get you to a decent doctor.'

She steadied herself, her hand on his arm, while she reached down and put on her shoes. 'I don't need a doctor. I'm not ill.'

He watched her struggling with her shoes. Where was the beautiful, interesting young woman in a blouse and smart grey skirt who'd opened the door to John Morris and him that first day at the Red Bluff house? He said, 'If you'd married one of your own mob, this wouldn't have happened.'

She bent and picked up the plastic bag and the small case. She looked at him. 'Are you jealous?'

'Of course I'm fucking jealous. I can't believe what you've done to yourself. Why? Why have you done this? Whatever it was you and I had, you've smashed it.'

She had left the damp-looking sketchbook and the pencil lying on the wet cobbles. He picked them up. 'Don't you want these?'

She glanced at them. 'It was a silly idea,' she said.

He took the case from her and put the sketchbook and pencil in his coat pocket. She put her arm in his and they walked down the steps together. He felt physically sick. Shaken. Bewildered.

Angry. He couldn't look at her. 'Where are you staying?' he asked her. 'We'll fetch your things.'

'I'm not staying anywhere. You've got everything there.'

'Jesus!' He caught a whiff of her. 'How long since you had a bath?'

She said, 'Leave me here, Robert. I'll manage.'

'I'm not leaving you!' He held her arm tightly. 'Just don't make me say anything else!' People going by looked at them. He stared them down. 'Bastards!'

They went to his pensione and Lena had a bath and went to bed. He sat by the bed and watched her sleeping. She looked like a child, small, alone, lost and confused, her pale eyelids trembling, her lips slightly parted. She was in his care. A wave of tenderness swept over him. He would write at once and tell Martin and Birte he had found her. They were his family now, these three people.

In the morning they took a taxi to the railway station. He bought tickets for Rome and they sat side by side in the waiting room. She leaned back against the wall and went to sleep. He wrote a postcard to Martin and Birte—on the other side of the card was a coloured picture of Perugia taken from the air. He marked with a small X the square where he'd found her.

Dear Martin and Birte,
I found her where the X is. She isn't very well, so we're going to England where we'll see a doctor. It isn't anything to worry

about. I hope you are both well. We'll be home soon. The weather is already cold here.

With love from us both to you two,

Robert and Lena

29

On the landing at the top of the stairs he set down her things and his suitcase. He waited for her to come up the last flight. She came up and stood beside him, an asthmatic wheeze in her breathing. 'Are you all right?' he asked. She nodded and coughed and said huskily, 'Thank God we're here.'

He put the key in the lock and opened the door. He stepped back to let her go in first, then he picked up their bags and followed her. They were in a small unlit entrance hall, with coat hooks and a box with shoe polish and rags. He found the light switch. They went into the passage. The door to the kitchen was open, sunlight coming through the tall narrow window and falling on the table in the centre of the room. There was a green vase with an artful arrangement of leafless twigs. On the left a door stood open to a bedroom. They went into the bedroom and he set their things down. She sat on the side of the bed and breathed. The sun was streaming through two large double windows, falling across the multi-coloured eiderdown on the bed and touching Lena's hair, which shone a dull bronze. He went over to one of the windows and looked out. The long front garden with its lawn and clipped hedge below, then the leafless horse chestnut trees along the street, a drift of smoke from the smouldering leaf piles in the gutter, the sharp familiar tang of the burning leaves in his nostrils.

He said, 'When I was a kid we used to raid these trees for conkers. We came from the estate in a gang and threw our sticks up into the trees and grabbed as many conkers as we could before we were chased away by a gardener or one of the ladies.'

She said, 'I'll go and have a shower.'

He turned from the window and looked at her. She was grey and exhausted. 'It might be a bath,' he said.

She got off the bed and stood looking at him. 'I haven't got anything clean to put on.'

He went over and opened his suitcase and took out a t-shirt and handed it to her. 'It'll come down to your knees.' They were no longer a married couple. They were two people persisting. He felt as if they were on a great mound of rubble. It was a bombsite from his childhood. He couldn't imagine that they could ever restore what they'd had and become again the people they had been. He would write to Martin and Birte. He should tell them the truth.

She said, 'Don't look at me like that.' She turned away and went out of the room, holding his t-shirt in both hands. A moment later he heard a door close.

He listened. The house was silent. He might have been alone. He was in England again. The familiar accents of the people had shocked him. He feared that he might be taken for one of them.

His old self lurking in him just below the surface. His parents and his young brother going about their lives only a suburb or two away, just the other side of Bromley, believing he was on the other side of the world, his sister gone long ago. He put his things away in the chest of drawers and the wardrobe. He didn't touch her things. He went out and investigated the rest of the flat. At the end of the passage was a large room that smelled of pine air freshener. He stood just inside the door. Two easy chairs and a couch covered in red and green floral fabric, two small round tables set at the sides of the couch and chairs, cut-glass ashtrays on the tables, a cheap lacquered sideboard against the wall with a large, empty cut-glass bowl in the middle of it. The room felt as if it had never been occupied. He turned around and went down the hall and into the kitchen. There was a telephone on the bench by the sink, a table with an oilcloth cover against the wall and two white-painted straight-backed wooden chairs, a dead clock on the wall, the sun shining through the narrow window onto the oilcloth. There was a faint smell of fresh bread but no sign of bread.

Lena stood in the doorway, wearing his t-shirt. She was pink from the heat of the bath. 'Don't look at me!' she pleaded. Her elbows and knee bones were sticking out, her thighs hollowed. She said, 'I'm going to have a sleep.'

He felt a rush of emotion and followed her into the bedroom and helped her to get into the bed, leaning over her and kissing her forehead. He tucked her in. She reached for his hand and gave him a tearful smile. 'I'm sorry.'

'You'll feel better when you've had a sleep,' he said. He drew the curtains and went out, closing the door of the bedroom behind him.

There was a note half concealed under the telephone. He picked it up and read it. *Welcome to the Tree house. Please help yourselves to ripe fruit in the garden.* The landlord, whose name was Donald Tree, had stamped the notepaper with a purple tree.

Robert left the house and walked to the high street. He bought tea and bread and vegetables for soup. When he returned, the landlord was in the hall downstairs. Robert said hello to him and he smiled and said, 'Do call me Don, please.' He was tall and very upright with a neatly clipped reddish moustache. He had an air of concerned authority about him and looked as if he'd spent his life in the military. Robert said, 'My wife's picked up something on our travels and I think she should see a doctor.'

'Nothing serious, I hope, dear chap,' Don Tree said.

'Lena suffers from the occasional asthma attack. I think she's got just a bit rundown from all the travelling we've been doing.'

'Understand you perfectly, Robert.'

Robert envied Lena the reality of her Australian identity. His own reality in England was a flimsy, make-do structure and he feared it would break down and this man would sense his Council estate origins. He could hear Donald Tree's tone modulate subtly: Ah, so you're from the Downham Estate. Robert hadn't realised quite how vulnerable he would be in England to his old childhood insecurities. He wished he was a bolder and more determined person and could laugh at these things. But he couldn't.

Lena was still asleep when he looked in on her. He closed the door softly and went into the kitchen and made vegetable soup. While the soup was simmering he had a bath. The sun was going down and was no longer shining into the kitchen. He put the light on and ate a bowl of soup and two slices of fresh bread. He sat there staring emptily at the darkened window and he realised he was exhausted. He couldn't finish the cigarette he was smoking and butted it in the ashtray. He got up and went into the bedroom.

Lena didn't stir when he climbed into the bed beside her. He fell asleep at once then woke abruptly into the deep silence of the night. He looked at his watch. It was eleven-thirty. He'd only been asleep for two hours. He drifted into an anxious half-sleep, then woke again, the dread in him that he was going to be sucked back into a life on the factory floor. Was that to be his true fate? In the dark, alone with her beside him, he was taken by the fear that he really belonged with his old schoolmates, the conker hunters, the ones who'd stayed behind. Here he was, inside one of the houses along the very street of their raids, as if the real hidden reason for his unwilling return to England had been decided by a force greater than himself, a force that would fling him back into line and set him down firmly, once and for all, so that he could never again make a break for it. You made your leap and you lost! Was this what they would say of him when they found out he'd returned from Australia empty-handed and defeated? The night was endless. His fear was endless. He had no answer for anything.

In the morning he got up and made a cup of tea and took one in to her. She turned and looked at him. 'You slept for more than fifteen hours,' he said.

She said, 'My mouth's dry. My breath must be awful.'

He set the tea on the bedside table. 'Sit up and drink this.' There were wrinkles and dark purple shadows under her eyes.

He went over to the windows and opened the curtains. 'Another fine autumn day.' He sat on the side of the bed and drank his tea. Neither of them spoke for some time. He said, 'We have to talk about things.'

'This is the best cup of tea I've ever had,' she said with feeling. 'It's so good to be in a real bed.' She reached across to him with her free hand and took hold of his arm. There were tears in her eyes. 'I didn't know where I was when I woke up just now. I really did think I was dreaming when you came in with the tea.'

'Don's given me the name of their family doctor. He's offered to give us a lift there in his car. He seems like a decent bloke.'

'I'm not ill,' she said. 'I don't need to see a doctor. I'm just pregnant. It's not an illness. Please don't make a fuss.' She withdrew her hand.

'You can't dictate your terms,' he said. 'You're going to see a doctor and that's that. Just imagine if you had an asthma attack. You're already weak as a bloody kitten. There's not an ounce of flesh on you.' How long would he be able to hold back? He looked at her. 'You've had some kind of a breakdown. I suppose it was brought on by your mother's sudden death. But whatever it is, we have to get some professional advice.' The idea of living with her made him feel sick and cheated. 'I'm just trying to be reasonable.'

She said with fierce determination, 'You're not going to tell me how to behave! I'm not here to be told how to behave. I know how to behave. You're not my mother.'

A dog was barking in the garden. Don was calling to the dog.

Robert wanted to grab her by the throat and shake her. He said, 'I don't deserve this. You're going to have to tell me about it sooner or later. I deserve to know.'

She set her empty cup on the side table and lay down.

He said, 'Was he a white man?'

She looked at him coldly. 'What difference does it make?'

'I just want to be ready for the unexpected,' he said.

She didn't say anything and turned to face the wall.

Someone was laughing downstairs. A woman's voice. The dog barking, Don calling to it, teasing. The sounds of a happy family.

Lena's voice was muffled by the blanket when she said, 'It was just something we did. Being on the boat was another world. You wouldn't understand.'

He waited.

After a while she said, 'I really don't want to talk about it. I might have another little sleep, if you don't mind.' She pulled the blankets up close around her chin.

He said, 'I'm going out.' He stood up.

'Where are you going?'

'To get a job.'

'You don't need to get a job. I've got enough money for both of us.'

'I'm getting a job,' he said. 'You do whatever it is you're doing, and I'll do what I'm doing. Okay? And maybe we'll get around to talking sense to each other sooner or later. And if we don't get around to talking sense to each other, then I guess we'll each go our own way with it, but I'm not going to sit around relying on your money and doing nothing while I wait for you to get better.'

She said, 'I need you. I don't want you to leave me.' She started to cry.

He stood looking down at her. Maybe she was going to say she was sorry. He was waiting for it. He knew he couldn't go back to Melbourne without her, but he couldn't see how he could go back to Melbourne with her either. If he told Martin everything, maybe Martin would dislike hearing such sordid stuff about Lena and would think less of him. And if he kept the truth from Martin, well, maybe it would eat into their trust. He took his white shirt from the chest of drawers and went out to the kitchen and ironed it.

When he came back into the bedroom she was sitting up. She had a notebook and a pen and was writing.

He went over to the wardrobe and changed into his shirt and put on a tie and then got into his three-piece wedding suit.

She said, 'You look amazing. Where are you going?'

'I'm going to present myself at the University of London appointments board and see what happens.'

247

He stood a moment in front of the mirror adjusting his tie. It was his wedding tie. Dark blue with small white polka dots. He felt strong and confident. 'What you're wearing makes all the difference in this country.' He turned around and walked to the door then paused and looked back at her. 'Promise me you'll behave till I get back?'

She said, 'I'm sorry for the mess I've made of everything.' She looked like she might cry again.

'It's okay,' he said. 'We'll work something out. It's going to need a bit of time. We can go back home when we're both good and ready; till then we'll make do here.' He went out the door. She called, 'Good luck!'

30

The young woman who interviewed him at the University of London read the Melbourne dean's letter—which advised that he would be granted a pass degree in the New Year if he decided not to undertake his fourth year. She said, 'Australian? But you're really English, aren't you? You're one of us.'

He smiled. 'I guess I'm both,' he said. 'Or perhaps neither.'

She looked playfully disapproving. 'Oh no,' she said, 'you'll always be one of us, Mr Crofts.' As if to be anything less than one of *them* would have been slightly shameful of him. She handed the letter back to him and said he should go and talk to the people at the Japanese Trade Commission. 'They're looking for an English graduate to do some market research for them. Their offices are in Marble Arch. Do you think you can find your way?'

He said, 'I've got a map of the West End engraved in my head.'

'Well there you are, you see,' she said, as if this decided the question of his identity. 'Only a real Londoner has that.'

He walked along Marylebone Road till he got to Edgware Road, then turned down towards Marble Arch. The London streets were intensely familiar from his days with his father visiting galleries and bookshops and later with his friend Ernie watching Cinerama and walking in the parks, dreaming their dreams of adventures and lying in the sun smoking where no one would see them. While he walked along the old streets the situation with Lena was playing itself over and over in Robert's head. He felt as if he'd been flung out of his orbit by her and couldn't think straight.

He reached the corner of Oxford Street and Park Lane and saw the offices of the Japanese Trade Commission. The receptionist, who was not Japanese, said, 'Mr Haida is expecting you, Mr Crofts.' She smiled and waved away as unnecessary the slip of paper the woman at the appointments board had given him, wafting towards him with her gesture a delicate hint of her expensive perfume.

A tall, elegantly suited Japanese man came out of an office and introduced himself. He shook Robert's hand and said he was very pleased to see him. He spoke English with an American accent. Meeting Robert seemed to make him happy. Robert was glad he was wearing the dark grey three-piece suit. They sat in Mr Haida's office on leather couches. A beautiful young woman, who was also not Japanese, brought in tea and biscuits, and Mr Haida and Robert chatted. Mr Haida said he was delighted the university had sent an Australian and he was interested to hear about Robert's experiences in Far North Queensland. The conversation was casual, and there was no particularly Japanese direction to it until Mr Haida said, 'Have you ever been to Japan, Robert?' Robert said he hadn't. Mr Haida said, 'They'd like you to visit Japan.' And that was it. Had this meeting really been a job interview? Mr Haida said he looked forward to seeing Robert on Monday, when he would introduce him to Mr Sugiura. He went with Robert to the outer office and shook his hand and smiled.

Robert walked up the ramp with the crowd of commuters at Chislehurst station and an old memory replaced his aching preoccupation with Lena. As he turned left at the top of the ramp and walked along the quiet suburban streets he found himself thinking about his father. When his father came home from the war he was convalescent for several months at Orpington Hospital with hundreds of other wounded soldiers. Robert's mother used to take Robert and his sister from Grove Park to Orpington every week to see their father. The Orpington train always stopped at Chislehurst. His father in his blue hospital uniform, grinning and hopping on crutches towards them across a wide expanse of green lawn, was vivid in his mind. His father had looked well and happy, a wounded hero returned. Nurses in vivid white stood back watching him and smiling. Everyone admired his father and Robert felt distant from him and wondered sadly if he and his father would ever again be close friends.

31

Don was in the hall downstairs when Robert came in the front door. He was looking startled and a bit confused. Robert said, 'Is everything all right, Don?'

Don set down his green watering can and stood close to Robert and put a hand on his shoulder. His demeanour was almost furtive. 'Look here, old chap . . .' he said. He glanced around awkwardly, as if he was afraid of being overheard. 'Two men came to see your wife earlier.' He paused and they looked at each other. Robert noticed how large his eyes were, deep brown, his eyebrows a little gingery like his moustache. Don drew a breath and squeezed Robert's shoulder with his strong fingers. 'When they left, one of them was carrying a bundle of towelling.' There was a question in his eyes as he leaned closer to Robert and whispered, 'There was blood on the towel.'

Robert stepped away from him.

'Do you think she's all right?' Don said. 'I've been waiting for you. I thought it better not to call the police.'

Robert ran up the stairs three at a time and let himself into the flat. Lena was lying in bed with the blanket pulled up. Her fingers were gripping the edge of the blanket. Her forehead was beaded with sweat. She turned her head towards him. 'It's gone,' she said. Her weak voice was muffled by the blanket. 'I've had an abortion.' She began to cry.

He sat on the edge of the bed and held her against him. She was crying, not frantically, not sobbing wildly, just crying quietly. He thought of the two men carrying the bloodied towels out to their car and driving away. How had she got in touch with them? When did she make the sudden arrangement? How did she pay them? A storm of questions in his head. He didn't ask.

The following morning she surprised him by getting up early and making them both a cup of tea. They sat across from each other at the table in the kitchen. She seemed to be completely recovered. 'I'm all right. Don't make a fuss. I'm really all right. I'm going to eat properly again. I want us to make a clean new beginning.'

He was seeing the child sinking slowly into the dark depths of the sea. Gone forever. A lost soul. How could that be the start of a clean new beginning?

She got up and began making toast at the bench.

He said, 'I need you to tell me about the abortion. How did you arrange it? Did you phone someone? Did you go out? How did you pay for it?'

He waited, watching her fiddling with the toaster. 'You have to say something,' he said. 'You can't just say nothing.'

She turned around and looked at him. 'Can it wait a bit? Please?'

He saw the pained look in her eyes. Was this for her a defeat of her womanhood? Was she afraid now of what she had done, how it might haunt her?

'Tell me about the job,' she said. 'I want to hear about it. Let's try and be a bit normal. We'll talk about the other thing another time. I can't talk about all that now.' She brought over a plate of buttered toast and set it on the table. 'We'll go shopping and I'll get some decent marmalade for you.' She pulled out her chair and sat down and poured another cup of tea. She sat munching a piece of the warm buttered toast. 'So, you had an interview? What were they like, the people?'

He looked at her for a long moment without saying anything. 'I need to know just one thing,' he said. 'Do you still have feelings for the man who gave you the child?'

'Oh, for God's sake, of course not!' she said with irritation. 'I never had feelings for him. Feelings! God! Please don't make me talk about it!'

They sat in silence. The heating pipes groaned and pinged and the excited dog was barking out in the garden again.

She said, 'Do you want to come shopping with me this morning? I need to buy some new clothes. I've got nothing decent to wear.'

He ate a piece of toast and drank a second cup of tea. 'I can't force you to tell me anything if it's too painful for you. But I feel as if I'm in a kind of vacuum if you don't tell me anything. I can't pin down any details. If you won't tell me anything, I'll imagine the worst. That's all. I'm here, you know. It's me. I'm still me.'

'I know it can't be easy for you,' she said. 'But can we just give it a bit of time? I'll tell you everything you want to know when I feel stronger. When I'm in charge of myself again. Right now I feel as if I'll break in half and fall in a heap if I have to deal with any more.'

He lit a cigarette. 'At least we're talking. It's something. It's better than the blank silence.'

'We can't become us again just like that. At once. We have to find our way a step at a time.'

'You sound like the professional social worker talking now.' It wasn't easy for him to trust what she said. 'What are we going to tell Martin and Birte? We can't tell them nothing. I have to write to them. You should too. They're worried about you.'

'Just for now,' she said, 'can you tell me about how you went looking for a job? Then we can go shopping together like ordinary people. I desperately need a bit of normality.' She put her hand on his. 'What did they say to you at the Japanese Trade Commission? Where was it? Are you going to have your own office?'

'It overlooks Park Lane. There's a view of the park. The guy who interviewed me was very handsome. A tall Japanese. He told me he went to McGill University in Montreal for five years and has been out of Japan for so long that he probably won't any longer be quite Japanese enough when he goes back. He twigged that I was an imposter. He seemed to like me for it. I think he's probably an imposter himself. Someone who's become disconnected from his past.'

'He sounds interesting.'

'Yes. We got on. I liked him. It was all incredibly casual. If we hadn't liked each other, he would have politely shown me the door.'

'What will you be doing?'

'He didn't say. I think they just want a young non-Japanese in a smart suit somewhere about the office. The way they have beautiful blonde English girls for reception and as secretaries. Part of the show.'

On Monday after work, he bought a bottle of brown ale at the off-licence outside the Chislehurst station. When he walked into the kitchen there was a large stoneware jug on the kitchen table, an arrangement of hothouse daisies and green leaves. Lena had lamb chops under the grill and was mashing potatoes in a yellow bowl. She was wearing a grey woollen roll-neck jumper and new jeans. She'd had her hair cut and styled and was wearing makeup. She was not her old self, but was a woman in whom her old self had taken up residence. Perhaps, if she were truly sane and she put on weight again, she would become entirely her old self. When he came through the door she looked up at him, her expression hopeful, expectant and a little worried. He said, 'You look terrific.' He went over to her and kissed her. She said, 'So do you.'

She didn't look terrific, but at least there was no sign of the disorder of her mind that had overwhelmed her since he'd found her in Perugia. He set the beer on the table and went into the bedroom and changed out of his suit and tie. Perhaps the dramatic change—the liberation of her demented spirit, which seemed to have been triggered by her mother's unexpected death—perhaps this change was going to go on forming in her. As he pulled on his jeans he realised this was the first time he'd had such a thought. The idea that she wasn't going to revert to the young woman she had been, the one he fell in love with, but was going on to become this other woman. Would they resume their sex life? The question was in the very front of his mind. It was difficult to imagine them making love again. He couldn't quite see it. But perhaps they'd manage it. They'd have to. He wasn't going to be celibate.

He went out to the kitchen and took two tumblers down from the cupboard and opened the beer and poured two glasses. He held one out to her. 'Dad's favourite beer.'

She took it from him. They clinked their glasses. 'What shall we say?' she said.

'To us!'

'To us,' she echoed.

They drank and looked into each other's eyes. Just possibly, it occurred to him, the bond between them—which was something not to be understood but to be felt—had been mysteriously strengthened. In a way he felt that. He lit a cigarette. 'I didn't want to marry you. But I did want you to be my lover and my friend.'

She didn't say anything to this but smiled and set her beer on the table and cut another small slice of butter and put it in with the mashed potatoes. 'Pepper!' she said and frowned and looked around. 'I don't think we've got any.'

He looked through the cupboards. There wasn't any pepper.

She dished up and they sat down to their meal. She had one chop on her plate and a small spoonful of mashed potato.

He enjoyed the meal and the beer. They'd taken some kind of step forward. There had been two liberating deaths for her: her mother's and her child's. He had been absent from both. Her double refusal of motherhood. Both deaths, in their way—in the way that is not locked to rationality and to facts and histories but is locked within our souls and is known only by our intuition—part of the price she was being called on to pay for the realisation of her particular secret, her liberty. Her cry, *I am fucking free*, ringing on and on; more prophecy than fact. He pushed his plate away, the three chop bones forming a Y on the plate. He lit a cigarette and refilled his glass with beer. 'You're turning into a good cook.'

She said, 'Nonsense! Anyone can grill a couple of chops.' She collected the plates and the cutlery and carried them over to the sink.

He said, 'Come and sit down. I'll do that later.'

She set the things on the sink and turned around. 'I want to meet your parents.'

Without thinking he said, 'I've decided not to tell them we're here. I've realised I need to get home to Melbourne and make a start on my writing. I've wasted enough time. The job was a mistake.' He didn't want his parents to meet her. It was complicated. There were too many old issues. He thought he'd left those issues behind for good when he left England. But here, back in England, he knew those old issues would soon come alive again and insist on being dealt with. Issues with his father in particular. A thoughtless word would be enough to rouse them to new life. He was afraid of what might happen if his two worlds were to meet, if the equation were to be completed, so that one side might measure him against the other side, so that he might himself be required to measure his new reality against his old discarded self. Once upon a time, when he was barely sixteen years old, he'd had a vision, a beautiful clear dream, an idea that had carried him around the world. The idea had faltered and had seemed to fail entirely. Now at last a new horizon, as empty as the first, had begun to entice him: the possibility of becoming a writer of the kind of novels that Martin would admire. He wanted to get on with it. He wanted to make a beginning. He had decided not to go back to the university to complete his honours degree. He now knew his way among books and was confident he could find the reading that would sustain him. And he had Martin's friendship. He said, 'We're going home.'

'Not before we visit your parents,' she said.

'We're not going to visit my parents,' he said and lit a cigarette.

She reached for his cigarettes, shook one halfway out of the packet, then changed her mind and pushed it back in and shoved the packet away from her. 'Now it's you who's being irrational,' she said calmly. 'You knew my mother. You knew my life at home. You know all about me. Now I want to know about you. It's important to me. I want to see you with your parents in your old home. Then I'll know who you are. Are you like your father or are you like your mother? Or will I see something of you in both of them? I *must* meet them. You have to trust me to decide for myself. I'm here in England with you now. We'll probably never be here together ever again. Now is the time.' She watched him, waiting, a mixture of determination and anxiety in her eyes.

He smoked his cigarette and stared at the oilcloth on the table. Someone had burned a small round hole in it. He rubbed the burn hole with his finger and looked up at her. 'It's a funny thing,' he said.

'What is?'

'When you left Red Bluff and I was there on my own I missed the sound of the piano. I went into the sitting room a couple of times and struck the keys. But that only made it worse. Every now and then I heard you playing a familiar piece.'

She said, 'We have to meet your parents. That's all there is to it. I'm not going home till we do.'

He watched her get up and go over to the sink and begin washing up their dishes. 'You're like your mother in some ways.'

She turned and regarded him levelly for some time. 'You see? That's what I mean. Whether you like it or not, I'm going to meet your parents. You'll just have to accept it. I can't imagine why you're being so weird about it.'

He didn't feel like having a head-on collision with her just then, so he let it lie for the time being.

That night she cuddled up close to him. He lay beside her

feeling uneasy and unsure. Then she put her hand on him for the first time since she'd left Red Bluff to go to Italy.

Neither of them said anything after they'd made love. There had been such an acute tension, almost a feeling of embarrassment or bashfulness about it, that they didn't know what to say. So they said nothing, but lay side by side holding hands in the dark. And eventually they went to sleep.

In the morning he took her in a cup of tea before leaving for the office. He went into the office every morning for the rest of the week and read the newspapers and had lunch with Mr Haida and caught the train home in the evenings. On Friday when he got home Lena was sitting at the kitchen table writing in her notebook. She had arranged a bunch of hothouse flowers in a vase by the window and was wearing makeup. Beside her on the table was a letter. She didn't close the notebook when he came in, as she usually did, but looked up and said brightly, 'How was your day?'

He put the bottle of beer on the table. 'I told Haida I wanted to be a writer and wouldn't be staying long,' he said. 'So who's the letter from?'

She said cheerfully, 'Your mother.'

'My mother doesn't know we're here.' He picked up the letter and slid the single sheet of paper out of the envelope.

My dear Lena,
What a lovely surprise to hear that you and Robert are in England. And so near to us! Robert didn't say he was plan-ning on coming over. It's just like him to surprise us. I used

to call him my difficult one! We can't wait to meet you. I do hope you can come either for lunch or afternoon tea next Saturday, if you're not too busy. Please don't feel you need to change your plans for us. We don't have the phone on unfortunately.

He put his mother's note back in the envelope and placed the envelope on the table and looked at Lena. She gave him a sweetly innocent smile.

He said, 'I guess you win.'

'It isn't a competition,' she said.

A surge of anger rose in him. He turned and went out into the hall, then opened the door and went down the stairs and out into the street. He just had to get away from her. She could do that without a word to him! He walked fast at first, down to the corner and turning into the street on the left. There was no one about. It was always so quiet. A dog barked at him from behind a hedge and he jumped, his heart batting against his ribs. 'Fuck you!' he yelled. The dog became frenzied. A woman popped her head up from behind the hedge and gazed at him with a startled look. He almost shouted at her, but held it back. On he went, striding out. Then he swung around and went back the way he'd come. The woman watched him approaching. As he went by he said hello. She didn't react but stood staring at him, the dog barking madly. He went into the house and up the stairs. In the kitchen Lena was still sitting at the table.

He said, 'You don't know or care what's at stake for me in this.' He stood looking at her. It wasn't only anger but sadness he was feeling now. 'You've had everything in your life. You've never had to struggle for anything. And now you sit around doing nothing and going on believing you're special and must be looked after and taken care of while other people work and struggle for the things they want.' His feeling of the injustice of the way she was behaving. She went to speak and he jumped in, 'No! You don't give a fuck, do you? I know what I want and you're blocking me from doing it. What the fuck do you want? Just tell me. I'll believe you. I'll help you do it. What is it that you want?'

She said calmly, 'I don't know what I want. If I knew what I wanted to do with my life, I'd be doing it.'

'So you're envious and you want to block me. Is that it? I'd like to understand. I really fucking would.'

'I didn't ask you to drop everything and come chasing after me.'

'But you knew I would. Have you written to Birte? I bet you haven't. You only think about yourself.' He felt weary of the game she was forcing him to play. He sat down. 'Give me the bottle opener.'

She reached across and opened the drawer next to the sink and handed him the bottle opener. He opened the quart of beer. 'Do you want one?'

'Yes, please.' She reached over and took two glasses out of the cupboard without getting up and watched him fill each of them carefully to the brim. He handed a glass to her. She took a sip.

'Cheers,' she said. 'Not knowing what I want from life haunts me day and night. I don't know what to do about it.'

He drank some beer then took his mother's letter from the envelope and read it again. 'You've read my mother's letters. Plenty of times. You must see this is not her style?'

'It didn't occur to me.'

'She's nervous. She's worried about meeting the middle-class wife of her difficult son.' He met Lena's gaze. 'The instant I read this note, I knew I had to give in and go with you to see my parents. Anything else would be the behaviour of a madman. You've got me. Haven't you? Are you happy now?'

She said, 'You didn't leave me much choice. I thought you'd be more angry.'

'I am angry. It's inside anger.' He lit a cigarette then got up and went to the window and looked out at the lit-up house next door. Huge and grand and apparently deserted. He'd never seen anyone going in or coming out. He turned around. 'If you haven't got anything planned for dinner, there's an Indian place near the station. We could give it a try.'

She said, 'I thought I'd make an omelette for us.'

'Is the omelette for us, or is it just for me?'

'Don't start, please. Let's just have one evening without discussing my diet, can we?'

He sat down again and drank some more of the beer. He held the glass up and looked at it. 'Dad mixed this with brown ale. He called it black and tan. It's funny the things you remember.

I'd never drink this in Australia.' He looked across at Lena. 'Mr Haida has an identity problem too. There are people like me all over the world. He said he envies me my need to be a writer. He doesn't have a need, he said. He lost it, he says, by staying too long in one job. He's cheerful on the outside and sad on the inside. I like him a lot.'

'Will you write to him when we get home?'

'I don't know. What's the point?' He got up from the table and went into the bedroom to change out of his suit. He could hear Lena getting the meal together in the kitchen. She had fucked some bloke on the ship coming out and he hadn't felt betrayed by it. Writing to his mother without telling him felt like more of a betrayal. The thought of seeing his parents made him anxious. He wondered if his ideas about these things were normal.

He put on his jeans and hoped Lena had thought to buy mush-rooms. He didn't like bland eggy omelettes. He went back into the kitchen and sat down and watched her at the gas stove. He was hungry. 'Dad will show you how to make a real omelette.'

She said, 'We should take them something. What do you think they'd like?'

'Mum would probably like it if we had the telephone installed so she could call my sister and chat to her grandchildren. Dad would think it was a hint from me that he should have put the tele-phone on for Mum years ago himself. He'd think I was suggesting hc was a failure and was too poor or too stupid to think of it.

He'd feel rebuked. It's probably a good idea. I'll check with the phone people.'

'Think of something before Saturday,' she said. 'Something that will please them both. Not something that's going to start a row with your dad.'

'I'll see what I can come up with.' He watched her in silence for a while. 'And you and I will go together in the morning and book our flights home to Melbourne.'

'We'll go to Sydney,' she said.

'Sydney?' Another surprise to wrong-foot him. Another little manoeuvre in her complicated negotiations. But he couldn't have cared less. So long as they were going home and he could start writing. He had imagined himself writing in Keith's study, his own books and Keith's books around him. Now he saw an empty room in Sydney, sunlight pouring in through a long thin window, reflecting off the polished floor, dazzling his vision.

'Melbourne for me is like Downham for you,' she said. She turned around from the stove. 'Try to understand that.'

'So why are you forcing me to return to Downham?'

'It's different. I need to meet your parents.' She shook her head. 'I don't know what I want from life. I wish to God I did. I don't expect you to understand. But I hope you can put up with it. I don't want to pick up where I left off. I'll never live at the Red Bluff house ever again. It would defeat me.'

32

———

They got off the Bromley bus opposite Grove Park station. It was a cold blustery Saturday with a spit of rain in the air, women dragging unwilling kids by the hand, men with their coat collars turned up against the chill of the wind, the smell of stale beer wafting across the road from the pub, a pale sun struggling to come through, the clouds grey and streaked with silver rushing along close overhead. He remembered these clouds. There was a nostalgia for him in the memory, a touch of sadness at the sight of these perfectly recollected clouds. The clouds had not changed, but something had been lost. He didn't think he would ever be able to talk about it, this subtle loss of meaning. In England his emotional life was like a room filled with boxes marked *Never to be opened*.

Lena had bought herself an expensive new black overcoat. They walked across the road together and he turned to her and said, 'You look really good in that coat.' It suited her. She looked cosy and at home in it. Safe from chills. No one could have guessed she was a starveling underneath. She even looked interesting.

Possibly sexy. She had a grey woollen scarf tucked into the collar of the coat, and a small dark grey woollen hat. After crossing the road she stood in the shelter of a shop doorway and refreshed her lipstick. They went on up the hill past Dr Hopman's house with its bright red front door. Dear Dr Hopman, who had once come in the night during the Blitz to see Robert's sister and had stayed for breakfast and raced him to see which of them could finish his boiled egg first. Robert stopped to read the brass plate. Dr Hopman's name was no longer there. The door was still red, the surgery still a surgery. The red light above the door. His chest was tight with memory and love. The strange beautiful pain of it. His bold leap carrying him to the other side of the world, to the limitless plains of the Gulf Country with Frankie and his mob, and here he was again, standing outside Dr Hopman's old surgery, just as if time had collapsed in on him and he had never made the leap but had only dreamed it.

Lena squeezed his arm. 'It's going to be all right.'

They turned down Bedevere Road at the corner where his father had given a last wave when he returned to the front after a brief leave, his uniform and his kitbag and his gun, his arm raised, signalling his love to his son. *You're in charge now, son. Take care of your mother and your sister.* Robert, a small boy, sitting in the window of the flat, his face pressed to the glass, gazing at his father till the very last second, his heart stilled by his terror that he was never to see his father again, the nightmare of the telegram boy running up the stairs to their door. His dad! His deep puzzling love for him rendering Robert helpless. Now he was afraid of seeing him.

'There it is,' he said. And he pointed to where the dark brick three-storey block of flats stood four-square at the far end of the street facing the T-junction with Pendragon Road. Their old top-storey flat set in a mansard roof with three dormer windows overlooking the gardens below. Home. Flanked on either side by cottages. The arch of the central entrance facing them at the bottom of the hill like an open mouth, the street lined by mature elm trees, leafless now. 'My bedroom was the last window on the left,' he said. 'They'll be watching from the other two windows. Waiting for us. They'll be as nervous as I am.' He laughed. 'I've often imagined this.'

Lena said, 'But it's beautiful. You said you lived in a housing commission estate. This is lovely.'

The streets were deserted. No gangs of boys. No broken fences with palings missing. No broken windows. No rubble of bombed-out houses, their old adventure playgrounds. The bomb damage repaired long ago, the pallor of the new bricks beside the old, the lives of the dead forgotten. Gardens with the wintry remains of flowers and shrubs, privet hedges neatly clipped. One or two cars parked by the kerb.

They reached the bottom of the hill and went in through the arched entrance and climbed the stairs. Two flights of concrete stairs to each floor, the iron handrail freshly painted black, the stairs scrubbed. His vivid dream of jumping from the top step of the last flight and finding himself held up by a magical force, floating gracefully to the bottom. A dream repeated again and again when he was five or six years of age. And every time he reached that top step, the dizzying temptation to make the leap.

This was that same place. But it was not that place. *Home* was somewhere else. This was the place of his childhood in fact only. And he understood, with a sudden conviction, that facts were not enough for reality.

His father opened the door to them. Behind him the small entrance hall where they had hung their coats and taken off their shoes. Coats hanging there now in the shadows behind his father, the smell of the cloth. Except for his receding grey hair his father looked unchanged, the pallor of his skin unlined, tight across his broad forehead. That memory had been correct. His resemblance to Martin was safe. It was true. Robert was glad he hadn't made it up. His memories were not to be entirely contradicted by the facts. He said, 'Hi, Dad.' He hesitated, wondering for an uncertain moment whether to embrace him and seeing at once that it was not on. His father had never been one for displays of affection. 'This is Lena, Dad.'

'How are you, son?' They didn't shake hands. 'Your mother saw the pair of you coming down Bedevere Road.' His dark Glasgow working man's brogue had not softened. He would never be English.

Lena stepped up to him and kissed him on the cheek. They embraced each other warmly and without hesitation. Robert had never seen his father do this, not even with his mother. Lena took his arm and they went ahead of Robert into the front room. Robert followed them. It was the room he remembered.

His mother was standing by the sideboard, one hand to the edge of the polished wood, her glasses glinting in the light from the windows. The flat had always been bright, even on the gloomiest days, sitting up there above the other houses. Robert went up to his mother and put his arms around her, and they held each other. She said softly in his ear, 'I had a feeling you were here. I just knew I was going to be seeing you soon.'

He was moved to find that her smell was still the pure and lovely smell of his mother. His mother's smell! They stepped away from each other and she laughed, perhaps so as not to cry, the emotion of the moment going through her. He had never seen her cry. She looked at his father and Lena, his father helping Lena off with her coat. 'Before you know it,' his mother said, 'he'll be wanting to show her his London and the countryside of Kent.'

Lena came over and she and Robert's mother embraced briefly. His mother squeezed Lena's bicep. 'You're looking a bit peaky, darling. Is it the travelling? You could do with a bit of building up. Is he not feeding you properly?' She was as direct with Lena as Birte had been with him at their first meeting, assuming the right to an immediate intimacy. Robert realised he'd been wrong to think she would be nervous at the idea of meeting his wife. His mother's North Country accent had mellowed, but there was still a touch of Irish in it somewhere, a faint echo of her own mother and her own distant beginnings, something yet cherished by her from her childhood.

Lena said, 'What a beautiful room.'

Robert experienced a little thrill of delight to hear her approving of his parents' style, the warm homeliness of their living room. The gas fire was burning. 'You did away with the coal fire then?' he said.

'We had to,' his mother said. 'The Council changed them over when the new regulations came in. Do you remember the pea-soupers? You got bronchitis every winter. Do you still suffer with your chest these days?'

'I've never had the flu since I left.'

'Keeping your father's chef's hats white was a terrible struggle. Everything was black with the soot in those days. I'll make us a cup of tea.' She gave him a private smile and squeezed his hand and went out to the kitchen. She did not close the door. He didn't feel it would be quite the right thing to join her, but he wanted to. There were things he wanted to talk about with her. He was sure his father wouldn't mind being left on his own with Lena.

The sun had broken through and was shining into the room, the leafless branches of the old elm tree outside the window black and still. A little wave of sadness went through him. It was all there: the polished sideboard with the ticking clock, the big square table in the middle of the room, covered with a Persian rug, the china cabinet with its shelves of treasures his father had collected over the years—the Cadogan teapot and the precious old porcelain coffee set with the paintings on it, and the Chinese jade pieces, the collection of little Japanese ivories, old men carrying burdens of one kind and another. It was all still there, their lives going on with it. And the secret drawer in the bottom of the china cabinet where his dad had kept his collection of the erotic drawings by the Frenchman Félicien Rops. His mother's silent toleration of them. Were they still there? And the bookshelves over to the left of the fire, filled with his father's collection of poetry and literature, Burns and the Glasgow poets, the set of Scott's Waverley novels, all read and reread and loved nearly to death over the years. And the pictures around the walls. His father's own watercolours and the two precious sketches by John Sell Cotman, his father's hero and idol, picked out with his quick eye one grey morning at the Bermondsey market.

Robert watched his father taking a folio from the shelves to show to Lena. His dad said over his shoulder, 'Brian Rush went to America. He married a beautiful girl from Los Angeles.'

Brian had lived next door. He and Robert were friends off and on. Never anything serious. He was an only child and was never one of the gang out in the street or on conker raids. A studious loner, so he had seemed then, always welcomed into the front room by Robert's father, the two of them sharing books. Brian's dad was a gloomy man with massive hands, like the hands of a giant. A stoker on the night shift at the gasworks.

'Good for him,' Robert said. He had not really liked Brian all that much.

'When his father died, Brian came home and took his mother back to the States with him.' A pause for effect. Then, 'You weren't the only one who left the estate.'

Robert said, 'Are you still painting?'

Lena said, 'I'd love to see your drawings, Mr Crofts. Robert has told me how much he used to love going into the country with you for the day and sketching and painting.'

Robert caught his father's eye and they exchanged a look in which there was for an instant a clear grain of that love of those old innocent days, the fleeting edge of its wing brushing them both, something not of the present but composed of memory, like a fleck of gold in a fast-running stream. His dad had hoped then that Robert would become an artist, inspired by his influence. Robert might have told him that the skill had saved him from despair when he drew his picture of the fighting man. But how to tell his father that? The desperation that had gripped him then, it was not something for telling.

Robert pulled out a chair and sat at the table and watched the two of them. His father wasn't going to ask him about his writing. And probably not about anything else. His father was in his own world, showing Lena his books. A greater mystery in the books for him than was in his own drawings and paintings. Many of his books were early editions and he was proud of them. She was admiring the 1820 first edition of Keats's *The Eve of St Agnes*. Robert knew the book well. His father was looking at Lena with admiration. Robert heard him say, 'It's yours, Lena.'

'Oh no!' she said. 'I couldn't possibly take it, Mr Crofts. It's precious. It's your book. You treasure it.'

Robert knew she had no hope. The book was hers now, just as Frankie's hat had become John's in that terrible instant. Unlike that one, this gift was happening sweetly. His father was smiling. There was still something handsome in his looks. He touched Lena's shoulder. 'I've enjoyed it for many years. Now it's yours.' This was his delight, to give precious gifts to people he loved. And he had decided to love Lena. Robert saw it. Robert knew what love was in his father and what the refusal of it was.

She looked at the book in her hands, then she leaned and kissed him on the cheek. The two of them engrossed in the delicate moment of it. Robert was proud of him. The sacredness of gifts for him, sealing friendships and speaking of love without ever needing the words for it. That was the way it had always been with his father. He was happy to see his beloved volume in her hands.

'I'll treasure it always,' she said. She turned to Robert. 'Look what your father's given me!'

Now that Robert saw him standing there being himself, the man and not his memory of the man, Robert knew that as far as his father was concerned his son had done what he had done 'out there' and that was his son's own business and there the matter ended for him. There was to be no enquiry into his successes or failures. And despite his father's love of literature, or maybe because of his excessive reverence for the authors of the past, the idea that his son hoped to become a writer would not greatly impress him.

Sitting there at the old table where they had eaten their meals together when he was a child, watching Lena and his father going through the books, Robert relaxed. He knew it was all right. He would thank Lena for making him visit them.

His mother came out from the kitchen. She was carrying the tea things on a black lacquered Chinese tray with pink and white peonies painted on it. There was a seed cake on a flowered oval plate. He said, 'I remember that little plate, Mum.' She set the tray on the table and touched the plate with her fingers. 'You gave it to me.' He had no memory of giving her the plate. 'There's not a chip on it,' she said proudly and she looked at him and put her hand on his. 'It's lovely to have you home with us.'

She pulled out a chair and sat down. 'Do you get parrots in Melbourne? I'd love to see parrots flying around in the trees. I always feel so sorry for them sitting in their cages at the zoo, their little shoulders all hunched up with the cold. I always think they are asking me to help them. Their eyes are so intelligent.' She looked at him. 'Do you get them?'

'We do, Mum. Yes, lots of them. They fit in very well with us. Do you think your people might have originally come from an island somewhere with parrots in the trees?' He was seeing how exotic she was. As a child, to his eyes she had just seemed normal, herself; now he was noticing her olive skin, her raven hair, still without a trace of grey, her dark eyes. She was small and light-boned and she was beautiful. He said, 'You must have had romantic dreams of travel yourself when you were young. Didn't you? Before you met Dad?'

'I wanted to go to South America. One of the sisters in the convent in Chantilly was from Peru. She was beautiful and mysterious and we all loved her. I would have joined the order and gone with her to Peru if she'd asked me to. Did I tell you in one of my letters that I revisited the convent at Chantilly last year? Sister Clementina was still alive. She remembered me. I sat with her in her room and we held hands. She was ninety-four.' She laughed with the pleasure of the memory. 'My French came back to me. It was like being a girl again.'

He said, 'You look younger talking about it, Mum.'

'Your father would stay at home if it weren't for me.' Her eyes were alight with a mischievous intelligence that he remembered from the days of the Blitz. He envied her the lightness of her touch with memory and experience. 'I love travelling!' she said. 'You got your wanderlust from me, you know.' She laughed again. 'Do you mind my saying that?'

'Of course not. It's lovely to hear you say it. We always loved each other. All of us. Didn't we?'

'We did, darling. We did. It's a pity your brother's away on school camp. They say it's a challenging winter hike with his schoolmates in the Yorkshire Dales. He'll be sorry he missed you.'

'I would have liked to see him,' Robert said. 'How's he getting on at school?' A school camp was an unheard-of idea when he was a boy. His brother was obviously not the hoodlum of the streets that Robert and his mates had been, but inhabited a world far richer in possibilities than the world they had known.

'Do you have to go back to Australia so soon? Lena said in her letter you'd be leaving on Tuesday.'

Lena and his father came over and sat down. Robert's mother poured the tea and handed the cake around. He didn't answer her question and she didn't ask it again. She and his father wouldn't probe.

Lena was enjoying talking to his father about his drawings. Robert watched her crumbling her piece of cake and pushing the pieces around on her plate, trying to make it look as if she'd eaten some of it. He had hoped she would eat normally in the company of his parents. She caught him looking at her and frowned. He looked away.

His mother still had lovely skin, her arms smooth and unblemished, just as he remembered her when he was a boy. The post-war gloom and poverty that he had left behind in Downham had vanished, however. There was no trace of it. This was a different world. He'd had no part in the making of it, but had been imagining all these years that everything had remained as it had been the day he left England.

Watching his wife and his father become friends, he was glad it had happened this way. He was grateful to Lena for persisting. He had not dreamed his parents' love for him. Writing was the real leap for him now. The leap from which in the end the quality of his own reality must be shaped. Now he must give substance to that dream.

When they were leaving the flat, Robert's father held him tight against his body and said with emotion, 'I love you, son.'

Robert was too moved to reply. He and Lena went down the stairs. On the top step of the last flight Robert paused. Lena turned to him. 'What is it?'

'It's nothing,' he said.

She said with astonishment, 'You're crying!'

33

My dear old cat Gus died last night. I got up to take a pee and he was a dark shadow lying inert on the mat inside the back door. I spoke to him. He didn't move. I bent down and touched him, speaking his name. 'Hey, Gus, old boy!'

Later this morning I wrapped him in my best towel and carried him out to the apple tree and dug a hole for him there. I wept helplessly as I placed him in the hole, his little head sticking out of the folds of the towel, his once-beautiful eyes sunken back into his skull and clouded over. He was eighteen. When I stood up abruptly after shovelling the earth in on him, I felt dizzy and rested my back against the scabby bark of the old apple tree with my eyes closed, waiting for the dizziness to pass. I was seeing the bloodied towel in the hands of the men who had visited Lena all those decades ago; two men and a bloodstained towel, something I had not seen with my own eyes but which had been reported to me by our landlord, Donald Tree, vividly before me now, an image from memory and imagination, the past touching my emotions with its savage presence, as it will.

It was the only child Lena ever had. She was never again to fall pregnant.

I stood there with my back to the tree, thinking back to that time. I had scarcely known her. We had scarcely known each other. What kept us together? It isn't enough to say love. We clung to each other. There was never any suggestion from either of us that we would not go on together. We must have still believed in a future life together. We never talked about her abortion. She refused to. Not having been with her that afternoon when it happened, I was haunted by my imaginings of how it must have been for her. I always felt slightly sick whenever I tried to imagine the actual event there in that bed in the house in Chislehurst, her terrible vulnerability, her thin body being violated by those two anonymous men with their instruments and bloodied towels. She told me nothing. She hid it deep inside herself. She kept it so strictly to herself that I sometimes wondered if it had really happened. I said to her once, 'Do you sometimes think the abortion never really happened?' She gave me a peculiar look, an expression of pain in her eyes that rebuked me and made me uncomfortable.

I ask myself now, did I wrap Gus in my best towel as some kind of unconscious attempt to pacify my guilt about that time? My guilt, not for the commission of a crime, but for my lack of empathy for Lena's situation. I am certain that the abortion of her only child was a life sentence for Lena. I am sure now that she not only never forgot it, but spent much of her subsequent life dealing with it in a richly creative way that projected the experience outwards and made of it something physical and real, something that satisfied her deep need for the private expression of an aesthetic value to her existence.

The abortion was to become a determining experience for Lena. Unlike me, she could never have imagined it hadn't happened. She needed it. In a way that I could not then have understood, she kept the abortion of her child as a secret treasure within herself—almost as though she kept the child within her, a permanent state of gestation, her control of her thin body and her child a weapon of defence against the world. The experience made her the woman she eventually became, and of course in a way it also unmade her. The loss of her only child was to become the central contradiction at the heart of Lena's art. She never attempted to share with me this central truth. She didn't want to share it. It was her own private reality. She understood something essential through the pain of it. So it stayed with me as a thing that was incomplete, unfinished and puzzling, a thing I had to deal with in my own way if I were ever to quiet the ghost of it within myself. And of course my way is to write of such things.

I gave Gus's fresh grave a last look then walked across the lawn and put the spade back in the shed. It had begun to rain, a soft rain from a grey sky, no wind, a cool stillness over the garden. The grass would soon grow over him. I went into the house and made my morning coffee, the sound of the steady rain on the roof. A good day to be inside. I carried my coffee into the warm study and sat down here at my desk and began to write. It is what I have always done, either to avoid the pain of these memories or to better understand them. I'm not sure which it is. Or is it simply to hide? To distract myself? To secure my inner peace against the torrent of memory? For there is something ruthless about old age. Old age unseals the buried memories of our past and refuses to allow us to forget. In old age those things we refused to think about in our youth because they were too uncomfortable come out of the grave and stand before us and demand their right to a place in the story of our lives. They are not polite, as they were when we were young and strong, and are no longer obedient to our refusal. In old age, with death closing in upon us, we lose our power over these troubling memories and they command us. The tables are turned. Deal with me now, or go to your grave unshriven! That is the choice we're given.

I sipped my coffee and considered the moment when Lena and I returned to Australia from England. She had succeeded in reducing herself to a figure resembling one of Giacometti's fleshless standing nudes. Ironically, her strong jawbone was more prominent than it had been when she'd first begun to worry about it at Red Bluff, telling me that night in a panicked voice of her fear that her face was getting fat—the first sign of the transformation that was to take place in her, had we only known it then. I was a young man, and when I saw her naked I felt the shock of loss, a keen nostalgia for the beautiful sexy young woman I'd first met and married. And a terrible regret at being cheated of the sexual pleasures that I was certain were my due. That she had become pregnant to some unknown man on that cargo boat played tricks with my mind. And yet—and it is important for me to find a way of saying this—there was even then in the extreme refinement of her physical being a fascination that she had not possessed before. A fascination that was only partly sexual; a perverse intensity that both denied and invited sexual thoughts. I believe my father was entranced by this, the absent, ethereal quality of her smile, and would have liked to paint her portrait. This quality seemed to be a compensation for her loss of flesh, and she appeared to enjoy an obstinate sense of advantage in starving herself. It was a source of power for her. When she thought herself unobserved she often wore a private knowing smile. It was impenetrable. If I spoke of it she denied it. What she had or wanted was an advantage over reality. That is how it seemed to me then. Not just control over herself: an advantage over her embodied self. Just as I was to find an advantage over reality in the world of my writing, where memory and imagination became indistinguishable from one another. And it is also true that I was never able to share this with her. In some ways she and I were a matched pair, and perhaps it was our recognition of this that kept the bond between us so strong.

I see these things now with the wisdom of hindsight, but at the time my response to Lena's condition was entirely conventional. I repeatedly tried to convince her to see a doctor. She refused: 'I'm not ill.' She was so confident about this that I began to think perhaps she really wasn't ill but was attempting something I simply didn't understand, and which she herself was either unable or unwilling to speak to me about, and most probably also didn't fully understand, her fasting a response to an inner compulsion that she felt was right and necessary for her. The peculiar appropriateness of my father's gift to her of Keats's *The Eve of St Agnes*, in which the heroine starves herself—*goes supperless to bed*—in order to raise her sensitivity to a higher imaginative state. It all became part of Lena's claim on freedom—the hard road of it. I thought for a time it might kill her. And of course it might have killed her. She was testing the limits. And there was a period when I don't think she would have cared if it had killed her, and might even have felt some kind of satisfaction about it.

34

Their plane landed in Sydney in the middle of a hot and steamy summer day. The blast of damp heat struck them as they stepped from the plane and they knew at once they were in another country. Sydney was unknown to both of them and made them feel vulnerable and disoriented. They didn't know where to go. They knew no one and had nowhere to stay. They rented the first flat they looked at. It was on the top floor of a three-storey block of new yellow brick flats in the inner west suburb of Leichhardt. The block was so new the stairwell still smelled of fresh cement. None of the other flats in the block were let. They dragged themselves and their suitcases up the stairs after the agent. Behind them the heavy street door to the lobby slammed with a crash that made them both jump, their nerves tingling with fatigue and anxiety, a booming reverberation going through the empty building and making it shudder.

The door to the flat the agent showed them opened directly from the upper landing onto a room that was to be their living and dining and kitchen area all in one. The door to the bedroom and the tiny bathroom were off to the right of the living space. That was it.

Robert walked over to the far side of the room and looked out the only window. Below him was a car park, the roof of the agent's iridescent blue saloon shining in the fierce sun. Across the way an identical block of flats was being built, a yellow crane swinging a cement bucket through the air.

Lena said, 'We'll take it.'

Robert turned around from the window. She took her cheque book out of her bag. The agent gave her his pen and she leaned on the bench and wrote out a cheque for the bond and a month's rent in advance then signed the lease without reading it. She handed the cheque and the pen to the agent. He put a copy of the lease on the bench and placed the other copy, together with Lena's cheque, inside his black satchel. He thanked her and shook her hand and she thanked him and went to the door with him and shut it after him. She stood with her back against the door, her eyes closed. She opened her eyes and walked over to where they had set down their cases against the wall and arranged herself on the bare floor, as if this was going to be her camping spot. The floor was made of a pale false wood laid over a concrete base. It was hard and unyielding.

Robert said, 'You'd better unpack your coat and some clothes and put them under you.'

She didn't reply.

He stood looking down at her, this strange woman with whom he had chosen to spend his life. She was curled into herself, lying there on the floor beside their cases, her back to him. She sometimes frightened him. He didn't know what it was that kept them together, but he knew he would be hopelessly lonely without her. 'We've come this far together,' he said. He would write to Martin.

The thunder of a jet going over gaining altitude at full throttle made the door and the window rattle. He went out and down the stairs and staggered into the desperate glare of the roaring street. Crowds of people rushing along the footpath in both directions, the sun's glare blinding. He stood still, stunned by the heat and the white pulsing sky above him. He had meant to buy supplies and furniture and the things they would need: cups and knives and forks, towels and blankets . . . He could see the second-hand furniture store. It was a little way along the road. He had seen it from the taxi. A green awning casting the front of the store in black shade, edges and legs of pieces of furniture piled onto the footpath. He couldn't move towards it. His throat was thick with the pulse of his blood. The sky and the sun and the noise a scream in his head.

He was standing outside the second-hand shop. He couldn't remember walking there. A pale blue Olivetti portable typewriter sat in the centre of a wooden table in front of him. Someone had put a sheet of paper into the roller. Robert stepped into the deep shade of the shop's dense interior and stood in the dark, unable to make out any detail.

The man understood his needs perfectly. A table and chairs, a double bed, the table with the typewriter and the typewriter itself, a box of assorted cutlery, two thick mugs and a teapot, a mattress and plates and so on. It all went into the back of the ute and the man's son brought the things to the flat and he and Robert carried them up the stairs. Then Robert went out and bought food. He couldn't remember afterwards whether Lena went with him or if he went alone.

He set up the little table under the window with the typewriter at its centre and a straight-backed kitchen chair and a ream of foolscap paper and at nine o'clock that night he began to write. He was exhausted, hallucinating, desperate to enter his own reality. He could not take another moment of dealing with his life and the mysterious needs of his troubled wife. He slid into the safety of his own world at once and without effort, breathing gratefully the free air of it, the image of himself and Frankie waiting for him. He might have been writing with his eyes closed. Thinking it onto the page. It was his cure. His medicine. His drug. It was long overdue. He was oblivious to his surroundings. The writing burst upon him. He didn't struggle with it but let it take him and it rolled out ahead of him; he knew it, it was written in his heart. He didn't resist.

> The two of us sitting on our night horses watching the dawn, the sweet smell of the Mitchell grass drifting across the savannah, the cattle rousing from their night camp. Me and

Frankie, the pair of us, the jingle of our horses' bits. The relief riders coming out and greeting us softly. And we rode in and gave up the night horses. Frankie went to the blacks' camp and I squatted by the cook's fly and ate my damper and beans and the gristly piece of salt beef and I drank down the scalding black tea and I made a cigarette and smoked it. Frankie and I met up again on our morning horses and rode out to check the isolated billabongs along the anabranches of the river, and those mysterious gilgais way out on the plain, looking out for signs that they had been visited by cleanskin bulls—the wild mickies, as we called them. Those loner beasts hating us getting close to them in the open, and they turned to face us and Frankie rode in on the head of the beast and wheeled away and I slipped in behind and grabbed the young bull by the tail and wheeled away, dumping him in a cloud of dust. Which was what we were there for and we had our system for dealing with them. Just now we were enjoying having nobody there to second-guess our performance. Getting away from the camp and heading off on our own out onto the dry flood plain. That's what we liked to do. The cool morning silence of the whispering Mitchell grass. Nothing between us and the infinity of that vacant horizon line. Frankie and me squatting next to our horses by a small depression in the plain, a gilgai of his Old People, known to him in his bones. Our mounts with their heads down, loose-reined, bits clinking, sucking their fill of the same water we were drinking ourselves. The low morning sun glare off the shivering plain so intense we had pulled the brims of our hats down. Squinting out there towards that emptiness, the dizzying line between the land and the perfect emptiness

of the white sky—an absence inclining us to muse on our
own paltry existence. Specks we were, out there; ants to the
lords of creation. And we were compelled to look. If we did
not look, we felt the tug of that vacant horizon in our minds,
and sooner or later we turned and looked towards its
consuming vacancy, shocked again by the emptiness, the
secret it withheld from us. Early morning yet and that line
still a precise demarcation between the earth on which we
rode and the heavens that stood above us. By mid-morning
the horizon would be lost to a dancing pulse of heat haze. We
were done with drinking water and we shoved our quart pots
back into their leather pouches and buckled them and we
rolled smokes and lit them. The smell of our tobacco the
perfume of luxury to us, a comfort nothing else could
provide. Beside the gilgai a hard-grown mimosa bush,
a precious cluster of sweet-smelling blossoms on the single
spindly branch of it that was not dead, the rest fit only for
kindling. Besides the trampled Mitchell grass the old mimosa
was all that grew there on the rim of that gilgai. No other
shrub or tree, but a vast intimidating nothingness to a white
man like me, pressing its emptiness against my mind. Frankie
and me and our horses but a small detail of composition
beside that hard-grown mimosa hanging on to its remnant
life out there, alone in the wildness of the place, shedding its
sweetness to the wind, standing on the edge of the small
depression where a man or a beast might find a drink.
I asked Frankie how it was such gilgais came to be out there
on the plain. He looked at the standing water and said
nothing for some time. Then he said, 'Well, they are just here,
old mate.' And he looked at me and grinned. I knew he

would not tell me more. I did not ask him for more. I knew better than to do so. I was sure he harboured in himself a deeper and richer knowledge of the place but was forbidden by the law to speak of the sacred origins of such features, for all such things were sacred and had their stories, each part holding all the other parts in place. That much I knew. A web of belief of the country and its ways I would never share and had no wish to trespass on. The story belonging to Frankie. It was never to belong to me. My story something else, its pieces broken and dispersed, rootless. I knew enough of Frankie's country to know I knew nothing much of it. My respect for the richness of it lodged in my love of my friend. There was no deeper exchange to be had in it, only the distance of my willing ignorance against the calm intimacy of his knowing. In our friendship we had that between us. Even before Frankie and I rode back into camp the old men would have known if he had betrayed his place, and would have punished him for it according to their law. He rightly feared the old men and respected the law that bound him to them and to his country. Just how those old men would have known such a thing is beyond me. But I had seen it. Their knowing of things that were unspoken. The grim elder, the holder of the knowledge, a wrinkled and bearded old man who had never given my presence among them a second glance, his eyes deep set and twinkling in his black face sheened with sweat. A man resembling the trees and rocks themselves of his own country. A man entirely contemptuous of my momentary existence among his people. For him I was no more than a pale flickering at the edge of his vision. This same old man had predicted with eerie accuracy the

impending arrival of a mob of cattle from the west two weeks
before we saw the first sign of their dust way off across the
plain one chill morning as the sun was coming up. When
they drew close later that day a dozen silent blackfellas stood
off from the great piker bullocks they were driving. The old
knowledge man was the only one of Frankie's mob to venture
to speak with the newcomers in their own language. He
knew their language and knew where they came from and
how long they had been travelling without anyone ever telling
him these things. Those wild men sat their horses and stared
emptily through us and would not come alongside us on their
still mounts, their long hair and beards gleaming in the sun,
their horses unshod, iron-hooved beasts with eyes like the eyes
of their riders, seeing distance. Two white men with them,
brothers, whose speech I could not follow, their tones so
deeply bound in with the language of the blackfellas they
travelled with. Frankie said they were wild men and could
not be trusted. They were seeking permission from the old
man to come in to water their mob and move on through the
country. Those wild black riders did not smile or respond to
our friendly hand signals but stood off on their horses, silent,
watchful and aloof. An old man among them stepped his
horse up to meet our old man and they both got down and
squatted on the ground and talked, a curl of smoke rising
between them. It was a deep protocol beyond even Frankie's
understanding. I watched it unfold, mesmerised. That
meeting out there between those two old men troubling and
inspiring me. For I knew myself to be looking on at a dimension of existence I had never dreamed of. I was an invisible
stranger for those old men and counted for nothing with

them. When they were done and rose and climbed onto their horses and turned away from each other, the wild men eased their roany mob of old pikers along with no shouting or yelling but with just one sharp whip-crack parting the stillness of the air. They did not look back at us. We might not have been. We watched them until they and their dust merged into the mirage of distance and they became a dance along the skyline, intermittent and flickering, then gone. And they might never have been, except for the churn of mud in the long waterhole where their beasts had milled and drunk their fill—those slow, heavy old beasts, walking to the slaughterhouse; a silent mob with no cows bellowing for their calves, no frantic calves searching for their mothers, just defeated old pikers from the scrublands of the far west. Frankie told me later they were making for the railhead at Kajabbi, a spur line north of Cloncurry, where there were yards for loading beef cattle in those days before the road trains cut out the rail. They had been on the drove from the west for months. I did not ask him how they knew to navigate their way through this country that was strange to them and hundreds of miles from their homes. It was the kind of question only a fool would ask. But the fool in me wondered all the same how they did it, finding their way from waterhole to waterhole in that vastness where there were no mountain peaks or outstanding landmarks to navigate by, but only the infallible map of the stars at night. And what guide were the stars if you were seeking water for a thousand head of cattle? I could not even begin to guess the answer to such a question of life and death. Seeing those two old men squatting on the ground, their patient mounts standing loose-reined behind them, I experienced an acute sense of having no place in their country or in the meaning of their lives, and if Frankie had not been my friend and beside me I might have decided to leave and have done with that country right then . . .

Robert inscribed the truth of it in simple unadorned prose. His way of telling it an echo of the calm truth Frankie and he had known together in the vastness of that country, the silence and the stillness of the endless Leichhardt scrubs, a land where they themselves became the substance of their own dreams, the mirage of their steady advance across the plain dancing on the vacant skyline, the yellow cloud of fine dust rising above the shuffling herd. It was where the story lay, waiting within him for the telling. The poetry of it. If Frankie were ever to read it, it must be for him the way things had been for both of them. The abrasion of his life, the knowledge of injustice in the conditions of his days and in the days of his mob, the corrosive cruelty of their lot as outcasts in their own country, their terrible loss of dignity and freedom in the face of the white man's indecent overlordship. Robert heard the sad condition of injustice as the steady background hum of his story. The subdued anger and the quiet decency of the black stockmen in the face of their humiliation.

35

———

Robert loathed having to emerge from the zone of his writing and re-enter the world of the flat and Lena and their daily needs. The two worlds did not know one another and had no desire to know one another. And when the world outside his storytelling insisted and broke in on him he was irritated and angry and had no patience to attend to it but thrust it aside and went on with his work. He ceased to listen. He didn't hear her when she called him. And at last she no longer called but stayed in bed and shut the door. There was no room in him to care. He didn't care. So he didn't see her downward drift over the weeks and months and had no sense of its seriousness. Or if he did have some sense of it, he was unable to respond. He cared only for his writing. It was for him a trance of days that became weeks and months. He was drunk with it. Drugged. Nothing could distract him. He was an addict. And when he was not writing he was nervous, agitated, anxious to get back to it.

Each morning he woke early and got out of bed, showered, dressed, ate a bowl of cereal, made tea and lit his first cigarette.

Then he sat down at the typewriter and wrote, following the richly layered prompts of his memory and imagination. And at six-thirty each evening he got up from the desk and walked to the university and cleaned the offices in the Woolley Building. While he was vacuuming the floors and emptying the wastepaper baskets and manoeuvring the polisher along the hallways, the story of Frankie and himself was tense in his mind. If someone spoke to him, he was listening to his own story and failed to hear them. He was blissfully in thrall to the seductive illusion of creating his meaning through writing. Deferring reality. Deferring his duties and his worldly worries. His responsibilities neglected. He didn't question his purpose in writing. He didn't pause to measure the value of what he was doing or reflect on the harm or the good that might come from it. He was seduced and did not resist.

Robert's lifelong faith in writing as the source of his salvation was established in him during those weeks and months. The dimension without time won him. He was more alone with people around him then than he was while he was writing. He carried afterwards no memory of what Lena had been doing during that period. When he thought about it there was nothing there. He had no sense of her during that time.

So the crisis, when it came, was for him sudden. He was innocent of its approach. It was so sudden he left a sentence unfinished and never returned to it. As usual, when he got home from his cleaning job that evening he went straight to his table by the window and began to write out the scenes that had been

entertaining him while he was at work. Her cry, which he realised had been repeated, eventually claimed his attention and he
stopped typing and listened. He didn't hear it as a human cry
but as the feeble sounds of an injured animal. When it came
again it sent a chill through him. The instant he stood up he
realised, with a shock of the obvious, that it was Lena making
that desperate sound.

He went over and cautiously opened the bedroom door. The
light was on, the same naked bulb hanging from the centre of
the low ceiling that hung there the day they moved in and which
Lena had objected to and said he must get a shade for. She had said
it was squalid. He remembered her using the word with distaste;
it flickered in his mind now as he stood at the door looking in at
her lying in their disordered bed, the sheets unwashed, the room
dense with their smell. His own familiar staleness and the indefin-
able quality of Lena's lonely struggles throughout the days of his
neglect. The heat of summer was long past. She was clutching
the blanket around her chin in just the way she had clutched the
covers after her abortion. With a shock of guilt he saw her as a
lonely, frightened, lost young woman, a woman aged before her
time. Her hair wet with sweat. The hairs sticking darkly to her
forehead and the pillow, her cheeks hollow, her skin yellow and
tight across the bones of her face. She stared at him, her mouth
open, her eyes huge, filled with fear and panic. Without a word
she pulled the covers down and lifted her nightdress. Her stomach

was bloated and tight, her belly button like a small mouth, twisted out of shape by the pressure.

He said, 'Jesus Christ! Look at you! I'll get a doctor.'

When the doctor arrived he curtly asked Robert to leave the bedroom. It was after midnight. Robert stood outside the bedroom door trying to hear what was being said, but the doctor was speaking softly and Robert could only catch the odd word. The doctor was in there with her for at least a quarter of an hour. Robert was filled with intense feelings of guilt and remorse and fear. With him she'd lost everything familiar to her: her friends, her job and her colleagues, even her piano and her love of music. That was how he saw it. He blamed himself.

The bedroom door opened. Robert stepped away as the doctor came out.

The doctor closed the door behind him and only then turned to face Robert. He was a tall man, in his mid-forties, clean-shaven, fit-looking, lightly tanned, dressed in a linen suit and tie, his bag in his hand. His manner was cold and disapproving, his tone severe, even contemptuous. 'Listen to me, young man,' he said, keeping his voice low, speaking slowly and with deliberation. 'If you don't get a proper job and smarten up and lead a decent life your wife may not get over this.' He waited. Robert said nothing. 'Do you understand what I'm saying to you?'

Robert felt humiliated standing there in front of this man. The doctor's attitude confirmed his self-doubt. He was incapable of defending himself.

'Your wife has told me the whole story,' the doctor said. 'She tells me you have a university degree. I want you to give me your assurance that you will get a job, and that you will look after her and begin to lead an orderly and normal life.' He waited.

Robert understood that for the doctor his neglect of Lena and his obsession with his writing were some kind of unspeakable perversion. He said, 'All right. I hear you. I'll get a proper job as soon as I can.'

The doctor stared at him for a long time, a look of dislike in his brown eyes. The malevolence of his gaze. He used a term then to describe Lena's condition, which Robert forgot at once. Robert stood before him, angry, ashamed and confused, miserably aware of the doctor's contempt.

The doctor shook his head, as if their situation defied belief. 'My God! People like you . . .' He left it at that.

Robert let him out and watched him going down the stairs. He wanted to yell after him, 'Fuck you! You wouldn't have a fucking clue!' What did this man know of them?

The foyer door crashed closed behind him, sending its booming reverberation through the sleeping building. It was after one in the morning. Robert closed the door and went into the bedroom and sat on the side of the bed. He took Lena's hand. Her skin was clammy, her fingers limp.

She looked up at him. 'I'm dying, aren't I? What did he tell you?' She started to cry, small helpless gulping sobs rising up from her chest. Her breathing was congested and he had a dread that she might have an asthma attack.

He said firmly, 'No, you're not dying! Okay? Stop panicking!' He squeezed her hand. 'He said I had to get a proper job. And I will.' He felt anything but confident of this, but he said it firmly and with conviction. 'You mustn't panic. It doesn't help.' He tidied the strands of hair that were lying across her face and he bent down and kissed her forehead. 'It's going to be okay. We'll live differently. I've been selfish. I'm sorry.'

She said, 'No, it's not you. It's this place. It's like a prison.'

He looked around the barren bedroom, their dirty clothes on the floor, a wet towel in the bathroom doorway. It must have looked squalid to the doctor. Robert realised he'd never really taken any notice of it.

They looked at each other. 'You're a crazy girl, you know. But I do love you. Why is that?'

She smiled and wiped at her tears with the sheet and took hold of his hand again. 'I need you,' she said. He thought she was going to start crying again. 'Promise you'll never leave me.'

He wanted to remind her that it was she who had left him and that if she hadn't left him they wouldn't now be in this position but would be living comfortably in the house at Red Bluff. 'I'll never leave you,' he said. It was true. 'I promise.' She held tightly onto his hand.

'You left me when you started writing your book,' she said. 'I've been lying here for months being tortured by that incessant tapping out there on your typewriter. You've hardly glanced at me. I thought I was going mad. If I tried to talk to you, you just weren't there. You didn't listen.' She lay there looking at him. 'You're back! It's so good to have you back.'

'Has it really been that bad?' It was true, he supposed. He hadn't given her a thought. He might as well have been on the moon. It couldn't all be his fault, though, could it? It occurred to him that it was only after her asthma attacks ceased and her mother had died that she'd begun worrying about her face getting fat and had started fasting. Wasn't that the problem? Her fasting? Her physical weakness? He felt suddenly exhausted and couldn't think about it anymore. He stood up. 'Do you want a cup of tea?'

'Yes, please. And it's not your fault. I'm responsible for me. I've always been responsible for me.'

'Okay. Of course you are.' But it was too large a claim for her to be making at that moment. 'Are any of us really wholly responsible for ourselves?'

'It's no one's fault,' she said. 'That's all I meant.'

➤

He slept soundly for the rest of the night and woke late. The early jets going over hadn't bothered him. He asked Lena how she was feeling. She said, 'Much better, thanks. What are you going to do?' She looked anxious when she asked him this. He said, 'I'll go and see the people at the university appointments board.'

'You don't have to do this.'

He looked at her. 'Yes I do. We can't go on like this.' He waited a moment, but she didn't say anything, just patted his hand, as if to imply there was nothing to be done.

He got up and went out into the living room and put the kettle on. He glanced guiltily at the pile of manuscript sitting on the table beside his typewriter, a half-filled page still in the roller. The thought of it made him feel he wasn't yet properly facing up to his responsibilities. But he wanted to go to it all the same. Thinking of his writing now, at this moment, wasn't it like thinking about making love to another woman when your wife was ill in bed? He didn't care what it was like. He wanted to be with his writing.

He took in her tea and picked up the dirty clothes and the towel and had a shower and a shave and put on a clean shirt and his suit and tie and he went in to the university appointments board offices and asked their advice. They suggested he apply for a graduate research position with the Commonwealth Public Service in Canberra. 'They're looking for graduates at this time of year.' Like orchardists, he thought, looking for seasonal fruit pickers in the autumn. Well, okay, I'll go and pick fruit in Canberra if that will save Lena. He filled in the forms and went home to the flat and told Lena what he'd done. She got up and sat at the table in the living room. She said, 'And I'll try to eat properly. We must do this together, you and I. We must find a proper way to live.'

36

Robert received his letter of appointment a week later and the following morning they walked out of the flat. They took with them a couple of suitcases and abandoned the rest of their things: the bits and pieces of second-hand furniture, the cutlery and plates and cups, their joyless bed. When Lena was already out on the landing, he took a final look around. They were putting behind them the failure they had made of Sydney. Abandoning a poor, half-hearted attempt at a life. And perhaps that was why he didn't take the manuscript of *Frankie*. He saw it sitting there beside the typewriter, and he wanted to go over and pick it up. But he didn't. His legs didn't take him across the room. Instead, he slammed the door behind him and joined Lena on the landing and took her arm. Going down the stairs, an image of the half-filled page sitting in the Olivetti's roller was a vivid icon in his eye, a silent scream in his skull. The manuscript of *Frankie*, paused in mid-stride. Was he abandoning writing forever? He didn't ask. He didn't want to know. He was doing what he was doing.

On the street he hailed a cab and asked the cabbie to take them to Central Station. At the ticket office the woman laughed at his request. 'There's no such thing as a Canberra train, love,' she said. 'The train doesn't go to Canberra. You can get a coach or you can get the train to Goulburn then catch the bus to Canberra. Most people fly.' He didn't believe her—surely there had to be a train to the capital of Australia—but the man in the queue behind him said, 'She's right, mate. There's no train to Canberra.'

He bought tickets for the coach. He picked up a packet of sandwiches, two Granny Smith apples and two takeaway teas at the kiosk. An hour later they were in the coach threading its way through the labyrinth of inner-city streets towards the highway. The man across the aisle from them said, 'We're a band of pilgrims going to a new frontier.' They all laughed and his girlfriend hit him on the arm and told him not to be silly. But Robert thought he had something. Lena and he weren't the only travellers who knew nothing about their destination. Whatever else, and despite the bliss and the pain of *Frankie*, the way they had done things in Sydney had not been right. There had to be a better way.

He insisted Lena have the window seat. She soon dropped off to sleep in the warmth, her head against his shoulder. He could smell her hair, the shampoo she'd used that morning. He ate the sandwiches and one of the Granny Smiths and smoked a cigarette. Lena slept till they pulled in for a refreshment break. She sat up and rubbed her eyes as children do. He said, 'How are you feeling?' She looked out the window, then turned to him, an expression of joy in her eyes. 'God, I'm just so glad to be out of that flat! That place was killing me. Let's get off with the others and have a cup of tea and stand in the sun for a minute. I want to feel the sun on my face.'

They got out and stood in the sun. He wanted to tell her the Leichhardt flat hadn't been killing him but was where he became a writer. He wanted her to know he had not been dying there, but coming alive. But he didn't tell her. It would have had the feel of boasting about another lover.

She astonished him in the cafe by eating a coffee scroll with her cup of tea. When they were back in their seats on the bus and humming along the highway again, she turned and looked at him, her gaze thoughtful. She tucked her arm firmly in his and said, 'I think part of our trouble is that I need other people more than you do.' She set his hand in her lap. 'You don't seem to need other people at all.' She smiled. 'It's okay. I don't mind. I love you the way you are.'

He said, 'I don't need people. It's true.' He was silent then, thinking. 'Everything you do affects me,' he said.

She kept hold of his hand in her lap and they looked into each other's eyes and neither spoke. She leaned and kissed him on the lips then turned away and looked out the window at the landscape rushing by—golden paddocks, a scatter of pale sheep, empty clouds standing in the sky, low wooded hills in the distance. The paddocks daubed with the shadows of the clouds. Time made visible. He could have stayed on the bus forever, postponing his future.

➤

Robert took up his appointment as a research officer in the education section of the Department of External Territories. The department was in a ten-storey building opposite a large open space covered in mowed grass and a dispersal of trees. Behind the building there was a car park. Each floor of the building was crowded with hundreds of people sitting at desks in open-plan offices. He was determined to fit in and make the best of things.

He was on the seventh floor and his desk was beside a window through which he had a view over the open grassland with its orderly trees. In the distance there was a hill with a radio tower on top of it. A red light on the very tip of the radio tower was flashing on and off at regular intervals. It was hard not to keep checking on that red light. It might have been warning him, and the rest of the inhabitants of the capital, that something was going to happen soon—perhaps the pressure inside the hill was reaching a dangerous level and they should all clear out before it exploded. Every time he looked out at the red light blinking he half expected to hear a siren. But no sounds came from the outside. No traffic noise, no bird calls. No sound of the wind.

The people at the desks around him made him welcome and wanted to know where he'd come from. Everyone in the office, it seemed, except for the young woman who carried the files up from the basement and placed them on their desks and had been born in Canberra, was from somewhere else. Being from somewhere else, Robert found himself in the majority.

His boss was a Frenchman, Claude Debussy, an easygoing man with a gentle sense of humour. Robert thought he was joking when he introduced himself, but Claude Debussy was his real name. He set Robert the pleasant and interesting task of reading the history of educational reform and institutional design in the liberated African ex-colonies. Why not the history of Papua New Guinea? Robert asked him, since that was where the college they were planning was going to be built. But no, first it seemed they were to make themselves thoroughly familiar with the institutional failures, and the one or two meagre successes, of the newly independent African states. Robert soon learned that the same humiliating conditions that Frankie's mob endured had been suffered by all the indigenous peoples of the colonised world. The challenge was not only to overcome the problems of liberation itself, but to deal with the intractable evil of their old conditions under their white overlords, the stains of which, both moral and economic, had become too deeply etched into the shattered native cultures to be easily removed. Frankie and his mob weren't even halfway there yet.

There was virtually no public transport, so Lena bought a car. Everyone had to have a car in Canberra; it was a city designed for cars. She also found a house to rent, and rang Dr Eady and asked him to have some things sent up from Red Bluff, including furniture, her Rönisch and a selection of their books. She took a part-time job as a social worker at the Canberra hospital. They were glad to see her.

Robert watched her regaining her strength. Even putting on a little weight. And he saw that she was piecing together a commonplace life for them, 'I think it's time we had a dog,' she said one evening when he got home from work. 'We can go walking with it in the bushland round here.' She'd had a dog when she was a little girl. She wrote to Birte and posted the letter without showing it to him. This puzzled him but he didn't question her about it. He decided she was putting on a very good act, but he said nothing in case she saw through the act he was himself putting on. He feared they were tying knots too complicated to ever unravel again. The game was deep. He saw no alternative and stuck with it.

In his more optimistic moments he accepted cheerfully that he and Lena were just like everyone else, except that they didn't have any children. They were average middle-class people, in other words. He had joined *them*, as she had once accused him of attempting to do. He was being encouraged by his boss to believe he might rise to a senior position in the bureaucracy.

➤

They were sitting in their living room watching the effect of the sunset over the forested hills. The full-length windows looked out on the surrounding bush, with a distant view of the Brindabella Range. He was drinking beer and Lena had a cup of her weak black tea. Earlier she had been practising her scales. Neither of them had spoken for some time, mesmerised by the beauty of the evening, when she said, in a voice that was quiet and cautious, a tone in which provocation may have had a place, 'So why did you leave your manuscript of *Frankie* behind?'

He couldn't believe what he was hearing and must have looked startled, because she at once said, 'I'm sorry. I just thought, that's all . . .' She let it trail off.

He looked at her with shock, hurt and disbelief. He couldn't answer her. He was choked with sudden rage. 'You're asking me *why?*' It was his father's rage. It boiled up in him. She had fucked another man and that had scarcely touched him. This struck him like a hot knife in his chest. He stared at her. He could settle the question then and there. The voice in his head urged him, Get it done! Get it over with once and for all! Put an end to the pointless tyranny of this tortured marriage to this mad manipulative woman.

He stood up. He was trembling. He had to get out of the house before he killed her.

She said, 'Where are you going?' There was a touch of fear and excitement in her voice, as if she thought she might have pushed him too far this time, just to see what he would do, to test him, to find the limit of his forbearance.

He went out the door and slammed it behind him.

He walked into the darkness of the forest. He was breathing hard, his brain boiling with wild impossible thoughts. He hated her. He stood in the rustling night, the elaborate silence of the scrub, his heart pounding. He felt cheated. Betrayed. He'd believed they had made an unspoken pact of silence about abandoning everything in Sydney, including his dream of becoming a writer. The doctor had said she might not survive. Now she was thriving. With a pang of regret he realised he'd left his cigarettes on the coffee table. He could see the light of the house from where he was standing among the trees. He leaned against a tree and looked up at the clouds swimming past the early stars, a thin remnant of pink still visible in the sky. What was he going to do? He'd accepted his defeat as a writer. His sacrifice had been sincere. He had meant it. And he had meant to stick to it. He had believed they were doing it together. Hadn't she also given up her search for some special meaning to her life? She'd had the piano tuned and was talking about taking lessons again. She had settled, it seemed to him, for being the person she'd been brought up to be. Her distress in Sydney had frightened her. She just wanted to be normal again, the piano-playing social worker. A product of her mother's world. Or what were they doing here in Canberra if that wasn't the case? He was bewildered and angry. Hadn't she understood anything? Hadn't he given up his writing in mid-stride *for her*? Hadn't he talked himself into this heroic renunciation for her sake? He said aloud, 'Fuck her! I'll write *Frankie* again. It will be better this time. It will be stronger. I promise you!'

He stayed there among the trees for some time, leaning against the rough bark, listening to the night, the faint hiss of traffic along the wide Canberra boulevards at the bottom of the hill. He said, 'I'll be a bureaucrat and a writer. You'll see. I'll do both.'

He walked back to the house. He didn't have a key and had to ring the bell.

Lena opened the door at once. She looked worried.

He said, 'I'm going to write *Frankie* again.'

She said, 'I'm glad. I hoped you were going to say that.'

They made love again that night. Neither of them was unkind but both understood it wasn't going to work for them anymore. The lust was gone. Out the door and gone. A dry paddock between them and their private dreams of sex.

On the weekend they went together and bought an expensive new portable typewriter and a new desk and office chair and a pale pinewood bookcase and they set them up in the spare bedroom. And that afternoon he unpacked his books from the boxes Dr Eady had sent and set them in the shelves of the bookcase. Lena came and stood in the doorway and told him dinner was ready.

'It looks wonderful,' she said, and she went up to him and kissed him on the lips.

'Yes,' he said, looking around. 'It's not too bad, is it?'

'It's wonderful. Come and have your dinner.'

After dinner he went back into the spare room, which they were to call the study now, and he closed the door and sat at the desk and he smoked a cigarette and gazed through the uncurtained floor-to-ceiling windows into the dark mass of the trees over beyond the bare earth of the garden where the bulldozer had scraped off the vegetation so the house could be built.

He rolled a sheet of paper into the typewriter—it was a Helvetia, not an Olivetti. Lena was playing the piano. Scales. Her fingers running up and down the keys like a rabbit at a wire fence looking for a way out. He tapped out the title, *Frankie*. Why call it *Frankie*? It was himself too, wasn't it? He couldn't remember how he had begun. He thought hard but no image came into his mind. He stared at the paper in the roller with the title in the middle of it and said aloud, 'Frankie and me.' It sounded silly and made him feel embarrassed.

He smoked another of the tailor-made cigarettes that he had changed to. The tobacco was hot and dry in his throat and he got up and went out into the kitchen and fetched a beer from the fridge.

Lena was sitting on the little round stool at the Rönisch in the front room. She paused in her playing and smiled at him. 'How's it going?'

'It's going well.' He flourished the bottle of beer and went down the passage and into the study. He shut the door and sat in the office chair and drank the beer and smoked another cigarette and looked out the window into the dark.

How to start? Where to start? Where had he begun in Sydney? He hadn't thought about it then but had just started. It had started itself. He sat staring out into the night, drinking the beer and smoking the cigarette. He decided to write a summary, just setting out the various stages of the story with no detail. This happens and that happens, that kind of thing.

➤

On Sunday he went back into the study and sat at the desk. He heard Lena go out the front door. A while later she came back. She began playing the piano. The sound of the piano was loud and insistent and it was all he could think about. He went on with the summary of his story. A dead, mechanical exercise. The room was chilly. He would buy a heater. And maybe get some curtains. Magpies were finding things to stab at in the bare ground. He felt sick. When he got up to leave the study on Sunday evening he screwed up everything he'd written and decided to buy a wastepaper basket.

➤

On Monday morning he was glad all he had to do was to put on his suit and tie and go into the office and read about post-colonial life in Kenya. It had shocked him to discover over the weekend that his imagination couldn't be coerced, but could hide in its black hole and refuse to be enticed out into the open. It wasn't enough simply to want to write. Did he want to write? There had to be something else. Whatever that something else was, it was missing. He felt burdened and unhappy when he thought of the shiny green Helvetia waiting for him on his new desk in the spare room of their rented house on the hill at the edge of the forest, the red light blinking on the mountain, warning of the coming disaster.

After dinner he went into the study and sat on the floor next to the bookshelf and looked at Camus's *The Outsider*. It was a book that everyone had read at university. Where was the magic? He opened the book and read the first sentence: *Mother died today. Or, maybe, yesterday; I can't be sure.* It was all very straightforward. He read a couple of pages and was soon engrossed in the story and forgot to think about the words. He was confident there was nothing unusual or special about the writing. It was just ordinary words strung together. One simple sentence after another.

He took Lena's copy of *Jane Eyre* off the shelf and opened it. *There was no possibility of taking a walk that day.* He put the book back in its place and picked out Aldous Huxley's *Brave New World. A squat grey building of only thirty-four storeys.*

He lit a cigarette and leaned his back against the wall. All he had to do was write the story. Emboldened by this discovery, he got up and sat at the desk. He put a fresh sheet of paper in the typewriter and sat staring at it. The spirit in which he had written *Frankie* in Sydney was missing, and he was unable to conjure it up. He realised Lena had stopped playing the piano some time ago. Was she listening for the tick-tick of the Helvetia?

He had thought he knew how to write. He felt rebuked. It was as if he had returned to the home of an old friend and knocked on the door, and discovered his friend had left years ago without ever telling him. Nobody was home. Kenya. The Mau Mau. Jomo

Kenyatta. The Kikuyus' fight for freedom. That was real, the reports and histories he was reading in the office. He felt very lonely. Empty. He missed himself. Where was he? It was *him*. He was the friend who wasn't at home. Maybe this was a punishment. He smoked another cigarette and looked at his watch. It was nearly ten. He would leave the study at ten-thirty and Lena would say, 'When can I read something?'

37

The weeks became months and Robert became increasingly dispirited. Lena worried about him. But apart from that she seemed happy. She met work colleagues for lunch and coffee in Manuka and found a new piano teacher and she began to plant out the garden. She stopped asking when she could read some of his writing. He stopped writing. One night he stayed up till first light the next day writing a long letter to Martin. A confessional outpouring that went on for twenty pages. He told Martin the whole story, from the moment he had found Lena sitting on the steps in Perugia to his present state of despair. He shared with his older friend his agonisingly conflicted feelings about his abandonment of the manuscript in Sydney. The last sentence of the letter was just as simple as Camus's first sentence: *I've lost myself.*

He didn't post the letter, but kept it in a drawer in his desk. He was going to post it sometime. Then one day he took the letter out and read it. The self-pity disgusted him. He screwed it up and shoved it into his metal wastepaper basket.

Lena's new friends at the hospital were young women like herself, with private school and university backgrounds. She even found among them an association with her old Melbourne life. Lena practised her piano every evening and began going to concerts and recitals. He stayed home. He could see that the lie was working for her. She might even have begun to believe in it. And the more he saw her finding her way, the more lost and desperate he felt. He hid it. His own lie he knew to be too deep to ever become a reality for him. He started opening a second bottle of red wine after dinner every evening instead of only on weekends. He watched them both eroding, as if he was someone standing outside looking in. Morally and spiritually, their lives were eroding. Although she remained frighteningly thin and continued to eat very little, no one ever commented on it. He supposed they assumed she'd always been like that. Men didn't ogle her, however, as they used to do when he first knew her. She had neutralised the issue of sex. They rarely attempted to make love. His torment was private. Outwardly he appeared to be sane. He had sex with married women they met at parties. 'Fuck me, Robert!' they said, pain and desperation in their voices, and he did. It was deeply dispiriting. The emptiness of it shamed him. He sought refuge in drink and meditated on the idea of suicide. In Japan it was an honourable way out.

On the downhill side, the house next door was a large rambling single-storey white stuccoed dwelling with deep timber verandahs. The man drove a green Peugeot and the woman drove a red Mustang. They kept to themselves. There were no local shops and no public transport. When Robert and Lena ran out of milk or cigarettes or bread they had to get in the car and drive to the nearest shops, which were several miles away. Their car was a two-tone Holden station wagon with a grey roof and cream sides. On the days Lena was working at the hospital, she dropped him off at the office on her way and picked him up again in the evening. On the other days he drove himself to work. The car smelled of the factory. Being behind the wheel made him want to do something dangerous. When he was alone in the car he had to restrain the urge to jam his foot on the accelerator and speed wildly along the roads, weaving in and out of the sedately moving traffic.

Time passed. The study remained unvisited.

One morning a new young man of around Robert's age began work in the office. During the morning tea break he came over to Robert's desk and introduced himself. 'Hi,' he said. 'I'm Phil. Phil McCrae.' They shook hands. He stood a while, leaning his hip against Robert's desk and looking out the window, telling Robert about himself. He said, 'You should come and have a drink with us and meet the crowd on Saturday.' Phil wrote his address on a piece of paper and handed it to Robert. He was tall with long dark hair, confident and comfortable with himself, the son of a local grazier. His family had been in the region for several generations, early settlers there long before the area became the site for the capital. He was working in the office part-time and was reading modern American literature at the university and planning to go to the States for further study once he had his master's degree.

He viewed the Canberra bureaucracy as a bit of a joke. Literature was his passion, he said, especially the modern American novelists. With a slightly embarrassed laugh, he confessed that his aim was to become a writer. A novelist, he said. He was a charming and very engaging kind of man.

Robert noticed that Phil gave the impression that when the time came for him to write his novels he would write them with ease and flair. He seemed to believe he was destined to be a novelist like one of his heroes: Hemingway or Henry Miller or Norman Mailer. He had a lovely open smile, his teeth as even and white as John Morris's teeth had been. He'd recently married a girl from Goulburn. He spoke with evident knowledge and enthusiasm about the native trees of the area and said Robert must go hiking and camping with them in the mountains. 'You should come cross-country skiing in the winter, you'd become a fanatic for it.' His enthusiasm was kindly and generous. Robert felt he was modelling himself on someone he'd read about in one of the books of his heroes.

Lena and Robert drove to Phil's place on the Saturday afternoon. On the way they stopped at a bottle shop and bought half a dozen bottles of beer. The house was a big weatherboard bungalow in the old suburb of Manuka, the guttering sagging and the paint peeling. There was the impression in this part of town of being in a real city, a failure of the perfection, a place with a human past.

The house was set back off the road behind a decaying picket fence that was being pushed out over the footpath by a tangle of cotoneaster bushes. A single spreading oak tree in the middle of the neglected lawn. A battered green Land Rover parked in the dirt drive.

They got out of the car and walked to the front door. It was open. Robert called, 'Hello!' and they went in. The hallway was narrow and dark. On the left side, against the wall, builder's planks resting on house bricks supported hundreds of paperbacks. There was a smell of incense and the sound of Indian music. They came out of the passage into a large open living area. The room was cluttered with books and journals, a pile of newspapers beside the fireplace, rugs on the bare timber boards, odd pieces of furniture, wine bottles and glasses, fruit in bowls, chips and nuts spilled across the rug, pictures on the walls. A large sofa with frayed red cushions in front of a fireplace, a red and green rug flung carelessly over its back. A young woman was sitting on the sofa. She was wearing a summer dress and sat easily with her legs crossed, open leatherwork sandals on her tanned feet. She turned and looked across at Robert and Lena. She didn't smile or say hello, and when Robert met her eyes she hesitated for an uncertain moment then looked away. She gave the impression of being alone. The smell of incense and dope.

Phil was standing by French doors looking out onto some kind of field or vacant block, the double doors wide open to the day, the afternoon sun shining through the tree into the room. There were people sitting around talking and drinking. Phil turned around and called a greeting and started over towards Robert and Lena. He was holding a glass of red wine and smoking a cigarette. Robert looked again at the woman sitting on the couch. She had her arms folded across her chest and was looking at an older man with a woven headband and long hair down over his shoulders who was lying back in some kind of canvas camp chair beside the fireplace. She was frowning, as if something had been said that upset her, or maybe she disapproved of the man lying back in the chair. It wasn't an ordinary camp chair of the portable kind that might be taken on a picnic, but was a superior-looking piece of furniture, solidly constructed from some dark wood such as teak. It made Robert think of English explorers in Africa in the nineteenth century who would have had porters to carry this kind of chair. The hippie with the coloured headband was smoking a joint. He wasn't passing it around.

Robert introduced Lena to Phil. Phil kissed her on the cheek and said, 'It's good to meet you, Lena. Robert's always talking about you.'

This wasn't true. Robert couldn't remember telling Phil any more than the bare fact of being married.

'Thanks for the beers, Rob. Put them down anywhere. Come and meet Ed. You guys will get on. Ed's a bit of a wild man. He's a very fine artist.'

Ed, the man with the headband, looked up at them from his English explorer's chair and grinned, his gaze on Lena. He said, 'Hi.' Two of his front teeth were missing, and there was a mischievous gleam in his blue eyes. His girlfriend, Mary, was sitting on the floor beside his chair hugging her knees and staring fixedly into the empty fireplace. She didn't look up or respond in any way to their greeting when Phil introduced her. Robert thought she was probably about sixteen years old, if that. Ed was somewhere in his middle thirties, maybe older. His face was lined and tanned, as if he spent a lot of time outdoors.

Phil introduced them to his new wife, the woman sitting on the sofa with her legs crossed, her smooth knees catching the sunlight and Robert's lustful attention. When Phil introduced them she looked directly into Robert's eyes, as if she meant to challenge or rebuke him. Her name was Ann. Her lips reminded Robert of the lips of the French actress Jeanne Moreau. She was wearing glasses, heavy dark frames with lenses as large as the lenses of Birte's glasses. They suited her. Around her neck she had a fine gold chain with a small locket or ornament that nestled in the hollow of her throat. Her hair was thick and dark and wavy. Phil said, 'Ann's completing a master's degree in French literature and teaching French part-time at the university.'

Robert said, 'Are you hoping for a scholarship to the States too?'

She asked Phil for a cigarette. He shook one out of the packet and lit it for her. She blew out smoke and turned to Robert. 'Does that surprise you?'

Phil laughed. Robert gathered that Phil expected him to be impressed with his wife. He *was* impressed with her, but not with her ambitions. He thought she was beautiful and sane and very sexy and had her life together, and he envied Phil.

A burst of laughter behind him made Robert turn around. Lena was perched on the arm of Ed's chair. Ed was looking up at her and grinning, the gap in his front teeth, his eyes alight with interest, a demonic dero. 'Lena and meaner,' he said. They both laughed.

'You guessed it, Ed. So watch yourself.'

He offered her the joint and she took it from him and put it to her lips and took a long slow drag on the thing, as if she knew what she was doing. Ed watching her, an expression of delight in his blue eyes. Robert wondered if he was seeing the Lena of the boat journey to Italy. A stranger to him. She seemed to be able to play with conviction the game of being whomever she wanted to be. Here, suddenly, she was this flirtatious woman of lightness and cheekiness. A woman he had never seen. Had not even guessed at. She and Ed delighting in a clearway to each other's lightest side, a twist of perversity in it, making them edgy with each other.

There it was. Robert was angry. He was *still* angry. He was always angry inside these days, the thing in him growling below the surface, thumping along with his desperation, pacing up and down. He had lost faith in himself. He was suffering. It had all briefly seemed clear to him and even settled; now he did not know where he was going any longer. What was to happen? In the night he wept with the terror of it. Was he punishing himself for putting writing second? For putting Lena and her game of life and death first? Was she playing with him now, flirting with this hippie? He watched the two of them carrying on. She knew he was watching. He had abandoned his dream for her. He was resentful and insulted by the way she was carrying on with Ed in front of him.

He took the beer Phil was holding out to him and he thanked him and watched Lena take the joint from between her lips and hold it out in front of her, her eyes closed, her chin lifted, sunlight etching the sculpted bones of her face, posing for Ed, posing for them all, slowly releasing the fragrant smoke from between her parted lips. Robert could see how she might be sexually interesting to someone who didn't know her as he knew her. He felt a stab of jealousy at the sight of their pleasure in each other.

Robert turned away from Lena and Ed. Phil had wandered off somewhere. Ann was watching him. He had surprised her, her gaze fixed on him. She coloured up. He said, 'How far into your master's are you?'

She butted her cigarette in the ashtray on the arm of the couch and stood up. 'I'm expecting to finish at the end of the year. It was nice meeting you.'

'You're going already?'

'I have to walk the dog.'

He said, 'I'll come with you.'

She smiled, a little challenging and perhaps a little regretful, some melancholy thought edging through her mind. 'I'd really rather you didn't.'

He said, 'You're escaping this circus.'

She regarded him critically. 'And what do *you* believe in?'

'Myself.'

'My God, you just say that!' She laughed.

He said, 'I was lying. And you?'

'I have to walk the dog.' She held his gaze, a sad smile in her eyes, then she turned and walked away, going out through an internal door on the far side of the room, at the last minute looking back at him quickly. He wondered if he should follow her. Did she mean him to?

Phil touched his arm. 'Come and have a look at the paddock, Rob. It was Dad's father's. This was the original homestead. Dad gifted the paddock for a public space so they'd never build out the view from this room. He grew up here, looking out at that view. We scattered his ashes over there by the laburnum and had a party. It was what he wanted us to do.'

Robert said, 'So this is your house now?' He was dreaming of being alone with Ann, dreaming of a perfect understanding between them, dreaming of being in love with her.

'Mum lets Ann and me use it,' Phil said. 'She doesn't like being here without Dad. She lives in Goulburn.' He turned to Robert and grinned, showing his beautiful teeth. 'Rent-free.'

Robert went with him out through the open doors onto a stone-slabbed patio.

They stood looking at the view, drinking their beers and smoking. Phil said, 'So what do you think of Ed? You'll have to get him to show you his pictures. He's the real thing.' He smiled, calm, easy, all was cool with him. Ed was another of his heroes. Phil was an open, easygoing man, content with his own perfection, ready to admire it in others. Robert was sweating into his shirt, an image of Ann holding his gaze that fraction of time longer than was needed, her dark eyes asking her own question. Had she meant him to follow her, or was he being crazy to even think it? He needed to know. He took a long drink from his beer. Ed and Lena were laughing. He heard her say, 'So what? I can ride a bike.' They both burst out laughing as if it was the funniest thing ever. Robert had never smoked dope.

Phil clinked his glass. 'Cheers, mate! You look deep in thought. What d'you say we nip down to the shops and pick up some Chinese?'

When they got back with the takeaways, Ed's girlfriend was curled up asleep on the couch where Ann had been sitting, one hand under her cheek, her thin hair fanned across her face. Robert wondered if her mum and dad knew where she was. Ann wasn't there and there was no sign of Ed and Lena. He went out into the paddock. They were lying on their backs in the sun beside an enormous azalea bush. He stood off, spying on them. Ed was openly flirting with her and she was enjoying it. Men didn't flirt with Lena anymore. They hadn't for a long time.

She and Ed were passing the short end of a joint—the old one or a new one?—back and forth between them and looking up at the sky and mostly just laughing about nothing. Had he ever seen

Lena this carefree? He couldn't think of any time when he had. Ed was making her happy. He was pointing with exaggerated excitement to a bird he'd seen way up in the dazzle of the sky and was trying to make her see it. 'There! There!' he yelled, his arm extended, index finger pointing. She sat up and leaned over him, sighting along his pointing arm. 'I can see it! I can see it!' she cried. Ed pulled her down to him and kissed her. She didn't resist. A stab of affront went through Robert, sharp and sudden, a spear in his side. He was fascinated and stirred by the sight of them. A strange perverted kind of excitement in it, a feeling of loathing, an *excuse* for violence. Sex and violence swirling together, a free ticket to beat the shit out of this hippie.

Lena looked across and saw him. She rolled off Ed and sat up, laughing. 'My serious husband's standing over there watching us, Ed. I don't think he approves.' They both convulsed with wild laughter, rolling around on the grass, struggling and giggling, Ed dropping the joint in the grass and groping around for it.

Robert walked over and stood looking down at him. He met Ed's blue eyes and held his gaze. Ed grinned his gap-toothed grin and reached his hand up to Robert. 'Give us a hand up, Robbie, old mate. I'm getting stiff in my old age.'

Robert didn't take his hand.

Ed giggled and rolled onto his stomach and stood up. Lena held out her hand and he helped her to her feet.

'I think we're being told off,' she said. She stood looking at Robert. 'You're out of focus.' She laughed helplessly, staring at him as if she couldn't work out why he was standing there in front of her.

Ed gripped Robert's shoulder with his fingers and steadied himself while he reached down and adjusted his sandal. Their eyes met and he gave Robert a cheeky grin. He was like a boy, a boy in a man's body, something innocent and yet deeply manipulative about him—edgy, cunning, working things out, his eyes shifting their focus. Robert saw in his eyes that he was amused by Robert's desire to give him a hiding, not cowed by the threat of it. Robert felt a grudging respect for him.

Robert said, 'We've brought some Chinese.' Lena slid her arm through his and pressed herself unsteadily against his side. The three of them walked across to the house. Phil was sitting on the floor with Ed's girlfriend. They were eating steamed dim sims and drinking beer, talking earnestly about the meaning of life.

38

It was two in the morning when they arrived home. Robert pulled into the drive and sat with the headlights playing over the garage. He had a headache and was feeling nauseous.

Lena said, 'What are you waiting for?'

'I've never seen anyone walking on our street. It's weird. We're living on the side of a hill in the middle of nowhere. No shops, no people, no signs of life. Nothing. That hill's been there since the beginning of time. Now we're here.'

She opened her door and stepped out of the car.

He followed her. He walked over to the demarcation line between the end of the suburb and the beginning of the wilderness. It was marked by an abrupt bulldozer scrape in the shallow soil at the edge of their block. He unzipped and took a long steady piss, directing it into the fleshy clay. The bare clay glistened with his piss. He thought of the slaughtered pig in Warren's yard one winter morning when he was a boy, the pallid flesh aching in the savagery of its death, the skin scraped clean of hair, the cold stillness of it, the pig screaming in his head, steam rising from its entrails in a bucket beside the carcass, its blood curdling in a bowl.

Lena was standing at the front door watching him. He zipped up and went over to her and put the key in the lock. The faintly chemical smell of the new building materials whenever they entered the house from the fresh air. The stillness and the silence. They didn't turn the lights on. She stood in the middle of the long front room, the shadow of a woman.

She said, 'You and I have never made a home.'

He was lighting a cigarette, the match flaring in the half-dark.

'Give me one of those,' she said. 'I need something. My throat's aching.'

He went over and gave her a cigarette and lit it for her. They had both drunk a lot. Robert had no memory of the drive home. He had been thinking about Ann. She had not returned to the party.

Lena took a drag on the cigarette. 'So Phil's another novelist?'

He didn't say anything. He was looking out into the dark.

She was watching him, waiting for him to say something. When he didn't speak she said, 'What's happened with your rewrite of *Frankie*? You're not writing, are you? You promised you'd do it. You *swore* you'd stick at it.'

He could see the silhouette of the dark forest going up the slope. Not a sound out there. No bells, no car horns, no trams, no Saturday night drunks. No sirens. Nothing. Just the forest. He felt as if he was waiting for something. His life at a standstill.

He hadn't answered Martin's letters. He was letting everything good and worthy fall away from him. He was drifting out in the blackness on his own, this house a chamber of solitude.

She said, 'You used to be so strong and determined. I was frightened of you when we first met. I admired you. What's happened to you? You've given up!'

He turned around from the window. Her dark shape against the pale windows on the other side of the room. He stood very still, looking at her for a long time.

She said, 'You're giving me the creeps!'

'We're supposed to be enjoying nature out here. Have you got that? Those people in the office with me every day, keeping their heads down, keeping out of trouble, hoping for a promotion, forever checking the gazette to see if their position has been confirmed or if someone's appealed against them, talking about the size of the house they're building. Surrounded by parks and forest and perfect roads. This is it. You don't think it's fucking weird?'

'You *have* given up,' she accused him, her tone flat, final.

'You want to have it out here and now? You want to accuse me of something. But it's not just me. It's us. Our lives aren't real anymore. I can't be a writer here and I'll tell you why: because I'm not here. I'm lost.'

'You're drunk. You're talking rubbish.'

'And that shit this afternoon, you and Ed rolling around in the grass almost fucking each other. Was that rubbish too? Or is that how you want to live? Living here is killing something in both of us. You know that. The sooner we face it the better for us. I don't know what else we have to do, but if we stick with this it will finish us.'

'I like Ed,' she said, a fierceness in her voice. 'We weren't fucking. We were playing. Ed's free. He's himself. I feel as if I've known him forever. He's got energy. He's not blocked the way you are. You're just making excuses. People who really have something to say write their books even in prison. People write no matter what their circumstances. They do it because they have to do it.' Her cigarette glowed in the dark. 'I used to think you were one of those people. You're not.'

'And you?' he said. He felt strangely calm, disconnected, unprovoked.

'What about me?'

'What sort of person have you decided to be?'

'I didn't make any promises.' She walked across to the coffee table and stubbed her cigarette in the ashtray. 'I'm going to bed.' She left the room.

He said quietly, 'You start this stuff, then you walk out. We never settle anything. On Monday morning I'll get in the car and go to the office in the park and enjoy the view of the trees and the grass.' He laughed.

➤

Robert was hanging out the washing on the clothes hoist behind the house when he heard a car door slam. It was followed by the sound of voices. He finished hanging up the clothes then went in. Ed and Lena were standing at the kitchen table. Lena was holding up an unframed canvas. She looked at Robert as he came in from the laundry. 'Look what Ed's given me.'

Robert went over and stood next to Lena at the table. She was holding an oil painting of a grey-haired old woman sitting on a red-painted garden bench at a red-painted table in a green garden. The woman had a glass of beer in one hand, a cigarette in the other, and a cat on her lap. She was in three-quarter profile, looking off into a vacancy of daydream. The cat faced the viewer, its golden-yellow eyes looking straight at Robert as he stood there looking back at it.

Lena said, 'It's a portrait of Ed's mum. Isn't it wonderful?'

The old woman was as scrawny as Lena. There was something poignant and beautiful about her. A vanished life. A life used up and gone. The knowing cat gazing directly into the eyes of the viewer was surely the artist himself. The picture had been painted with great feeling. Robert said, 'Yes. It's wonderful.' He looked at Ed. 'I like it a lot.'

Ed gave a sideways grin and said, 'I'm glad you like it, Robbie.'

Robert saw that Ed was sensitive about his work, believing in it, knowing it had worth. 'Where did you do your training?'

Ed laughed. 'Self-taught, Robbie. Like Gauguin.' He was wearing a khaki shirt with two button-down breast pockets, a black-bound notebook sticking out of the left shirt pocket along with a red pencil. His woven headband holding his long hair back off his face. There was something in the headband that reminded Robert of Frankie's woven hatband, subdued colours from nature plaited together. The green and red in the painting. Robert thought Ed had probably made the headband himself.

Ed looked at Lena. 'I'm going to do a portrait of Lena when I get back.'

Robert said, 'Where arc you going?'

Lena said, 'Ed's won an important art prize in Adelaide.'

'Congratulations,' Robert said.

'Ten grand,' Ed said. 'I'm gonna be rich.' He laughed, his gappy mouth wide, letting it all out.

They went onto the balcony at the side of the house and Ed got out his black sketchbook and started drawing Lena. She sat on the boards with her back against the railing, her eyes closed, the sun in her face, Ed sitting maybe a yard away squinting at her. Robert left them to it for an hour then carried out three beers. Ed took the beer and passed his sketchbook to Robert. Small, exquisite likenesses in which he'd uncannily captured the strength of Lena's features, and even something of her elusiveness, in a few simple pencil lines.

Robert leaned down to Ed, holding the sketchbook open. 'This one's just brilliant. It's Lena.'

Ed took the sketchbook from him and carefully tore out the sketch and handed it to Robert. 'For you, Robbie.'

Ed said he couldn't stay for lunch. 'I've got to go and front Mary's people.' He looked sheepish. 'I had a row with her old man. I'd better straighten things out with him before I head off.'

Lena said, 'Do you love her?'

Ed pursed his lips and thought about the question. 'Yeah, I suppose I do.' He smiled. 'She's bloody pregnant, so I'd better love her.'

Lena laid her hand gently on his arm and asked in a concerned tone of voice, 'Will Mary have an abortion then?'

'Jesus! No way!' Ed recoiled. 'We want the kid. If her old man doesn't kill me, the brat's gonna have a proper daddy.' He giggled. 'Fuck, I can't wait!'

'Any chance of that?' Robert said. 'Her dad killing you, I mean?'

'I reckon he's been giving it some thought.' Ed smiled. 'He's not a happy pappy right at this minute.'

Robert wondered if Ed had had a proper daddy himself.

They went out with him to where his Land Rover was parked in the drive. Lena hugged him and thanked him emotionally for the painting of his mother. There were tears in her eyes. They stood and watched him leave. He tooted the horn and hung out of the window and waved and yelled something as he turned into the road at the bottom of the drive. They stood a while, the elaborate silence of the forest rising around them, birds somewhere high up the hill crying and wailing. They turned around and went back inside the house. Robert wondered if she was thinking of Mary's fortunate child. He said nothing. The clothes would be dry by now. He went on through to the back and took the basket out to the clothes hoist and unpegged the shirts and handkerchiefs and towels and folded them into the washing basket.

39

The minute Robert walked into the office, Phil came straight over to him, looking pretty pleased with himself. 'Shake my hand, Rob,' he said. 'I've been awarded a scholarship to Harvard.'

Robert shook his hand. 'That's great news, Phil. Congratulations!'

'Yeah. Pretty good, eh?' Phil stood looking at him, expecting something more, waiting for Robert's eager questions so he could unload his excitement.

Robert set his satchel down and sat at his desk. 'So when did you hear?'

'I got a fax last night. I haven't slept much. We'll have a few cleansing ales after work.'

'My shout,' Robert said. 'And how about Ann? How did she go?' He managed to mention her name without his voice stalling. She was leaving. Nothing had come of their moment, imagined or real. He could still see that look of vague discontent in her eyes, the way she had held his gaze then looked away with almost a shrug of regret. Was he making it up? His inner voice insisted it had been real. He believed his inner voice.

'Ann missed out,' Phil said. 'She's going to try for something at the Sorbonne. It could make things a bit complicated, me living in the States and her in Paris. But I guess we'll jump over that one if and when we get to it.'

'When are you leaving?' Robert said.

'We'll stay with my brother out on the farm for a couple of weeks over Christmas then head to the States in the New Year.' He rested one buttock on the edge of Robert's desk and looked down at him—a happy man, eager to share his good fortune. 'It's lucky you and I met when we did. We're all in transit to somewhere else in this place.'

Robert said, 'We don't have any plans to leave Canberra.'

'But you will,' Phil said. He looked around at the sea of heads bent dutifully over their desks. 'This is not you, mate. Don't try telling me you're going to be doing this for the rest of your days. I'm not going to believe that.'

Robert said, 'Have you heard from Ed since he went over to collect that prize?'

'You don't *hear* from Ed. Ed just turns up.' He stood up and stretched and looked out the window. 'God, I feel so fucking good!' He laughed. 'We'll have a farewell party closer to the time. I hope you and Lena are going to be around for it.'

➤

It was an evening party. Cars parked along the kerb and up the driveway. Robert drove around the corner and found a spot and he and Lena walked back to the house. He was carrying the beer. A starry summer night, the smell of the bush on a drift of air from the mountain. Lena holding his arm, being close, concerned for him. She said, 'This place sometimes makes me feel like a refugee in my own country.' He squeezed her arm.

People going into the old house ahead of them, a knot of friends greeting each other in the doorway, talking and laughing, inching aside to let them in, smiles and apologies. The tabla player's fingers frenzied, candle flames wavering as if in time to the flickering rhythm of the drums, the shuffling darkness of the hallway with its smell of books and incense, a press of bodies. The living area seething with people, loud with laughter and talk, the air already thick with cigarette smoke. Lena said something but he didn't catch it. He headed for the bathroom and set the beers among the ice in the bath.

When he came back into the big central room Lena was standing over on the far side by the open doors to the patio and the paddock. She was talking with Phil and another man, a drink in her hand. One of the crowd now, no longer a refugee. He looked around the room but he couldn't see Ann. He made his way over to the fireplace and stood in front of a large rectangular painting that was sitting on the mantelpiece, leaning against the wall. He had no memory of having seen it there before. It was difficult at first to make out what was going on in the picture. Small figures and details of the interiors of rooms in a child's idea of a house open to a blue sky in which an old-fashioned plane was circling, leaving a white smoke trail behind it, tiny pieces of text written in here and there across the canvas, as if the artist had been telling himself a story by painting it, things flying through the air between the people, a brown loaf describing a perfect arc above the heads of an old man and an old woman, both looking up to watch it fly. The whole thing detailed, colourful, highly active, the numerous figures agitated. In the bottom left-hand corner of the canvas a bubble of writing inscribed with a fine brush in green against the brick-red background: *The Food Fight with Daddy—Family Life in Girilambone, Christmas 1953.* The year of Robert's first Christmas in Australia. Beside the bubble of text a signature, also with a fine brush in vivid green: *Ed.*

A woman's voice close behind him said, 'Hello, Robert.'

He turned around. Ann was looking directly at him, that slightly puzzled, questioning look in her dark eyes, as if she wasn't quite sure of what she was doing but was doing it anyway. He felt a start of excitement. She had sought him out! He said, 'Hello, Ann,' and held her gaze.

The intensity of his look made her shift uneasily and look past him at Ed's big painting. She was wearing a soft grey t-shirt and faded blue jeans, her arms bare. Her face without makeup, her brown hair loose. The dark circles under her eyes, her Jeanne Moreau lips.

He turned to look at the picture with her. 'The story of Ed and his home life, I guess? Where the hell is Girilambone?'

She didn't reply but continued to stand beside him. He said, 'You and Phil have a lot of friends.'

Her brown eyes serious, fixed on him. 'They're Phil's friends.' She looked around, pointing out people. 'They're the climbing club. And there's the cross-country skiing club. Over here is the gliding club. In the corner over there, that's the literature club. And dotted around the room are his school and university friends. They hang together in clumps. Phil needs to be surrounded by friends.' She looked at him. 'And then there's Ed. The artist friend.' She paused. 'And now there's you. The mystery friend.'

'And what about you? You don't need friends? You don't join Phil in his hobbies?'

'I have one good friend,' Ann said. 'She'll be here. I'll introduce you.' She kept staring at him. 'So what do you really do?'

He offered her a cigarette. She thanked him and took it from the packet. He lit it for her, then lit his own. 'What do you think I do?'

'I think you're unhappy.'

He was surprised. 'That's pretty honest of you.'

'What's the point of anything else?' She took a drag on the cigarette.

He considered her. He would have liked to tell her how incredibly attractive he found her, and how deeply dissatisfied she made him feel with his life. The big frames on her glasses had a strangely calming effect on him.

She said, 'Why are you smiling?'

'I like your glasses.'

She laughed. 'What an odd thing to say. So, do you have any dreams or are you just gliding along with it all?'

'I've dreamed of being a writer.'

'Then why are you here being a public servant?'

'Wanting to write isn't enough,' he said. 'There's something else. I don't have it.'

They stood looking at each other.

'It's complicated,' he said. 'I'd like to explain. But I don't think I can. Writing has a will of its own. For me, at any rate. I can't force it to happen.'

She said, 'That could sound like an excuse for not facing the difficulty of it.'

'It might be. I'm not sure. And you're going to America?'

'What does me going to America have to do with it?'

'I'm not sure. Who knows? Maybe we'd be friends if you weren't going to America.'

She looked around for somewhere to butt her cigarette.

He said, 'I'm sorry you're leaving.'

She gave him a sad little smile. 'Thank you. Phil knows people at Harvard. He's done some work with them. They were here at the ANU. Friends. They're supporting him. Encouraging him.' She seemed to be trying to decide something, looking at him. 'Tell me; I shan't ask you any more questions, but tell me, I want to know: have you really given up your dream of being a writer?'

'I have, and I haven't.'

'I believe you. Deep down we still have our secret dream even after we decide we've abandoned it. There is something in us that won't allow us to finally let the dream go. We need it.'

He liked her a lot. More and more. 'And what about you? What's the dream you can't let go of?'

'My dream changed. I wanted to be a dancer. Badly. Passionately. Until I was about sixteen. But my mother refused to let me take dancing lessons. And so the dream changed, because it was refused expression for so long, and gradually it became something else.' She looked at him. 'I've come to believe I should be living in Paris. I feel as though I'm meant to be there. As if something is waiting for me there. I don't know if I ever will. And don't laugh at me,' she said.

'I'm not laughing.'

'You were smiling. I don't like Harvard. I'll be lost there. I feel lonely walking around that place. I don't fit in.'

'But you'll go with Phil?'

'Of course. I'm his wife.' She waved her hand about. It was a gesture of fatality. 'It's what we do. Isn't it?'

'You mean your duty?'

'Something like that.'

'Phil said your mother's French?'

'Mum has spent her life regretting her decision to marry my dad and move to Australia. *It was my big mistake*, she says. It's her regular whinge. No one listens to her. No one has ever listened to her. Mum hates Goulburn. I think she might hate all of us: her family and Australians, the lot. She doesn't have any friends. She spoke only French to me until I was ten. She's caught in a bind she can't unpick. That's Mum's story. She'd quite like it to be my story too, so she could say, *I told you so.*'

'And if you go to France, you might regret leaving Australia and make the reverse of your mother's mistake.'

'Mum would enjoy the irony of that. She'd say she had passed on her curse to her only child. For Mum it would all be part of the family's destiny. Nothing to do with her real needs or desires or dreams. Mum believes in fate. She was raised a Catholic but she doesn't believe in God and she hates the priests. For her we are all pawns in a mysteriously elaborate plan. The moves in the game have been decided for us long ago. The end game is known, just not to us. That, Mum says, is the mystery that entices and infuriates us—not God, not religion, but the end game that's kept secret from us.' She switched abruptly, as if she thought she might be boring him. 'Have you seen the paddock? It's a clear sky tonight. The best thing about Canberra is the stars on a clear night.' She waved to a woman who had just come into the room from the front hall and was standing looking around. 'There's Sylvia!' She was suddenly animated, forgetting herself and her mother. 'Come and meet her.'

He said urgently, 'Don't give me the slip, will you?'

She gave him a quick look and laughed. 'I won't. I promise!'

They went together across the room. Ann and the woman embraced, holding each other close. He was reminded of the way

Lena and Birte had hugged the first time he met Birte. Ann turned to him, holding the other woman by the hand. 'This is my friend Sylvia.' She was smiling happily. 'This is Robert. Robert's going to be a writer.' There was a private smile in her eyes for him.

Sylvia and Robert greeted each other and stood a moment, silent, waiting for the other to speak first, then they both said something at once and laughed.

Sylvia put him in mind of an airline stewardess. She was wearing a dark blue blazer with gold buttons and a blouse with a choker collar and gold pin. Her hair was yellow blonde, her lips red, her eyelashes black, long and false. She didn't seem to be at all the sort of woman he would have imagined being Ann's close friend. Her body was round and plump, her cheeks smooth and pink, like the cheeks of a toddler. She said, 'What sort of writing, Robert?' Her eyes wide, a look that might frighten a butterfly.

'God knows,' he said.

She said wistfully, 'I should like to write a novel one day.'

Ann took her by the arm. 'Let's go out into the paddock and look at the stars.' She hustled Sylvia through the throng towards the open doors and the patio. The table in the middle of the room was crowded with wine bottles. Robert grabbed an open bottle of red wine on the way past. Obedient to Ann's instructions, the three of them lay down side by side on the grass, like people executed by a firing squad. They lay on their backs looking up at the astonishing display in the night sky and said things like, It's amazing! It's hard to believe how many stars there are! It's wonderful!

'We are on the edge of the universe looking out into space!' Ann said, her voice awed.

Sylvia said, 'Are we looking *into* the Milky Way or *out* of it?' But no one knew the answer to this.

Lying on the edge of space, the warmth of Mother Earth beneath them, the summer night, the noise of the party behind them, candles casting a shimmer of light out into the night, the shadows of people flicking back and forth, the tabla thrumming along at an incredible speed, a blur of finger notes. Robert knew it was a moment he would remember always, lying out there under the stars with Ann.

He said, 'I would have missed this. This sky!' It was easier to speak to her in the dark, not looking at her, not having her gazing at him with that serious, enquiring look of hers.

Ann's voice came softly out of the dark beside him. 'I dream of being a French cat in a village living with an old woman who knows my secret.' It was as if she confided her dream just to him.

He said, 'You can tell me the cat's secret. I won't tell anyone.'

'Promise?'

'God's honour.'

'It's not something that can be spoken. *You* have to dream it too.'

He spread his arms, being a crucifix, and filled his lungs with the fragrant night air. His outstretched fingers touched Ann's fingers. She didn't move her hand away but left it there, being touched by him in the dark of the beautiful night. He longed to tell her something memorable, to fix himself in her mind so that she wouldn't forget him when she was living in America but would remember him and think about him always. But he could think of nothing memorable. 'You'll be gone from Canberra next week,' he said. 'Do you think we'll ever meet again?'

There was a long silence.

Ann said, 'Do you believe in knowing things that can't be spoken?'

'The best things to know are those things that can't be spoken,' he said.

At this he felt her fingers move against his, not holding his hand but touching him. No touch had ever felt so intimate to him, so gratifying, or so exciting. He closed his eyes to believe more intensely in the touch of her fingers. He whispered her name, and heard her whisper back, 'Robert.' As if she tested the sound of his name on her lips.

40

It was a bleak winter, the frosts persisting well into October. Robert received a letter from Phil. Phil didn't mention Ann. Robert had been hoping for a letter from her, but when he considered it, he saw the wisdom of her silence. Words were so heavy and clumsy and might easily erase the delicacy of their memory of their night under the stars. *You have to dream it too.* He kept her words close.

The air of Canberra's winter had the smell of real cold in it, a cold he hadn't known since he was a boy with a weak chest growing up in London. He had the flu. It was hanging on and he had developed bronchitis, which he hadn't been able to shake off. The doctor told him he must stop smoking or he would damage his lungs. He hadn't had a cigarette all day.

He was in bed reading when Lena came in from work. She came into the bedroom still wearing her coat. He caught a whiff of Hermès Calèche, the expensive perfume she'd begun to wear. It was another sign of her recovery, her self-assurance. She had lost her terrible pot belly but hadn't put on any flesh. He had accepted that her fined-down state of being was to be permanent. She was in control. No longer the victim. She said, 'I've got some news that will cheer you up. I called Martin this morning. He's coming to visit us. He'll be here tomorrow. I said you'd meet him at the airport.'

Robert set the book aside. 'I never sent that long letter I wrote him,' he said. 'I've betrayed our friendship.'

'That's nonsense!' she said. 'Martin doesn't see things in that way. He's not judgemental. Martin loves you, and he trusts your love for him. He knows you've been struggling. He doesn't expect you to be anything but yourself.' She patted his leg through the blanket, the way a nurse or a mother might reassure a sick child. 'I bought some fish for your dinner on the way home. Will you get up for it, or shall I bring it in?'

'What sort of fish?'

'Flathead.'

They looked at each other.

She said, 'I was lost when you found me in Perugia. I couldn't have gone on from there without you. Martin has always been a part of that.' She went over and stood looking out the window, her back to him. It wasn't easy for her to speak of those days.

'I was in a strange place when you found me. It's hard to believe now that I could have gone there of my own free will. But I did. I'd reached a point where I couldn't bring myself to care any longer about what was to happen to me. I don't want you to go to a place like that. I don't think I'd cope if you did. I would feel guilty for the rest of my life. I didn't know before then that it was possible for us to believe our lives were worthless. Which was naive, I suppose. I was at the end that day when you found me sitting on the steps of the cathedral. I'd tried to do those drawings of people and I'd realised they were just stupid and that I had no skill for it. I didn't care anymore. I wasn't going to try to help myself. I suppose I must have thought at some stage that I had to test my resolve in this absolute way.' She sounded puzzled when she said this, as if it still troubled her. 'I'd gone a bit crazy on the boat. I'm ashamed when I think of it. I'm not sure what I was trying to prove. But whatever it was, I was in the grip of it for those months.'

She turned around from the window and looked down at Robert. 'You stood by me at a time when I thought I was no longer worth anything. I must have been repulsive.'

'I needed you too,' he said. 'It wasn't just to save you; it was to save myself as well. I doubt I would have gone in search of you if Martin hadn't convinced me you'd leave a trail. He said you'd be easy to find, especially if you were trying to hide. He made it sound possible. He was confident you'd be expecting me.'

'You haven't regretted it?'

'I've had my moments.'

They smiled at each other. 'I wasn't surprised when you walked up to me. Martin was right.' She was silent a moment, then she said with feeling, 'Dear Martin. How well he knows us both.' She stood looking out the window of the bedroom towards the forest. Neither spoke for a long time. Then she said, 'I'll cook your fish.'

He said, 'I'll have a quick shower.'

➤

The following afternoon Robert was waiting in the arrivals lounge when Martin's plane landed. He watched it taxi to the end of the runway and turn slowly as if it meant to go back the way it had come, then hesitate a moment and begin its stately approach to the terminal. He was nervous. He couldn't believe that for more than a year he had neglected this most important friendship of his life.

Martin came down the steps with the other passengers and walked towards the doors, which the ground staff had opened, the cold air flowing around the people waiting, the chauffeurs with their signs. Robert was seeing Martin now as other people saw him: a middle-aged man of medium height, his hair grey and receding from his broad forehead, a man wearing an old-fashioned black overcoat, his black shoes polished, glasses glinting in the pure limpid light of the Australian inland—a light Renaissance painters like Botticelli would have given their eye teeth for as a model for the light of celestial promise. He was carrying a small brown leather case. He saw Robert as he came through the door and a smile lit up his eyes. At once Robert was remembering the consoling reality of Martin's physical presence, his warmth, his generosity, and the wisdom of his precious silences—silences as filled with meaning as Frankie's had ever been.

Robert started towards him. Martin set down his case and opened his arms and embraced Robert, holding him firmly against the lightness of his body. He said with feeling, 'I've missed you!' At once Robert was liberated from his fear of having failed to live up to the beauty of their friendship.

Martin picked up his case and put his arm through Robert's. 'So, are you well? Lena said you've had the flu.'

Robert said, 'I'm better. And you?'

'You've still got a bit of a cough.'

'It's nothing.'

Martin paused and looked about him. 'Do you know, I've never been to Canberra before.' He was evidently delighted. 'You'll have to show me everything.'

They walked out of the terminal together, Martin's arm in Robert's, and crossed to the car park.

➤

After dinner that evening the three of them were sitting watching the purple and green clouds lowering over the Brindabella Range, cold grey streams of snow angling downwards from the troubled weave of the clouds across the horizon, the peaks disappearing into the darkness of the winter storm. Martin said, 'I haven't seen snow clouds since I was in Russia.' He smoked his cigarette and sipped his vermouth, the ice clinking in his glass, gazing at the distant turbulence of the storm.

Robert was moved to see how content Martin seemed to be. They were sitting with the lights off, the electric heater spreading a soft reddish glow through the room, giving an illusion of home-liness to the barren house. As the storm darkened the sky, the uncurtained windows began to stare back at the three of them from the blackness, a blackness populated by their own ghostly reflections, their faces reddened by the glowing bars of the heater.

Martin leaned forward and set his glass on the coffee table and balanced his smoking cigarette on the edge of the ashtray. He excused himself and stood up. He left the room and went into the spare bedroom, where they had set up a bed for him. He returned a moment later carrying two books.

He went up to Lena's chair and kissed her on the cheek. He handed the smaller of the two books to her. 'Birte sends you this little gift with her love.' Lena took the book and thanked him. He said, 'We can talk later.'

He stepped across to Robert and handed him the other book. On the white cover there was a dramatic black and red title, *The Last Temptation*. The word *Last* rendered as a violent red slash. In the centre of the cover an image of a tortured hand with a massive nail driven through it. At the very bottom of the cover, in small red capitals, the name KAZANTZAKIS.

Martin said, 'It was his final novel.'

Robert opened the book. On the blank page facing the inside cover Martin had inscribed in his neat hand the words, *To my friend Robert, with love, from Martin.* Robert looked up at him and thanked him.

Martin nodded and turned away and sat in his chair. He picked up his smoking cigarette and put it to his lips. He said, 'Kazantzakis was in Berlin during the working-class struggles of the mid-twenties.' His gaze was directed into the dark beyond the windows. 'He became a friend to some of the Berlin members of our movement.' He drew on his cigarette. 'He was one of my heroes.' He said this softly, as if he wasn't so much giving them information as reaffirming the truth of the claim for himself.

Lena handed Robert the book. 'Look what Birte has given me.'

He took her book and gave her the Kazantzakis to look at. Birte's gift to Lena was pocket-sized, the covers decorated with an elaborate fawn and pale yellow crisscross pattern, in which the diamonds of the intersecting diagonal lines were filled with smaller diamonds. The title and author were printed on a pasted-on label. The lettering was the old Gothic script of a Germany of the past. He was unable to make out the title, but the author was Stefan Zweig. He opened the book. On the title page, in browned and faded ink, there was a handwritten dedication. Birte's name stood out. The rest of the inscription was indecipherable to him. He handed the book back to Lena. 'It's beautiful,' he said. 'What's the title? I can't read it.'

She took the little book from his hand. *'Brennendes Geheimnis,'* she said. *'Burning Secret.'* She looked across at him and smiled. 'Your flu has gone. You haven't coughed once all night.'

Martin said, 'Birte's mother gave Zweig's book to her at the border, after Birte was released from prison in Germany during the war and was being escorted into exile by the police.'

They both turned and looked at him.

'The police refused to let her mother go into exile with her. Birte never saw her mother again.'

Lena looked down at the book, her lips moving silently as she read the German text to herself. A large tear was sliding down her cheek, catching the red glint of the heater. In her left hand, behind the book, she held between her fingers the single sheet of a letter from Birte that had accompanied this extraordinary gift of love from her old teacher and dearest friend. Lena closed the book and pressed it against her breast with both hands. She stood up and walked over to Martin. She leaned and kissed his cheeks, first his left and then his right. One of her tears fell into his thin hair where it was swept back off his forehead. She straightened and stood looking down at him. She set the book aside on the low table and he reached up both his hands and she took his hands in her own. They stood like that for a long moment. Neither spoke.

At last Lena said, 'I'll make fresh coffee for you both.' She let go of Martin's hands and picked up the book and went out to the kitchen, carrying her precious gift with her.

Martin and Robert sat in the silence. Martin said, 'Lena wrote to Birte and told her about Sydney.'

Robert looked at him. 'She's better. I mean emotionally. She's strong again. But I think she's always going to be terribly thin from now on.'

Martin said nothing for a long time. Then he said, 'And you? What about you?'

There was so much to say that Robert didn't know where to begin. He said, 'I feel as if I've completely lost my way. I can't write here. It just doesn't work for me. The job's not so bad. My boss is a good man. Everyone's kind.' He fell silent again. This wasn't what he had meant to say. 'I was writing happily in Sydney before Lena's crisis. I thought that was it. I really believed I was on my way with it. I spent every day at it. Now it's just not there anymore. I don't seem to have the ability to feel it any longer, not in the way I felt it while I was writing in Sydney. It isn't enough to want to write.'

He turned and looked at Martin and saw that the older man was still looking into the darkness outside.

Robert said, 'I feel as if I've betrayed something. I'm not sure what. Whenever I try to write the story I was writing in Sydney there's a dead blankness inside me. I feel as if something has closed down.'

He waited, but still Martin said nothing.

Robert said, 'You've been mistaken to believe in me. That's what I really think.'

Martin turned to him. He looked into Robert's eyes for several long seconds, then he said, 'Every one of us betrays something. Everyone who is compelled to search for meaning and purpose in his life is forced by circumstances to betray his finest hopes. Sometimes again and again. We all founder in our struggle to find our way. Our way to our own truth. Success in the end is to survive these repeated failures.' He gestured at the book lying on the coffee table where Lena had set it. 'Kazantzakis took many wrong turns before he found his truth. He despaired many times. It was the same for all of us. I and my comrades, each of us in our own ways, we all made terrible mistakes and misjudged the realities of our situation a hundred times.' He lit a cigarette and drew in the smoke. 'So long as we don't give up, that's all.'

Robert said, 'And you don't think I've given up?'

Martin made an impatient gesture towards the windows with both hands. 'This situation here in Canberra is no doubt perfect for some people. It is such a beautiful place to live. It is unique among the cities of the world. That was obvious to me as we drove here from the airport. I'm sure it is a fine career here for many of your colleagues. But for you it is the wrong thing. The wrong place.' He spoke with vehemence. 'I am sure of it. For you and for Lena this life you are living here is not the right thing.'

He paused, reached for his glass and drank off the last inch of vermouth.

'You haven't given up. I can see that. You are still troubled by your failure. To have given up is to have become apathetic and embittered, or fatalistic. I know. I have seen such tragedies many times. It is my own tragedy. Friends I loved. To give up when you have struggled is to enter a bitter, hard place. It is to be driven to extreme behaviour in the desperate search for a solution to your pain and your disappointment. Giving up is harder than going on. I understand this. I still love those friends who took their own lives. To do that required great courage.' He looked directly at Robert. 'I believe you are one of those who will persist.'

'It means everything to me to hear you say that.'

'And to me,' Martin said with force. 'To be *able* to say it. Don't imagine it means nothing to me.' There was a fierceness in his eyes and in his voice Robert had witnessed only briefly once before, when Birte accused Martin of making a mistake in giving Thomas Mann's novel to Robert. 'Our friendship has given me hope too,' Martin said. 'Don't forget that. You are not the only one for whom friendship is important.'

Robert said, 'As soon as you and I are together and I hear you talking like this, my energy and my belief return.'

'We're fortunate to have met each other. I have the same revival of my spirits when I think of you. Birte and I love you and Lena. We look at you both with hope in our hearts.'

Lena came out with the coffee and biscuits. Martin and Robert drank coffee and Lena nursed her cup of weak black tea and they talked about Melbourne and the school where Birte was deputy head. They didn't talk about Perugia or the dead child or London. They were tired and the three of them had fallen silent, when

Martin asked just one question. It was late and they were staring emptily at the glowing bars of the electric heater, when he stirred and drew on his cigarette and roused himself.

'So for how long do you plan to stay in Canberra?'

Everything was in that one question. Everything that Lena and Robert had been unable to speak about openly with each other. The whole dilemma. It was the one crucial question silently haunting them both—where to look now for a place and a style of life that would suit them? Neither of them had an answer. Since leaving Lena's family home in Red Bluff they had been to Italy and London and Sydney and then here to this place. Was there some magical place that they had not yet thought of where they would find themselves at home? If they were to leave Canberra now, wouldn't they be running away again? This thought was in both their minds. They had been afraid to ask themselves the question.

And when Martin casually asked it, at that moment when they were all tired and ready for sleep, Lena and Robert looked at each other, and each waited for the other to speak first. Martin said no more but left his question hanging in the silence.

Eventually Robert said, 'We haven't decided what we're going to do next.' Saying it out loud made it seem as if he and Lena had been talking about it already and might even have been on the brink of deciding something.

At once Lena said, 'We never planned to stay here forever, Martin.' She looked at Robert. 'Did we?'

'No, of course not.'

She turned to Martin. 'Robert doesn't have the time to write.'

'It's not that I don't have time,' Robert objected. 'I do have the time. Other people make time to study and to do other stuff. Look at Phil and Ann and everything they did apart from working. It's not time, it's just that writing and Canberra don't make sense to me.' He didn't want to say that in coming to Canberra in obedience to the Sydney doctor's instructions he had been required to renounce the idea of being a writer. But that was what he believed he had done. He believed he could not have abandoned *Frankie* and committed himself to a life as a public servant in Canberra the way he had without making this renunciation. For him at the time of Lena's crisis in Sydney, discarding his manuscript hadn't been just a renunciation of the manuscript but a renunciation of the whole complicated edifice of his dream of becoming a writer. Without at first realising it, he had discarded himself as well as *Frankie*. The alternative at the time, and he knew this, was to abandon Lena. Frankie would have said he'd laid a curse on himself and that he would need to move away from the hollow ground he'd created with this curse if he were to restore the life of his dreaming.

Robert hadn't had a cigarette all evening. Now, without thinking about it, he lit a cigarette and sucked the smoke back into his lungs. His tender throat closed tightly over the smoke and he leaned forward and coughed harshly into his hands. It was some moments before he could get his breath. 'I'm sorry,' he said. He stubbed the cigarette out in the ashtray. Lena was looking at him with concern. When he looked at her she said, 'You've still got a touch of that bronchitis. Please don't smoke!'

They were silent, the creaking and settling of the new timber in the house frame as the cold outside began to bite. The storm had not reached them. A sickle moon appeared and disappeared between broken clouds. Robert could feel the cold around his ankles from the glass of the uncurtained windows. There would be a frost again in the morning.

Lena said, 'I've always dreamed of having a little place in the country.'

He looked at her with astonishment. 'Since when? I've never heard you say that before.'

'Since forever,' she said defensively.

'It's news to me.'

'You don't know everything about me. When I used to go riding with Dad we'd talk about it. A little place in the country where we could be happy. There were paddocks and open country the other side of Sandringham in those days. Dad and I used to tell each other stories about our imaginary place in the country. It was his dream. It was my dream too. Somewhere where we could grow our own vegetables and be self-sufficient. We would have an orchard.'

She sat smoothing the cover of Birte's book in her lap.

'Other people have done it,' she said. 'I don't see why we couldn't. You know about outside work and farming and that sort of thing. You could teach me. Dad always had a good vegetable garden.'

'We haven't got any money to buy a farm with,' he said.

'I didn't say a farm. Anyway, we could use some of Mum and Dad's money.' She was watching him. 'I know what you're going to say, but we wouldn't be spending their money. We'd be reinvesting it. The place in the country would still be there if we ever wanted to sell it again. It would just be moving the money from one kind of investment to another.'

Martin said, 'Birte and I bought factories when we received our compensation from the German government. We could just as easily have bought flats or shares or a place in the country. A farm might have been a better investment in the long run than the factories have been. A great many factories have been built in Melbourne by developers since we bought ours and rents have gone down instead of up as the agent said they were certain to. And there's always something for us to attend to, either with the factories themselves, the roof or a crack in the wall, or with the people who lease them from us or trouble with the neighbours. Problems you don't think of when you buy things like that. We can't just own the factories and live off the rents and forget about them, which is what I thought we were going to do. Birte was more realistic. Every week there's something. Birte attends to it.' He smiled, no doubt thinking of Birte yelling at the agent down the phone, and lit another cigarette.

Robert envied the way Martin smoked without any concern for his health, enjoying every puff.

Martin said, 'I think a place in the country sounds like a good idea.' He looked up and grinned at them. 'I'd come and stay with you for holidays. I could help. My father and I were workers. I haven't forgotten how to handle tools. The country air would do us all good.'

Lena said, 'I really would love to have an orchard. I've always wanted to be able to look out of my room at an orchard. Dad loved fruit trees in bloom. Plums and apples and pears. That's why Mum and Dad went to Japan for their honeymoon. It was his idea, to see the cherry blossoms in the spring.'

Martin was holding his cigarette delicately between two fingers, the smoke drifting about his head, his gaze on Lena, listening to her with evident pleasure, his legs crossed at the ankles, his socks wrinkled, a strip of white leg showing. He was leaning back in his chair, his hairless cheeks waxen in the ruby light of the electric heater, a sense from him of deep unlimited patience, an extraordinary pleasure in listening to Lena's rapture, as if listening to music. He murmured, 'A cottage in the country.'

➤

They drove Martin out to the airport on Tuesday morning. Lena didn't work at the hospital on Tuesdays and Robert was still on sick leave. The two of them stood in the departure hall and watched

Martin's plane lift away from the tarmac and fly into the blue distance.

She took his arm and they walked out to the car park and climbed into the Holden. 'Imagine Martin coming to stay with us when we have our little place,' she said. 'Wouldn't it be wonderful.'

41

They drove over the border into New South Wales and were soon on a minor road, the narrow strip of tar spearing straight ahead through open grazing country, the day cold and bright. Every now and then a stock truck or a utility passed them going the other way. They drove for maybe an hour through flat, dry, withered-looking country, where the storm had obviously not softened the grip of the drought, skinny sheep nibbling the roots of the grasses, a few red cattle gathered here and there under a scatter of shade trees.

They crossed a bridge over a dry riverbed and came into the town of Braidwood. Robert drove slowly down the main street. Utes and cars nosed into the kerbs. A few people about. Two men standing by a stock truck watching them go by. Robert raised his hand from the wheel and the men raised their hands. Old Victorian buildings, two-storey shops and agencies on each side of the street.

Lena said, 'Who were they?'

'No idea.' He turned and looked at her and grinned. 'Just being friendly,' he said. 'They haven't seen the Holden around before and were wondering who we were.'

She said, 'Let's stop and have a look. We can ask someone about places for sale.'

He parked outside a two-storey brick-and-stone building with a cast-iron balcony. It was the Australian Estates office. There was a cafe next door, a single-storey weatherboard shop with a canting false front and no verandah. A signboard over the door— ROYAL CAFE. Nothing less. They went in. There was a blower heater going and it was warmer inside. A fan in the ceiling moving the warm air down over them. A smell of fruit. On the counter small piles of shrivelled apples and oranges and spotty bananas along with a box of potatoes and another of brown onions. Behind the counter, shelves along the wall stacked with rows of tinned food— Heinz baked beans, Spam, IXL peaches in syrup and pineapple chunks. Bottles of tomato sauce. The cafe area was in the back, up a low step. They went up the step and sat in the first booth on the left. The sound of country and western music coming from the back. Slim Whitman lamenting the loss of Rose Marie. A voice out of Robert's past. Half a dozen dead blowflies littering the sill of the sash window beside them in the booth, their living mates battering against the glass. The window looking out onto a dirt laneway, kids' broken toys, a mattress leaning against the wall, two rusting forty-four-gallon drums lying on their sides. Across the laneway facing their window an unpainted weatherboard wall with a small four-pane window. Every pane of glass in the window broken.

A handsome Greek in his mid-forties came out from the back and walked over to their booth. Lena looked up at him and smiled. 'Can I have a cup of black tea, please? Not too strong.'

He turned to Robert.

'I'll have tea and two rounds of ham sandwiches, with hot English mustard, if you have it.'

The Greek said, 'We have the mustard. Tomatoes with the ham?'

'Just the ham, thank you.'

When he'd gone back into the kitchen to prepare their order, Lena said, 'Wow, what an amazing-looking man.'

Robert said, 'And it's not just his good looks.' There was a self-contained grace about the Greek that had impressed them both. Robert said, 'Zorba.'

When they'd finished their sandwiches and tea the man came back to their booth to collect the dishes. While he was putting the dishes together he said, 'You folks down from Canberra for the day?'

Lena said, 'We're looking for a small farm to buy. Is there anywhere around here you'd suggest we could look?'

The handsome Greek arranged the dishes on a tray then set the tray aside on the table in the next booth. He offered his hand to Lena first, then to Robert. 'Dom Alvanos,' he said. They introduced themselves. He had an open, relaxed, slightly ironic smile. 'I'm not a local,' he said. 'Maybe you've guessed that. You won't find anything to suit you up here on the tablelands. They're all big cattle and sheep properties up here. The old families hold on to their country. If you keep on out of town past Nomchong's hardware until you hit the gravel, you'll see a sign to the Araluen Valley after you cross the creek. There's no bridge. But there's no water in the creek either. You might find something to suit you down the valley. I've leased a piece of country down there myself. Look out for the sign for Big Oakey Creek. That's it.'

The unsealed road down the mountain was steep and narrow with one tight hairpin bend after another, and the gravel surface was washed out in places. The inside of the car was soon reeking with the hot carbide stench of the brakes, the windows wound down, the scream of cicadas out in the forest. Robert was silently praying, Dear God in heaven, let us find a place for ourselves in this valley of Dom Alvanos! A priest had once told him we pray without knowing we're praying, but Robert knew he was praying. The phrase *Dear God in heaven* was his mother's.

Half an hour or so later they came out of the last bend and saw the valley opening out ahead of them, a scatter of dwellings, spirals of smoke rising into the still air, one or two horses and the odd cow and calf, heads down grazing on the sparse winter feed, a horse with its head pushed through the second wire of a fence lipping at a milk thistle. Orchards of peach trees over on the right, lines of trees, a tractor spraying between the lines. It was close-fenced country, smallholdings and orchards. The purple hills rose up in the distance on the far side of the open ground. They drove along a short strip of bitumen. A single-storey pub standing alone thirty metres off to the right of the road, a big old quince tree out the front, the ground thick with yellow globes of fruit. A white ute with two shivering dogs chained in the back, catching the edge of the shade from the tree. The sign across the front of the pub, ARALUEN HOTEL, square letters in faded pink, the paint peeling. The door was wide open.

Lena said, 'Pull over. Let's talk to the people in the pub.'

Robert pulled off the road and parked beside the ute, the two dogs watching them. They walked across the dusty patch in front of the pub and went through the front door into the sudden dark. There was no one in the bar. A smell of beer and roasting lamb, the back door open to a view of the yard beyond, a red International truck with a cattle crate and a clutch of forty-four-gallon fuel drums, a rusting Willys jeep, brown chooks pecking the ground. Robert called but got no answer. A radio playing somewhere. They waited. Robert called again.

They went out to the station wagon and drove on. Ruins of stone buildings and deserted brick houses standing in isolation among overgrown gardens here and there by the side of the road.

Three or four kilometres further on the valley abruptly closed in. They entered a narrow dirt track, following the twists and turns of the creek, overhung by the festooned branches of big old candlebark trees, the glare gone off the shaded road, and with it a stillness. Heavily timbered ridges on their left hand, the cutting on their right hand dropping away steeply to the bed of the creek, a good flow of clear water down there despite the drought.

'Keep an eye out for Dom's Big Oakey,' Robert said. 'If I take my eyes off this road we'll be over the side.' The road was so narrow he could not see how two vehicles could pass one another. If they met someone coming the other way, one of them was going to have to back up. Every couple of kilometres they crossed a gully coming out of the hills to their left. There were no causeways or bridges, the crossings just the tumbled rocks of past floods. He slowed the Holden to a walking pace, lifting and bumping over the rocks, the dif bottoming on the biggest of the rocks with the hollow sound of steel on stone. They had been negotiating this road for some time when Lena yelled, 'Big Oakey up ahead!' She was like a kid on an outing.

He pulled up in the middle of the gully. They got out and looked over the iron gate that stood across the front of a cleared patch of ground. A few acres worked up by the plough, tucked into the groin between steeply timbered hillsides. An iron shed over to the left. A mechanical cultivator parked over to the right. The worked country ridged up, brown stalks lying along the furrows. 'Dom's been growing potatoes here for his shop,' Robert said.

They stood a while, awed by the wildness of the place, birds calling back and forth among the timber.

They got back into the station wagon and drove on. A couple of kilometres beyond Dom's Big Oakey they crested a rise. Below them over to their right the creek abruptly left the road, flowing away in a wide loop, a line of tall casuarinas along the creek sweeping in a curve, enclosing a cleared area of forty or fifty acres, a weatherboard house, a barn and cattle yards. Ahead of them on the road a man was leading his horse behind two cows and calves, his dog off to one side. The cows were Herefords, their hips poking up, their guts hollowed out, the calves bothering them for a drink. The man turned around and looked back at them.

Robert pulled up alongside him and called a greeting. The man stepped over to the car window and touched the brim of his hat to Lena. He was an old man, brown and vigorous, his features heavily lined, his nose flattened and pushed over to one side like a boxer's. His abundant white hair touching the shoulders of his leather jacket. In his dark eyes a glint of amusement.

Lena and Robert introduced themselves and the man said his name was Ray McFadden. Robert asked him if there was anywhere for sale around there. Ray McFadden turned his head and gestured down to the house below them in the paddock. 'She's been on the market for three or four years. You'd need to be a young man to take her on.' He took a packet of Champion Ruby from his shirt pocket and stuck a paper to his lower lip, rubbed a pinch of tobacco between his palms then took the paper from his lip and rolled a smoke, nipping the whiskers from the ends and lighting it with a match. He shook out the flame of the match and looked at the wisp of smoke from it before flicking it onto the road with his thumb. Robert had not encountered a man like him since his Queensland days and his instinct was to trust him. Seeing Ray McFadden standing there smoking his cigarette, Robert felt a hopeful thrill of possibility. He believed Martin would also approve of this man. They would sit together in their comfortable silence and they would know one another at once. Robert believed and hoped that he belonged in the company of such men.

Lena nudged him. 'Are you getting out?'

He stepped out of the car and stood beside Ray. The day had warmed up. The three of them looked down onto the house and barn with the yards and, directly behind the barn, the line of trees along the course of the creek. They stood considering the scene. The warmth triggered a sudden rise of a cicada chorus, the shrieking waves of sound flowing back and forth in the forest behind their backs. The roof was gone off the house, sheets of roofing iron scattered over the paddock, black wattle trees growing up here and there, patches of blackberry spreading along a fence line.

Ray said, 'A storm took her off a couple of years ago.' He took the cigarette from between his lips and examined the end, then pinched a strand of tobacco and put the cigarette between his lips and sucked on it. The smell of the smoke in the fragrant air was making Robert wish he still smoked.

Lena asked, 'Do you think it would be all right if we went down and had a look around?'

'There's no one going to stop you. There's been no one down there for years.' Ray smiled, his eyes filled with the enjoyment of the moment. She smiled back at him and Robert had the thought that here was a man who appreciated Lena just as she was. Ray didn't have to tell them he lived on his own. Robert knew he did. Ray gestured down the hill. 'The bank's on the back of them

Wilson boys and I know they're dead keen to sell. They was buying up country all over the shire before the drought. Jim Forbes is looking after the sale for them. They was intending to winter heifers down here but they never did stock the place and I only seen them the once. They come down here in a blue and white Pontiac motor car half the size of a house and just about ripped the bottom out of her in Big Oakey. You'll find Jim at the Australian Estates office in Braidwood. You could call in on your way back and talk to Jim. He'll do the right thing by you. Tell him Ray McFadden sent you.'

Lena asked, 'Are they really orange trees down there?'

Ray said, 'Old Patrick Waddell put them orange trees in the year I was born. Betty used to always give us a box of them to take home whenever I come up this way as a boy. She called them my birthday oranges.' He drew on his cigarette, squinting down at the orange grove. 'They sweeten after a couple of frosts. They'll be good eating now.'

'They're beautiful trees,' Lena said, and she glanced at Robert, looking for a sign from him, her enthusiasm in her eyes, the sun in her hair. Robert smiled to see the eagerness in her.

They stood a while longer, reluctant to say farewell to Ray McFadden, his presence making them feel welcome. He smoked, the reins looped loosely over his arm, his brown gelding hanging its head, eyes closed, sleeping on its feet, its long mane knotted up. The two cows had moved on, nipping the dry rubbish on the roadside, their calves bumping their saggy udders for a pinch of milk. The dog lying close by, her eyes not quite closed, keeping a check on Ray. Kookaburras starting their cackling, working themselves up to a high pitch of excitement, then falling silent as if they were waiting for applause. In the distance the sound of an aeroplane high up in the blue somewhere.

They talked some more. Ray told them he lived two kilometres further along the road, his hand going out and gesturing in that direction. His place neighboured the one they were looking at. He had three thousand acres. 'Mostly hilly scrub,' he said. 'Like this place. Some nice creek flats like the one you're looking at. It's healthy country.'

When Ray had moved on, Robert turned the car at a gate and drove back up the hill. They went in over the cattle grid, the familiar rumble of the tyres, and swooped down the loopy track to the yards. They passed the ruin of another house on the high creek bank up the hill from the yards. Robert said, 'There's material there to repair the cottage with.'

There was a closed gate across the road between the stock yards and the barn. He pulled up at the gate and they got out of the car. The crouched form of a dark scrub wallaby raced away from the side of the barn and charged into the casuarinas, leaving a little spurt of dust in the air. The barn stood fifty metres from the house on the rocky bank above the creek, its roofing iron intact. Beside the barn, the set of heavy timber cattle yards. A solitary dunny standing behind the house looked like a sentry box. Between the dunny and the yards six orange trees in two rows of three, old and healthy-looking trees, trees of character, bright oranges set among the deep green of their leaves, as if someone had been decorating their branches with Chinese lanterns.

There was so much of Robert's past in this scene, the rural past he had made for himself after leaving the Council estate as a boy of fifteen, his magical time with Morris Aplin on Warren's farm in Somerset, then journeying alone to Australia. The first small cattle station he had worked on, where he had been the only hired hand and had become part of the family. He might have returned home to find the old place derelict and deserted. It was as if he looked into his own past and saw that he was no longer there. And he was stirred by a feeling of sadness and nostalgia. Lena and he stood together by the car looking at the orange trees. He said nothing to her about his feelings. He didn't want to encourage her to convert her mother's blue-chip shares into some marginal hillbilly farm in the scrub just so that he could have the peace of mind to write. But all the same, and without a need to consider it, he was at once in love with this wild little patch of country and saw in it a haven from the despair that had come over him in Canberra.

They walked over to the orange trees and picked an orange each. She held the orange to her nose and closed her eyes. 'Smell that! I haven't smelled an orange like this since I was a kid.'

Robert peeled the thick skin from his orange and broke off a section and put it in his mouth. It was running with juice and sweetness. 'These trees must have deep roots to produce fruit like this in a drought.'

They stood in the sun eating their oranges.

She wiped her lips with her handkerchief and said eagerly, 'Let's look in the barn first.'

They walked back to the gate and Robert lifted it and dragged it half open, where it was sagged on its hinges. They went through and stood outside the wide entrance to the barn, looking into the dark cavern of the interior. As he followed Lena in, two owls flew out over their heads. Lena said, 'Do you think they're good luck?'

'Sure to be,' he said.

The barn was on two levels. They were on the ground level in a parking bay for machinery, a workshop at the far end. An unglazed window over the workbench. To their right a set of three steps led up onto the main floor. Lena went up the steps and Robert followed her. She stood looking around. 'It's enormous.'

The flooring of this upper level was made of broad pit-sawn timber planks. They were worn smooth with use. The tall iron walls and roof were supported at the corners by enormous tree trunks, the roof heavily beamed and artfully structured. 'It's beautiful,' Robert said. 'I wonder why they needed a barn like this?'

Stone jars and bottles and pieces of rusty iron, old iron bedsteads, two hurricane lamps hanging on wire from a crossbeam, a bench with a blacksmith's vice and a carpenter's vice. A long row of tins ranged against the wall on a bench. He went over and looked into them. The tins were filled with an assortment of nails and screws, coach bolts, nuts, washers, split keys and other bits and pieces whose uses were familiar to him. Remnants from a way of life in which nothing was ever thrown away, but was only ever set aside for possible reuse at some future time. At the far end of the bench was a pile of iron heads from old hand tools. He counted several mattocks, axes, adzes, picks, wedges, hoes, worn-down plough shares and tiller feet. Rows of horseshoes strung along the side wall, arranged in fours, hind shoes and front shoes in pairs. Dozens of fuel drums and oil cans. There was a tarpaulin covering something on a crossbeam. Laid across the tarpaulin were several halters and bridles. He went over and lifted the end of the tarp and looked under it. Three stock saddles and a pack saddle. Lena came up and stood next to him. He set the bridles and halters aside and took the tarp right off, sending a shower of dried bird shit and dust into the air.

Lena reached out and fingered the steel hooks on the pack saddle. 'Goodness, what are these for?'

He hadn't seen a pack saddle since the last camp with Frankie. He told Lena the hooks were where the panniers were hung. He looked around but there was no sign of them. He was thinking of lifting the heavy panniers off the pack saddles when they came into camp in the evenings. He covered the saddles with the tarp and laid the bridles and halters over it. Lena had wandered away. A sunray of dust motes in the air where they had intruded.

He was crouched down trying to prise open the lid of an iron box with writing on it when Lena came up behind him. She said, 'Look what I've found.'

Lolling in the crook of her arm was a stained old doll, fine wood shavings poking out from a rent in its stomach. Lena touched the open wound. 'I can sew it up,' she said. The doll had a sad-looking face crudely painted on its round head, faded pink lips and blind eyes. No hair. Lena looked down at it where it was nestled against her t-shirt. 'I wonder if the little girl it belonged to lost it or threw it away?' She looked at him. 'I don't think she would have thrown it away, do you? You don't throw away a doll just because it's old.'

He said, 'Maybe her parents told her she had to leave it behind when they left.'

'If she could speak she would tell us the sad story of what happened here.'

He wasn't sure if she meant that the little girl to whom the doll had belonged would tell them the story or that the doll would tell the story. 'What is it?' he said.

'Don't laugh, but I feel as if she's been waiting for me to come and find her.'

He said carefully, 'Or maybe it's you who's been waiting to find her.'

'Isn't that what I said? I'm going to keep her. She's never going to be tossed aside again.'

'You sound as though you mean it. Will you give her a name?'

'She has a name. We just don't know what it is.' She walked across to the small doorway and stood looking out towards the orange trees and the cottage, her back to him. 'We should go and have a look at the creek before we go over to the cottage,' she said.

Her sudden change of mood had distanced her from him. He got up from his crouch and walked over and stood next to her at the open door.

'It's so peaceful,' she said. 'You could write your novels here. They would be as beautiful as this place is.'

He said, 'What did you think of Ray?'

'Ray is a gentleman of the old school. My father would have trusted him at once.' She was silent for a moment. 'We've met two lovely men today. It's a sign.'

They went out of the barn and turned down towards the bank of the creek. The bank was too steep near the barn for them to get down. The barn had been sited above the reach of floods. They walked on a little way below the barn, following the wallaby track down to the line of casuarinas, and they stood on the bank in the dappled shade and looked at the clear stream flowing by.

She said, 'Smell that sweet water.'

The slim trees around them, their needles whispering in the gentle movement of the air. The far bank of the creek a shelf of rock, on their side a silt bank sloping into the water. A green sunlit hole under the rock bank. He said, 'Keep still a moment. See that green lizard over there watching us? That's a water dragon.'

She turned to look where he was pointing and the lizard flicked into the water and was gone. 'I missed it!'

'I reckon there'll be plenty more of them,' he said. 'I'm going in.'

'It'll be freezing,' she said. 'It's been running through the frost all night.'

He took off his clothes and stepped into the water. It was bitingly cold. He gave a yell and ducked under and pushed off from the bank. He rose up out of it, yelling with the cold and shedding water around him in a spray of sunlight. The water was up to his chest, a coloured mosaic of river stones and yellow sand on the bottom, glints of mica. A shoal of small brown stripy fish gathered in the disturbance around his legs. He called out, 'It's wonderful!'

She took off her t-shirt and jeans and her underclothes and set the doll on them. Naked in the sunlight she stood on the bank facing him. Then she walked into the water and, with a slow elegant movement, slid beneath the surface, swimming past him under the clear stream and surfacing against the rock face of the far bank, the water to her chin. She didn't cry out with the shock of the cold but stood silently, the sun in her eyes, the water reflecting the light upwards across her features, looking around her with wonder at the ferny rock bank. He was remembering her swimming away from him out towards the rusting hulk of the sunken ship at the beach that day, confident and unafraid of the sea, beautiful then, now scrawny and aged.

He said, 'Water's your element.' He climbed out and palmed the water off his skin then put his clothes on. His body chilled and refreshed.

Lena swam across and stood in the shallow water, her back to him, wringing the water from her hair. Every one of her ribs stood out sharply in the clear light, her buttocks fleshless, reduced to the bony structure of her pelvis and hips, the sunlight through the casuarinas etching the lines of her skeleton, something strange and poignant and slightly repellent about her, something unreal that eluded and fascinated him—as she had always eluded him. His bond with her was beyond his understanding. She was so intimate, so much his familiar, and yet she was still a mystery to him. A deep stream of her inner life was unshared with him. And he was sad thinking of the lost beauty of the tanned young woman in the expensive black swimsuit; and he couldn't help himself in that moment from asking her the forbidden question, the foolish question. It was uttered before he considered it. 'Would you put on weight if we lived down here?' He was imagining making love in the sun on the bank of the creek with the tanned young Lena who had seduced him with her beauty and the promise of her intensity.

She went on wringing out her hair, then she bent forward and shook it out, running her hands through it. 'The water smells beautiful,' she said. She turned around and stood looking at him without saying anything for a long time; not a cold examination, but with a kind of wonderment. 'And if I were to put on weight, would you write a great novel? Is that to be our bargain?'

He said nothing.

She said evenly, 'We're both doing our best. That's what we're doing. It isn't everything the dream of love is supposed to be, but it's the best we can do. It's us, isn't it? This is who we are. You and I doing our best. That will have to be enough, won't it? Haven't we learned not to make foolish promises to each other and to ourselves? It's harder than we thought it was going to be. We've learned that. It's not as simple as we thought it was. We're no longer the people we were then.'

He said, 'I shouldn't have asked you that.'

'No, it's all right. You should have asked. Especially now. Here! Today! So long as you don't expect to get the answer you're hoping for you can ask me that any time you like.' She stood there, naked and thin as a starving prisoner—the prisoner of her compulsions. The shifting shadows of the trees on her, as if her skin undulated. She stepped out of the water and stood beside her pile of clothes. 'You know what you want to do. Maybe you can do it here.'

'I believe I could try,' he said, and he meant it. He could see himself repairing the cottage, the two of them living in this little cleft in the valley, growing their vegetables, running a small herd of breeding cows. He didn't quite dare to imagine himself writing. But he would not be an alien here, he did know that. And Ray McFadden would lend his support and encouragement. He would be a fine neighbour to have. And Martin would come and stay with them. He could see it all. A new beginning. Another new beginning.

'And you can't promise more than that, can you?' she said. 'We can do our best.' She was looking across at the orange trees and the little cottage. 'There's a quality of peace here that I believe would have saved my father's life. In Canberra there's no room for ideas as small and uncertain and vulnerable as ours. I've made my peace with this small thing in my own mind, and it is safe there and maybe it will become something. I can't say and I'm not going to try to say. Who knows if I will put on weight? I don't want to put on weight. It's you who wants me to put on weight. Let's be clear about that. I'm glad for you that you know what you want to do and I hope you will do it. If you don't do it, I have seen that you will go down the same deadly track I went down myself. I wouldn't forgive myself for that if you did.'

He said, 'I don't see a long-term alternative for me but writing.'

'And if I stay at the hospital in Canberra I'll go on doing what I'm doing and one day I'll wake up in that terrible house in that terrible suburb and I'll know I've missed it, whatever it was. Something beautiful. Something that was mine. My *meaning*. It is this serious for me.' She stood looking at him. 'You looked grand, you know. Standing there naked in the sun with the water coming off you just now. I wanted to kiss your body.'

'Thanks,' he said. He felt helpless.

She smiled. 'And don't tell me I look grand too, or I'll chuck one of these rocks at your head.'

'I believe you would,' he said. 'But as a matter of fact, you did look grand.'

She said, 'I suppose there are springs coming down from these hills or it would have dried up in the drought by now.' She looked up quickly, as if the idea had suddenly struck her. 'I bet Ray would love to have us as his neighbours.'

They stood looking at the sparkling water, the small brown fish reclaiming their domain.

She said, 'I feel as if I've known this place all my life. There's so much to think about. So much to say.'

He said, 'I wonder how big it is. It might not support us.'

She laughed. 'Now you're being careful. I've made you careful. I fell in love with a cowboy. You were the freest man I'd ever met.'

'I didn't have anything to be careful of back then.'

'Being careful of our possessions is being trapped by them,' she said. 'It's not what we have, it's our state of mind. It's what Dad did. He did it for Mum's sake. Now you want to do it for my sake. Being careful is what killed Dad. It's what killed them both. Dad should have chucked his city job and taken on a rundown place like this. He would have come alive. Instead of that the hope slowly drained out of him until his heart weakened and he died. By then he was filled with bitterness and regret. Being careful is what killed the fear and the excitement and the intensity in my parents' lives. They risked nothing and lost their dreams. They risked nothing and lost everything. Their lives were smoothed out from being careful, as if a bulldozer blade had ploughed through their dreams the way the dozer must have ploughed through that block of land where we've been living.' She leaned down and picked up her pants and put them on. 'I know about that,' she said. 'I know about people being careful.'

Robert said, 'Look at that!' He pointed. A white-bellied sea eagle was floating silently over the cleared paddock beyond the line of trees. 'She's looking for a rabbit, I'll bet.'

Lena said, 'She's beautiful.'

They stood very still in the shade of the casuarinas watching the great bird gliding over the country. Its cry a sudden warning or lament as it swung abruptly away and gained height and was gone.

She said, 'I feel as if we've been welcomed here. First Ray and now the eagle. I've never seen a sea eagle that close before.'

She looked at him. 'I'm happy. Shall we go and look at our new house now? Did you notice there's a wattle tree growing up through the middle of it?'

'There'll be rats,' he said.

'So we'll get a cat.'

42

It was a warm summer morning in Canberra and Robert was out in the driveway in his singlet helping the man who'd come with the moving van. He'd asked them to send two men but they'd sent only one. He was unfit and in his late fifties. His name, he said, was Oliver Green. Lena's Rönisch was enormously heavy and the truck didn't have a hydraulic lift. Oliver Green would not have been able to get the piano to the ramp on his own, let alone up it and into the truck. He and Robert had manoeuvred it onto the ramp and were struggling to push it further up the slope towards the open back of the truck. Robert had his shoulder padded with a towel between his skin and the sharp edge of the wood, Oliver on the other side of the piano, his face contorted with effort and anxiety, a trembling bead of sweat trying to cling on to the end of his nose.

Lena was standing outside the front door watching them, a hand held to her mouth, ready to cry out in horror if the Rönisch crashed to the concrete driveway. Or maybe she was half hoping to see the end of it. In some ways, the beautiful instrument must have been a reminder to her of her failure to be the person her mother had hoped she was to become—this weighty symbol of family love and the dutiful life from which she had struggled to liberate her spirit.

Oliver and Robert paused to gather themselves. Robert knew it wasn't going to happen. They were underpowered for the job.

'You ready, mate?' Oliver said hoarsely, and the drop of sweat let go. 'On the count of three, give it everything. One, two, three, *heave*!'

Together they put all their strength into it. The piano inched up the ramp a few meagre centimetres then stuck fast, the ramp bending alarmingly under its weight. They paused again, the piano rocking gently from side to side like a boat at anchor, Oliver and Robert catching their breath, staring at each other across the width of the piano's polished veneer, Oliver's thinning hair plastered to the skin of his pale skull. Robert smiled, hoping to give him confidence. Robert was worried Oliver was going to have a heart attack and die before they got the piano in the truck. To get the great instrument all the way up the ramp and to then tip it forward onto the floor of the truck had begun to look like it was a job that was beyond them. But how to get it down again now that they had it halfway up was just as big a problem.

There was a sudden roaring, as if a Harley was coming up the hill at full throttle. Ed's Land Rover came flying around the bend, its rusted-out muffler bellowing. He pulled up and jumped out and, without a word of greeting, stepped onto the ramp between

Oliver and Robert, laid his back against the piano and shouted, 'Heave-fucking-ho, you fuckers!'

The three of them kept her going, yelling encouragement to each other. The instant the piano's weight tipped it forward onto the level floor of the truck, Ed jumped down to the road and bent over, his hands on his knees, and had a violent coughing fit. Mary was sitting in the front seat of the Rover with her dress up around her thighs looking like a very pregnant schoolgirl. She was staring at Ed with a look of dismay on her innocent face, as if it had just dawned on her that she was partnered with a sick old man who was about to die and leave her and her kid without a daddy.

Lena ran over and took Ed by the shoulders. 'Ed! Are you all right?'

He straightened up and grinned at her.

She said, 'I'll get you a drink of water.'

He waved her away. 'I'm okay! I'm okay!' He sucked in air and coughed a couple more times. He fingered the crushed butt of a cigarette from the pocket of his jeans. He lit the butt with a match and took a deep drag on it, his eyes closed, the lit butt touching his lips, pinched delicately between thumb and forefinger, sucking the smoke hungrily into his lungs. 'So,' he said, opening his eyes. 'You guys are heading out? What's going on?' He'd lost another front tooth. Had it fallen out or had someone hit him?

Lena said, 'We bought a farm, Ed.'

'Fuck off!' he said. 'You're fucking kidding me!'

The pair of them, he and Lena, delighted with each other. Watching them, Robert decided they must have been lovers in a previous life.

An hour later they headed off in a column for Braidwood and the valley. Lena and Robert in the Holden following Oliver Green's brown truck, Ed and Mary coming on behind in the Land Rover, making their way to freedom and the simple life in the country—this was the story Lena insisted on. The sign coming up on them, YOU ARE NOW LEAVING THE AUSTRALIAN CAPITAL TERRITORY. Lena reached across and tooted the horn. Ed flashed his lights in their rear-view mirror.

Once they were in New South Wales the road narrowed to two lanes and began following the natural undulations of the landscape instead of cutting through it.

Robert said, 'So, do you reckon Ed and Mary are going to have their baby with us? Are we going to become a little commune down there?'

Lena said, 'You know Ed doesn't have plans. He just lets things happen.' A minute later she looked across at him. 'Would you mind all that much if Ed and Mary did decide to stay with us for a while?'

'Let's see how it goes,' Robert said. 'They may leave tomorrow. They may not even stay the night.'

She reached across and put her hand on his leg. 'We're not going to let anything spoil this, are we? I can't wait to have a swim in the creek.'

The farm was to be an investment, and Robert was to run it. That was Lena's idea. After all, she said, 'You know about these things.' And, of course, he would also write his novels. She was confident there would be time for both. It was not clear what she was going to do herself. Apart from an enthusiasm for growing their own vegetables and planting an orchard, she didn't talk about having any special plans.

The place had turned out to be vastly larger than they'd imagined. All up it was fifteen hundred acres, most of it leasehold and too steep and heavily timbered to be productive. The main freehold section was a forty-acre portion around the house. Several other smaller freehold blocks were dotted along the creek. Most of these had originally been gold leases. The lower boundary of the property was the Deua River, which the creek they had swum in joined at a place Ray called the junction. The main river was their boundary with Ray's place. Up the river, Ray said, was wilderness: hills and forests and wild cattle.

As he drove through the dry summer landscape behind Oliver's truck that morning, Robert was thinking that this new beginning they were making had better work out. He had the feeling it was probably his and Lena's last throw of the dice.

Oliver stopped in the high street in Braidwood. Robert pulled in and parked next to him. Ed came in beside them. They all got out and stood around together. They had packed the essential stores from the Canberra house but Lena said she was going to buy some fruit and vegetables from Dom Alvanos at the Royal.

Mary offered to go with her. Robert said, 'You just want to perv on the beautiful Greek.' Mary said, 'How did you guess?' Ed went across the road. Robert watched him go into the Commercial Hotel. A minute later he came out carrying a cask of red wine which he put in the back of the Rover.

There was an old farmhouse table upended against a shopfront near where they were standing. It was the same type of table as had been in the kitchen where Robert had his first job in Australia. He went over and asked the man how much he wanted for it. The man considered the table. 'Three pound ten,' he said. Robert gave him the notes, then ran his hand over the surface of the table, which had experienced years of scrubbing with sand soap and was pale and smooth with a lovely undulation in the grain. Oliver helped him put the table in the back of the truck. The sun and the country town and the old kitchen table made Robert feel happy. There was only one thing missing. He went into the general store and bought a packet of Champion Ruby tobacco and some papers and a box of matches. He came out and stood in the sun and rolled a smoke. Oliver came over and stood with him. Ed and Mary were sitting in the front of the Land Rover cuddling. Robert passed the makings to Oliver and Oliver thanked him and made a cigarette for himself. The two men stood in the sun smoking their cigarettes and watching the activity on the main street. The old Victorian buildings and the utes and stock crates nosed into the kerb, knots of women and men standing around talking as if they had all the time in the world, the smell of cattle from the stock truck parked nearby.

They got back into their vehicles and drove on across the granite tablelands and down the winding Araluen mountain road into the valley. They unloaded everything directly from the back of Oliver's truck onto the raised floor of the barn through the side door, the Rönisch sliding in without a hitch.

They were all tired out, and after a meal of baked beans on toast the four of them camped on the floor of the barn. Robert woke in the grey light of early morning and got up and went outside and took a pee around the back of the barn. A hunch-backed wallaby saw him and fled. It was just getting light, a night chill in the air. A mist rising along the line of the creek among the grey shadows of the casuarinas. Standing there looking at the scene, the situation of the cottage and the barn seemed to Robert more tightly enclosed by the densely timbered hills than he remembered from their first visit, the buildings and yards clustered into this narrow pocket of cleared land at the bottom of the valley, the immense stillness of the morning, birds making a racket in the timber. The place seemed smaller and older and more distantly abandoned than he remembered it.

He fetched their large saucepan from the boot of the Holden and walked down to the creek. He kneeled at the edge of the deep hole where Lena and he had swum and sluiced his face with the cold water then cupped his hands and drank. The water was sweet and fresh, the smell of it in the still air. A small bird dropped from an overhead branch of a casuarina and dipped into the water then flew straight up again and perched on the branch. It made a small twittering sound repeated rapidly, then dipped down to the water's surface again. It was not a bird that was familiar to him. It showed no sign of fear at his presence there by the pool's edge.

He carried the saucepan of water back up to the barn and filled the billy they'd used for tea the previous night. He gathered dry gum leaves and sticks and lit a fire beside the barn on the spot where he'd heated their beans, and set the billy on the sticks. He squatted and watched the flames catching at the wood, shifting a stick here and there to adjust the heat. The deeply familiar smell of the smoke in the morning air and the billy set among the flames convinced him he had returned into his past. He knew himself to be at home there and wondered if this peculiar rural isolation was to be the only reality he would ever know and be at home in.

Lena came out of the barn and stood close to the fire, her hands held out to the flames. 'You look the part squatting there,' she said.

Ed came out and the three of them squatted around the fire and drank the tea. Robert cooked eggs and bacon. Mary did not put in an appearance. After breakfast the three of them went over to check out the cottage. The rising sun was striking the tops of the farthest hills. Lena said, 'It's so beautiful. I can hardly believe we're really here.'

The cottage was set into the side of the hill, two stumpy stone-and-brick chimneys jutting from the wall facing the barn. The chimneys had once been painted white, but the paint had flaked and peeled, leaving the stone and old brick mostly bare. The three of them went in under the verandah, round posts supporting the roof, along the front wall of the cottage a square four-paned window and the door. The door was scraped back on its failed hinges, just as they'd left it from their first visit. Inside was one long room the width of the house. Robert stepped into the pantry on the left as Lena and Ed came through the door. The pantry had a three-paned window looking out onto the hill up towards the road. It was probably the oldest part of the house, and was constructed of split slabs, daylight showing through the cracks between the slabs where they had shrunk over the years and the filling between them had fallen out. A handmade cupboard with adzed timber shelves from floor to ceiling. Rat shit scattered over the shelves, the ceiling sagged in and damp-stained, straw and dried grass hanging out the ceiling cavity. The roof tin was still in place over the pantry.

He went out into the main room. Lena and Ed were standing looking up at the sky. The tin was completely gone from the roof over this part of the house and the room stood open to the elements. A slender black wattle sapling reaching up from under a broken floorboard, spearing into the sunlight above them, where it sprouted leaves and thin branches. The three of them stood admiring the little tree. Ed took a notebook from his shirt pocket and made a rapid sketch of the sapling. Lena said, 'We couldn't leave it, I suppose. Could we?'

Robert walked over and took a look at the iron stove tucked into its stone niche against the end wall, a four-inch square of thick glass mortared into the stone at the back of the niche to shed daylight onto the hotplates. He opened the fire door, a litter of old grey ash, the smell of something stale in the disturbed dust. 'Let's light the stove and see how she goes,' he said. When he turned around he saw that Ed and Lena had gone already along the passage that led from the middle of the kitchen to the rest of the cottage. To the left of the stove was a wide open hearth, a deep stone hob either side, an iron bar across the chimney cavity, two chains with hooks hanging from them, like something from a medieval torture chamber. A blackened log from the last fire still lay among the ashes, white splatters of bird shit patterning its crusted face.

He followed the others down the passage and looked into the room on the left. It was the room immediately behind the pantry. The roof iron was still intact over this back part of the house, so it was shadowed and darker and seemed more abandoned and even mysterious, as if something had been said and was waiting for a response. The room he stepped into was square, with space enough for a double bed with a foot or two to spare either side. A low black-painted set of shelves sat under the window. Robert decided at once that this room would be his study. He went over to the window and looked out. A view of the side of the hill, looking up towards the road and the heavily timbered slopes above the road. Dense banks of blackberry thickets. He went out and looked into the room across the passage. It was identical to the one he had just been in, except here there was a window that gave onto a closed-in verandah at the back of the house. Through the window he could see Lena and Ed standing at an open door. Both these small square rooms were fitted with a loose sliding door to the passage.

The materials and workmanship at this end of the cottage were cheap—thin fibro-cement sheeting on the walls, and the thin material of the doors, their panels not fashioned from solid timber like the front door and the door to the pantry. The kitchen and the front of the cottage were meant to last, the walls of stone and weatherboard fitted with quality timber window frames and solid doors from the previous century. He saw the construction of the cottage told a story of declining fortunes and a gradual abandonment of traditional values and materials. Time and skills had been lost, and the last people who had lived here had turned from the old ways entirely to a more makeshift way of life. Then they had left, leaving behind them the signs of their own decline. It was a narrow neck of marginal country, offering no one a fortune but only a living to be scraped together. The history he'd seen written into the cottage gave him the impression it was unlikely any young people remained in the neighbourhood. What future could there be here for them?

Ed and Lena were looking out from the back door into the fenced garden, beyond which there was a small paddock of five or six acres, and beyond that a section of humpy broken ground, mostly covered in blackberries. The garden fence was made of split timber posts and rabbit netting. The garden was around forty metres square. Through the tall dried-out docks, thistles and slender grass heads, he could see that the garden had once been divided into beds, some of which had been ridged as if the gardener might have been growing potatoes. There was a three-foot drop from the back door to the garden. There were no steps. A claw hammer lay on the floor of the verandah beside the door. Where Ed had kicked it aside it had left its hammer shape. Robert leaned out of the door and looked down. A wooden box with a collection of rusted tools rested against the stump immediately under the door. Lengths of sawn timber among the couch grass, white-ant tunnels along their surfaces. Here the look was not only of something unfinished and temporary, but a sign that the occupants had thrown down their tools and left in a hurry, almost as if someone had shouted to them to get out at once. Ray McFadden would surely know the story of what had happened here. Cheap glass louvres, a number of them broken, ran the length of the verandah at chest height.

Lena turned to him. 'We'll need to get the electricity and the phone reconnected straight away.'

Ed said, 'There's a couple of oil lamps in the shed. They've still got oil in them.'

'We'll need electricity for the fridge,' Lena said. She sounded just a little impatient with Ed's idea of the oil lamps. None of them had slept well in the barn the previous night.

Robert stood with them looking out at the dense weed growth in the garden, sheets of roofing iron lying where they had been blown up against the fence, twisted and bent by the force of the wind. The morning was still, the sun warming the air. Distant bird calls and that faint familiar rustling and shifting in the air that is the peculiar summer silence of the bush. The shimmering haze of millions of tiny insects going about their business for the day. Robert knew the others were waiting for him to set the direction of how things were to go.

He said to Ed, 'Let's make a start and get the tin on.' He jumped down to the ground and dragged the box of tools out, freeing it from the weave and tangle of the couch grass. 'We'll build these steps when we get the chance. We'll need to get some new timber. This stuff's had the dick.'

Ed and Robert collected the twisted sheets of roofing iron from the garden and the paddock and stomped on them to straighten them out. They worked steadily side by side all through the day, coming off the roof only for a ham and salad sandwich and cup of tea at noon. It was dusk and nearly too dark to see by the time they hammered the last piece of iron onto the trusses over the front section of the cottage. Lena had spent the day sweeping out the rooms. She looked grey and exhausted, her clothes clotted with dust and sweat. They were all tired and dusty, their limbs aching and their skin tense with dried sweat. Ed went over to the barn and called Mary and the four of them went down to the creek and stripped off. Robert let himself sink into the cool water. The moon was coming up over the hills.

Afterwards, he lit a fire beside the barn and cooked sausages. Ed and Lena and Mary stood watching him. Ed said, 'Can I have a potato in the ashes?'

They stood around the fire watching the food cook and drinking wine in cups from Ed's cask. Lena said to Robert, 'I need to sleep in our bed. Can we take the bed over to the cottage after we've eaten?' He said it was too late and they'd shift their stuff over to the cottage in the morning when they were fresh. She didn't have the energy to insist. There was a look of utter weariness in her eyes. She had eaten only half a potato and drunk a cup of black tea. Her hair was still damp from the creek water. He put his arm around her shoulders and held her against him. She rested her head on his shoulder. 'Do you think it's going to be all right?' she said. He said, 'We'll be in the cottage this time tomorrow with the stove lit and a proper meal inside us. It's all going to be fine.'

43

Robert stood looking out the door of the barn. The sharp brightness of yesterday's sky was gone out of the air and there were clouds low over the high hills to the west, the rising sun touching the peaks with pink. Robert said, 'It looks like rain.'

After breakfast they stood looking at the piano. Ed said, 'I reckon I can get her into the cottage no worries.' They watched him back the Rover up to the loading door of the barn. The Rover's tray was a couple of inches below the bottom of the door. They pushed the piano across the floor and eased it onto the tray. The Rover sank and groaned and settled under the load. Robert stood on the tray steadying the beast while Ed put the Rover in low-low and drove over to the cottage, easing slowly across the uneven ground. He crept over the cattle grid that protected the garden from stock and backed up to the door-without-steps. The tailgate of the Rover was level with the floor of the verandah. Together they edged the Rönisch onto the bare boards. Robert saw Mary watching them from the entrance to the barn. He waved but she didn't wave back. She had a blanket around her shoulders and was clutching the ball of her stomach. She stood there looking like a figure in an old photograph. Lena turned and looked at him. 'Now we're really here,' she said. Robert thought she was going to say more, but she didn't. They pushed the piano up against the wall and Lena lifted the lid and stood looking at the keys.

Seeing her standing at the piano like that, undecided and on the point of striking the keys, Robert hoped she was going to play a few bars of something familiar; a Chopin nocturne would have been ideal. Just a few bars, to give the moment its completion. To make their presence real.

Slowly, she lowered the lid and turned away.

By lunchtime they had all the furniture and their belongings in the cottage. Lena hung the portrait of Ed's mother over the hearth in the kitchen. The painting immediately looked as if it had always been there, the cat's yellow eyes following them around the room. Robert stacked the cartons of books in the small square room with its view up the hill towards the road, and set up his desk and swivel chair. The Helvetia sitting there in its green case, an intact ream of foolscap typing paper beside it, a shaft of sunlight striking the wall, the air filled with a light disturbance of dust, the faint smell of rats—the real owners of the house. There was space enough beside the desk for the pine shelves and the black-painted shelves.

In the front kitchen the old farmhouse table he'd bought in Braidwood filled the centre of the room. Like Ed's painting of his mother, the table looked as if it had always been there. There was a stack of old building timber in the barn, hardwood slabs and pit-sawn planks that had lain there seasoning for maybe a generation or more, materials for plans that had never come to anything. Robert and Ed put together a couple of benches for sitting around the table. Mrs Soren's floral easy chairs and the sofa looked far less elegant than they had in the sitting room of the Red Bluff house. Here in the cottage they might have been given as charity to a family of poor people—squatters in an abandoned cottage. The chairs and the sofa made the kitchen look squalid. Lena took one look at them and said, 'Put them out of sight on the back verandah, for God's sake.' Robert said he'd move them later. But he didn't. Other, more urgent tasks got in the way, and in the end they got used to them being there.

Ed set up a temporary encampment for himself and Mary at the far end of the back verandah, the piano forming a buttress. He said he and Mary would sooner sleep with bedding on the floor than use the single bed Lena and Robert had bought for the guest room when Martin visited Canberra. So they left the single bed in the barn. Robert saw that the barn was as much a depository of the history of the area as was the construction of the house. The future confidently envisaged by the people who had accumulated the things in the barn had never arrived but had become their past.

Robert had just lit the fire in the iron stove when there was the distant sound of an engine. He straightened and went out onto the front verandah. It sounded like a tank was approaching up the road, the belching roar of an open throttle. Ed and Lena came out and stood with him. Mary stayed inside on the couch, her blanket spread over her, her eyes dreamy and filled with wonder and an infinite sense of absence from their preoccupations, already more with her child than with her old self. An ancient black Standard Vanguard with no number plates and no muffler came down the road towards the cottage trailing a pall of smoke in the still air. The car pulled up outside the garden grid and fell silent after a long shudder. Ray McFadden stepped out. He was carrying a pup in his arms. Robert was struck once again by what a handsome old man he was, his white hair down to his broad shoulders, the amused intelligence in his blue eyes, the quiet confidence of his walk as he came over and presented Lena with the pup. Lena took the warm bundle in her arms and looked into its eyes. It gazed back at her with a look of perfect trust. 'He's one of Tip's new litter,' Ray said. 'I kept two of them. You fellers need a dog. There's a dozen rabbit traps and two short-handled tomahawks in the boot.'

Lena looked at Robert and said, 'Can we call him Toby? I had a dog called Toby when I was a little girl.' She cradled the pup against her t-shirt.

Ray said, 'He'll be a good working dog, Lena. You don't want to fuss over him or you'll spoil him.'

Robert introduced Ray to Ed. Ray narrowed his eyes and looked long and hard at Ed's beaded headband and his long sun-bleached hair, then he nodded and reached out to shake Ed's hand. 'How are you, Ed?' He raised his voice when he said this, as if unsure whether Ed would speak his language. Ed smiled and said, 'It's a pleasure to meet you, Ray.'

Robert thanked Ray for the traps and the tomahawks. Ray said, 'Don't let me forget them.'

Lena set the pup down beside the door and invited Ray in for a cup of tea. The pup leaned against the wall and watched the feet going by into the kitchen. Robert paused before going in and bent down and ruffled his ears. 'You on guard there?'

Ray walked over to the armchair on the left-hand side of the hearth and took off his hat and set it on the floor beside the chair and sat in the chair. He said, 'Just as well you got the tin on her. We're getting rain in a day or two.' He hadn't seen Mary. She was still curled up on the couch.

Robert checked the fire in the stove and set the kettle on the front hotplate.

Ray said, 'There's three horses belong to this place. They've been running up the river on my country. You'll be needing them, Robert.'

Mary sat up. Ray turned and smiled at her. 'Did I wake you up, dear?'

She said, 'I wasn't sleeping. Who are you?'

Robert said, 'Mary, this is our neighbour, Ray McFadden. Ray, this is Mary.'

Ray said, 'You haven't got long to go, my dear.'

She looked down at herself and made a smoothing motion over the ball of her stomach with both hands. 'He's moving around.' She looked up and smiled at Ray. 'He's a boy.'

Ray said, 'You know that for sure?'

Ed was sitting on a box at the table, sketching Ray's profile.

Mary said with confidence, 'Oh yes. I do, Ray.' She looked down at her stomach again. She spoke softly, her voice filled with a dreamy love for her unborn child.

'You have a name for the little feller?'

Ed got up and moved onto the couch beside her. He leaned down and pressed his ear to her stomach. Mary covered Ed's head with her hands, as if she was blessing him. He said, 'He's going to be our little Wild.'

Lena said, 'You're calling him Wild?'

Ed laughed. 'Wild and free. Like the wind.' He sat up and kissed Mary on the mouth. 'That's our boy, eh?'

They snuggled together, Ray sitting there smiling at them.

The kettle was boiling. Robert wrapped a tea towel over his hand, picked up the hot kettle and carried it over to the table, where he poured the boiling water onto the leaves in the teapot. He went back and set the kettle on the side of the stove. He could feel the heat coming off the iron—the old familiar smell of wood smoke and hot iron, something of the memory of home in it, an image in his mind of the kitchen on the Exmoor farm on dark winter mornings, Morris's wife moving about in her apron by the light of the kerosene lamp.

Lena said, 'I'll pour it in a minute. Sit down and talk to Ray. Will you stay and have something to eat with us, Ray?'

Ray said, 'Thank you, Lena, but I ate a breakfast with Peggy Mallon an hour ago. Do you mind if I smoke?'

'Go ahead, Ray.'

He made a cigarette and lit it. 'You've got plenty of feed on this place, Robert. It's dry feed but it's good. There's been no stock on here for a number of years. You should get your boundary fences in good repair quick smart and I'll take you up to the Braidwood sales and we can pick up a couple of yards of in-calf heifers for you. They'll do well here.'

Lena was standing at the table with the tea things. She said, 'How much will the heifers cost?'

'They won't cost you anything. Jim Forbes at the Australian Estates office who sold you this place, he'll be happy to stock her for you. You'll pay him back over three seasons with half the proceeds of your sales of the vealers each year and them heifers will become the basis of your breeding herd. If we get this rain now, prices will be going up again. Everyone will be looking for breeders. You wait. I've seen it a dozen times after these big droughts.'

Lena poured the tea and handed cups around. She had buttered a few Jatz biscuits and set them out on one of her mother's flowered plates. Ray took one of the biscuits and thanked her. He munched a while then drank some tea and took a pull on his cigarette, staring into the cold ashes of the open hearth in front of him. 'I'll take you over to Cooma, Robert. We'll get you a good Hereford bull from old Jack Francis. Jack's a good friend of mine. He'll let you have one of his bulls at a fair price. His line is bred from the original Vern sires from England.'

Lena said, 'And will Jim Forbes pay for the bull too?'

'No he won't, Lena. You will pay for the bull yourselves and you will not be sorry that you did.' He drank the last of his tea and looked into his cup. Lena asked him if he'd like another. He gave her a smile and passed the cup to her. 'You need to put in for the mail contract, Robert,' he said. 'We've had no one running the mail now for a year. You'll be sure to get the contract. We're all hungry for someone reliable. It's cash in hand at the end of each month.' He gestured towards the door. 'And you can cut yourselves a load of wattle bark with them tomahawks I left on the verandah for you. There's a feller still buying tanbark in Moruya.'

Lena handed him a fresh cup of tea. He thanked her and turned to Robert. 'You shoe horses, Robert?'

'Yes I do,' Robert said.

'I might get you to put a set of shoes on that old gelding of mine when you've got a chance. My back's getting a bit past it these days.' As he said this he reached around and rubbed his lower back.

Robert said, 'I'd be glad to. Whenever you want. Just give us a yell.'

Lena was sitting up at the table watching Ray, her chin in her hands. She said, 'Why did they need such an amazing barn on this place?'

Ray lifted his hand and pointed through the wall. 'That barn of yours was a great event when they built her. When I was a boy the old people still talked about setting up those corner posts. We used to have weekly dances there. They put her up after the men came back from the First World War. A lot of them fellers from the valley never came back. There was a need for a place where people could get together. There was a whole community of people down here in the lower valley in those days. All these small freehold sections of yours up along the creek, they was each owned by a different family. That's why they're called John's and McLeary's and Mallon's and the rest of them. There was families all through the timber and along the creek in those days. Now there's just one or two left. The men cut props for the mines and fossicked for gold and picked fruit in Araluen. We had a Lower Araluen school then. She's still there opposite my place, next to the church. The priest hasn't come up the valley this far for it must be twenty years. Old Father O'Halloran used to keep his racing stallion on my place. That filly of yours up the river is out of him. Cotton Patch was his name. They kicked Frank O'Halloran out of the priesthood and he went and got married.' Ray sat back, gazing into the dead hearth. He drank off his tea and reached for his hat and stood up. 'That barn of yours was the centre of life down here. Thank you, Lena. I will call in tomorrow and see how you are all getting on.' He turned to Robert. 'You go up to the pub and see Aunt Molly about that mail contract today. She will sign you up on the spot.'

After he'd gone, Lena looked at Robert and grinned. 'Ray's got your work organised for you. Catching horses and running the mail and fixing the fences and shoeing his horse for him.' She laughed. 'I think that might be just the beginning. You're going to be busy.'

Ed leaned across from the couch, offering his profile of Ray for her inspection. She took the sketchbook in her hand and looked at it. 'God, it really is him! You've got a magic eye, Ed.' She handed the book to Robert. A few quick lines, assured and confident, Ray's mane of white hair mostly a blank area, a touch of the pencil sufficient indication, the heavy line of his broken nose below his brows. Robert felt a sharp pang of jealousy. 'It's brilliant,' he said. He was dismayed by the ease of Ed's freedom. It was so simple for him. He and Ed exchanged a smile in which there was a perfect understanding of their difference. Ed said, 'Thanks, mate.' Robert thought of his typewriter sitting in its case on his desk in the back room, the knotted complications of his need to write. He handed the sketchbook back to Lena. She sat looking at the drawing, Ed watching her. He said, 'Ray's an old Roman centurion. He must have been a real heartbreaker when he was young.'

Robert stood up. 'I'll go and see about this mail run.'

The pup was at the door. He stood up and stretched and followed Robert. Robert scooped him up and carried him over to the Holden and set him on the passenger seat.

44

Robert woke in the night to the sound of Mary's voice. He sat up and listened. She wasn't speaking loudly and sounded calm. He couldn't catch what she was saying but he knew what it was. He got out of bed and pulled on his pants and went around onto the verandah. Ed had his torch on and was searching for something. He saw Robert and said, 'All right if I take the Holden?'

Robert said, 'I'll get the keys.' He went back into the bedroom. Lena was sitting up. 'The baby's coming,' Robert said. 'They're taking the station wagon.' He picked up the keys and took them to Ed. Lena got up and put on a dressing-gown. Ed was bundling up their things. Mary giving him instructions. Lena asked Ed if he'd like a cup of tea before heading out.

'I think we'd better get to Canberra pronto,' he said. He was grinning. 'Do I look terrified? Because I am.'

Lena said, 'You look happy, Ed. Like you should.' She kissed him on the cheek. When she turned away, Robert saw the twinkle of tears in her eyes. Something clenched inside her had never eased its grip, a fragility in her that cried out for a steadying support.

Without him, he could imagine her destroying herself. He longed for the day when she would find her meaning, and wondered if she ever would.

He helped Ed load their stuff into the station wagon and Lena and he hugged them both and wished them good luck. Robert and Lena stood side by side out on the verandah and watched them drive up the road. Ed gave three short blasts on the horn as they went out over the cattle grid. They watched the flash of the Holden's lights through the forest canopy till they disappeared. The pup hadn't moved from beside the front door, his eyes blinking up at them. Robert said, 'We should bring him inside with us.' Lena said, 'I think he's happy out here. If he wants to come in, he'll make a fuss.'

There was no moon. The forested hills were dark and heavy, encircling them, a touch of rain in the air. They got into bed and lay in the silence side by side, the rain tapping on the tin.

Lena said, 'I'll miss him.' That was all.

45

———

Rain was coming down steadily. When Robert went outside to take a piss, a grey mist of cloud and rain was drifting down the valley, obscuring the tops of the hills. They ate their breakfast, the fire going in the hearth. Robert said, 'Another twenty-four hours and Ed and Mary wouldn't have got out.'

Lena said, 'Maybe the baby knew the rain was coming.'

It rained for a week, the creek roaring in the nights. The gullies were running a banker, carrying a fresh wave of rocks and debris across the road. Robert collected firewood in the back of the Rover. He kept the big hearth alight as well as the iron stove.

They heard nothing from Ed and had no way of contacting him.

So the time had come. They were alone and free to live their dreams. Except for the three days in the week when he had to run the mail—Saturday, Wednesday and Friday—each morning after breakfast Robert went into the study and sat at his desk and he wrote the story of himself and Frankie. But it was soon clear to him that this was no longer the story he had written in Sydney. Somehow it had turned into another, more complicated story.

Something larger and more demanding in its scope. Something less private. No longer the intimate celebration of friendship, but an idea now; an idea concerning justice and injustice.

He worked in the study each day from breakfast till lunchtime. For the first hour Lena played the piano. He liked to hear her playing. It made him feel more cocooned and alone with his work to know she was out there with her music. He soon discovered, however, that after four or five hours working at his writing in the privacy of his room there was an awkward and irritating mismatch between the demanding realities of the farm and the house and his relations with Lena, and the peculiar illusion of meaning brought on by writing. And when he came out of his study to have his lunch, his writing was reluctant to give way to the everyday needs of the farm. He was irritated at the thought of the chores that were waiting for him—shoeing Ray's horse and mending the boundary fences and rebuilding the tank stands and gathering firewood. He ate his lunch in silence.

Lena said, 'When do you think you'll go up the river and catch the horses Ray told us about? I'd quite like to come with you.'

Robert sat back and pushed his plate away and lit a cigarette. 'You know what I need?' he said. 'I need a modest little apartment in the city. St Kilda would do nicely. With a cafe round the corner where I can meet friends and strangers when I finish writing for the day.' He looked at her and grinned. He didn't tell her that Ann would be there in the cafe waiting for him and they would go back to his flat together and have wonderful sex.

She got up and went over to the hearth and stood with her back to the warmth of the fire. The rain had eased up half an hour ago. Now it was coming on harder again. She said, 'I love the sound of the rain on the roof.'

'Ray says it's raining money.'

They were both silent a while.

She said, 'Aren't you happy?'

'I was joking. I'm not complaining. I'm fine. It's just that writing puts me in a funny mood. It takes a while to come down from it, or out of it. When I stop writing for the morning I feel as though I need a reward. Something exciting. Thinking of the chores waiting for me isn't what I want. It takes a minute or two to adjust.'

She said, 'Music's like that.'

They looked at each other. 'Our two worlds,' he said. 'Don't worry, I'll fetch the horses when it stops raining, and I'll do all the other things that need doing.'

'And I'll make a lovely vegetable garden for us.'

'And an orchard?' he said.

'We'll make the orchard together.' She stood looking at him. 'I love this place. I feel as if we're meant to be here.'

➤

Driving along the road on his return run with the mail, his next stop Ray's place, then the Mallons and last of all the Hemler family, Robert looked down on the cottage. The sun was shining, a drift of smoke from their chimney, Lena bent over in the vegetable garden, Toby lying on his back, belly up, beside her. She stood up when she heard the Rover and turned around and waved to him. He tooted the horn. She was wearing a pale scarf over her hair and from the distance of the road looked like a peasant woman. She might have been down there in that hollow all her life, dutifully scratching a living from the stony soil. The beauty of the setting among the forested hills always moved him to a mixture of joy and sadness. The beauty and the isolation. The solitary figure of Lena working in the garden. It astonished him. Lena Soren, head prefect at the Methodist Ladies' College, dux of her class in German literature, a concerned social worker, transformed into a peasant girl. Was her struggle for meaning over? Had she found her place here in this remote valley? The confident girl in the smart swimsuit, sophisticated, educated, passionate. It was like a fairy tale in which the princess turns into an old woman of the forest.

Ray was standing at the road gate waiting for him, the Standard grunting and jumping and belching smoke beside him. He was clean-shaven and dressed in his three-piece town suit and was without a hat, his proud head of hair shining in the sun, his new fibro-cement cottage set back from the road behind him, his stock yards in need of repair, the original kitchen of his old place still standing, a small slab hut with its tin chimney, a relic from the valley's old days, the new growth of wattle trees coming up where he'd once cleared the ground and was now letting it slip back into wilderness again, his youthful energies spent.

Ray greeted Robert. 'I'm going up to Sydney for a few days to see my nephews. One of them's getting married again. I'd be glad if you could slip down and feed Tip and make sure there's water for her and the pups. I'll leave Beau in the yard for you to put those shoes on him. If you catch them horses of yours, I'll take you up the river when I get back and you can give us a hand to get the cattle in. You'll get to know the country. We might need to do a bit of work on these yards first.'

Robert smiled at Ray and wished him a good trip to Sydney. He even added foolishly, 'There's no hurry to get back, Ray. Take your time.' Perhaps he *was* a fool. But that's who he was.

Ray said, 'I'll call over and see you and Lena when I get back. Old Beau won't give you any trouble. He's inclined to lean on you, but he doesn't kick. He never has kicked out.'

He climbed into the chugging car and drove off. Robert looked after him. 'There goes a happy man.'

46

On the day, Lena decided not to go with him up the river to look for the horses. She said she wasn't feeling too good and anyway the weeds were getting ahead of her in the garden and she hadn't realised, she said, that he would be leaving so early. She came out of the kitchen and stood at the door and watched Robert going through the frost, Toby at his heels. Lena was clutching her dressing-gown around her against the cold morning air. She called after him, 'I hope you find them.' He gave a wave as his answer. He had the feeling she was looking forward to being alone and having the place to herself for the day.

He went on over to the barn and picked out a halter and lead rope and he walked down beside the high creek bank to the bottom of the small paddock. He picked up Toby and crossed the creek on a fallen willow, then followed the far bank down to the junction with the river. He stood on the bank of the river and smoked a cigarette. There was a movement in the air here and the mist was drifting off the water, the air clear above, the tops of the casuarinas sticking up like pines. He was admiring the sweep of the river where the creek water flowed in. A deep green hole carved out by the creek when it flooded into the river, a wide sandbank making a perfect beach this side of the hole.

Robert picked his way between the boulders along the steep riverbank for some way then climbed up onto what turned out to be flat, lightly timbered country, the base of the heavily forested hills rising abruptly a kilometre from the river. He walked out onto the flat, a sudden openness and the morning smell of the eucalypts. The day had begun to warm up. There was good sign of cattle having recently been grazing there, but no sign of horses. Toby flushed a rabbit and took off after it with a yelp of helpless excitement. The air was still and warm and there was the great silence of distant bird calls. He had stopped resenting having forfeited his writing this morning. His mood was lighter now as he began to recover the beauty of being alone in the bush, always that uncanny sense of human absence that made him want to turn around, half expecting to see a figure watching him from among the timber.

Three Hereford cows and their calves were camped in the shade of a stand of black wattle. Over on the edge of the cleared country close to the rise of the hill where the forest began, he saw a stone ruin. He made his way over there to take a look at it. The roof and most of the walls were gone, lying scattered on the surrounding area, the old beams cluttering the inside where the rooms had once been, rooms where people had lived their lives, eating and drinking and sleeping and making love and getting sick and dying. He stepped around among the rubble, looking for whatever was there. The ruin had been scavenged, someone coming here for building materials for their own place. There was that empty silence about it, the hollowness in him of knowing he stepped among the remains of forgotten people. A pack saddle had fallen from a rotted beam. A big old lemon tree shading the place on one side, its branches heavy with lemons, the air rich with the citrus smell of them. Someone had lit a fire not so long ago in the stone hearth. He wondered if it was Ray, out looking for cattle, boiling his lunch billy.

He walked on, leaving the ruin behind. On the far side of the open country the hills closed in again where a deep green cleft led up towards the ridge. The gully had a seep in it and there was fresh horse dung and hoof prints scattered about. Robert said to Toby, 'They will be up here in the cool.' He went on in among a glade of ancient wild apple trees. A family of striking yellow-and-black birds were making a fuss, squawking and jumping about in the branches, warning him off. He had never seen these birds before and was curious to know what they were. He stood watching them for some time, Toby beside him looking up at the larrikin birds as if he was thinking they were the reason for walking all this way up the river.

The three horses were feeding in a soft green glade. The old brown gelding looked up and gave a low throaty rumble of welcome to see him. The creamy mare blew out a startled whistle and trotted stiff-legged in a circle, her tail up, her eyes wide, snorting, expecting the other two to set off with her. The old brown stood his ground. The young filly gave a sideways jump then stood looking at the dog.

Robert walked over to the brown gelding and gave him one of the apples he had brought. The old horse was glad to see a man again and pushed his head into Robert's chest, pushing him back and looking for another apple. He did not object when Robert slipped the halter over his ears. Robert led him over to a fallen tree and sat on the log and rolled a smoke. The old horse took the slice of bread from Robert's hand, his eyes dreamy with the pleasure of it. Robert sat smoking and looking at the creamy. She stood well back, watching. There was plenty of feed about. The horses were all in good condition. The creamy was interested but she wasn't going to come too close. She was not so trusting of men as the gelding. Robert wondered who had owned her. She was a beautiful-looking thing. The filly, her daughter out of the priest's stallion, was narrow in the chest and small-rumped, just as Ray had described her. She shook her head at Robert. He said, 'You don't like being stared at. Is that it?' She knew herself addressed and perked her head and took two or three prancing little steps towards Toby, who gave a squeal and hid behind Robert. The filly wheeled away and kicked up. Robert gave Toby's ears a scratch. The gelding reached his nose down and snuffled at the pup. Toby yelped and rolled onto his back. Robert stroked the gelding's nose. The horse half closed his eyes, his long lashes black and elegantly curved. Robert said to him, 'You have had nothing but kindness from men.'

He was in no hurry to leave the soft light of the glade and did not resist the feeling that he was being observed. He had camped alone one time by a great stone on which there rested an old flat iron, far up in the headwaters of Coona Creek on Reg Wells's station, when he was sent out to hunt brumbies. His horses both stood close by his fire that night and did not feed on the level green of the creek flat he had chosen for the night camp. A woman, he was told by Reg when he recounted the experience to him, a mother and wife, was murdered with that flat iron. Robert had known nothing of that story when he set up his camp that night. But whatever it was that remained of the woman's brutal death had kept him and the horses awake all that night. Being observed by such spirits was not all that new to him.

He stood up and led the old gelding out of the gully onto the sunlit flat and climbed on his back. The creamy and the filly followed their old leader at a respectful distance. When they reached the river Robert stepped off the gelding, picked up Toby and climbed on again. Setting the dog in front of him, he urged the old plugger into the water. The current was strong there and the dog might have made it alone and he might not have. Robert had not wanted to risk him. Toby enjoyed the ride and the old gelding did not object. Robert walked the gelding on down the far bank of the river and set Toby down. He did not look back but heard the other two splashing across behind them, the thud of their hoofs and the snorting as they cantered up the bank.

Robert rode the gelding into the big yard and slipped off his back. He noticed Toby running over to the house. He looped the lead rope over the rail at waist height and propped the gate open. Then he went over to the barn and fetched a couple of tight slices of the hay bale Ray had left for him and a scoop of the milled oats and set the oats and one of the slices of hay in front of the gelding. Robert set out the other two slices of hay one either side of the gelding, not too far off but not so close that he could reach them. Robert went into the dark interior of the barn and waited in the shadows until the creamy and the filly finally gave up ducking and diving around the gate and tucked their backsides and scooted right into the big yard where the gelding was enjoying his feast of oats and lucerne. The creamy and the filly crowding the gelding in their nervous excitement. Robert went over and closed the gate on them.

Robert put a set of shoes on the creamy the next day and took her for a ride up the creek. She was skittish at first but soon settled, and it was clear she was a well-mannered horse and, like the gelding, must also have had a caring owner.

47

————

Soon, sooner than anyone expected, Lena was having to plant her summer salads again. She had done it once, but it hadn't stayed done. She began ordering vegetables from Dom Alvanos. The weeds soon took over. The fabled orchard had not been planted. The orange trees remained as they had been when she and Robert had first seen them. The hills remained the same. The same trees continued to grow where they had grown before. Robert's book was nearly finished. He hadn't let her see it.

A momentary excitement broke the routine when Robert finished repairing the boundary fences and Ray took them both up to the cattle sales in Braidwood. Instructed by Ray, Robert bid successfully on a yard of thirty in-calf heifers, and he and Ray and Lena followed the stock float down the mountain and watched their beautiful red-and-white cattle slide and clamber down the ramp into the yard. After the truck had gone Robert opened the yard gate and he, Lena and Ray went over to the house and watched the lovely beasts find their way out of the yard and begin to graze on the fresh green pick of the hillside. By evening there was no sign of them. In the morning Robert saddled the creamy and went out to look for them. They had not gone far. When he breasted the hill over onto John's and saw his heifers grazing peaceably on the flats along the creek, he felt a thrill. Some had already made their way up the gullies and into the hills, as if they had long been accustomed to the tight clefts of the lower valley. Toby went with him and they stood together, horse and rider and dog, at the top of John's clear-felled paddock the other side of the hill from the house. Robert rolled a cigarette and watched. And watching, he felt a new sense of responsibility on his shoulders.

➤

Lena took to going for long walks into the bush. She climbed to the summit of hills and sat alone and gazed out at the vaster view she had achieved, seeing weather changes before they became apparent in the valley, meeting shy king parrots and rock wallabies and finding discarded mining equipment from the old days. And every morning after breakfast Robert sat on his swivel chair in the study and added to the pile of single-spaced typescript pages beside his typewriter. The closer he got to the end of the story the more eager he became to continue working and was reluctant to come out for lunch. At times he worked on the book in the evenings and on into the early hours of the morning. But sooner or later the awkward process of re-entering reality had to be faced, and he felt that great wave of discontent and hunger for the sublime diversion of exquisite sex with his imaginary Ann.

Then, one Wednesday morning when he picked up the mail at the pub in Araluen, there was a letter from Martin. He parked along the road and opened the letter and read it:

I will come and see you soon. Birte has not been well this year and we haven't been able to travel. I am looking forward very much to seeing you and Lena and helping you with your farm work. You know my father and I were also skilled workers. Perhaps I have never told you this. I don't know the word for our trade in English. We made a living sewing the fancy stitching that you see on shoes and boots. Like you, dear Robert, I have a deep respect for the manual skills and for the values of working people. I would feel happier for you, however, if I knew you were enjoying the company of other writers and one or two intelligent friends, as well as the pleasant company of Ray and the local farmers that you speak about in your letters. I would also like to hear your impressions of the book I gave you on Karl Liebknecht. You've not mentioned it. I hope you are leaving time for serious reading.

A phrase from the Liebknecht biography was, in fact, Robert's epigraph for his book: *Karl Liebknecht understood his political activity in the interest of the proletariat as a fight for equality and justice.* It stood as Robert's homage to what he took to be Martin's expectations of his writing, and as a justification for his private struggle to write something that would resonate beyond the narrow compass of his own experience.

48

That winter was cold and wet, with frequent frosts and even a light covering of snow on the hills one day, the creek often running a banker. By the time spring came around the heifers were all doing well in the hills away from the constant wet. Robert rode out on the creamy mare and checked them from time to time, Toby, a grown young dog now, tagging along and getting weary.

Lena walked every day, rain or shine. Thin as she was she didn't seem to feel the cold. One morning when Robert went outside to take a piss, a ginger cat was sitting on the verandah gazing fixedly at Toby. Toby staring back at it. When Robert came out the cat stood up. It yawned and stretched then jumped down and rubbed itself against his legs. Toby made a careful approach and sniffed it. The cat ignored him. Toby was required to accept his inferior status and it wasn't long before he and the cat were lying close together.

The grass on the flats began to grow at the first touch of spring and the cattle began grazing on the open slope above the house. Robert and Lena were astonished one morning to see the first calf suckling at its mother's teats. Lena said, 'You've become a farmer.' He looked at her. 'And what about you?' She didn't reply. 'The calf is beautiful,' she said. And it was, shining in the morning sun as if it had been groomed and polished. Robert said, 'Are you content?' He knew she wasn't content. She had stopped playing the part of the simple peasant woman. Ray called in to see them from time to time and often stayed to eat his evening meal with them. He dozed in the armchair in front of the fire, and when he woke he always said, 'Well, I'll see you fellers later,' and he picked up his hat and put it on his head and said goodnight. Robert and Lena always went out with him and watched him drive away.

Robert had been up on the ridge behind the house since lunch, dragging broken old barbed wire together and cutting new fence posts. It was a hot sticky windy day up there among the trees, the flies and a thousand other insects finding his sweat irresistible. He was unable to endure it a moment longer and picked up his tools and made his way down to the creek. He started the pump and went on up to the house.

When he came into the house he called to Lena but got no answer. Toby wasn't around. He went down to the back verandah and stood looking into this room which he rarely visited. The Rönisch had been standing silent for a long time. The first thing that struck him was the rescued doll, which was usually sitting up on the closed lid of the piano. It was slumped against the wall under the louvres. The doll looked as if it had been thrown against the wall, violently, its limbs twisted under it, its head facing back over its shoulder on its stumpy neck. Two old ledgers which he recognised from the tin box in the barn were lying on the floor. One of them was lying open. On the open page were delicate pencil studies of the bits and pieces she had found on her daily explorations, notes inscribed beside each sketch. He crouched down and read the notes. They recorded where she had found each article. Every entry was dated. Robert turned the page of the heavy old quarter-calf ledger. On the right-hand page there was a heavily overscored pencil drawing of the doll. The drawing was utterly different to the careful little studies of the found objects. The agony of the doll's violent abandonment was convincing. On the left-hand page Lena had written something in pencil. The notes were not written in the finely disciplined hand in which she had written her notes about the found objects, but were scrawled carelessly across the page on a sharp diagonal, as if with a little more freedom, a little more flourish, with another leap of conviction, the pencilled words might themselves become the sensuous lines of an expressive drawing.

Crouched there looking at this writing he was remembering the postcard she had sent to Birte and Martin from Florence. He couldn't recall the name of the artist whose picture was on the postcard, or what Lena's message to Birte and Martin had been, but he remembered vividly the impression of the picture itself: a group of figures huddled under a shattered tree, battered by the violence of a storm, the wild swirling lines of the drawing, its freedom and energy. He also remembered the dramatic change in Lena's handwriting on that card, the large looping scrawl.

He could hear the tank overflowing. He'd have to go down and turn the pump off. She'd left the ledger open. Was that an invitation to him to look at it? She'd kept these drawings to herself. She hadn't even spoken about them, let alone offered to share them with him. Her drawing, even more than her wandering in the bush, seemed to be a cherished private matter with her. He set about deciphering her notes with a feeling of trespass. He knew he was looking at something utterly authentic and meaningful and could understand her reluctance to share it with him. She was sure to be afraid he wouldn't see the seriousness of it for her. How to believe our dreams and little creations will have meaning for others as well as for ourselves? He understood such doubts. He had them every morning when he sat down to begin writing. The farm work was its own justification. No one would ever ask him why he fixed the fences or cared for the animals. It was obvious to everyone why he did these things. But drawing and writing had no such obvious meaning. With difficulty he deciphered the words Lena had scrawled across the page of the ledger facing her drawing of the contorted body of the doll:

Finding meaning by drawing the same image over and over again.
FIERCE
Self-portrait emerges
* I am a fierce, intense little woman

* I am a helpless doll
* I am a comical vessel containing an unruly brood of
thoughts and feelings
—this I MUST TAKE FURTHER !!!!
Is this my own nursery tale?
Jagged
Watchful
Grey
STIFF—girl
My world—my home & garden—a broken doll
Joy—collapse

He was moved by the desperation of these intensely private inscriptions. Had she really come to see herself as a helpless doll? A comical vessel? This tortured image of herself dismayed him. But it also fascinated him. There was something terrifyingly real about it. As if, with this poetry, if that's what it was, she had cut into the deep anatomy of her dilemma. It was ruthless and determined. A nakedness in the images of herself that impressed him hugely. He couldn't have written such vivid words himself. There was an honesty in it that he knew himself to be incapable of. He read over her wild scrawl several times.

The words made him wince. To think of her solitary suffering, keeping it all to herself, unable to speak to him about it. He turned the page. A drawing of the doll lying face down, as if it had fallen forward onto the ground or been roughly pushed, its face thrust into the loose surface, scumbled smudges of charcoal blurring the outlines of the figure, giving an impression that it was melting into its surroundings. The violence again. The pencilled caption: *Sketch of a dead toreador.* Beside the drawing, stuck onto the page, a small glossy photograph cut from a magazine. The carcass of a bull being dragged through the dust by a tractor, a chain around the buts of the bull's horns. And a long note, written in a clear hand:

> Ray told us one frosty winter evening when Robert and I were sitting with him by the hearth that the previous owner of this place was driving his tractor across the hill above the cottage when a chain he was dragging became hooked on a stump and whiplashed around his neck. He was killed on the rise above the house. I can see the stump that killed him when I stand at our front door. He had seven children. He comes into my dreams. One night I went out into the moonlight to pee and he was standing looking at the house, the chain looped around his neck, his hands holding the loose ends of the chain. He was looking directly at me. His eyes were deep and were fixed on mine. I was not afraid of him, but knew a kindred link with him and with the pain of his futile struggle. We did not exchange words, that dead father and I, but exchanged the empathy of our deepest emotion. My hero! My saviour! The abandoned Barn Doll! My child!

The dreadful cry of Lena's anguish startled him. She had not written *that dead man and I* but *that dead father and I.* Robert thought of her own dead father who might have saved his life if he had possessed the courage of his dreams. Fathers, dead prematurely, crying out in the final days against the failure of the dream;

mothers holding the keys to the cage; and children, her aborted child in the form of the discarded doll. He saw it all hopelessly knotted together in a tangle that could never be unravelled. And she had exposed it here. Made poetry of it.

He turned back to the page where Lena had left the ledger open, and stood up. He realised the pump had stopped. It must have run out of petrol. His fingers trembled as he rolled the tobacco and touched his tongue to the paper, sealing it. He lit the cigarette and drew the smoke into his lungs. Set up on the lid of the piano and across its top, and ranged along the wall under the louvres, were the souvenirs Lena had brought back from her explorations into the bush. An old sauce bottle. A rusted can with a dead bat in it, the bat black as a crow and desiccated: a bat mummy. A dry root shaped like an arm without a hand. A range of coloured stones from the creek. A black stone Aboriginal axe, its cutting edge chipped ragged. A piece of iron from a machine.

He went to the kitchen and got the fire going in the stove and put the kettle on. After he'd eaten his lunch he made a stew for the evening. Lena would push the potatoes and carrots around on her plate and maybe take a few spoonsful of the gravy.

➤

That evening they were sitting by the hearth drinking a cup of tea after dinner. He had said nothing to her about her drawings and her poetry. The moment for him to speak of them hadn't arrived yet when she said, 'I've decided to go and visit Birte.'

It flashed into his head that she was going to share the ledger with Birte.

He said, 'Martin's coming up to see us soon.'

She was looking into the fire. 'I hate to think of Birte being ill. She was always the strong one. Despite what she went through in the war, she was never ill. All through school, I don't remember her ever taking a day off. No one ever had to substitute for her.' She turned to him. 'In six years. It must be a record. I need to reconnect with her properly. I know she'd love to see me. It would cheer her up. Maybe I shouldn't wait till Martin's been? What do you think?'

He was thinking of the fierce self-flagellation of her words. 'I think you should go when you want to.'

She said, 'You'll be all right here, won't you? Ray will come up and see you nearly every day. And you have the mail run. Will you start a new book, do you think?'

'Not till Martin's seen this one.'

'I wish you'd let me read it.' She picked up the poker and thrust it into the smouldering log, sparks flying up the chimney. She turned to him. 'I think I will go then. If that's all right?'

He knew she had already decided to go. He asked her lightly, 'Do you still believe in this? The farm, I mean? What we're doing here? Does it still make sense to you?'

'Of course I believe in it. Don't be silly. You know I love this place. I love it here! I just need to go and see Birte. Do you understand? I hope you do.'

'When will you go?'

'Maybe you could give me a lift to Canberra on Saturday after you've done the mail run?'

So there it was. Lena was on the move again.

49

——

Martin came to stay when the nights in the valley were cold and windless, the sky clear, sounds carrying through the forest with a strange clarity, distant places drawn near by the gleaming prism of the air. Lena had recently returned from visiting Birte in Melbourne. Robert picked Martin up at the airport in Canberra. They stopped in Braidwood to buy supplies and it was late in the afternoon when they drove into the farm, Toby running up the road to greet the Land Rover, racing them down the hill barking. The night chill was already settling, a pale mist drifting in the hollow by the creek, where the casuarinas lay in the deep shadow of the hill to the west.

Lena came out of the house and met them at the garden grid. She and Martin embraced then stood beside each other on the small square of lawn at the side of the house. They were facing the horse paddock and she was describing to him the lay of the land, pointing to where the creek had its junction with the river, the boundary of their land and the beginning of their neighbour's place, their friend Ray McFadden. Martin was wearing smart

Italian sunglasses with a striped business shirt and dark tie. He looked very European. He had taken off his jacket and Robert was holding it for him, along with the small leather suitcase he'd brought. Standing there in the late sunlight beside Lena, Martin seemed to Robert more youthful than he ever had in his home in Melbourne. He stood very straight and alert, his hands on his hips, as if he surveyed a field of active operations that were being described to him, a dilemma confronting him to which he was confident of finding the solution. Robert noticed he was wearing onyx cufflinks, the polished surface of the black stones catching the last of the sun when he moved his hands. Robert was nervous. Martin would ask to read his book. He so longed for, and dreaded, Martin's verdict that he refused to let himself dwell on it.

Martin turned to Lena and said something to her and she smiled and took his arm. The only concession to being in the country Martin had made in his clothes was to loosen the knot of his tie.

Lena had made up the single bed for him on the back verandah and had placed a wicker chair and a low table under the louvres near the piano. She had made the back verandah look homely.

In the morning after breakfast, while the three of them were still sitting at the table in the kitchen and the fire in the hearth was burning brightly, the old grey box cracking and popping, sparks flying up the chimney, the iron hot, Martin eased back his chair and lit a cigarette.

Martin turned to him. 'So, tell me, Robert,' he said. 'How's it going with you?'

It was the question Robert most wanted Martin to ask him and most dreaded to hear. Robert said, 'I've finished my novel.'

'Can I read it?'

'Now?' Robert said.

Martin shrugged his shoulders.

Lena reached over and put her hand on Robert's hand and they looked at each other. Robert got up and went into his study. He picked up the thick wad of typed manuscript and held it a moment before he turned around and went out into the kitchen. Martin was standing by the window above the sink looking up the low hill, the snaking curves of the access road a pale feature of the view. Without turning around he said, 'It's very beautiful here.' He turned and smiled at Robert. 'I don't imagine you have so many interruptions.'

'None at all,' Robert said.

As Robert handed the manuscript to Martin, a terrible doubt assailed him.

With the manuscript in his hands, Martin turned to Lena. 'Have you read it?'

She said, 'You're its first reader, Martin.' She stood close beside Robert. They watched Martin walk down the passage to the back verandah. The house was tensely silent for a moment, then they heard the creak of the wicker chair and the metallic snap of

Martin's brass lighter. Lena kissed Robert on the cheek. 'It's all right. Do something! Occupy yourself!'

'Are you going to be here?'

She said, 'I'm going for a walk to Big Oakey to see if Dom's beans are ready to pick. He said we should help ourselves.'

'Shall I come with you?' he asked.

'Do you mind if I say no? I love to walk along the road on my own.'

She went out and Robert stood listening. He heard the rustle of a page being set aside. He went out and drove the Land Rover down to the junction to collect firewood. A previous owner of the block had ringbarked twenty or thirty acres of timber there and the ground was littered with the grey carcasses and limbs of long-dead trees. He loaded the back of the Rover and sat on a log and smoked a cigarette and tried not to think. But in his head he could see Martin setting each page aside, slow and careful, his eyes scanning the following page with close attention, bringing his rich intelligence to bear on the words. In this hope-filled scenario Martin was deeply absorbed in a story he greatly admired. In the other version, which was equally insistent, he was coldly disapproving of what he read. The two versions switched back and forth in Robert's head.

He drove home and stacked the wood out in the paddock near the dunny. He carried an armful in and set it down beside the door under the verandah. He went down the passage to the back verandah. Martin was sitting in the wicker chair, half turned away from the door, a page in his hand, his glasses on his nose, a cigarette held close to his lips in his free hand. Robert said, 'Would you like some lunch?' Martin lifted his hand in a gesture that said, please don't disturb me. Robert went back into the kitchen. He was hungry. Martin called, 'A cup of tea, Robert, if you're making tea.'

The day dragged on. Robert took the Land Rover down to the junction again and fetched another load of firewood. Lena was home when he got back. There was washing on the line in the garden and she was reading by the fire. The stove was alight, the kitchen cosy. He went over to the hearth and sat beside her. She smiled. 'It won't be long now.'

'Have you been to see him?'

'I took him something to eat. Don't worry. He's nearly finished.'

'Did he say anything? I don't think he's going to admire it.'

'Don't be silly. Of course he'll admire it.'

The cigarette Robert was smoking was making him nauseous. He tossed it into the fire.

Lena set her book aside and stood up. 'I'd better go and get the washing in.'

Robert felt hollowed out from the tension of waiting all day. He got up and sat at the table and rested his head on his arms. A few minutes later he heard a board creak in the passage and sat up. Martin came into the kitchen. He was carrying the thick wad of manuscript. He didn't look at Robert but dumped it heavily on the table beside him, discarding it with evident relief.

Martin met his eyes. He said sadly, 'Why don't you write about something you love?'

Robert realised at once that Martin hadn't given up on him. That was what mattered most. Robert had secretly known all along that there was something dishonest about the book, but had somehow tricked himself into going on with it. Now he could admit that he had been lying to himself. Somehow, and he wasn't sure how this worked, it had been easy to fool himself. But Martin hadn't been fooled. Robert hadn't loved this book, but had tried to impress with it. And Martin had seen this and had no intention of putting up with it. Robert was glad to be rid of the unseemly burden of it. He stood up and went around the table and embraced Martin. 'Thank you,' he said with feeling.

Martin looked at him and laughed softly. 'So why don't we have a drink?'

The irony, surely, was that he'd written his first, his abandoned, version of *Frankie* out of love, without really noticing then what he was doing.

The three of them sat by the fire talking and drinking wine until late into the night. There had been some talk earlier between them about friendship and betrayal. Martin told them in a few simple sentences the story of how he was betrayed by his Polish comrade when they were stationed on the western border near the Oder River. The first German armoured assault of the war fell on them and they were overwhelmed and made a run for it, following their retreating officers towards Warsaw. Martin's

Polish comrade saved his life initially only to betray him later to the Nazis as a Jew.

Early the next morning, before Lena and Martin were up, Robert got up and went into his study and wrote Martin's story out in detail. The scene gripped him, the dark and the shells and the fear and the exhausting run in the ditches at the sides of the fields. He called the story by the ironic title 'Comrade Pawel'. He wrote it out of love for Martin. He gave Martin the story to read when they were gathered in the kitchen for lunch. Martin stood by the kitchen table and read it. He didn't sit down. And Robert stood by his side, confident that the older man was going to approve of it. When Martin had finished, he set the last sheet on the table and turned to Robert.

'You could have been there!' he said, and he clasped Robert to him. He was moved.

Robert still could not quite believe he had got the details right. How could he have? he asked himself. After all, he had *not* been there. He said, 'But the soldiers' caps, the woollen caps I've described—are they right? Is that really how it was? And the trucks pulled up behind the trenches, with the officers drinking?'

'Yes! Yes!' Martin said, impatient with his doubts. 'It's all there.'

It was the first time in his life that Robert had written above himself. Had written, that is, with an assurance beyond the realities of his experience. He had found a direct imaginative link to the story through his love of Martin and his longing for the deepest empathy with his friend. Martin's story was a gift. Martin had entrusted the story to him and he had made it his own. They were both moved by the outcome of this strange and wonderful exchange. They had been waiting a long time for it.

Late the following evening they were sitting by the hearth. Martin was smoking a cigarette, a glass of red wine on the stool beside his chair. He looked happy and content. Out of one of his long silences earlier he had said, 'I feel at home here.' The companionable mood of this statement had remained with them. They had fallen silent, the three of them staring into the fire, the creaking log sending a curl of blue smoke into the chimney cavity, its underside glowing red.

'Ed, and us three, and Birte,' Lena said. 'The five of us, there's hardly a thing in our histories that's common to us, and yet we've all given each other so much from our love and our friendships.' She looked at Martin and then at Robert. She seemed to feel she'd asked a question and was hoping to hear an answer.

It occurred to Robert that this was just the kind of thing Birte might have said. He heard Birte's voice in Lena's statement. But Birte wouldn't have left it at that. Birte would have demanded some kind of explanation from them. Robert wasn't surprised Lena had included Ed among their little group. He said, 'You make it sound as if it's nearly over for us.'

She turned to him quickly, alarmed by the suggestion. 'Do I? No I don't,' she objected. 'Of course it's not nearly over. We've only just begun. Did it sound like that to you, Martin? As if I meant it was nearly over?'

Martin was sitting in what had become known as Ray's chair. He didn't say anything for a while. Robert had begun to think he wasn't going to respond when he leaned forward and tapped his ash onto the stone lintel of the fireplace. 'Being here has been a new beginning for you both.' That was all.

A plover screamed its alarm in the horse paddock and was answered by its mate. Toby gave a low woof by the door. The pair of plovers was nesting down there somewhere. Toby was on his mat outside the kitchen door, listening to the night, being on guard. He had disdained the use of the warm kennel Robert had made for him. The ginger cat had adopted it as her new home. Robert got up and gave the log a couple of whacks with the iron poker.

In the morning Martin went with Robert to help him repair the boundary fence which had been washed away by the creek again. Robert gave Martin a shirt and a pair of his old jeans and found a hat for him in the barn. Martin's feet were small enough for him to wear a pair of Lena's work boots.

They worked side by side, for much of the day up to their waists in the cold water of the creek. As the day wore on, Martin showed no sign of being fatigued. He used the heavy bar and the fencing spade and the pliers as if he was familiar with them. Robert saw from the first how Martin stood with his weight positioned over the bar, both hands gripping it close to his chest, his head bent, sighting between his feet where the chisel end of the heavy steel would strike the ground to greatest effect. There was nothing clumsy in Martin's movements. He wasn't going to strain his back or exhaust himself, as someone new to manual work might have done. The impression of fragility he could sometimes convey was not to do with physical weakness but was more a reflection of his inner world. Martin's easy familiarity with work tools was something in their pasts they had in common. It made no difference that Martin had grown up in Germany and Robert in England. Martin saw at once what was required down there by the creek among the casuarinas. He strode into the cold water up to his waist, dragging the twisted wire free from the flood debris and later realigning the fence posts on the banks. The two men kept pace with each other and found a rhythm that required no words of instruction. Robert wished Ray had been there to see them. He wanted Ray and Martin to meet. Until Martin came to visit them, there had been nothing to connect Robert's life as a worker and his life as a writer. Now here it was, unexpectedly with Martin, as if both Martin's past and his own reached out and met at a point of perfect understanding. Neither man spoke of this. In the middle of the day they took a spell from the work and ate oranges and boiled the billy for a cup of tea and a smoke. Toby came down to visit them. He laid his head in Martin's lap and Martin stroked his ears and spoke to him softly. Toby blinked and gazed up at him with a look of dog rapture.

Before he went home to Melbourne, Martin said he would return soon and stay for longer next time. Working in the bush alongside Robert, he said, had restored in him an emotion he had thought he was never to feel again. He didn't say this emotion was optimism, but Robert couldn't help believing that was what it was. 'I was seriously hungry for the first time in years,' Martin said. They promised each other they would do it again soon.

50

_____

Robert couldn't wait to try his Martin story with a publisher. The day after Martin went home he posted the story to a literary journal in Melbourne. He didn't keep a copy and he didn't include an envelope with a return address but simply wrote a three-line note asking if they would be interested in publishing the story, which he said was true. Three days later he had a phone call from the editor of the journal. The editor asked to speak to Robert's father. Robert told him he had written the story himself. The editor said, 'It reads as if it was written by an older man whose first language isn't English.'

'Yes, that's right,' Robert said. 'It's written in the voice in which I heard the story, the voice of my friend. It isn't really my story. I only wrote it down.'

In a tone heavy with amused irony, the editor said, 'Ah, so you only wrote it down? That thing that writers do.' He said he would like to meet Robert. Robert told him that wasn't possible as he had a mail run and a farm to look after.

Robert wasn't surprised that the editor liked the story and wanted to publish it, but he was very pleased. He knew the story was right even before Martin had said he could have been there. The editor said he would send the page proofs in a couple of months. 'Your story will appear in the first issue in the New Year.'

Robert put the phone back on its hook and went out onto the front verandah. He said aloud, 'Success is good for your health.' He stood looking up the hill, Toby beside him, also looking up the hill. Three heifers with their shiny young calves were grazing on the hillside. The sun was shining. A deep wave of happiness was passing slowly through Robert's belly and up into his chest, easing out the old anxiety and replacing it with a golden softness. He said, 'So I really can do it.' He didn't say, I'm a writer, but that was what he meant. Just write it down. That was all he had to do. The simple truth. Never again attempt to impress. He felt ashamed when he thought of the awful book he had written. He would burn it. He would begin the story of Frankie this time with an account of himself on the farm in England. That was the way it had happened. He had loved those people and their landscape. The almost two years he spent working on the Exmoor farm remained with him, the details sharp in his memory. As the farmer's boy then he had been at the very bottom of the social ladder. When he arrived on the station in the Gulf he was elevated to a superior rung in the order of things. The bottom, the lowest pay and the least respect, was reserved for Frankie and his mob. Frankie's notional four pound ten a week and his own very real four pound ten a day had said it all. It was the perfect story of injustice, but it was also a story about people and places he had loved and it would live in his heart for the rest of his life.

He went into his study and sat down at his desk. He would have loved to tell Ann about Martin's story, but he didn't want to tell Phil. He rolled a fresh sheet of paper into the typewriter and began to write out what he thought was going to be a synopsis of this two-part story—his life as a labourer on Exmoor followed by life in the outback on the other side of the world. It was a story as familiar to him as his own body.

51

————

He came back from doing the mail run and put the meat and bread bags on the table and he went over and called down the passage, 'There's a letter here for you.' The return address on the envelope was the Prahran College of Art. He put the letter on the table. Lena came in and picked it up. She slit open the envelope and unfolded the letter and stood reading it. 'What is it?' he said. 'What do they want?'

She looked at him. 'It's from Margaret Hall.' She looked so excited he thought she might be going to press the letter to her breast.

'So, who's Margaret Hall?'

She sat down at the table and read through the letter again.

She had colour in her cheeks and her eyes were alive with excitement.

She said, 'I suppose I should have told you before.'

'Tell me now.' He sat across the table from her.

'When I went to Melbourne to see Birte we talked about our lives. I showed her my drawings and she said I had to take myself seriously and that I should go and speak with the people at the Prahran College of Art who were teaching a full-time three-year drawing course. I took my drawings and met Margaret Hall. She's an artist and one of the lecturers. We got on really well at once. She took me up to the studio and showed me drawings by students and staff and asked me if I thought I would fit in with their ideas. There were some unsigned charcoal and pencil drawings on top of a desk and I said, "These are the kinds of things I do." They were astonishingly like my drawings. More elaborate and more highly finished and larger but the feeling of them was like my own things. Margaret said the drawings I'd picked out were by Pam Hallandal, who runs the course.'

Lena stopped talking and sat looking at Robert, her lips compressed as if she was holding back the flood of things she wanted to say, her eyes shining. 'Margaret said she'd speak to Pam about me and would write after they'd had their meeting. I probably should have told you. I don't know why I didn't. I was frightened, I suppose. I didn't trust it. It just seemed too much to expect that they'd really make me welcome.' She picked up the letter. 'She suggests I come in to the college and meet them and bring in everything I've done so far.'

Robert said, 'This is wonderful for you. You must go. Of course you must.'

She said, 'We're both finding ourselves at the same time.'

'It's Martin and Birte,' he said. 'It's making sense. It's them. I don't think I can ever go back to being quite so helpless and confused ever again as I was before Martin read that dreadful bloody book of mine.'

'I just want to draw,' she said. 'I hope they don't ask me to explain why. I love doing it. While I'm drawing I feel calm and hopeful. I don't know why. I can't explain it. I don't really care about being an artist. That's got nothing to do with it. When I was talking with Margaret and looking at those drawings I felt as if I was among people like me.'

'There isn't anyone like you. You're a one-off.'

'Would you mind if I enrolled in the course, if they'll have me? It's three years full-time.'

'You have to do it. I'll miss you. It will be lonely here without you. But I'll be over the moon if you really have found what you've been looking for.'

'How good did you feel when the editor said he'd decided to publish your story? You looked like you'd been let out of gaol. Well, that's how I feel. This really is what I want to do. It feels right. I was terrified I was just kidding myself. I've been feeling my way in the dark for so long. I've made some terrible mistakes.'

'You've no idea how glad I am for you. You already look better. You're an intense bugger.'

'And look who's talking!'

They both laughed.

He got up and went around the table and sat on the bench beside her. 'This is going to work for you,' he said.

'It hasn't happened yet.'

'Your drawings are amazing. And the poetry. Those powerful images of yourself. I was blown away by them. It was powerful. Disturbing.'

She looked at him. 'You never said.'

'Leaving the ledger open while you were out walking seemed like an invitation. I should have said something. I've never been capable of that level of honesty. I knew I was looking at the real thing. It was all so raw, so open and painfully real. Those people at the college don't see that kind of stuff every day.' He took her hand in his. 'It hasn't happened yet but it's going to happen for you.'

She said, 'I should have been more ready to share them with you.'

'You shared them in your own way. Our way. Nothing's direct, is it? Between us. It's impossible to keep anything secret in this house.'

She said, 'Come and help me select some of the drawings for them to look at. I need a folio for their final decision. I'd love to see which ones you choose. Then, when I'm down there showing them to the women, when they pick up the ones you liked, I'll think of us and the way all this has gradually come to us.'

They went down the hall to the back verandah. It was a warm sunny day. She arranged some of her loose drawings against the back wall under the louvres. She opened the ledger to the page of the contorted dolls and the strange series of notes she'd made. They both stood back and looked at the display. She said, 'What do you think? I don't think I can decide.'

He crouched down and looked closely at the row of drawings against the wall and the strangely disturbing contorted dolls in the ledger. He was thinking of the two men carrying the bundle of blood-soaked towels from the house in Chislehurst. Two men he had not seen, but whom he remembered. He said, 'They all affect me. I look at them and I see a part of you that you've never been able to share with me. For me your drawings have a lot to do with all the things that you and I have never been able to talk about.' He turned and looked up at her.

She said, 'Don't start analysing it, please. Just tell me which ones affect you most strongly. Which ones would you take?'

He stood up. 'They belong together. They're a suite. *The Doll Suite*. I think the women need to see them all if they're going to understand what you've done.'

'I suppose I could take them all,' she said doubtfully. She bent down and turned the page of the journal. A drawing of a doll with a broken skull, dark empty eyes.

➤

In the morning it was raining. Lena stayed in bed until Robert took her in a mug of tea. She sat up and took the mug in her hands and thanked him. He sat on the edge of the bed and sipped his own tea. The fire in the kitchen was sending out little explosions. He said, 'Some of that last lot of wood we got was green.'

'It couldn't have been green,' she said. 'It's been dead since last century.'

'Maybe it's just damp.'

They sipped their tea and listened to the rain drumming on the tin.

She said, 'Do you think it would have made any difference if we'd had a child?'

Her question shocked him. Surely it came from that most deeply guarded part of herself, that fragile place to which she had never been able to admit him. He thought a thousand thoughts all at once and didn't know which of them to speak aloud. She had said *a* child, not children, or *the* child. He heard her question as an announcement of change, an announcement of the prospect of being on her own forever, for the rest of time, her life. In the deepest sense, of course, she had always been on her own. He knew that. He had seen that from the start. He said, 'It must have made some difference, mustn't it? I mean, there would have been three of us.'

'I've often thought of a little boy who looked just like you.'

How moved he would have been if she'd been able to tell him this when that imaginary little boy had still been a possibility for her.

She said, 'Promise me you really don't mind if I do the Prahran course.'

'It seems almost too much to dare think you might have found something at last that's going to make sense of your life for you. I not only won't mind, I'll bloody well rejoice.' They looked at each other, the years of her struggle between them. 'It will be the end of this little dream,' he said.

'No it won't!' she objected at once. 'Araluen has been my way of getting to it. This place will always be important to me. It's given me my sanity. My year of gardening changed something for me. It's been important for both of us. Some things are sacred. This place will always be with me, no matter what happens and no matter where I am.'

Robert said, 'I know that but you'll be in Melbourne. I'll be here on my own with Toby.'

'Why should my going to Melbourne be the end of this? I can come up here between semesters and over the long Christmas vacation and you can come down to Melbourne from time to time for a break. We can go to movies and the theatre together, and see Martin and Birte, and you can buy books. You'll be writing your novels and we can enrich our life here by connecting it to the city. We can live in two places. People do it. People even live in two countries. It can be another way of sharing our lives—not an end to what we have but an addition. I'd hate to lose the farm. I'd hate to think of being cut off from the creek and the hills.'

He was unsettled by what she'd said about the little boy. He was annoyed with her for saying it. It seemed to hark back to a time when she'd been attempting to manipulate his emotions, and he didn't trust her motive for saying it. He couldn't see where it fitted.

She said, 'Your father was showing me his pictures and you were talking to your mum when he said to me, "You know, Lena, I feel safe while I'm doing this." I thought he meant safe from his memories of the war. The horrors they lived through. All that.

Now I think he meant more than that. He said that while he was drawing and painting, the door to his nightmares was closed. That's how I feel. When I'm drawing I feel whole. Not safe, but whole. Strong enough to take the risks. If someone asked me why I'm drawing the broken doll I'd say because I feel as if I'm stealing time with her, and there's no other way for me to do that.' She looked at him and frowned and laughed at the same time. 'Can that possibly make sense to you? I didn't plan it, honestly. I started drawing her without thinking about why I was doing it. I was playing the piano one day and she seemed to be waiting for me to notice her. I rescued her. Now she's rescued me. That's how I see it. Is that too fanciful?'

'Nothing's too fanciful in this business,' he said. He was moved to think of his father sharing such a moment with her. Robert's father had never spoken of those things to him. 'Thanks for telling me about you and Dad,' he said. He was looking at her and was thinking of the past of Lena Soren, the plump girl in her tight jodhpurs before he knew her, riding her pony with her dad alongside—the dad who turned out to be a disappointment because he never took the leap she knew he was dreaming of.

52

————

Driving up to Canberra the pastures were looking green and fresh, the sheep and cattle shiny and content. He waited with her in the boarding lounge. When they called for passengers to board they stood up and embraced—the bones of her back under Robert's fingers, her frame under his hands, fragile and intensely familiar.

He said, 'Good luck. Be careful, won't you?'

She laughed. 'I'm only going to Melbourne, not Florence.'

He said, 'This is the second time you've left me.' And was immediately sorry for saying it.

She said, 'That's not fair.'

When she looked back at him from the gate he saw there were tears in her eyes. He watched her plane rise into the golden evening sky, glint once, and then again, a golden flickering in the sunlight, then disappear.

53

He drove the two and a half hours home to the narrow lower reaches of the Araluen Valley, the hemmed-in poor part of the valley, with its few old people still hanging on. As he passed the light of Betty and John's place, he thought, They'll all be dead in ten years and their shacks will be rotting into the ground the way the old shacks on John's and all the other flats are rotting into the ground, scavenged for materials. His headlights picking out the familiar road ahead, the tunnel of trees and the sudden drop-off to the creek. He had never felt so strongly before the sense of the lost history of the lower valley, the shadowed melancholy of the place. He wondered if a day would come when he would try to write about it, attempt to bring it back out of the silence for love of the place, the way he was attempting to bring back from the silence of his own past those magical days on Exmoor, wanting to set them beside Frankie and his mob on the plains of the Gulf.

He parked beside the barn and stepped out of the Rover and stood looking up at the sky. The night was cold and still, the sky clear, the Southern Cross sparkling, the creek roaring. Toby came over and greeted him. Robert said, 'Well, here we are, old mate. Lena's gone.' Toby gave a low woof and charged the ginger cat, who was watching them from the top of the strainer post at the corner of the garden, her silhouette against the sky like a Chinese lion. She looked down at the dog prancing around the base of the post, inviting her to come down and play—the idiocy of dogs and the regal disdain of the solitary cat. Robert went into the kitchen and lit the stove. He poured a glass of wine from the flagon and drank it off, then refilled the glass and sat down with it in front of the stove.

The crackling of the kindling pushed back the emptiness of the house. He sat close to the open fire door of the stove, his glass of wine clasped in both hands. He looked into the swirling flames, the heat on his face.

In the morning he was lying in bed working his way through a lavishly erotic fantasy with Ann when he heard the roar of Ray's old Vanguard coming up the road. He said, 'Shit!' and got out of bed and dragged on his pants and shirt and went out into the kitchen and stuffed a page of the local newspaper and some kindling into the stove and threw in a match. Ray's car door slammed and he came up onto the verandah, called a hello to Toby and stepped through the door. He entered the kitchen and tossed his hat on the table and sat in his chair.

Ray took out his tobacco and rolled a smoke. Robert set out two mugs and the sugar bowl on the table and cut two slices of bread. He said, 'So what's doing? You're early.'

Ray lit his cigarette. 'My nephew phoned last night. He wants me to see his doctor. I said I'd go just to quieten him down. It's his wife nagging at him about me. Sonja's a lovely woman. He's a lucky boy. If I'd met someone like Sonja when I was young I would be a different man now.' He laughed and coughed. 'I don't mind pleasing her at all.'

'Are you ill?' Robert said.

'It's nothing. There's nothing wrong with me. It's her worrying about me being down here on my own. I tell her I've been here on my own since I was eighteen and old Nancy and David Andrews passed on and left me the place. She wants me to eat more vegetables and fruit. But I never did eat vegetables or fruit.' He gestured towards the stove. 'That kettle's boiling.'

They drank tea and ate the bread with jam.

Ray said, 'Lena get away okay, then?'

'Lena's gone, Ray. I don't think she'll be coming back on any kind of a permanent basis. Maybe for a visit.'

Ray turned and studied him for a long moment.

Robert said, 'Well, that's it. I'm on my own just like you are. I reckon Lena's not a Sonja kind of woman.'

Ray said, 'I am very sorry to hear this. I had you two paired for life.'

'We are, in a way. We are the best of friends and I don't admire any woman more than I admire Lena. She has great courage.'

'Oh, I admire her too,' Ray was quick to come back with. 'That's not what I meant.'

Robert said nothing.

Ray said, 'It's not my business, but I don't think the single life will suit you.'

'You've done it.'

'Not from choice. I would have married Tess up there at the pub with Aunty Molly, but that Pommy bloke got in ahead of me.'

'You never had any other choices?'

'Well, I probably didn't look too hard. I always thought there was one woman and one man who was meant for each other and when they found each other that was that. Tess was that woman for me.' He looked into his mug. 'Any tea left in that pot?'

Robert leaned over and filled Ray's mug with the dark brown tea. 'She's a bit stewed.'

'I don't mind it stewed.' Ray drank. 'How's that bull of yours doing?'

'He's done his job. Every one of those heifers had a calf again this year.'

'He's a good type, that old feller.' Ray sat a while, looking into the dead fire. 'I'll go up to Sydney and see that doctor.'

Robert knew he was talking to himself, the way he did down there at his place on his own. Keeping a bit of conversation going. Robert was doing it himself. Talking to Toby more.

Robert said, 'I'll put some eggs on.'

Ray said, 'I never did live with a woman.'

'You stayed sane without a woman.'

Ray chuckled. 'I don't know about that.'

Robert got up and broke four eggs into the pan and set it over the plate on the stove.

➤

Three weeks went by and Robert was writing. He heard nothing from Lena. He thought of calling Birte and asking if they'd seen her, but he was afraid it might look to them as though he and Lena were doing a rerun of the Italian escapade. It was evening and he was in his room writing his Exmoor days, riding second horse with the Devon and Somerset Staghounds for old farmer Warren, when the phone rang and made him jump. It was his party line signal, two shorts and a long. Robert went out to the kitchen and picked up the phone. John said, 'A call for you, Robert. It's Lena from Melbourne.' Robert thanked him and waited till he heard John hang up before he said hello; John liked sitting on the line listening in. When Robert heard the click he said, 'Is it you?'

She said, 'I'm really sorry! Honestly! I've been meaning to call you every day but things have just been really hectic. So much has been happening. You won't believe it, but I've bought a house.'

'You bought a house?'

She went on, sounding a bit breathless with her news. 'I put Mum's place on the market and got a bridging loan from the bank. It's a romantic old Victorian terrace in South Melbourne. It was a boarding house for single women. The woman who was running it died. There's still one old woman living downstairs. I'll let her stay if she wants to. We said hello when I looked at the house. I'll live upstairs. There's a bedroom with a balcony at the front that looks out over a park and the railway. There's a kitchen next to the bedroom and then at the back there's a lovely bright sunny room with a view over a jumble of backyards. I fell in love with that room the minute I saw it. It seemed to be waiting for me. I'll use it as my studio. The house is wonderfully dilapidated and a bit smelly. I'm going to leave it just as it is.' She stopped talking abruptly, as if something had interrupted her.

Robert listened to the hissing on the line.

She said, 'What do you think? You can come down and see it. Get Ray to water the horses and feed Toby. And maybe he can do the mail run for a couple of days. I told Margaret Hall about us and the farm and she said it sounded enchanting. She'd love to come up and stay for a while and she and I can go out on drawing expeditions together. How has your writing been going?' Before he could tell her how excited he was about his book she continued. 'You were right about calling my pieces *The Doll Suite*. That's what Pam called them too. She was enthusiastic about them. It made them seem important. As if I didn't do them but someone far more interesting than I am did them. She made them seem mysterious and intriguing. They made me welcome. All of them. It was wonderful. I felt as if I'd arrived home at last. I've enrolled as a full-time student. Am I crazy? Tell me the truth. I just love it there. The whole atmosphere. They don't care about anything but their drawing.'

Robert had never heard her being so positive and enthusiastic about anything before. 'Of course you're crazy,' he said.

'I feel like I'm one of them. Honestly! They understand. They don't talk about understanding, but I know they just do. They accept me. They make me feel serious about what I'm doing.'

'You sound as if you're in love,' he said. And he did feel a bit jealous, a bit empty and alone and even abandoned.

'You're right. I *am* in love. I'm in love with my new life. It's everything I've dreamed.' She fell silent. He heard a train going by in the background and thought of the city, Melbourne, the dense activity. She said in a thoughtful voice, 'Why has it taken me so long?'

54

___

Once Robert was living alone on the farm, Ray came up to see him more often. Scarcely more than a couple of days went by between his visits. He called in the afternoon or early evening and they sat by the hearth and drank tea together and talked. Ray was respectful of Robert's ambition to be a novelist but was not able to take it seriously, so Robert did not talk to him about it. The farm, rain and the growth of feed, these were what concerned Ray, and the old days. The condition of his herd of breeders and their calves and the price of vealers when he came to sell the annual crop, that was Ray's familiar territory.

Robert thought he was looking older this evening. Ray hadn't bothered to shave and the grey stubble on his cheeks made his craggy features seem shadowed and caved in. He had declined to stay for dinner but had hung on anyway, the evening getting later and later. He sat dreaming and gazing into the fire, fallen into a long silence. Robert was very glad of his company, but he was also hungry and wanting his dinner. He saw in Ray the last of the old bushmen of the kind he had met when he first arrived in

Australia. Modest and decent men who often lived alone and took for granted the need of a neighbour's help or giving help wherever it was needed without being asked. Robert was comfortable and relaxed in Ray's company. He understood and respected the values of the man. And while Ray dreamed in front of the fire, Robert thought of the hunt for the Haddon stag across the bogs and clefts of the moor. He was writing this book from love and it was giving him a deep and sound feeling of satisfaction. Martin was coming up to the valley for a visit again soon. He was looking forward to getting his two friends together at last.

Ray roused himself and took the dead butt of the cigarette from between his lips and examined it. He said, 'I'll get you to give us a hand to bring in that old piker bullock in the morning, if you haven't got anything on, Robert.' He sat forward and eased himself up out of the chair. 'These chairs of yours swallow a man. I'd better get home and get some dinner on.'

Robert said, 'You are very welcome to stay and have a feed here, Ray. I've got plenty in that fridge.'

'I need to get home.' Ray looked around for his hat and put it on his head. 'We'll leave early if that suits you.' He warmed his back in front of the fire. 'You hear from Lena lately?'

'Oh yes, she always asks how you're going and sends her love.'

'And you send my love back to her too.'

'I always do.'

They went out and Robert stood by the verandah, Toby looking on, while Ray climbed into the Vanguard, the driver's side door giving out a squeal. He slammed the door and started the motor with a roar that woke elaborate echoes around the hills. Robert stood watching the Vanguard's headlights bouncing up the road. The next day was a Tuesday, a non-mail-run day. He had been looking forward to getting on with the story of the hunt.

55

It was grey light when Robert got out of bed and went out into the kitchen and lit the stove. He made a cup of tea and fed Toby and ate two fried eggs on toast. He put on his old leather leggings over his moleskins and he sat to pull on his riding boots. He put on his sheepskin jacket and the hat he'd scavenged from the barn soon after he and Lena arrived there and were still exploring the treasures of the barn. The sun wasn't up over the hill yet when he left the house. A low drift of white mist hanging between the orange trees and the barn, birds calling to each other in the timber. He fetched a scoop of milled oats and the bridle from the barn and walked over to the horse paddock gate. He didn't need to call the creamy. She whinnied and trotted up to the gate, eager for the oats. The old brown gelding and the filly standing off in the mist watching, knowing these early-morning rituals were none of their business. Robert rolled a smoke and lit it while he watched the creamy lipping her oats. When she was done he slipped the bridle over her ears and led her to the barn and saddled her.

He got up and let her step off and they rode over to the horse paddock and he leaned down and unlatched the gate. She didn't like this manoeuvre and he gave her time to deal with it. Inside the paddock he wheeled her around and she stood nervously to let him latch the gate. The old gelding watching them, the filly arching her neck and kicking up, then giving them the benefit of a stiff Spanish canter along the fence line. The filly's feet were hard and in good order and he'd never shod her.

As he rode out into the fine morning Robert was thinking to himself, So here I am, back where I was, sitting on a horse looking for wild cattle. He was resenting it and was thinking maybe he should be more selfish and just plain mean enough to tell Ray he was too busy writing to take the morning off. But here he was doing it. He turned at the far fence and whistled to Toby. The dog came out around the house and stood looking. He was still mourning the loss of Lena. After she left he seemed to have decided he wasn't Robert's dog.

Robert rode down the broken silt bank into the river. The water up to the mare's belly. He kept a loose rein, letting her feel her way nervously over the river stones, stepping daintily. She was sure-footed and had never stumbled with him. He left her alone to get on with it.

They rode up out of the water onto the grassy bank and went on in among a regrowth of black wattle, where Ray had once cleared the big trees off his country, the country reclaiming its natural state now he no longer attended to it. Six cows and three calves were camped among the stand of wattle. They stood up ahead of the creamy and stretched. Robert did a bit of a detour around them. The sun came up over the hill as he came out of the wattle onto the extensive river flats above Ray's place, the country bright and golden around him. Robert had forgotten to resent the interruption to his writing. He was at home on the horse and was doing the only work he had ever respected.

A quarter-hour later they came up to Ray's place, a low pit-sawn kitchen with a tin roof and tin chimney piece. No sign of smoke from the chimney. Beside the slab kitchen was a new fibro-cement two-man quarters. Robert stepped down at the yards. He opened the big gate on the main yard and propped it with a rock Ray left there for that purpose. If they were to bring the old roan piker down the river later with a bunch of coachers he wanted the way into the yards to be clear for them. He hitched the creamy to a rail. He was surprised then to see Ray's horse standing in the long paddock beyond the house watching him. He had expected Ray to be saddled up by now and waiting for him.

He walked over to the kitchen and ducked under the rail Ray had nailed across the gap between the kitchen and fibro quarters to keep the stock out. Robert called a greeting and stepped into the dark interior of the kitchen. The hearth was cold. A plate of half-eaten steak and sausages on the table and a half loaf of bread. Robert called again but got no reply. He was concerned now. He came out of the kitchen and stepped across to the fibro quarters. Ray was lying on the floor beside his bed. His old sweat-stained nightshirt ridden up around his skinny thighs, a powerful stench of vomit and shit.

Ray said, 'Give us a hand up, will you.'

Robert kneeled down beside him and pulled his shirt down. His bowels had let go and he had vomited. The vomit was congealed. 'Have you been lying here all night, Ray?' Robert got his hands under Ray's shoulders and lifted him into his arms and hauled him sideways onto the bed. Then he lifted Ray's legs and set them on the bed with him, as if they were separate things that had come adrift.

He said, 'How long have you been down?'

Ray gave Robert a faint smile and reached for his hand. He held Robert's hand and closed his eyes, his breathing shallow, his mouth gaping. He looked like a broken shell of the man Robert knew, his teeth blackened and worn down like the teeth of an old horse. He was caved in and drained of his beautiful spirit. Robert said, 'Ray, old mate, I'm going to call for the ambulance. Are you having any pain?'

'Get me a drink of water, Robert,' Ray said. 'I think I've had a stroke.' He seemed to revive a bit. 'I always thought my heart would give out like it did on old David Andrews and I'd fall from the saddle the way he did. Dead as mutton.' He gave a hoarse laugh and coughed, a sudden violent cough that he was unable to break, lunging forward and drawing breath, a high-pitched whistling in his windpipe. Robert went over to the kitchen and fetched a cup of water and he propped Ray up and held him while he took a drink.

He went back into the kitchen and rang John at the exchange and asked him to send an ambulance as quick as he could. 'Ray's had some kind of a collapse. He might have had a stroke.'

Robert fetched a bucket and a cloth from the kitchen. He filled the bucket with water from the tank and went into Ray's bedroom. He took off his sheepskin and hung it behind the door and he set to cleaning up the vomit and the shit. When he had done he asked Ray, 'Where do I find a clean nightshirt for you?'

Ray did not respond for a long time. Then he opened his eyes and stared into Robert's eyes. 'Promise me you'll get that old piker bullock, Robert.'

'I'll get him,' Robert said. 'Don't you worry about it. The creamy and me will have him in the yard before lunch.'

➤

The ambulance took him away. They came up from Moruya on the coast and not down the mountain from Braidwood. Robert drove up to Araluen and told the woman at the pub, but she already knew all about it from John at the exchange. She had called Ray's nephew and he was coming down to the Moruya hospital from Sydney.

Robert heard no more for a couple of weeks. Then one afternoon he had a call from the nephew. The nephew said Ray had a brain tumour and lung cancer and they were operating on him. 'I promised him I'd bring him down to see you as soon as he's back on his feet. He wants to know if you got the roan bullock.'

Robert said he hadn't got the bullock. 'I will be going out to look for him as soon as I can make the time,' he said.

The nephew said, 'I'll tell Ray you got him. It will cheer him up.'

Robert said, 'Ray will know you are lying.'

The nephew said, 'Leave it to me.'

Robert said, 'I would not like Ray to think I had lied to him about something.'

The nephew said again, 'Leave it to me.'

A couple of weeks later they turned up in a smart new Holden Statesman. The car came bounding down the road one afternoon, its dark purple iridescent paintwork gleaming in the sunlight. It pulled up by the garden grid. Robert went over to them. Ray and a man of around forty got out of the car. Ray's head was shaved. He had lost his lion's mane. He looked a hundred. Robert choked inside to see him.

Ray shook his hand and said, 'You get that old piker yet, mate?'

Robert looked at the nephew. He shook his head slightly.

Robert said, 'No, Ray, I didn't. But I will get him.'

'I know you will,' Ray said. 'I know that.'

Robert never saw him again. Ray died a few weeks later in a Sydney hospital. Robert didn't hear of his death until after the funeral. The nephew rang and told him. He said, 'I'd like you to take care of Ray's place, Robert. We've decided to keep it going for the time being.'

Robert said, 'I am already doing that.'

The nephew said, 'We need to make it official.' He said they would offer Robert a payment. Robert told him he would not take a payment for it.

———➤———

Lena wept when he called to tell her. Robert didn't weep, but he felt a sense of great loss. He sat by the fire and drank a few glasses of red wine and smoked a cigarette and gazed into the red coals and talked to Ray as if Ray was there with him. One thing he said was, 'The lower valley died with you, Ray.' That was the way it felt. An end to the old values and the old ways. Who, after all, was to persist with those old ways now? Those values had died with Ray McFadden. Robert knew it.

He went on playing his part, bringing Ray's cattle in for marking and bringing his own in, but after Ray was gone there was an emptiness about it. The meaning of it was lost. The meaning of his days centred more and more for Robert at his desk in the morning and the reliving of his story of Exmoor. He wasn't inventing the story, but was remembering it, rekindling its intimate moments in himself. He even kept the real names of the people. He could not bring himself to invent new names for Morris and farmer Warren and the great hunters and those people among whom he had found a place for a time.

But he could not work on the book twenty-four hours of the day and the silence of the long hours and the endless nights when he was not writing was oppressive. The one great moment he looked forward to was when Martin was to come to stay with him. Robert was hoping to have the Exmoor book finished by the time Martin arrived. He knew this Exmoor story was just as authentic as the 'Comrade Pawel' story, and he was eager for Martin to read it.

But things never seem to happen on their own. There is always a series of things that happen around the same time. As if some kind of vortex develops, tripping some kind of trigger and speeding up the passage of time. First Lena left and found a purpose for herself, a life with her artist friends that had taken on a deep and satisfying meaning for her; then Ray died, the man who had welcomed them to the valley and had become Robert's close friend. When Martin's letter came Robert kept it unopened till the evening. He kept it till after his evening meal, when he had a fire going in the big hearth. Then he sat down with a cup of tea and a cigarette and he took a knife and slit the envelope and slid the two pages out and unfolded them.

> My dear Robert,
> I have had news that I long ago despaired of ever hearing.
> Out of the blue I have received a letter from my sister's son in Israel. I had no idea anyone else from my family had survived. His name is Richard and he is a doctor and lives in Tel Aviv with his wife and their three children. I cannot tell you how much it means to me to discover that I have a family. This news has come like a sudden new spring into my life. I am going to Israel to stay with Richard and his family for a while. As this will almost certainly be my last and only visit

to Israel, I have decided to spend a year with them. So I'm afraid I will have to postpone my next visit to you.

I have received the copy of the journal with your story in it. Thank you for the dedication. I was moved to see it.

We see Lena, but not as often as we would like to. She seems to be very busy with her new vocation. Birte and I have never known her to be so free and so vividly energised by her life.

There was more. Robert could hardly bear to read it. He went out to his room and wrote a reply to Martin at once. He said how pleased he was to hear his wonderful news. He said other things too, light and without meaning.

56

That winter was bleaker than any Robert could remember having lived through. The weather stayed wet and cold for weeks and the creek was often in flood, the road to Araluen closed repeatedly. He saw no one. The rain thundering down day after day. Big Oakey and the gullies coming down off the hills roaring, rolling great stones and boulders over the crossings, old trees crashing down in the night.

The road stayed out for weeks and Robert was eating only tinned food and had no tobacco. During that time the darkly forested hills closed in more tightly over the cleared patch of ground around the house and barn and the pressure of his isolation was at times nearly too much to bear. He woke in the night and lay staring at the blackness of the window and could not get back to sleep, his limbs alive with a nervous tingling. Lying there hour after hour he began to wonder if he had walked into a trap when he had agreed to come and live on the farm with Lena, becoming the cowboy of her dreams. The dream they had shared of the cottage in the country had become his nightmare. As he lay there alone in his bed, the rain beating down on the tin, he felt fated to be on his own, alone with his own empty fantasies. Was he going to become like Ray? His life eaten up by solitary days here without a companion? The night panic of these thoughts thickened in him. Was it his fate to be led back always to his first choice in life? His leap to freedom nothing but a leap into loneliness. A loss of home and the familiar. Had he duped himself? His only thread of hope now was his Exmoor book. The need to get it finished was suddenly fierce in him. Without the book he would surely be done for. He struck a match and lit the lamp. He got up and put some clothes on and went into the study and began to write. He worked till the grey light crept in at the window, then left the work and crawled back into his cold bed, exhausted. He had seen the end of the story. It was almost done. He knew it was good.

He woke to a dripping silence. He went out onto the front verandah and marvelled at the beauty of the place: the hills black and smoking, golden patches of sunlight falling through dramatic rents in the clouds. His sense of his solitariness there overpowering, like a singing in the air. It awed him and frightened him and he knew he could never survive in the valley as Ray had survived, a strong and sane man till his humiliating end. How such a man could have endured his solitariness without losing his sanity was a mystery.

The creek had backed up from the flooded river and was a slow brown flood creeping over the lower paddock, the water coming in through the fence at the bottom of the horse paddock.

He could not tell if the level of the water was still rising or had begun to fall. He went down to the water's edge and hammered a stake into the ground.

By next morning the water had receded back beyond the horse paddock fence. After breakfast he set out in the Land Rover to see how far he could get. The narrow gravel road was covered with sticks and branches, weeds and grasses growing up through the surface, even little wattle trees sprouting here and there. The road looked neglected and abandoned, as if it had not been used for years, the lower valley uninhabited. He got through to the Araluen pub and picked up the mail there and bought some tobacco and wine.

The following day he left Toby and Ray's dog Tip with Aunty Molly at the pub. Before leaving he opened the horse paddock gate just in case the rains returned and the river rose again. He told Molly he was going to miss a couple of mails and drove up the mountain. He filled the tank in Braidwood and drove on. The other side of Yass he pulled out onto the Hume Highway and pushed his foot to the floor, the buckles on the tarp cracking and whipping behind him, the smell of old grease and exhaust fumes in the cabin, the beautiful open road rushing by. The day was fine, the road dry, the paddocks green and fresh, the taste of tobacco in his throat. He flew along the open highway hour after hour, stopping only to fill the tank then pulling out onto the highway again and flattening her. The old Rover's tyres were worn down to the wire, the wheels out of alignment, the steering wheel juddering violently in his hands. He powered the motor along full pelt till he hit the outskirts of Melbourne and was forced to slow to what felt like a crawl after the freedom of the Hume; snaking through the suburbs and crossing the Yarra River to the south side. He was exhilarated by the drive, his face burning with the wind. He was a free man. He had made his escape. He could do as he liked. He stopped off at a florist's shop on the corner of Clarendon and Market streets and bought a bunch of mixed blooms.

It was a small crescent of old Victorian terrace houses fronting on to a neglected section of grass, then the deep cutting of the railway line, and behind the railway line the solitary monolith of a high-rise block of Housing Commission flats, casting into afternoon shadow the house on the extreme left of the terrace. Number eighteen was the middle one in the crescent. It was still in full sun. He parked the Rover by the grass and sat looking across the road at the house, trying to imagine Lena living there, the girl from Red Bluff. He rolled a smoke and lit it. There was no sign of life along the crescent. A train rushed through the cutting behind him, the ground trembling, the air filled with noise. Then silence again. A tabby cat watching from the top of a gate post at the house next to Lena's. A magpie dive-bombing the cat from the branches of a gum tree. The cat curling its lip at the bird. It was Wednesday afternoon. The roaring of the city a general sound in the background. He had forgotten it. The voice of the city. His body was still vibrating from the violent shuddering of the drive, his blood still settling. Iron railings across the front of Lena's place, one dry-looking bush in the middle of the patch of garden, weeds grown through it. The gate was sagged off its hinges and looked to be permanently open. A balcony overhung the front porch. The fancy cast iron of the balconies on the houses either side of number eighteen had been replaced on her balcony with grey water-stained fibro-cement sheeting and louvres. A deep crack ran from the pediment above the balcony where it joined the next-door house down through the front brickwork to the bottom of the lower porch. A head-sized piece of the pediment had broken away at some time and the old brickwork was showing beneath the plaster. Downstairs there was what looked to be the original front door and one window. The door was painted dark blue, the paint flaked and faded.

He reached behind into the back and took the blanket off Ed's portrait of his mother and he cradled the bunch of flowers and stepped out of the Rover. He walked across the street and in through the gate. He wasn't exactly nervous, but he wasn't sure what to expect either. He set the painting down on the tiles and banged on the door with his knuckles. There was no knocker or bell. He stood waiting. Silence from within. He knocked again. Lena called down from the balcony above, 'I'm coming.' A moment later she opened the door. He thrust the flowers at her. 'So, here you are!' There was an odd momentary awkwardness between them.

She took the flowers and said, 'So here I am.' She looked at the flowers. 'Thank you. They're lovely.' Then she saw Ed's painting and her face lit up. 'Oh, you brought it. You're wonderful!'

He said, 'The kitchen feels a bit empty without her and that yellow-eyed cat.'

She said, 'You should keep it then. Really, it belongs in the cottage.'

He said, 'She belongs with you. You must have her with you.' He turned the picture face out and set it against the bottom of the wall. The colours were bright in the daylight, the yellow eyes of the cat vivid.

Lena and he stood looking at each other, uncertain what was to come next. Then, at some inner prompting, they hugged each other tightly. A flicker of arousal surprised him, a touch of their ancient Melbourne past. He stepped away. 'It's bloody good to see you!'

She laughed, delighted, colour coming into her cheeks. 'You sound as if you mean it.'

'I do mean it. I need you, your friendship. You learn stuff about yourself living alone in that valley.'

She took his hand. 'You must miss Ray terribly. I'm sorry I didn't have a chance to say goodbye to him. He was the life of that place. Come in and see my house. Have you brought a bag or something? Are you staying?'

'I came as I am. I didn't know if you'd want me to stay.'

'What an idiot you are,' she said fondly. 'Of course I want you to stay. Why wouldn't I want you to stay?'

She was wearing a black t-shirt and jeans, her old Italian sandals on her feet and a red and green bandeau over her hair. He picked up Ed's painting and followed her into the hall. She closed the door. The smell of the house was of an old musty dampness, something from a past time. The hall was dark, the air chill, light coming down from above at the far end, glinting on the wooden banister of the stairs, giving the impression that the upstairs was bathed in welcoming sunlight.

She went quickly up the stairs ahead of him, her tread light and swift. She said over her shoulder, 'I'll put these in water and we'll have a cup of tea. You must be starving. I bought rye bread at the market this morning.'

At the top of the first flight of stairs there was a half-landing, three steps continuing straight on towards an open door, and on the left a further short flight of stairs. She started up the stairs to the left. When he hesitated on the half-landing she turned back. 'Don't look in there. It's my studio. I'll show you later.'

At the head of the second flight of stairs there was a door immediately to the right, the upstairs hallway continuing on to the front of the house and the balcony, the sun shining directly into his eyes through the front louvres as he turned the corner, the bare wooden boards of the hallway a dazzle of reflected light. They went into the first door on the right. It was a kitchen. The reflection of the sun was shining onto the lino from a window over the sink. The lino was black, a worn black-and-white cowhide lying across it. He set the portrait on the table, leaning it against the wall. His red ochre fighting man was hanging on the wall above the table.

She said, 'I'll put your picture in my bedroom. He should be there anyway.' She lifted his drawing off its hook and set it on the table then picked up the portrait and hung it in place of his fighting man. She stepped back and looked at Ed's mother, then stepped forward and adjusted the hang of it. 'There! She's home,' she said. And she looked at him. 'Thank you!' She kissed him quickly on the cheek.

He said, 'Ed has replaced me.' He laughed.

'That's not fair. You've been promoted to the sanctity of my bedroom.'

'The sanctity!' he said. 'That sounds pretty good. She looks great there. The cat suits you. Ed would have a laugh.'

She picked up his chalk drawing and went out into the passage with it. He sat on a chair at the table and took out his tobacco. She came back a moment later and put the kettle on. While the kettle was boiling he watched her at the sink arranging the flowers in a tall green ceramic vase. He thought of her living here alone, happy and free with her own arrangements, just the woman tenant downstairs. She brought the vase over to the table and set it down then stood back and admired the flowers, the green and red of the portrait above them. 'I love being given flowers,' she said and she turned to him. 'It's so good to see you sitting here in my kitchen. I've been longing to show you my new life.'

He said, 'That sounds pretty final.'

She made no reply to this but set about getting the lunch. He smoked and watched her making the tea and arranging the slices of dark bread on one of her mother's old flowered plates which she'd brought back with her. She sliced a cucumber and put the slices on another plate beside the bread. She seemed healthier and more energetic, deeply settled now into her extreme thinness and comfortable with it. It seemed to him that she had achieved a point of contentment with her body, the violence of her old inner struggle, her demon, pacified. For the moment, at any rate.

She looked at the table. 'It's not much to offer you.'

'It's fine,' he said. 'I'm not hungry.'

'You should have let me know you were coming. I hope you're eating properly. You're looking a bit frayed.'

He laughed. 'You sound like your mother.'

She thoroughly surprised him then when she said, 'I suppose I am like Mum.'

'Do you remember what you said when she died?'

'Of course I remember. I'd rather not be reminded.' She was standing at the sink with her back to him, the teapot in her hand, looking out the window at the chequerboard of backyards and small laneways. 'But actually I don't mind at all being like Mum.' She turned around and looked at him. 'I'm not her, however. Being like someone in some ways is not the same as being them.'

She went over to the bench and put three spoons of tea into the pot. 'Your flowers are just what this room needed.' She paused, looking at the flowers in their tall green vase. 'I never thought I'd say this, but I'll be a bit sad when Red Bluff sells. The garden was horribly neglected. It looked sad and abandoned. The house needs new people to care for it. A new start with a new family. But all the same, I'll feel sad. Dr Eady died. Did I tell you?'

He said, 'I thought at one time that you and I were going to have a life there together.'

She brought the teapot to the table and sat down. 'That wouldn't have been possible.' She considered him. 'The dreadful tangle of my childhood and growing up was embedded in the fabric of that house. The smell of it when I went through the door with the agent was enough. I nearly turned around and left him to it. If I were to live there, God forbid, those old emotional knots would never have been unravelled for me.'

She poured the tea and handed him a cup.

He said, 'Would you mind if we sold the farm?'

'Don't be silly. We can't sell the farm.' She smiled at him. 'You're not serious. Our beautiful bathing hole? We both love the farm.' She sipped her tea. 'It's where you've found your voice as a writer. It's where I found my way as an artist. It's going to take time for us to work it all out, I know that. But we will. We're going on, you and I, but differently, aren't we? You said you need me. I need you too. We're part of each other. We need *us*. We've done it together all this way.'

'We're not doing it together now. I'm alone there. I can't stand it.'

'Yes, I know, it must be horribly lonely for you, and now without Ray, but we grieve and then we go on, don't we? And you're able to write there. It's making sense for you. I thought you were happy.' She was frowning, a tight furrow between her brows, a grey shadow in the circles beneath her eyes, as if the sun had gone in.

He said, 'It's not that simple.'

'How's the Exmoor book going?'

'It's nearly done.'

'That's wonderful! And you feel good about it?'

'Yes I do. I think it's just as good as "Comrade Pawel". Just as real. Even more real in a way.'

'We went to the farm so you could write in peace. Now that's what you're doing. You can't sell the farm just because you feel a bit lonely. You can't just give up. Where would you go? It's unthinkable.'

He realised she probably imagined he was thinking of moving in with her once the farm was sold. The idea obviously appalled her. 'Anyway, it's your farm,' he said. 'I don't suppose I can sell it if you won't.'

She looked up at him sharply. 'How can you say that? The farm is *ours*. Your name's on the title beside mine.'

He took a slice of the buttered rye bread and bit into it. 'You needn't think I'm going to turn up here looking for a home. It was your money.' He hated to hear himself saying this.

'It was Mum's money. Mum and Dad's. Not mine. I didn't do anything to earn it any more than you. And anyway, you've done all the work there.' She looked down at the bread and cucumber on her plate, her face sad. 'I don't want to talk about selling the farm.'

'It's okay for you; you've got your new friends and the college and you live in the middle of the city. There's action going on around you all the time. I'm stuck up there on my own with the mail run and no one to talk to. You've gone. Ray's dead. And Martin's gone to Israel to be with his family.'

She touched the bread but didn't pick it up. He thought of a thwarted child. 'What am I supposed to do about sex?' he said. 'I live like a monk up there.'

Her eyes were brimming with tears. 'Stop this. Please.'

'You and I,' he said, 'we haven't had sex for years. I feel like a cripple. Emotionally.' He had touched a sensitive nerve with her.

She said coldly, 'If sex is so important to you, find a mistress.'

'Where am I supposed to find a mistress? A *mistress*! You make it sound as if I'm looking for a mechanical transaction.'

'There are women in Araluen. In Braidwood. In Canberra.' Her voice was like stone. 'Get out and meet people.'

'And you wouldn't mind if I had a relationship with another woman? A full-on sexual relationship? You wouldn't mind that?'

She said steadily, 'I would hate you for it.' She looked up at him. 'I'd kill you.'

'So, I get a mistress, then you kill me? Is that the idea? Brilliant.'

'I'm just telling you the truth. Being reasonable has nothing to do with any of this. If you were fucking someone else I would hate you. Forever.'

'Well, I don't have a mistress, do I? So don't go working your-self up into a state of purple hatred about it. And I'm not likely to meet anyone anyway. Am I? Think about it. That's not me. I live like a monk because the truth is in some way it suits me to live like a monk. But I don't find being a monk easy. I don't find it satisfying and warm and encouraging to have to talk to people along the mail run over their garden gate three times a week and hear that Daisy had her calf and the tomato crop is lighter this year than last year. I have empathy, but not that much. And Toby misses you. He's sulking. Did you know that? He's waiting for you to come home. Dogs know stuff we don't know.'

She looked up quickly. 'Is he really? Poor little Toby.'

'That's right. Poor little Toby.'

'Bring him down here with you next time you come. I'd love to have him here with me. Haven't you got Ray's dog now?'

'Yes, I've got Tip. Toby was always your dog.' He reached for the loaf and the knife and cut a thick slice of the black bread and buttered it and took a bite. He chewed a few times then reached for his tea and drank half the mug off, washing down the masticated bread. He said, 'Look, I'm not sorry I said all that stuff. There's a lot of stuff you and I have never dealt with.'

She said quietly, 'You sound bitter.'

'Sometimes I'm bitter. It depends on the day and the mood and how the book's going and the rest of it. Sex in the silence alone. I suppose it's okay. It's not illegal. A bit humiliating, but okay. Bitter? Not generally. But, yes, sometimes. Eaten up with hatred and bitterness for an hour or two. Who knows but me?' He laughed.

'I'm sorry,' she said.

He said, 'There's no need for contrition. It's not your fault. It's not my fault either. It's just us. It's who we are. You and I. There's always been a price. Show me what you've been doing. I want to see it.'

She stood up. 'You might not like it.'

He followed her out of the kitchen and down the short flight of stairs to the half-landing then up the three steps. The far room was small and oblong and filled with the brightness of the late-afternoon sun that was shining down the long passage. Out the window in the backyard below a woman was hanging out grey-looking underwear on a clothes hoist. Lena said, 'That's Angela, my boarder.'

The floor was covered with paper. Dozens of pen-and-wash drawings of dolls stuck around the walls, overlapping each other, joined here and there by scrawls and lines and bits of masking tape—thoughts added after the drawings were put up. The whole room a work in progress. Several old dolls lying propped against the walls, a sad-looking trio on a threadbare couch, huddled together for comfort, or dead drunk, or just dead. On an easel was a half-finished nude study of a woman.

He said, 'So who's this? She's got a body like you used to have when we first met.'

Lena stood beside him looking at the unfinished drawing. 'It's Margaret. She's beautiful, isn't she?'

'Voluptuous,' he said. 'So you two pose naked for each other?'

'Of course.'

'Will you finish it? Most of these look unfinished.'

'They are unfinished. I like unfinished things. Art is like time. I mean, there's no point at which it's complete and finished. Your fighting man wasn't finished. You stopped doing it when it reached that point. You didn't complete it. It just came to a stop for you. You knew you'd done enough. Drawing is like that. It's one reason I love it. That's what makes your drawing still intriguing to look at today. You asked a question with it. A question without an answer. Finished work has answered something. It's come to a stop. Grand oil paintings are still and dead and finished.'

He said, 'You should write that.'

She laughed. 'I have written it. The art school published my essay in their journal.'

'Can I have a copy?'

'I'll give you something else,' she said.

The doll drawings were mostly rendered in pen-and-wash, while the nudes were a combination of heavily scored and finely detailed charcoal. In her naked studies of herself Lena's ravaged body was portrayed unflinchingly, a fiendish delight in deciphering crevices and details that another woman would have been horrified to see.

'They're powerful,' he said. 'Why do you exaggerate your decrepitude? You still have a lovely face, you know.'

She laughed. 'You don't need to say that. I draw what I see in the mirror.'

'The truth? Your truth? Is that it? You really have become an artist.'

'Thank you,' she said. 'I'm happy. And I want you to be happy too. I can't be fully happy if I know you're unhappy.' She slipped her arm through his and leaned against him. 'We're still us. When you get depressed on your own you must always call me. It doesn't matter what time of day or night it is. Just call me. You're not alone.'

They were standing in front of one of the more fearsome of the naked self-portraits. He said, 'There's something tragic about it. It's as if you've externalised the anxiety that used to torment you. You're calm now. The agitation's in your pictures.'

She was delighted. She kissed him on the cheek and waited until he turned from the drawing and met her gaze before she said with feeling, 'I'm free. Just like you were when I met you. Do you remember how completely free you were then? You didn't have anything, but you were free. How I envied you in those days! I looked out of my cage and I thought, my God, just look at that man standing there as if he owns himself. It made me weak at the knees to see you.'

'You're even living in a dilapidated house like the one I lived in back then.'

She considered him. 'We both have our sense of purpose. Our belief. We don't take it for granted.'

'My sense of purpose is fleeting. It's unstable. It doesn't hold. It disappears and I'm wondering what the fuck I'm supposed to be doing hidden away on that patch of hillbilly country.'

'But you do have your times of belief and purpose.'

'Anxiety and ambition, they're the only things that really hold steady. It's hard to know which is which sometimes.'

She went to her bedroom and came back with the ledger. 'I want to give you this,' she said. 'The dead toreador.' She opened the ledger at the drawing and handed it to him. 'This is a precious document for me, just as your fighting man is a precious document for you. I want you to have it.'

He stood looking at the fallen doll and brief inscription. 'Thank you. I knew at once when I saw this that you'd found something authentic.'

They were both silent for some time, she looking out the window at her boarder hanging out the washing on the clothes hoist. He was looking again at her half-finished drawing of her naked self. No doubt the decrepitude she saw in the mirror was a reflection of her inner truth, the terrible days of her degradation in Italy and the abortion in London. The stuff her truth was made of.

'Margaret wants me to have a show,' she said. 'But I'm not going to. I love the mystery of unfinished things. It's what keeps me going. A poet, I forget which one, called it the miracle of incompleteness. There's no point having a show. People aren't interested in the incomplete. There's no market for it.'

'I bet you there is.'

'The senior students and staff have shows and get caught up in the whole rigmarole of it, wondering if someone is going to buy one of their pictures. They walk back into the trap they spent years freeing themselves from so they could become artists. They begin working towards the idea of a show and it changes them, changes what's in their heads. They can't help it. We all want to be liked. I'm not going to do that. I'm outside and I'm going to stay outside. I just want to draw.' She laughed. 'Come on! Let's go and sit on the front balcony and watch the sunset.'

There were more dolls in her bedroom, the room at the front of the house next to the balcony. All naked. All harmed or broken in some way, picked up at opportunity shops, she said. Mostly. Others discarded on the street with the hard rubbish. Robert imagined her fossicking through piles of waste put out for collection on the roadside by home owners. A thin woman with a shopping trolley into which she crams the things she fancies. Rescuing dolls. Not a bag lady, but the doll woman of South Melbourne, her ageing body browned by the summer sun, her fierce spirit private, driving her.

There were two wicker chairs and a small round table on the balcony. She set a bottle of wine and two glasses on the table and brought an ashtray. They sat opposite each other and she poured the golden wine into the sparkling glasses, her mother's best, the glasses that had been kept in the sideboard for special occasions— Waterford, something like that.

She handed him a glass of wine and picked up the other one and held it out to him. 'To our lasting love, my dearest Robert!' Tears sprang to her eyes, making her at once older and more vulnerable and wonderfully beautiful in a way he knew only he would ever see; the private, the secret Lena he had come to know.

'To you, my Lena.' He was moved.

They smiled and touched their glasses and looked into each other's teary eyes and drank the luscious wine.

'God!' he said. 'We're not going to cry, are we?'

They both laughed.

He turned to the window when a train rushed by, and she said, 'The evening skies here are very different from the valley. That tower block against the more fiery evenings always makes me think it must have been built by visiting aliens. I never see anyone on the balconies.'

They looked out at the tower, crimson in the last of the sun— the burning tower.

'Do you think you'll come to the farm during your semester break?'

'Margaret and I are running a life drawing class in July. I'll come in the summer. We'll have Christmas together.'

'I'll hold you to that.'

'Melbourne feels a bit empty with Martin and Birte away,' she said. 'When they're home again we can all get together in their lovely front room. Just the four of us. The way it was.'

He didn't say anything. He knew things would never again be as they once had been. The crimson tower was turning grey. They sat in the silence until it was dark. There was no more to be said. He didn't want to stay any longer.

They went downstairs together. At the front door they embraced. She stood at the door watching him leave, silhouetted against the light. He put the ledger in the back of the Rover and started the motor, rousing the neighbourhood with the roar of Ed's beaten-up old Rover. He stuck it into gear and drove off, his arm waving out the open side, the brass buckles of the loose tarp already starting up their tap-tap-tap. Before he'd cleared the suburbs and hit the open road he was back in the world of the Exmoor hunt. Everything now depended on the book. He drove on through the night, the wind swirling around him, the smell of the country and exhaust fumes in his nostrils, his thoughts already far ahead.

57

The sun was coming up over the hills, the western summits of the forests splashed with gold. Aunt Molly was around the back of the pub feeding her chooks. She called to him, 'There's a dozen eggs on the bar for you, Robert.' He unchained the dogs and went around to the bar and picked up his bread and meat and the eggs. Tip and Toby jumped into the back of the Rover. He drove through the morning to the lower valley. He wasn't tired from the long night drive but was exhilarated. He lit the stove and cooked eggs and sausages and cut three slices of the fresh white bread and he made a pot of tea and sat at the table and satisfied his hunger. When he'd finished his meal he lit a smoke and poured a fresh mug of tea then went into the study and sat at his desk. He read the half-page he'd left sitting in the typewriter and began writing at once. *The hounds moan and bay and howl their mournful howls, but they don't turn aside until Perry's desperate shouts threaten them with hanging, and then they draw off, reluctant, complaining, growling and giving out that deep peculiar baying that is sinister and needs no explanation . . .*

He wrote steadily all morning, the sun coming through his window and warming the small room. The visit to Melbourne and Lena had woken him and given him a great burst of energy and belief. He wrote the last sentence of the story at ten minutes after midday. The great stag was dead, the story was done, the body of the deer broken and distributed to those who had been in at its death. He typed the last thought of the nameless boy narrator: *I wonder what it is that I am making my own way towards*. It was done. At no point had the story resisted him; it had unfolded before him as if it possessed a secret need to be told. He sat back and looked at the final sentence and read it over several times, then he took the last sheet of paper from the typewriter and set it on the pile. One hundred and seventy-five pages. *Hunted*. It was his first real novel.

He got up and went out onto the front verandah and stood looking out onto the sunlit hillside, the red cattle grazing peacefully on the abundant feed. He knew he had done something good. Something true and real. He rolled a smoke and lit it. He was about to go back inside and make a pot of tea when it occurred to him that something more final and complete than the story of Morris and farmer Warren and the great hunt had been laid open. Surely a different question had been asked by the book than the question he had thought he was asking? Writing it had laid open to him an understanding of the power of the stranger to disrupt a settled community; the stranger, himself in the story, the nameless boy narrator, like a pathogen unknown to the locals, against which they had prepared no defences. Their necessary adjustment to find a place for the one who had no place in their tradition. He had seen none of this before he wrote the story. He saw now that what he had written was a meditation on his own place in that closed society.

Standing there on the verandah looking up the green hill at the trees and the cows, Robert knew that the act of writing might also be a revelation of the self. He hurried back inside and stood at his desk and began to read the manuscript from the beginning. What had he really done? He read the opening lines: *The doctor told Morris yesterday that he shouldn't eat so much raw pig fat. It would probably kill him before he was forty* . . . Suddenly it seemed to Robert that the act of writing was to deal in the mystery of the self, the story merely a cover for this inner need. The key had been given him by Martin: *Why don't you write about something you love?* Only now he had discovered that to write of what he loved involved him in far more than he could ever possibly understand. A richness of future possibility seemed to lie in wait for him. All he had to do was to write of those things and those people he loved in order to lay open to his understanding the hidden sources of his own emotions and motives.

He sat at his desk and read the manuscript through from the beginning. He was reading something else, a story not of the visceral rush of excitement and fear of riding hell for leather down the steep combes and boggy hollows of the moor, but the hidden story, something he had not been aware of writing. Would readers of the novel hear this subterranean story, or was he the only one who would ever know of its existence?

He stood up and went into his bedroom and lay on the bed and closed his eyes. His head was buzzing. Something in himself had been completed by the story of Morris and the farmer and the great hunt. He drifted into sleep with the sound of the magpies warbling in the garden, the distant rushing of the creek over the rocks, the hum of millions of insects out in the sunlight, the stillness of the house inviting a rat to gnaw the shelves in the pantry.

When he woke he couldn't think what day of the week it was. He looked at his watch and saw he had slept for twelve hours with his boots and clothes on. He sat up and rubbed his hands over his face. He remembered lying down on the bed the evening before feeling utterly spent. He swung his legs over the side of the bed and stood up. He saw the day was fine and warm. He took a towel and his toothbrush and called the dogs and went down to the creek and stripped off. He plunged into the bathing hole. The little brown fish shoaling in the disturbed water, finding minute specks to feed on. The sun glinting and flashing in a restless pattern on the stones. Robert felt as if he was being lifted and carried forward on a wave of happiness. He surfaced and blew out water and shook his hair. He swam to the end of the deep pool and back then dived deep, clinging to a bulge of casuarina root, holding himself down there in the flickering waves of light among the little fish, the dogs pawing the water above him. He surfaced and climbed out onto the grass and dried himself off. He was hungry again, but first he had something he had to do.

He went over to the house and parcelled up the manuscript then drove up to the pub and left it with Molly to be posted on with the other mail. He was confident that whoever read the story would know at once it was authentic. He had addressed the parcel to a Melbourne publisher and included a brief letter: *Dear Sir or Madam, I am sending you this book in the hope that you will like it enough to publish it. Yours sincerely, Robert Crofts.* All he had to do now was to wait for their enthusiastic response. When he got home he gave the handle on the phone a good twirl and waited for John to pick it up. He asked John to put him through to the main switch in Braidwood. He called Lena's number and waited.

Lena's voice in his ear. 'Hi! Is everything all right?'

'Everything's very all right. I finished the book.' He paused. 'It's gone. I needed to tell you.'

'That's wonderful! And you feel really good about it?'

'I know it's good.'

'That's fantastic. I'm so happy for you. How long do you think it will be before you hear from them?'

'Well, the editor rang me about "Comrade Pawel" only three days after I posted it to him. So maybe a week? Ten days? What do you think?'

'And do you think *Hunted* is as good as "Comrade Pawel"?'

'Probably better. I feel very sure of it.'

'You sound wonderful. I mean, you sound really strong and happy and motivated.'

'There are things I'd like to talk with you about sometime.'

'What things?'

'I can't really say over the phone. They're the kind of things you can only say in person.'

'I'm intrigued.'

They both fell silent.

He said, 'Are you still there?'

'Yes, I'm still here. I was just leaving for college when you rang. I'd better go or I'll be late. I hate being late. Can we talk again tonight?'

'Give me a call.'

'I will,' she said. 'It's wonderful news. Let me know at once when you hear back from the publisher.'

'I promise.'

He put the phone down, a small empty space in his belly. He needed to celebrate with somebody. There was no one.

He went down the passage into his study and sat at the desk. He rolled a fresh sheet of paper into the typewriter. *Dear Martin, I finished my Exmoor novel yesterday. I'm very happy about it and have sent it to the Melbourne publisher you suggested . . .* He tore the sheet out of the typewriter and screwed it up.

He got up and went outside and fetched a spade from the barn and began turning over a new patch of ground in the garden for the peas. The cabbages and sprouts were just about done. A few swedes and turnips still sat in the ground, being nibbled by grubs. His mind wasn't on the digging. He needed a celebration. A drink with a friend or a lover.

He set the spade in the soil and went back inside the house and poured a glass of wine. He sat at the kitchen table and stared at the phone. Maybe there was someone he could call? He could think of no one. He was listening for the sound of a vehicle. There was no vehicle. He poured another glass of wine. Maybe he should begin another book? Have another go at Frankie and the Gulf. He drank the wine and sat. He thought of driving up to Canberra, but Phil and Ann weren't there. Who else would there have been?

He fed Toby and Tip. They still believed in him. He set down Toby's meaty bone by the rainwater tank. Toby grabbed the bone and hunkered down with it, as if he thought Robert might take it back.

58

Day by day, somehow, the weeks went by. He heard nothing from the publisher. Two months later he had still heard nothing. His new attempt at Frankie and the Gulf was resisting him. Every morning, except on mail days, he went into the study and worked at it. He hated it. It made him sick. He knew it was no good. He couldn't understand why. He read Camus again and Naipaul, and he saw how simple and straightforward their prose was. But it didn't help. His own words lay flat and dead on the page.

It was coming on to summer, late November, three months since he'd sent off the manuscript of *Hunted*. He saw the letter sitting on the counter at the pub one morning waiting for him. His eye picked it out and knew at once what it was almost before he was through the door. His heart gave a lurch. He ordered a beer from Aunt Molly, who was standing behind the bar sorting mail. She pulled the beer and set it in front of him. 'We're drinking before breakfast now, are we?'

'It looks like it.' There was no other mail for him. He drank the beer and eyed the letter. When he'd finished his beer he set the glass on the bar and picked up the letter. 'See you Friday, Molly.'

'See you, Robert.'

He had it in the pocket of his sheepskin jacket. He was saving it, like a kid with a special lolly, to be savoured alone in a private place, to get the full pleasure of it. He leaned the letter against the sauce bottle on the kitchen table and stirred up the fire in the stove and set the kettle on the hotplate. He kept looking at the letter sitting there. He was scarcely able to believe it had finally arrived and was not just that persistent aching hope in his mind. He had not given up. He poured a mug of tea and stirred in two spoons of sugar and lit a cigarette. He sat at the table and picked up the envelope and examined it.

The publisher's address embossed on the back. His own address written in black ink in a neat hand on the front: *Mr Robert Crofts, RMB18, Lower Araluen, NSW 2622*. His hands had developed a tremor. So it was true, our hands shake at a moment like this. The envelope was longer and more serious-looking than a normal letter-sized envelope. The contents were not bulky, but by the feel of it, there was not just a single sheet of paper inside. There was more to it than the dreaded rejection slip, that was for sure. And they hadn't returned the manuscript. This wasn't just a quick note saying your book's no good and we don't want it.

He took the bread knife and slit the envelope open. He took out the two sheets of paper and unfolded them. One was creamy white with the embossed letterhead of the publisher at the top, the other was green and filled with writing, no letterhead but his name and the title of his book across the top. He took a drag on his cigarette and closed his eyes for a second or two. Then he read the publisher's letter.

> Dear Robert Crofts,
> *Hunted* is brilliantly sustained and engrossing—and I've enclosed one of our reader's reports which you might find heartening.
> I'm very sad to say that I don't believe we could give the book the kind of distribution it requires.
> Thanks for your patience. We've been deliberating long and hard about how we could best be involved—but to no avail. Of course, we would like to see your next novel.
> With best wishes, etc.

His mouth had gone dry and there was a pulse thumping in his diaphragm as if he had been king-hit. After the first two-line paragraph he had experienced a flicker of ecstatic euphoria—*brilliantly sustained and engrossing*—so they thought it was *that* good! Then the second paragraph had dropped him into the void. He was shocked, puzzled and faintly humiliated by this cruel trick, to lift him up in order to drop him dead. Had he read it right? He read the letter through again, frowning at it. And then again. What had he missed? He stared hard at each word, in case it held a key to the true meaning of the letter. Didn't they long to publish books for their readers that were brilliantly sustained and engrossing? What more was needed? What hadn't he done?

He stood up, then he sat down again, anger blazing up in him. How could they praise his book so highly and still not want to

publish it? He could make no sense of it. He was angry and humiliated and felt sure they must be laughing at the idea of him reading
their letter. He picked up the green page of the reader's report.

> The book presents an archetypal situation and achieves
> mythic force. It's about the powerless outsider confronting the
> various power structures and hierarchies of an entrenched
> social system. The narrator identifies with the hunted stag of
> the title . . .

And that's exactly what it was. The reader had read the real
story behind the story.

There was more. A lot more. All of it praise for the strength
of the novel. He read to the end of the page then read it again. It
was obvious the publisher's reader had loved the book. They were
passionate about it. They had understood the real private story that
was hidden in it. He or she ended with, *In short, absolutely first class.*

But they weren't going to publish it.

They didn't want it. He was trying to believe this. He was
bewildered. Surely they meant to tell him something else? This
couldn't be all. He walked about the kitchen. He looked into
the fire door of the stove and shoved a bit of wood in. He was
pretending to be normal. It was as if someone had just died. He
said to the room, 'So how can I go back now and sit down and
write another brilliantly sustained and engrossing fucking novel
and send it off to them and have them fuck me over again with
their shit tricks?'

He went out onto the verandah and gave a great yell of anguished bitterness and frustration. Toby and Tip both got up and slunk away, their ears flattened, tails between legs, hindquarters tucked in. Tip slipped under the tank stand then poked her head out and blinked at him sorrowfully. The echo of his cry following the ridges, faint then loud again. Standing there hearing that echo, the conviction grew in him that he was trapped and alone and powerless to do anything about it. He went back into the house. He could not bring himself to look at the letter again. It burned inside him.

His meat order and the bread and groceries were still sitting on the table waiting to be put away, a blue-and-white box with the new bearing for the water pump. His regular weekly purchase of grog, two flagons of Penfolds red. He unscrewed the top of one of the flagons and filled his tea mug with the red wine and drank it. 'Fuck them!' he said. He wanted to weep. He refilled the mug and sat at the table facing the stove. He felt suddenly exhausted. During the winter the rain had come in through a crack at the side of the little square window in the wall behind the stove. It had left a brown stain on the whitewashed wall in the shape of Italy. Lena had painted the stone and brick of the stove alcove and the open fire white, hoping to make the kitchen look like a peasant cottage in Greece. She had never been to Greece, but she had seen the travel posters. As he had. They both liked the simplicity of the whitewashed look, the modesty of it. He sat there drinking for some time, then he laid his head on his arms and wept.

After a while he sat up and wiped his eyes then got up and went into the study and sat at his desk and stared at his books and smoked and talked to himself. He was afraid of what he might do. The hum of the deep rural silence lay over the house. He was tired, weighed down by the wine and his dismay. He lay on the floor and soon drifted into an uneasy sleep. When he woke it was dark. He wondered for an instant where he was, the hard floorboards digging into the back of his skull, as if someone was pressing a rock against him. His head throbbed. He sat up. He was going to have to tell Lena. He didn't want to tell her. He couldn't bear the thought of her knowing his book had been rejected. He felt shamed and embarrassed for the book—as a parent might feel for a beloved child who bore some kind of humiliating defect. He felt as if the publishers had had their laugh and had kicked his book aside and walked away. He had never before felt so confused and demoralised. Cheated.

Days went by. Then a week. Then another week. He didn't tell Lena. She didn't call; they spoke only when he called her. She was leading such a busy social life with her new women friends at the college he could imagine her totally forgetting his existence for long periods, unaware of the grinding solitude of his days and nights. Knowing nothing of his bitter failure. His feeling of isolation and helplessness. He no longer went into his study. He had begun to believe he was a failure. The Gulf story had gone silent in his head. Dead silent. A door had closed. He had given up.

59

Summer brought the bees to the garden and the peas and strawberries and lettuces ripened faster than he could eat them. He did think of writing to the publisher and asking them to return the manuscript. Without it he was naked. But he couldn't face the idea of addressing them. Apart from the mail run he never left the farm.

As the end of the year drew near the weekend shooters started arriving. The sound of shotguns and rifles at night, car doors slamming somewhere along the road, motors revving, men's voices shouting. He kept a check on Ray's place. It was empty and forlorn. He was afraid shooters might vandalise Ray's old kitchen. Leave their shit on the floor. Break down a door. Cut the fence. The sort of thing they did before they went home to their jobs in the foundry or the mine. After one particularly noisy night he decided he had better check on the cattle up the creek and make sure a young beast hadn't been butchered.

When he put the saddle on the mare he realised the old string girth was rotten. He stood with the girth in his hands.

He would have to make a new one. He would have to become fully his old self once again, the stockman with his useful skills. He got out his sewing gear from the box where he had put it in the barn. He untied the thong and rolled out the bundle on the bench. The needles and awls and hole punches for working leather and repairing the gear, the scarred ball of hard wax, the bobbin of twine. The sight of these things and the slightly sour smell of the wrapping reminded him of the day after he arrived in Melbourne and unpacked his gear at the boarding house, the stale air of that room, himself then. He was no longer that person. He had become someone else. He cut the old girth free from the saddle and tied one D to the vice and began to string the new girth, fixing the second D to the end of the bench. He sat on a fruit box and smoked while he did the job. He was out of practice and had to unstring it and begin again, his tensioning all out of whack and his end-weaving loose and crooked. He said, 'You're not even any good for this stuff anymore, Crofts. So what are you good for?' Toby and Tip sitting in the sun in the doorway blinking and scratching. Tip looked over towards him and squirmed and wagged her tail, raising a dust into the sunbeams.

Self-pity and a bottomless gloom sat with him as he struggled to get the girth strung in a workmanlike manner. He knew Frankie would have been disgusted to see his inept fumblings—he and his brothers had prided themselves on the beauty of everything they made, even a casual hatband plaited from wire grass and vines collected on the ride out from the night camp in the morning and strung together at the lunch camp. Frankie had educated him in their way of it—a way in which all things had their respect and their sacredness. As he sat there making a mess of the job, Robert felt he had betrayed everything decent he had ever known. Who should he have really become? Perhaps the mistake was to have left home in the first place. Somehow, and he did not know how, he had failed to make sense of his life after all.

While he worked he looked up every so often at the great timber crossbeam tying one side of the roof of the barn to the other side. It was a beam made for hanging. He was seeing a soft-twist cotton rope slung over the beam and tied off. A noose at the hanging end. His body weighting it taut, so it creaked if you listened hard. A slight sway still in the corpse. That rope would hum if it were struck. Someone would find him there. Not Lena and her friend Margaret coming for their summer visit to the country. He believed now that they were not coming. The blowflies crawling in his nostrils by then, in his eyes, the maggots in the cavity of his open mouth. Bloated and stinking, like the carcass of a dead cow. Only a dead man. His story ended. A broken promise to Ray McFadden to get his old piker bullock the last thought in his mind. Nothing done. Nothing done. His fingers fumbled with the twine.

But of course he wasn't free to hang himself. What would the dogs do? Toby and Tip sitting there in the sun relying on him for a feed. There would be no one to return their love or to feed them. For the horses, well, he could open the gate and let them return up the river to where he'd found them, and the big ginger cat would go on looking after herself. But the dogs wouldn't manage without him. Toby came over and Robert leaned down and scratched him behind his ears. Toby closed his eyes with the pleasure of it. 'It's all right, old mate,' Robert said. 'That's not the way I'm going.'

He thought he heard the phone over at the house. He wasn't sure of the call sign and paused, listening, his hands stilled on the twine. A few seconds later the two shorts and one long of his call sign. He got up and put the unfinished girth aside and walked out of the barn into the sunlight, Toby and Tip at his heels. It was a lovely warm summer afternoon, two weeks before Christmas, the blue thistle flowers out along the fence line and Lena's red rosebush blooming by the garden gate to the dunny and the orange trees, a dozen single-petal roses on it. He thought how beautiful it was, this place, sheltered below the road there in the lower valley. How modest and charming and optimistic the cottage, butted into the side of the green hill in the sun, the vegetable garden and the three horses in the paddock below, their coats shining with the oats, watching him now in case he was carrying a scoop of oats or a bridle.

He went into the kitchen and lifted the earpiece off the wall set. John had hung up. Robert gave him a buzz and he picked up at once. 'You nearly missed her, Robert. I was just about to disconnect her. You've got a call from a woman in Canberra. It's not Lena.'

Robert thanked him and asked him to put her through. He could hear John listening in, the wheeze and grip of his breath. Robert said, 'Hello, it's Robert Crofts here. Who's calling?'

'Hello, Robert. It's Ann. How are you?'

'Ann who?'

'How many Anns do you know?' She laughed softly.

He knew who it was. Her voice had not changed. He said, 'You're back in Canberra? How long have you guys been home?'

'I've been in Goulburn for six weeks. My mother was seriously ill. I came back to be with her.'

'Is she better?'

'Mum died last week, Robert. It's okay, I've been expecting it. She was ready to go. I'm staying with Sylvia for a week or two.'

'And what then?' he said. 'Will you be heading back to the States?'

She said, 'I'm not going back.'

He let the seconds tick by, wondering what was coming.

'I've been awarded a post-doctoral fellowship to the Sorbonne.'

'The Sorbonne in Paris?'

'Congratulate me!'

He said, 'Congratulations! So you're going to be living in Paris?'

'I'm going over after Christmas. In January. And how are you and Lena?'

'I'm okay. Lena left a while ago.' He wanted to ask if Phil was with her.

'Have you written those novels you were going to write?'

'I've done some writing.'

'Sylvia thought you might like to come to dinner at her place tonight?'

He was remembering Sylvia, the unexpected woman friend he had thought looked like a chubby air hostess. He said, 'Sylvia thought I might like to, or you thought I might like to?'

'We both did.' She waited, letting a little silence build between them. 'So will you come?'

He said, 'You sound just the same.' His voice had gone a little husky. He had the picture in his mind of them lying out on the grass in the paddock behind her and Phil's house that evening, looking up at the stars, arms outstretched, their fingers touching.

'So do you,' she said. 'You want to come?'

He heard something a little sad or wistful in her voice when she said this, as if she feared he might not be interested.

'It would be fantastic to see you,' he said. 'What time should I get there?'

'Just come when you're ready. I'll give you the address. It's in Garran. It's a new suburb, you won't know where it is.'

They were both silent.

He tried for a neutral tone. 'So how's Phil? I don't think I replied to his last letter. It's a while ago now.'

She gave a short laugh. 'You didn't reply to quite a few of Phil's letters,' she said. 'Phil's fine. He's at home in Boston. Have you got a piece of paper and a pen? I'll give you Sylvia's address.

It's the white house, the last one at the top of the hill. The lights will be on.'

He hung up the phone and went out of the kitchen and sprinted down to the creek, the dogs yelping at his heels. He snatched off his shirt and pants and dived into the bathing hole. He swam underwater to the far side and held on to the familiar root of the old casuarina, keeping himself submerged, looking up through the dazzle of the water, sunlight flicking back and forth among the tree shadows, the small brown-striped fish passing above him through the agitated water. The dogs' twisted reflections through the water on the silt bank, barking and pawing at the water and snapping at each other, their barks distant, muffled. Was he coming up again, or was he staying down in the fish world? Not hanged but drowned! He surfaced and yelled, 'She rang me!'

He waded to the bank, the silt squeaking under his feet as he came out of the water. The yellow soap lodged in the crotch of the tree. He soaped himself all over then stood a moment looking down, admiring his erection, soap dripping off the end of it— quivering, hard as wood. He said, 'Now don't you go getting any ideas! She's only invited us to a polite Canberra dinner party. You are an uncivilised beast.' He gave the beast a flick with his finger and dived into the water and swam down to the bottom again and washed the soap from his hair and body. He stayed down, sitting on the river stones, thinking thoughts about Ann, till his breath was used up. He surfaced and got out and picked up his dirty clothes and walked back to the house, the dogs trailing along, Toby snapping at his mother's ears, Tip pretending to be annoyed.

He went through into the bedroom and tossed his dirty clothes on the floor, got out some fresh gear and went back out into the kitchen. He stood at the kitchen table in his town shoes and pants and ironed a shirt. It was an expensive Italian white linen that Lena had bought for him in London. A real summer shirt. On the two or three occasions he had worn it, Lena had said how well it suited him and had looked at him with something like admiration in her eyes. He put the shirt on and gave his shoes a quick polish and went out to the Rover and told the dogs to take care of the place till he got back. 'I'm going to dinner with the girls tonight.' He climbed into the Rover and drove out of the farm and turned left at the road. Crossing Big Oakey Creek, the last golden touch of the sun flickering among the trees on the side of the hill. He went on through Araluen until he hit the winding mountain road to the tablelands. On into the evening, through Braidwood, and across the open grasslands of the southern highlands. Driving through the black night, getting closer to Canberra, he realised he hadn't been thinking about the real woman, Ann, but about his fantasy of her. So the real Ann had come back to bury her mother and had called him and asked him to come to dinner. His reaction while he was sitting at the bottom of the swimming hole was that she had snatched him from the jaws of death. But the person he was going to meet was not the forlorn fiction of his hopeless fantasies but the real flesh-and-blood woman, a complicated person he scarcely knew. What did she really expect from the meeting? It was true what he'd said to her on the phone, she did sound just the same, but it was also true that he scarcely knew her. He wondered if maybe it was Phil who'd asked her to call him. The thought sobered him.

The closer he got to Canberra the more anxious he began to feel. She was probably just being polite, asking Phil's old mate to join the dinner party. Another guest to sit around Sylvia's table in her white house on the top of the hill to exchange small talk with the smart Canberra people till one in the morning. Then go on home alone, half-pissed and angered by what some dickhead had said, about the failed novelist from the bush—those journos and out-of-office pollies and academics and their smart-arse ironies. As if they sat at the centre of the world and ruled it. Was a Canberra dinner party really an improvement on hanging himself from the crossbeam of the barn? What would be so bad about that, after all? He wouldn't know anything about it after the first couple of choking minutes. Lights out. Leave the theatre. Go home.

But, all the same, despite his doubts and anxieties, he wasn't going to turn around and go back. He was going, not to his Maker but to Canberra. He would sit and suffer and drink too much and maybe vomit in Sylvia's garden as he was leaving. But he would go, and he would endure it, and afterwards he would reconstruct his fantasies.

And there it was! The suddenness of the perfect city glittering in the wide realm of the black night. He remembered Ray telling

Lena they were the first people from Canberra he'd ever spoken to. It would have been all the same to him and to the Araluen folk if aliens *had* landed in the middle of the bush.

The lights of Sylvia's house were shining onto the tightly clipped grass, a border of small tightly clipped bushes, sprinklers sending up a gentle mist into the summer night, the long white house with the yellow lights within. A shiny low-slung silver Audi convertible parked in the drive. He drove in and parked the steaming Rover behind the Audi. Sylvia was standing at the door. As he walked up the path to her she smiled, her lips glossy and very red, her big teeth white and even. 'Hello, Robert, it's so lovely to see you.'

She was fatter than he remembered her. He said, 'You too. How have you been, Sylvia?'

She offered him her chubby cheek, and he leaned in and touched her cheek with his lips. Her skin was damp. She was wearing Hermès Calèche. He recognised it from Lena's perfume-wearing days.

She said, 'So how was the drive?'

'The drive was fine. Thanks for asking me to dinner.'

He followed her in. A steady throbbing pain had started up in his groin. A large blue suitcase was standing in the hall. They went into a big open-plan room, couches and chairs, mirrors and a couple of colourful posters on the walls, some kind of Asian matting on the floor, over by the kitchen a table laid for three, a single candlestick, the candle unlighted, glasses catching the lights. Lights everywhere.

Ann was sitting on a grey-striped couch, in front of her a low table fashioned from a slice of red gum, with a bottle of wine and three glasses. She was leaning back, her right arm resting along the top of the sofa, her legs crossed, her bare knees catching the light, just as he remembered them. Her Jeanne Moreau lips. Italian sandals on her feet. She was wearing a short-sleeved light blue linen dress with big white buttons down the front, her glossy brown hair curled around her cheek. Her large-framed glasses making her look more beautiful and more sexy than his fantasy of her had ever been. He'd forgotten the glasses.

He said, 'Hi, Ann. It's good to see you.' His groin gave him an extra-sharp jab and he flinched.

'Are you all right?' she said.

'It's nothing.' He tried not to flinch as the jab struck again.

'I'm glad you could come.' She looked him over and smiled. 'You're looking very brown and healthy. Country life suits you.'

Sylvia said, 'What would you like to drink, Robert? Is red okay? I'm afraid we didn't wait for you. We've been getting stuck into it.' She gave a nervous giggle and glanced at Ann.

The three of them sat around the red gum table. They clinked their glasses and wished each other good health. The stabbing pain in his groin abated, assumed a dullness. He eased his shoulders. Ann was watching him. He thought she was going to ask him something.

Sylvia said in her bright clear voice, 'You're driving Ed's old Land Rover. Do you still see Ed and Mary?'

'We haven't seen them since they left to have the baby.' He told them the story of Ed and Mary's sudden departure in the night in the Holden.

Ann said, 'Ed's a drunk and a manipulator.'

He looked at her. 'I'm sorry about your mother.'

She leaned forward and picked up her glass and took a drink of the wine. She looked bored, or fatigued perhaps, maybe wishing she hadn't suggested this dinner to Sylvia.

There was a long silence. No sounds of a city. The front door open to the night. No distant roar of traffic. The black silence of the bush out there. Miles and miles of it. Mountains and forests. Tiny lights glimmering in isolated homesteads. The humming of the refrigerator behind him in the kitchen. The large floor-to-ceiling windows uncurtained, the mist from the sprinklers drifting across the illuminated grass. A faint hissing.

He took out his tobacco and began to make a cigarette. Ann watched him.

Sylvia said, 'I don't think I've got an ashtray, Robert.'

Ann said, 'A saucer will do. Could you make one for me?'

Sylvia said irritably, 'You'll just start again if you have one now.' She got up and went back into the kitchen and rattled around in a cupboard. She came back and plonked a saucer in the middle of the red gum slab.

Ann said flatly, 'Thanks. I need a cigarette.' She took another sip of wine.

He decided she was either bored or nervous. He fashioned an extra-neat cigarette for her and licked it down. He stood up and passed it to her. She took the cigarette from him and waited, holding it between her fingers, her elbow on her knees, looking up at him. He struck a match. She put the cigarette between her lips and he held the flame to it and watched her draw in the smoke. He breathed with her breath. She raised her eyes and looked at him. 'Thanks.' She sat back against the sofa, releasing the smoke through her nostrils. She said to Sylvia, 'You should try it.'

Robert sat down again. The pulse in his groin like a blunt thumb now, nudging at him. He made another cigarette and lit it.

Sylvia said abruptly, 'I'll dish up.' She stood and took her wine and went back into the shiny kitchen area.

Ann was looking at him, making some kind of judgement. No doubt wondering if he was worth it after all. She had large dark serious eyes.

He said, 'So you've stuck with French literature?'

'It's what I love. And you? Have you written those books you were going to write?'

'I've written two. I haven't found a publisher for them.' In his fantasies he would tell her about the rejection of his Exmoor book and his strange abandonment of the manuscript of *Frankie*. And he would know that she would understand. Now, sitting opposite the real Ann, he had run out of things to say.

Sylvia called them to the table.

They got up and went over and sat at the table. Against the far wall was a small fish tank with a solitary yellow fish in it. The fish was so utterly stationary he wondered if it was a plastic toy. Sylvia lit the candle in the centre of the table. On their small plates a tiny amount of sardine with something green and mashed. Ann said something complimentary about the tiny offering and the table setting.

Ann said, 'Have you started work on something else?'

She's not interested, Robert told himself. She's just asking for something to say, to keep this terrible silence at bay.

They ate the sardine and the green stuff and drank the crisp chilled white wine. The let-down that is reality which follows our soaring fantasies. He couldn't imagine ever again being stirred by his desperately futile erotic dreams. Where was the permission for his imagination to even go there? The sterile house cast its pall over them.

They ate the meal, grilled whiting in the pan, filling the house with its smell and the smell of dill, and they drank the wine and struggled with their helpless broken attempts at conversation. Then suddenly it was time to leave.

Ann turned to him. 'You've got quite a drive ahead of you. What time will you get home?'

'It's about two and a half hours. I don't mind. It's a beautiful black night. I like driving through the bush at night.' He turned to Sylvia. 'Thanks so much for tonight, Sylvia. It's been a great evening. I guess I'd better be getting along.'

They stood. Sylvia embraced him lightly, keeping her body from actually touching him. 'It was lovely to see you again, Robert. We'll have to stay in touch now that we've made contact again.'

'For sure.' He turned to Ann.

She said, in a tone of confident command, 'Take my case out and put it in the Rover, will you? I'll get my coat and bag.' She looked directly into his eyes, challenging him. 'Is that a problem?'

'I guess not.' He thanked Sylvia again and went into the hall and lugged the heavy blue suitcase outside and put it in the back of the Rover. Ann came out of the house. She was carrying her overcoat and a leather satchel. She and Sylvia hugged and said a few words and Ann came over and climbed into the passenger seat beside him. She said briskly, 'Okay. That's that. Let's go!'

60

———

They drove in silence, the terrific racket of the Rover's broken exhaust, the smell of petrol fumes and the snap and crack of the buckles against the sides of the Rover, the warm night air rushing around them. They didn't attempt to make conversation.

They were going past Nomchong's hardware store in the deserted main street of Braidwood when Ann said, 'I spent my Christmases there when I was a girl. It hasn't changed.'

'At Nomchong's?'

'Rob Nomchong was Dad's best friend. They used to go fishing together and repair old cars. The Nomchongs were my second family.'

'What did your dad do?'

'He was a motor mechanic.'

So she was a working-class country girl from Goulburn who spent her Christmas holidays with the Nomchong family in Braidwood!

'You've got more of a history in this place than I could ever have.'

'I knew everyone in Braidwood once.'

———

They left the town behind and crossed the creek. It was a dirt road the rest of the way. He slowed down.

Ann said, 'I haven't been down the mountain since I was thirteen.'

'Why did you go down then?'

'We picked peaches one year for pocket money.'

He sensed the innocence of her memories and felt a sudden empathy for her. When she said she had picked peaches for pocket money he was once again with the woman who had lain on the grass and looked up at the stars with him. This shift in her mood a softening from her distant manner at dinner in Canberra, the stifling effect of the suburb lifting from her spirit as she encountered the places where she had spent her school holidays. Sylvia's perfect new white house on the hill with its dining setting and couches in the large empty room, the absence of any sign of the wear and tear or the confusion of living, the blankness of it had silenced them.

They entered the tunnel of the timber, the dense forests close against the splinter of road, and began at once the twisting descent of the mountain. She said, 'That smell! If I went blind I'd know I was home by the smell of the bush. Here nothing has changed.' She turned to him, excited by her discovery. 'Thank you for bringing me. I was afraid you might object.'

He turned in at the road grid and Toby came bounding up the hill to meet them. The house and the yards and the barn looked romantic in the Rover's lights, an isolated settlement deep in the valley, peaceful, old, bothering no one. A place to find peace and quiet, a place to think and work. That was just how it looked. The dream of a city dweller, a cottage in the country. He said, 'It's pretty rustic, I'm afraid.'

Ann said, 'I can't wait to see it in the daylight.'

The night was warm and still. He parked by the garden grid and dragged her suitcase out of the back of the Rover. They went together over to the house. Tip sneaked out from under the tanks and Ann crouched down and made a fuss of her.

'My neighbour's old bitch,' he said. 'She's the other one's mother. My neighbour died a while ago and she came home with me.'

They went into the kitchen. He said, 'Would you like a cup of tea? I'll need to light the stove to heat up the kettle.'

She stood looking around the kitchen. 'You live here on your own?' She sounded disbelieving. She turned and looked at him. 'I've been trying to imagine what your house would look like. This is it! I'm here.' She laughed. 'I can do without tea, but I wouldn't mind having a wash and cleaning my teeth.'

'I clean my teeth and have a wash under the tank tap outside or down the creek. I'll get a bowl for you from the barn if you'd rather. I take a bath in the creek. I'll get you a towel.'

'And what about the winter?'

'A tin tub in front of the hearth here.'

They were both silent, standing looking at each other, suddenly awkward. She held his gaze steadily but didn't speak. He said finally, 'My room's a bit of a mess. I wasn't expecting you to be staying. I'll make the bed while you do your teeth.'

He turned around and went down the passage and into his bedroom. He stood with his back against the door and steadied himself. His work clothes were lying anyhow on the floor. He gathered them up and whispered, 'Ann is here with you!' He stripped the bed back and remade it. He had no clean sheets to put on. The bed didn't look too bad. He lit the lamp and left it on the box beside the bed. He went out onto the back verandah and fetched the stretcher and put it in his study and put a blanket on it. He didn't know what to think.

He heard her coming down the passage. She went past his bedroom door to the verandah. 'Lena didn't take her piano? Is she coming back?'

'Just to visit. I'll get you a fresh towel.' He went out to the pantry and found a towel and went back down the passage. She was in his study, standing at the desk looking at his books. He said, 'You're over here.' She came out and went ahead of him into his bedroom. He handed the towel to her. 'Will this be okay for you?'

The lamp was casting a warm coppery glow over the small room. 'It looks lovely.' She turned and smiled at him.

'I'll get your suitcase.' He fetched her case and set it inside the door of the bedroom. She was sitting on the bed. She had taken her sandals off. She looked up at him and their eyes met. He held his breath for a second or two, waiting for her to say something. When she didn't speak he said, 'Well, I'll leave you to it. Goodnight then, Ann.' He went across the passage and into his study and slid the door closed behind him.

She called, 'Goodnight, Robert.'

He stood by the door listening to her going out and cleaning her teeth then coming back and sliding her door closed. He wondered if maybe he should leave his door open, as a sign to her. He sat on the camp bed and took his boots off. He put his head in his hands. Holy Mother of God! How do you know? How can you tell? Do you just take the risk and say something straight out?

He lay there listening, his blood loud in his ears. He thought he heard her stealthily sliding her door open and held his breath, straining to hear. A low steady snoring was coming from the other room.

⤙

He got up and put his clothes on and went outside and fed Tip. There was no sign of Toby. He took a piss behind the dunny. The sun was just coming up over the hill behind the house. A soft summer morning. It was going to be hot later. He came back inside and lit the stove. No sound from her yet. He might have still been on his own in the house. He crouched by the stove, feeding sticks into the fire box, imagining her sleeping in his bed. He would take her a cup of tea in a minute, knock gently on the door, wait for her sleepy voice, then slide the door open. So how did you sleep? You were snoring! The beginning of intimacy. He might sit on the side of the bed while she sat up to drink her tea. He closed the fire box door and set the kettle on the hotplate. He stepped out onto the front verandah and lit a smoke.

Ann was walking towards the house from the creek, the yellow towel he'd given her over her shoulders, Toby stepping along beside her. She was wearing black shorts and a green t-shirt, her tanned thighs catching the morning light. It was years since he had seen a strong healthy young woman walking towards him like this. He thought with shame of Lena's wasted legs, her knee bones and pelvis sticking out of her tight skin. He pitied Lena and pitied himself. The terrible strangeness of their improbable union—precious beyond words, beyond thinking. How they had cast themselves out into such a bewildering place. Ann was so beautiful and so, so filled with the vigour of her life and her youth. A woman with a purpose about which she seemed to have no doubts. The sun shining on her.

She called, 'Good morning! Your creek's magic. I saw a brown snake.'

She came up onto the verandah and stood beside him, looking out onto the hill.

'There's plenty of snakes around at this time of the year,' he said. He caught a delicious whiff of the fresh creek water on her skin and turned to look at her. 'So how did you sleep?'

'I had a perfect sleep,' she said. 'I haven't slept so well since I was a kid.' She paused and met his eyes. 'But then I was sleeping in your bed, wasn't I?'

He didn't know what to say to this. Imagine if he were to tell her he'd been toying with the idea of suicide only yesterday. He was not as sane as she was.

She looked at Toby. 'What a lovely intelligent dog you are.' She leaned down and ruffled the dog's ears. 'He saw the brown snake first and let me know. So we both avoided it.' She straightened. 'What have you got for breakfast? I'm famished.'

They went into the kitchen. The kettle was boiling furiously, the lid rattling. He went over and took it off the hotplate and set it aside on the iron hob. With the toe of his boot he closed the damper. Toby stood at the open door looking in at them, his tail going from side to side, his ears half cocked. 'He's glad you're here,' Robert said. 'It's been a bit quiet around this place.'

While he cooked eggs and bacon and made toast, Ann sat at the kitchen table reading his story in the Melbourne literary journal of Martin's escape through Russia and China. He kept looking over his shoulder at her from his place at the stove, imprinting the image of her on his brain. 'You don't have any doubts about your life, do you?' He said it without thinking.

She looked around at him, frowning. 'For Christ's sake, whatever makes you say something like that?' She didn't wait for a response but went back to reading the story.

He said, 'You would love him, Martin, if you met him. He's been up here. He's gone to Israel.' She didn't look up or say anything. He set down a plate of eggs and bacon beside her and set his own plate across the table from her.

She put the journal aside. 'God, this smells so good.'

He sat opposite her and they both ate. He loved the pleasure with which she was eating the breakfast he'd cooked for her. She was so physical and so robust and so filled with a need to deal with her hunger. To see her eating with such an appetite satisfied something in him. No picking and poking around at the food, no nudging it to the side of the plate. Her plate was empty and she was wiping it clean with the last piece of toast. She took a drink of tea then set the mug down on the table. 'So how long is it since Lena left?' she asked, looking up at him, her wonderful Jeanne Moreau lips shiny with bacon grease.

'She's been gone a while,' he said. 'Lena's got her life sorted out, thank God.'

'Will she be coming back?'

'Just for visits, like I said. How about you and Phil? Will you two be getting back together?'

She said, 'We should go outside in the sun. It's such a beautiful day now. Phil's happy being an academic in Boston and having affairs with his students. I was in his way. Anyway, my place is in Paris. We're not enemies. There's been no hostility. We just don't need to make the kinds of compromises any longer that living together has required us to make for years.' She stood up and started clearing away the dishes. 'I liked your story about your friend Martin. Can I read your Exmoor manuscript?'

'I don't have the manuscript of the Exmoor book,' he said. 'The publisher didn't send it back.'

She said severely, 'Well, you must get it back from them. You didn't keep a copy? That was a bit silly.' She was standing looking into the sink, the dirty plates in her hands. 'Where do you do the dishes? Not in here by the look of it.'

'Leave them there.' He got up and they went out onto the verandah and stood looking up the hill. He wanted to tell her how beautiful she was in her green t-shirt and black shorts, but he didn't trust himself. He had a dread of spoiling things between them, upsetting the delicate balance of this careful friendship. She gave the impression of being relaxed and sure of what was going on between them. He had no way of deciding if she thought of him as her potential lover or just a friend. He did know that it was beyond him to take any kind of initiative. Whatever it was to be, it would be up to her to decide. He told himself to calm down and let it play out.

She said, 'This lower part of the valley intrigued us when we were kids. We heard stories about it. Lower Araluen . . . It always sounded like it was a place where old-fashioned people still lived in their old secret ways, the lower ways that we didn't understand. I imagined the women wearing bonnets and long skirts that swept the dust. I wanted to wear a long skirt and to walk in the dusk in my imaginary Lower Araluen. The Nomchongs had friends down here. Descendants of their ancestors who'd helped to build the water race for the goldminers a hundred years ago. They talked about your barn. It must have been your barn. I don't imagine there's another one like it anywhere in the valley. We were always begging Uncle Bob to bring us down here so we could explore, and he always said he'd bring us next time. And of course next time never came.' She looked at him. 'Now it has come and I'm here with you.' She studied him for a long moment. 'How strange is that? Me and the Nomchongs all those years ago. And then you found your way here ahead of me. As if you'd come down here to wait for me.' She laughed.

He said, 'Maybe some things are meant to be.' He felt foolish at once for saying it.

'What did the publishers say about your Exmoor book?'

'You can have a look at their letter if you like.' He made the offer readily and without thinking. It seemed natural, even a relief to share his humiliation with her. He'd kept that from Lena, and Lena had in the end, it seemed, forgotten to ask what had happened with his book.

They went back inside. Ann fetched her glasses from the kitchen and came into his study. The glasses made her look serious and even more beautiful. He had set the camp bed against the back wall. She stood looking out the window at the sunlit hill, waiting for him to produce the letter. The native grasses on the side of the hill had seeded, a pale carpet of faintly stirring buff. He found the publisher's letter and the green reader's report and handed them to her. 'I felt too depressed by this nonsense to write back to them,' he said.

He watched her reading the letter. When she had read the letter she turned to the reader's report. He was impressed by the way she'd become focused and serious the minute she was doing something she understood to be important. He could imagine her in some grand library in Harvard, standing among the stacks, a book open in her hands. Except she wouldn't have been wearing that faded green t-shirt and those black shorts. He wanted to stop time and keep her there forever.

She put the reader's report under the publisher's letter and read through the letter again, then turned to him. 'Well, I can't understand why you felt humiliated by this. A rejection letter reassuring you that you've written a fine book in their opinion is a reason for celebration.' A frown was furrowing her forehead, her eyes large and questioning through the lenses of her spectacles. 'The story's set in England, isn't it? And you were English yourself. It's obvious. You must send your book out to English publishers.' She tapped the Melbourne publisher's letter with her finger. 'These people can't publish it because they don't have the right distribution for it here. They tell you this.' She waited for him to say something.

She was a schoolteacher now, kindly, caring, considerate of his future, but unwilling to compromise her authority; she was someone in the know, changed, not deeper but more definite. He was about to speak, say something inconsequential, when she said, 'Why don't you write to the editor of the journal that published your story about Martin? You could send him a copy of this reader's report and he'd know you were serious. He'll know people. He might be able to make some suggestions. Phil's had fifty rejection letters, none of them as encouraging as this one. He'd be over the moon if he got this. These people had no need to send you the reader's report. It was kind of them to do it. They wanted to encourage you. You should write to them too, and thank them and ask them for your manuscript back.'

She set the letter and the reader's report on the trestle beside his typewriter. 'You can't let things like this depress you. It's unrealistic.' She put her hand on the manuscript beside the typewriter. 'So what's this one about? Publishers always want to know what you're working on next.'

'It's about my time working up in the Gulf with Aboriginal stockmen. I haven't got the right feel for it. I don't know whether I'm writing a book about myself and my friend or a book about injustice. It's got all tangled up for me. I've got to step back and sort it out. I haven't been able to face it for a while.'

Her tone wasn't exactly severe, but there was an element of reprimand in it, a sense of disapproval, a wish to correct him, to penetrate his ignorance of such things, to defuse the pointlessness of his isolation. 'You're working with cattle and horses again now, here. Of course it's confusing for you. You wrote freely about England from here. Now you need to get away from working with cattle to write freely about your time in the Gulf.' She shrugged. 'Well, that's what I think.'

'You're probably right.'

She put her hand on his arm. 'I want to see the Deua River while I'm here. Uncle Bob used to tell us how beautiful it was. It can't be far. And it's such a perfect day. Will you take me to see it?' She took her hand off his arm. She stared at him for a moment. 'You frightened me that night. The first time we met.

The intense way you stared at me when you came into the room. I was scared of you. Then, at our farewell party, we lay down out in the paddock and looked up at the stars and you reached for my hand. You didn't say anything. You didn't make any demand. I felt sad. I understood something about you. You seemed incredibly solitary. When your fingers lay quietly in mine that night I knew how vulnerable and alone you were under all that intensity you were projecting.' She smiled.

'I've wondered if you've ever thought about that night.'

'I think about it all the time. Don't you?'

'Pretty much every day, I guess.' They stood looking into each other's eyes—it was the moment in the Hollywood movie when the man in the white tuxedo with the thin moustache and the irresistible crooked grin takes the woman boldly in his arms and kisses her and she responds hungrily to his manly embrace, while in the background the jazz band begins to play something soft and sweet. Robert swallowed noisily. 'I'll take you down to the junction,' he said huskily. He cleared his throat. 'We should go before it gets too hot.'

In the kitchen he handed her a straw hat. 'You'd better take this.' She took it and stood looking at it. 'It was Lena's gardening hat,' he said.

She set it back on the table. 'We never wore hats when we were kids.' She ran her fingers over the surface of the table. 'I love these old pieces of furniture. They've seen the days of our forebears.' She looked up. 'Was it here?'

'I bought it in Braidwood.'

'It was somewhere like here. You must leave it behind when you go. It belongs here more than you or I ever will.'

'When I go?'

'Well, you can't stay here forever.'

They went out and the dogs got up and stretched and went along with them, Toby going ahead in the hope of surprising a rabbit, Tip sloping along at their heels. They went down into the casuarinas and walked along the bank of the creek.

There was a kind of perfection in the day for him now, walking along the bank of the creek in the dappled shade of the casuarinas with Ann beside him, their little journey together to the junction. He felt sad and happy. 'You're right,' he said.

'About what?'

'All of it. I suppose.' How had Ray survived? That good man's sane endurance had been a deep mystery to him. Ray would have been as incapable of seducing a woman as he was himself. He smiled to think of Ray struggling to find something to say to a woman he was attracted to. It would not have been in him to find the words. He and Ray were the same in that. Only a bold invitation from the woman herself would have moved Ray to speak his heart. The confident seduction of girls and women was Ed's territory. Ann hadn't responded to Ed's charms.

They emerged from the casuarinas and the Araluen Creek opened out ahead of them into a wide sandbar, the clear waters running into the cloudy flow of the Deua River, the two waters keeping to their own course for fifty metres before merging in a deep hole along the far bank of the river, like strangers meeting and keeping clear of each other till something draws them together.

He stood with Ann in the shade of an enormous blue gum whose vast canopy hung out over the river, hanging there for hundreds of years before they came along and stood in its broken shade. The sun was well up now. Ann said, 'I'm going in.' She stripped off her t-shirt and shorts and set them beside each other on the sand and she took off her bra and pants and put them down on her clothes. Then she took off her glasses and put them under her pants, and without looking at him she walked away from him across the sand in the sunlight. He stood watching her, on her naked back the shadows of the great blue gum's patterning. Toby ran out after her but stopped at the water's edge and dug a hole for himself, pretending he had found something valuable. Tip lay back behind Robert in the shade on the cool sand, her chin on her paws.

Robert stood on the bank watching, enthralled by Ann's beauty. His fear was that she saw him as only a dear friend and brother, while he longed to be her lover—that familiar tormented play of thought around the erotic filaments of his mind, nothing real, nothing of flesh and blood, no firm thing to grasp except himself, and the hollow futility of the discharge, the emptiness of that emotion. He knew it too well—the masturbating monk in his wintry cell had known all about the sadness of that game. And here she was, not the lusted-after fantasy of his lonely winter nights, but the real woman stalking naked across the sand for him to admire.

When she reached the end of the sandbar she waded in a couple of steps then dived, the ripples spreading out into the slow ease of the current. She stayed down for a long time until he began to worry she might have hit her head on a rock. She surfaced against the far bank, where the water was deepest, the bottom scoured to bedrock by the force of countless floods. She seemed distant now, small in the vastness of that landscape of river and ancient trees and forested hills rising in the distance against the shimmer and glare of the summer sky.

He heard the cry and looked up. A pair of wedge-tailed eagles riding the thermals high above her, their cries remote, the high-tuned cry of an unearthly freedom. He thought then of Ray and how he was gone from this place, his deep familiarity and love for it; he would have passed this pool on his horse so often. Robert longed to hold to something permanent and strong and good. He feared to be alone again and wanted to be in love with Ann. And he wanted her to be in love with him. And he feared it would not happen as he longed for it to happen and that soon he would be here alone again with another winter.

She waved and called to him. He took his clothes off and walked across the sandy beach, dived in and swam through the sunlit water to her side. They swam in the big waterhole together, yelling out to each other like children. 'I'm here at last!' she shouted. 'It's so beautiful, Robert.'

He kept a careful distance between them. He didn't want to risk scaring her with his weird, inarticulate intensities ever again. If she wished him to be more than a friend, she would tell him so in a very direct way. Or the possibility of such a thing would fade into their past lives forever, the regret of lost possibilities. Back then, at that party, when they had lain out there on the grass and looked up at the stars, neither she nor he had been free to think of being lovers. They had left it there, that brief touch of their hands in the dark, that certain look in their eyes. And they had each kept that moment, cherishing it in their memory, their intimate moment together among the stars, either the promise of something great and lasting, or a passing thing of no moment.

They came out of the water and walked back along the sandbar into the shade of the gum tree. They got dressed and he rolled two cigarettes and handed her one. They sat on the sand and smoked and looked out at the water and the trees along the far bank. An azure kingfisher dived from an overhanging wattle tree, its metallic plumage flashing in the sunlight. She pointed, saying excitedly, 'Look! Look! A kingfisher.'

They watched the bird fishing. In the distance, somewhere up the river, a cow bellowed for her calf.

They sat side by side in the silence, the fragrant smoke of their cigarettes lingering in the warm summer air. The kingfisher had moved away and found a new spot to fish from further along the far bank.

Ann said, 'You love this place.' She was silent again, then she said, 'You have to sell it and get out.' She turned and looked at him. 'You can't risk being stuck down here alone for another winter.'

He said, 'It's not that simple. Lena would hate to lose the farm.'

'Let her live here then. We can't have everything. And it is that simple if you decide it is.'

61

———

Walking home later, the sky was purple and green over the hills to the west behind them. A lurid glow through the timber. He knew the lower valley was an enchanted place and, like all enchanted places, was possessed of melancholy and death and loss and the sadness of lives past and forgotten. If he'd been capable of it, he would have confessed to her just then that the lower valley had no future, only its past. But she knew it already. The sun dipped behind the hills as they were walking up to the house. He carried an armful of wood into the kitchen and set it down by the stove. He was about to feed the dogs when Ann said, 'Let me do that. I need to do something. It will make me feel as if I belong here.'

He stood looking at her, the pieces of meat and bone in his hands. 'You can belong here if you want to belong here,' he said.

'You know that's not true,' she said. 'People like us can never belong in a place like this. But there's nothing to stop you coming to Paris with me.'

He handed her the two pieces of meat. 'Which is which?' she said.

'This one's for Toby. The other's for Tip. So why aren't they the same? Well, I'm not sure. It's just the way they prefer it. Give Tip hers by the tank and take Toby's over to the grid. They like to be private while they're eating.'

'What are you laughing at?'

'I had an image of you being a hillbilly woman down here feeding your dogs.'

'I could do it if I had to,' she said, and turned away and went out to feed the dogs.

He had the fire going in the stove when she came back into the kitchen. She said, 'I was standing out there looking up at the hill. I was so moved by the sad beauty that hangs over this place. Like all these places, it's haunted. It doesn't really have a present. Not in any human sense. Perhaps that's what it was we understood about it when we were kids. The evenings coming down and only yourself and the dogs. The idea of it scares me.'

'Don't worry,' he said. 'There have been plenty of times when I nearly didn't keep going. But someone had to stick around to feed the dogs.'

She said, 'You and Lena arrived here at the end of days for this place, really, didn't you? I don't mean the history; I mean the old way of life and its values that must have hung on here for a long time after things had moved on further up the valley. It's what Uncle Bob used to talk about. Twenty years ago, when we came down to pick peaches, the community in this part of the valley would have still been fully alive, old-fashioned even then, but active.

The locals would have still been having their dances in your barn. Now there's just the shell of something that no longer exists. And soon even that shell will be gone. It's beautiful, heartbreakingly beautiful. But it's ghosts. The sadness is part of its beauty. The sadness would overwhelm me.'

He said, 'Are you okay with vegetable soup for dinner? It's mostly pumpkin.'

'That would be lovely.'

'You could pour a couple of glasses of that red wine if you like. You sound like my old mate Frankie. Frankie would have said what you just said about this place, only he would have said it in fewer words. Ghosts were one of his favourite topics.'

She poured the wine and handed him a glass. 'Lena was right to leave. Her treasured piano sitting out there on your back verandah gathering dust and going out of tune says it all. It's the sadness of its beauty that holds you to this place. I suppose that's the kind of man you are, isn't it? You love the idea of the melancholy and the solitary life. But you can't really do it, can you? You can't make it work.' She reached and clinked her glass against his. 'Promise me you'll sell up and get out of here.'

He took a swig of the wine and set his glass on the table and he picked up the pumpkin he'd left sitting there. 'I grew it this year,' he said. 'One of the few vegetables I did grow. Isn't it beautiful?'

She gave him a long, serious look. She wasn't interested in the beauty of the pumpkin.

He hacked it into quarters with his Chinese cleaver from Nomchong's store. Its innards were a rich dark gold. 'Ripe! Look at that!'

Ann was sitting by the hearth looking at the ashes. Something wasn't quite right between them now and needed correcting. He said, 'I'll leave. You're right. If I stayed I'd probably shoot the dogs sooner or later and hang myself from a beam in the barn.'

They were finishing their soup when the storm broke over the house. The tin rattling and the chill air rushing through the cracks, flinging the door open with a bang. He jumped up and slammed the door. He lit the fire in the hearth and they sat close up to it while the sticks caught, drinking the wine and smoking, listening to the violent crashing and thumping, the roaring of the wind in the timber, the rattling of hail on the roof.

The storm passed as suddenly as it had arrived and there was just the dripping of water from the guttering and the gurgling of the overflow from the tank. He asked her about her interest in French literature. She said she was writing a study of the French novelist Marguerite Yourcenar, and then she fell silent.

'Tell me more,' he said. 'Who's Marguerite Yourcenar? Should I read her books?'

She sounded grumpy when she said, 'I don't particularly want to talk about French literature.' She sighed and got up and went out and looked into the night, then came back inside and sat by the hearth again. She looked at him a couple of times, as if she was waiting for him to say something.

She set her glass on the hob and stood up. 'I'm going to clean my teeth.' She went to the bedroom and fetched her toilet bag and went outside. He heard her talking to the dogs. When she came in she stood looking at him. He said, 'Is everything okay?'

She laughed and shook her head. 'Oh, everything is very okay. I'm going to bed. All right?' She didn't wait for a reply from him and she didn't say goodnight but just went down the passage and into the bedroom.

He waited a few minutes then got up and followed her down the passage. Her lamp was on and she'd left her door open. He stepped into his study and took his shirt off. He set the camp bed down beside the desk then stood up. There was a moment of intense silence. He felt it a fraction of a second before she called out, 'For God's sake, Robert, you're not going to sleep in that room on your own again, are you?' She sounded as if she would weep with frustration.

He stood still for three of the longest seconds of his life, then he went across the passage and into the bedroom. She was lying on her back in his bed, the sheet covering her nakedness. She sat up, the soft lamplight across her shoulders, glinting in her hair, her breasts modelled in the meeting of light and shade.

'Are you coming to bed with me or not?'

He was trembling. He sat on the side of the bed and pulled his boots off. She ran her hand down over his back. He stood up and took his pants off and she moved across and he got into the bed beside her. They held each other close, his heart battering wildly at his ribs, their naked bodies pressed to each other, their breath coming in gasps, her Jeanne Moreau lips against his. She reached down and guided him into her and she sobbed and cried out.

He stayed deep inside her, their lips searching for each other, their hands caressing and exploring each other's bodies.

He rolled away from her and lay on his back. He reached over and took hold of her hand. They lay side by side in the silence recovering. He laughed. 'I'm saved! I can't believe you came to me.'

She propped herself up on her elbow and kissed him on the lips. She caressed his cheek and said softly, 'Why didn't you race me off that night when we lay under the stars together?'

'You made a coward of me.' He ran his fingers gently across her lips. 'Your lips.'

She said, 'I wanted you to take my hand and run away with me.' She lay down close beside him again and they gazed into each other's eyes. She said, 'You and I here together. I've dreamed it a hundred times.' She smiled. 'I'm glad you're such an idiot with women.'

'There's nothing I can do about it.'

'I don't want you to ever do anything about it.' She put her hand down between his thighs. 'You're beautiful. You're my lover.'

He gasped and closed his eyes. Slowly they began to make love again.

When he woke she was lying against him, her breathing even. She was fast asleep. For the first time in years the warm body of a naked woman lying beside him in his bed instead of the bony chill of Lena's wasted limbs. She stirred and opened her eyes. 'I was dreaming I was weightless,' she whispered. 'I could move in any direction by thinking about it, without any physical effort. I woke in the dark earlier and saw you sleeping beside me. I pressed my hand to the cleft in the muscles of your back. I kept my hand pressed against you so that I would know you really were lying next to me. And then I dreamed of the perfect state of lightness. I wanted to tell you something. But you were sleeping so silently and so deeply that I didn't dare disturb you. I had a terrible thought that we must both die one day and be alone again.'

He kissed her. 'I'm never going to die. I promise. Neither are you. Not for a hundred years at least.'

She gazed into his eyes. 'Come to Paris with me. You'll write freely about the Australian outback there. The outback will seem distant and romantic to you again. Paris will give you your freedom. I'll introduce you to lots of good people. You'll learn French. The life of the city will make you realise how real the world can be. I mean it.'

'I'll come if I can be your lover.'

'You can be my lover.'

They held each other close, whispering their dreams and fears.

The warning cries of the plovers woke him. The grey light of dawn through the verandah louvres. They had slept with their arms around each other, their legs entangled, her belly against his, her breath warm and sweet in his face. He looked at her sleeping there close beside him and whispered her name. 'Ann! You are here with me.' Again he brushed her perfect lips lightly with his fingers.

62

Two days later he drove her to the Canberra airport. She was catching a flight to Sydney, where she would connect later in the day with her flight to Paris and her new life. They held each other in a long farewell embrace. She said, 'I'll write as soon as I get there.'

'Have you got somewhere to live?'

'They've given me a room in the student building.' She smiled. 'No male visitors allowed.'

The final boarding call was coming over the PA. 'You'd better go,' he said.

They kissed one last time and she walked away, out through the door onto the tarmac. At the plane's steps she turned and waved. He stood at the window and waved back. He watched her go up the steps and disappear.

He took the road to Braidwood and pulled up at Dom Alvanos's Royal Cafe and went into the Australian Estates office next door. The woman on the counter told him Jim was out inspecting a property. 'He'll give you a call later, Robert. It's not urgent, is it?'

When Jim Forbes called, Robert was in the kitchen at home eating his dinner. The place felt still and quiet without Ann there. Toby sat in the doorway listening while they talked. Jim said, 'There's a demand in Sydney and Canberra for bush blocks. I'll put ads in the *Sydney Morning Herald* and the *Canberra Times*. You should sell the twenty-seven titles of your place separately.'

Robert felt sad to think that it would no longer be a farm but would be a jumble of weekend blocks for city people. He was himself destroying the last vestiges of the old ways in the lower valley.

Jim was enthusiastic. He said, 'We should be able to get thirty-day contracts. The market for small picturesque blocks is hot.'

Robert put a call through to Lena. When she picked up he said straight out, 'I've decided to sell the farm.' He waited, but she said nothing. 'I have to get out. I'm going to Paris. I hope you're not going to make a fuss.'

She said calmly, 'Why Paris?'

'You remember Phil's wife, Ann? She's living there. She visited me for a few days.'

'And?'

'Yes, and. All that.'

'Are you going to live with her?'

'No.'

Lena was silent a while. He waited. She said, 'I'm not going to make a fuss. But you know I hate the thought of selling, of never being able to go back to Araluen. And I hate the thought of you living so far away, with someone else. How long are you going for?'

'I don't know.'

'You sound different. You don't sound like you.'

'I can't stay here on my own. Jim Forbes said it's a perfect time to sell. He's going to put the ad in as the first-ever release of hobby farms in the beautiful Araluen Valley.'

'Hobby farms. How dreadful. It will change everything.'

'Everything has already changed. It's not like it was when we came here.'

'Do you really have to do this?'

'I'm doing it. It's my way out.'

'I didn't know you were feeling so negative about being there.'

'You've been busy.'

'Did you ever hear back from the publisher?'

'They turned it down.'

'Oh, I'm so sorry.'

'It's okay. I'm over it. Do you want to have Toby down there with you?'

'Of course I'll have Toby here. You'll sell the cows and calves. What will you do with the horses? And Tip? It sounds so awful.'

'Jim says breeders are at a premium. We've had great seasons and everyone's restocking. I'll let the horses run back up the river on Ray's place. Give them their freedom too.'

'And who will do the mail run?'

'Someone else. Not me.'

There was a long silence. She said, 'Are you in love with Ann? Tell me you're not.'

He hesitated.

'You *are* in love with her, aren't you? You bastard! God, I hate you.'

He didn't say anything.

She said, 'I remember her. I thought she was cold. A distant, aloof sort of woman. I can imagine her being an academic. Those big glasses of hers. I didn't particularly like her.'

He still said nothing.

'So you really are leaving me. I didn't think you would do this. I thought you understood us. What we have.'

'You left me,' he said. 'Twice. So, yes, I suppose I am leaving now. I need a new life. I love this place. It's harder for me to leave than it was for you.'

She cut in. 'Let's not start an argument. When do you imagine all this is going to happen?'

'Jim will put the ad in next week and we'll take it from there.'

'It makes me feel as if you've left already. I'll come up for a last visit. The whole idea of hobby farms. Those people from Canberra swimming in our swimming hole. Doesn't it make you sad?'

'According to Jim you're going to make a huge profit on what you paid for this place.'

'It's not me. It's us. We'll share it, half and half. Mum would have wanted that.'

'That's very generous.'

'It's not generous. It's fair. I love you. I'll always love you. You'll always be my cowboy. You're the only man who has meant something real to me and I want you to be happy. I want you to find the right place for yourself and to get your books published. And make no mistake, I also hate you for falling in love with Ann.'

'I didn't say I was in love with her.'

'You didn't have to.'

Was he in love with Ann? Did it matter whether it was love or not? 'I love you,' he said. 'I'll always love you.'

'Fuck you, I know you will. You're a bastard, Robert Crofts!'

He smiled.

She said, 'After I left I thought of you on the farm every night and I felt comforted and secure and I told myself, If this doesn't work out I can always go home.'

'This place will always be special to us both.'

'It meant everything to me that you were there. Let's not lie to each other about us, about who we are and who we've become. It's always been us together, hasn't it? Even when we've been apart. I couldn't bear it if I thought you were going to Paris to this woman and were denying our reality. Tell me you're not doing that.'

'Of course I'm not doing that.' He spoke gently, sadness in his tone. How to convince Lena that she and he would always be . . . would always be what? There wasn't a word for it. 'There aren't any words for this,' he said. 'We both know. We just know.'

There was a long silence.

He said, 'I'll write to Martin.'

'It will make them both very sad.'

'They're grown-ups. They'll understand. Martin understood perfectly when you went on your crazy jaunt to Italy. He knew exactly how to react.'

'Do you think the four of us will ever be together again? The way we used to be?'

He said, 'Do you think we will?'

'There's so much letting go in life, isn't there? Of things we love.'

63

Three months later Robert stepped out onto the verandah for the last time. There was no one left to say goodbye to. The Rover was packed. Toby was with Lena in Melbourne, and Tip was on Jim Forbes's farm, the horses running free and wild up the river, the way he'd found them, the cattle sold. For the first time in his life, Robert had money. Enough to buy him three or four years of writing if he was careful. Lena hadn't made it up from Melbourne for a final visit, a last swim in the sacred waterhole. The place was deserted. It felt as if the place was waiting for him to leave now. Just the plovers crying out their warning in the horse paddock. Nothing would change when he left.

He stood in the doorway looking back into the kitchen. The log in the hearth creaking, sending up a curl of smoke, a bowl of bright oranges on the table. He might just as easily have stayed, put a rabbit stew on the stove for dinner, peeled a few spuds, had a glass of wine and a smoke and talked to himself. It was no longer his kitchen. The sadness of that was something he could not express. It was still his kitchen, no matter what. It would always be his kitchen.

His thoughts refused the loss of it. The price of his freedom could only be managed in instalments. The farm and Lena giving him his freedom in the end. He closed the door and walked across to Ed's old Land Rover. He rolled a smoke and lit it before starting the motor. The busted exhaust echoed around the hills as if Ray's old black Standard Vanguard had woken to life again. 'Ray.' He said his dead friend's name aloud. He drove out over the grid and onto the road and he didn't look back.

64

———

He rested his forearms on the sill of the casement window and leaned out. The big soft snowflakes drifting down, brushing his bare arms like the wings of butterflies. He was wearing only a singlet but he wasn't cold. He held his hands out to catch the snowflakes, remembering the way he had done this when he was a child. The concierge was crossing the yard below him. She looked up and signalled to him and he waved back. He had mail. He closed the window and put his shirt on and ran down the six flights of stairs. He carried the letter back up to his little flat and closed the door. It was from the English publisher whom the editor of the Melbourne journal had recommended to him. He sat at the painted table Ann had found for him at a local flea market and slit the letter open. They wanted to publish *Hunted*. *Everyone here loves your beautiful story.* They were offering him a modest advance.

Robert slipped the letter back into its envelope and placed it on the table beside his typewriter. He sat smoking a cigarette, looking out at the snow coming down. He was calm. The past six months in Paris had calmed him. The generosity of Ann's affection had calmed him. They didn't live together. That wasn't it.

He felt no great surprise at the publisher's letter and seemed to be looking on at himself, the young man sitting in that room overlooking the courtyard. It was as if he was not himself but this other person who took a close interest in the unfolding of this young man's fate. His pleasure in knowing his Exmoor book was to be published was a gentle cool pleasure; it was quiet and it satisfied him. He would write and tell Martin. He was already halfway into his new Gulf book. That's where his mind was now, back in the Gulf with Frankie. That book was no longer about anger and injustice but was about the beauty of a friendship between two young men, himself and Frankie—boys really, as they had been then, but men in their hearts. Ann had been right. From the distance of Paris he had seen the truth of the story he had to tell. All the other things were there, the adventure and the injustice, but for him they were not what the book was about. He got up and put his jacket and overcoat on and he put the letter in his pocket and went down the stairs.

Ann was sitting at their usual table towards the back of the cafe. She was reading. She looked up and set the book aside and he leaned down and they kissed. 'You're early,' she said.

He sat down, took the letter out of his pocket and handed it to her. She read it quickly, 'That's wonderful! They love it.' They stood up and embraced. 'You must be over the moon.'

'It's odd,' he said and sat down again. 'It's been so long coming I'm not really all that excited. I'm not taking it for granted, I don't mean that. I just don't feel madly excited—as I would have, I'm sure, if I'd got this letter while I was on the farm.'

She looked down at the letter in her hand and said, 'It's a very small advance.'

'It's money for my writing. It's a start.'

She was reading the letter again. 'They want you to come over from Paris to meet the team.' She looked up. 'And they'll release it in Australia sometime in the New Year.' She took his hand in hers. 'I'll take you to lunch. We'll have champagne.'

The waiter set Robert's coffee on the table beside him. He drank the black coffee and set the cup back in its saucer.

They walked arm in arm along the street. The snow had stopped falling. The street was bathed in pale yellow sunlight. They walked along the narrow footpath together, enclosed in their happiness. The cafe she took him to was noisy with laughter and talk. The proprietor came out from behind his counter and greeted Ann as if they were old friends. He shook Robert's hand and led them to a corner table at the back. They took off their coats and a tall Tunisian waiter took the coats from them and spoke to Ann in French. She ordered champagne. They toasted each other and she said, 'To your book!'

He said, 'And to your phone call from Canberra inviting me to dinner.'

They sipped the champagne and held hands across the narrow space of the table, looking into each other's eyes.

'I was so nervous I nearly didn't call you,' she said. 'How different our lives would have been if I hadn't phoned.'

He tightened his grip on her hand. 'And here we are together in Paris!'

'And now you really are a writer.'

When they left the cafe they walked along the quai to a bridge. Leaning on the rampart they looked at the river and the famous skyline, then they turned to each other and kissed, a long, lingering kiss. And when they at last drew apart she said, 'I didn't know it was possible to be as happy as this.'

They held each other close and looked with wonderment into each other's eyes. He said, 'Life can never be better for us than it is now, right at this very moment. I want to keep this moment on the bridge forever. Will you stay the night tonight?'

She squeezed his hand. 'Of course I will.'

They turned and walked across the bridge and on to the square before the great facade of the cathedral. They stood gazing at the elaborate Gothic architecture of the front. She said, 'Will you go back to Australia for the release of the book there?' It had begun to snow again. Being home in Melbourne when his book came out had been the first thing he had thought of.

'I don't know. What do you think? Should I go back for it?'

She said seriously, 'Of course you should. But I don't want you to.'

'Well, I might not. Let's not talk about it now. You're going to show me Voltaire's manuscripts in the library. I love this quiet snow.'

'Snow is always quiet.'

He reached and took her hand. 'Don't look so sad.'

'I'm not sad.'

'Yes you are. You are especially beautiful when you're sad.'

'If you go back for the release of your book,' she said, and she turned to look at him, 'will you come back to Paris?'

'Of course I will. Come on, take me to Voltaire! We're doing good things today.'

They stood, arm in arm, watching the birds circling the cathedral towers, crying their strange heartfelt cries of knowing.

PART THREE

65

When I opened my email yesterday morning I got a shock. My past hurled itself into my face as I sat here at my desk. My French translator, Françoise, had forwarded to me an email she'd received from Ann. It is the first communication I've had from Ann since I left Paris and returned to Australia for the release of my first novel forty-three years ago. A painful guilt that has lain corrosively on my conscience unattended for more than forty years was revived. That time in Paris with Ann, a time long before my wife and I had our children and watched them grow to adulthood and become successful in their chosen fields and have children of their own. That remote time, a lifetime ago. So long ago you might think its details must surely have been forgotten by me and overlaid with such an entangled depth of subsequent experience as to be difficult, or even impossible, for me to access. Despite this remoteness in time, the instant I realised the email was from Ann, I saw an image of myself standing at the open casement window of my sixth-floor apartment in rue St Dominique that day, leaning out and watching the snowflakes falling softly into the courtyard below. And I pictured Ann, not as an old lady in her seventies, as she must be now, but as the lovely young woman I knew then.

I sat here at my desk for a long time, reading and rereading her email, which she had written to Françoise in French. I was trying to imagine the person she had become. But my memory resisted this brutal transformation and insisted on presenting Ann to me as the shining young woman who had walked away from me naked in the sunlight across the sandbar at the junction of the Araluen Creek and the Deua River that day, the shadows of the blue gum dancing across her skin. That is the woman who stood in my memory's eye as I translated her letter. An image as clear and as present to me as if I had seen her only yesterday. Her letter greatly disturbed me.

We didn't live together for that year in Paris. Neither of us wished to re-enter with each other the labyrinth of marriage. I kept to my flat in rue St Dominique and she kept to her rooms at the university. She visited me most days and we often spent our nights together and cooked our meals in my little flat. When I returned to Australia I knew her address and could have written to her. She didn't have an address for me in Melbourne and must have waited in a torment of suspense for some word from me, her hopes of hearing something gradually fading. Had that experience left her with a scar that still burned in her mind whenever something happened to remind her of our days and nights of love in Paris? There was cruelty in my failure to write to her. I returned to

Australia after a little over a year in Paris to be present for the release of *Hunted* and to look for a publisher for my book on Frankie and the Gulf. I was by then missing the Australian way of life and the bush. I promised Ann I would return. She came to Charles de Gaulle to see me off. 'You won't come back,' she said. I never saw her again.

Within a week of arriving back in Melbourne I met the woman who became the enduring love of my life and who bore our children. The woman with whom I have grown into my old age. The companion of my years. We began living together two days after we met. From the first there was no doubt in either of our minds that we would spend the rest of our lives together.

There is also no doubt in my mind now, and never has been any doubt, that I should have written to Ann at once and told her what had happened. Leaving the valley and joining her in Paris saved my life and ended my long period of isolation and failure. And, of course, I still loved her, my memory of her, our youth and the intensity of our hopes and emotions then, the wondrous liberation of our meeting. The way she and Paris calmed me. None of this was forgotten, but it was cruelly neglected by me. At first I simply put off writing to tell her I'd fallen in love. Then, gradually, I began to realise I wasn't going to tell her. Now I shan't remain silent. I don't want to remain silent. My reply can't be the letter I didn't write then, and I'm not sure what it can be. She hints at sickness in her email and says that she has just read Françoise's translation of my latest novel. She then quotes from an interview of mine she found on the internet: *C'est moi, le 'woman friend' à qui Robert fait référence en parlant de son roman* Lovesong *sur son site: 'I sold my farm in the Araluen Valley and went to live in Paris, invited to go by a woman friend who, when she visited me at Araluen, had seen how jaded I was by my solitary life on the farm, and how unlikely I was to ever become a successful novelist if I were to remain there.'*

Reading in the interview my reference to those days, Ann must surely have known herself included in the world of my writing, and been made aware for the first time in more than forty years that I hadn't forgotten her. What I said in the interview might even have seemed to be a secret message to her. She was right when she said that I loved the farm and the lower valley: I did. I still love them. Until she provided me with a way out, I also hated and feared the farm and knew myself to be trapped there. Until Ann's invitation to dinner in Canberra I'd been deprived of my liberty.

I thought all day about what I would say in my letter to her. I wrote and rewrote that letter in my mind a hundred times. But I didn't write it in the email. I woke at two and couldn't get back to sleep. I lay in my bed till four, then I gave up the struggle and got out of bed and went out to the kitchen. The garden was in cold moonlight. Still and beautiful and silent. I made a cup of tea and took it into the sitting room. I put on the light and stood in front of the fireplace looking at Lena's painting of the open door—an open door through which another open door can be seen, the sense that someone has just left the room, the air still disturbed by their passing, the sense of loss. The picture is unfinished, as all her pictures were. She didn't like finished things. They silenced her, she said. There is no more to be said when something is finished. That was her claim. She hadn't given the picture a title but had left the enigma of it with me. Why must our memories always be touched by melancholy?

I sat on the couch, Lena's painting above the fireplace, a vertical image, a welcome distraction for me from my torment over the letter to Ann that I knew I must write. I sipped my tea and looked at Lena's picture. I was seeing her slip around the corner of the far room, leaving the house of her dreams. She was always sparing with colour, until the end. This painting came close to the end. Something was always held back and concealed from view. That knowing smile of hers. Her secret life.

I've been invited to speak to the women's book club in the prison again. I asked if the note-taking woman would be there. They told me she'd been released. I would have liked to meet her again. But I suppose something was settled at our first meeting. I always want more. I wanted more from Lena. Her withholding of herself was surely partly what kept us together. I only now seem to be fitting the pieces together at last. I shan't locate all the pieces, of course. How could I? Some things are not recoverable. Those missing pieces are the negative shapes in our stories. It is they that define for us what is really there. The inescapable truth of Lukács's horizon line. The sentence at the beginning of 'Comrade Pawel', my very first published story: *To our front, towards the west, stretched a plain without a single feature to interrupt the distant skyline.* Written half a century before I had thought of any of this, the resolute connections, the tyranny of narrative. Martin's voice in my ear transformed into my own truth.

I've always seen this late painting of Lena's as a depiction of the presence of absence, just as the note-taking woman in the prison read in my work a preoccupation with absent mothers. Perhaps there was something that Lena and I had both forgotten. Something we'd overlooked. Something left unresolved along the way—like the manuscript of my first attempt at *Frankie*. In my memory it still lies on the table in that Leichhardt flat.

She died suddenly. There was no warning. Abruptly, from one day to the next, Lena ceased to exist. Her death shocked me and left me with a terrible emptiness. She is one of my present dead. There are a number of them. Martin and Birte among them. They inhabit my soul.

The friendship that blossomed between us after we separated was far freer and more generous than our relationship as a married couple had ever been. Once we no longer lived together, once we'd got rid of the impediment of our vows, we were able to share the important things with each other. Separation cleared the decks for us to have the friendship I'd told her mother we should have had from the beginning. I haven't forgotten her terrible struggle, a far more painful struggle than mine ever was, the heroic way in which she made of her obsession with thinness a positive project, a form of self-protection, a way of becoming who she was physically as well as with her art. Her project was her body. The abandoned doll. I spoke to Lena on the Friday and wished her well for her trip to America. Then, at three in the morning, I received a call from the woman who shared the house with her. There was no traffic at that hour but all the same it was an hour and a half from here to the hospital in Melbourne. A nurse showed me into a small private room on the seventh floor.

There was a single bed in the room. Lena was lying on her side, her left arm out of the covers, dangling slackly over the edge of the bed. The nurse had not bothered to tuck her in properly. The room was cold. Strands of her thin hair were slicked across her face. She wasn't attached to any machinery. There were no wall connections in the room to fix machinery to. It was clear that no drips or other life-supporting apparatus were ever used in this little room. The room was dimly lit, the shade drawn half down over the window, partly obscuring a view across the city to the bay. The greenish glow of the first signs of a summer dawn.

I sat on the chair and gently pushed the strands of hair off Lena's face and tucked them behind her ear. I took her hand in mine. 'Well, you silly old thing. What did you want to go and do this for?' Her fingers slowly closed over mine, a sense of a grip; then, as if a wave passed through her, her fingers loosened again. I sat holding her slack hand in mine. The faint smell of something chemical, or just the smell of sickness. I couldn't detect any sign that she was breathing, but I knew she wasn't dead. I shall turn eighty at the end of this year. Lena and I were the same age, so it must be seventeen years ago now that she had the stroke. She was sixty-three. The same age as her mother had been when she had her fatal stroke. It was as if her mother's authority had hibernated in her for decades, waiting for its moment to make a lie of her daughter's claim, 'I'm fucking free!' A claim only a young person could have made. She had been due to fly to St Louis on Monday to view their famous collection of the works of the German Expressionist painter Max Beckmann. She adored Beckmann's work and was inspired by it to attempt things she might never otherwise have been bold enough to imagine. When I spoke to her on the phone that last time she told me she was feeling anxious about the trip. I told her it would be wonderful and to be sure to send me a Beckmann postcard. 'Just go and enjoy it!' I said. She had often cooled at the last minute and cancelled trips she'd spent years imagining and organising. 'It's important for you to see Beckmann.' She thanked me for stiffening her resolve. 'You're right. I'll be fine once I'm on the plane.' We were both silent a while, not wanting to hang up yet. I said playfully, 'Would you like me to come with you?' She said, 'Ah, if only.'

The nurse came in and whispered, 'Are you all right, Mr Crofts?'

When I answered her I also spoke in a soft voice, the noises from the rest of the hospital building distant and muted, night sounds, like the low light. 'You don't expect her to recover consciousness then?'

'I'm sorry, Mr Crofts, but I'm afraid there's no chance of her waking.'

The nurse and I looked at her. The nurse said something, touched my shoulder, and left the room. I said, 'They tell me you're dead. But I can't believe it.' I took Lena's hand in mine again and I leaned forward and kissed her forehead. 'Lena! Dearest friend and companion of all those struggling years of ours.' I pressed her cold hand to my forehead. The grief of her loss gripped me, and I wept. I had never felt closer to her than I did at that moment, nor more helplessly excluded from her presence.

I'd raised the blind and was watching the sun coming up over the bay, struggling through the haze of Melbourne's polluted air. It was a rather wonderful sight; the sun looked as if it was made of solid gold, an Inca mask of great weight being drawn up by a massive force from the depths of the past. When I turned around, wanting to tell Lena to look at the sunrise, I saw at once that she had gone. I was reminded once again that the dead have nothing in common with the living. I was never to see Lena again. When I scattered her ashes it was 25 September 2000. A stormy day, waves crashing onto the rocks off Red Bluff. The waves rising up and snatching at me. A real Lena day. I would have told her about it. When I shook her ashes from the canister the updraft caught them and flung them back in my face. My clothes and hair were plastered with a mixture of sea spume and her grey ashes. What a laugh she's having. The madness of it. Her will, to get me to walk along the old beach from those days together. And I did. She had her way. The wild girl in the elegant black swimsuit, out of my reach, having the last word. Lena.

What did we leave unsaid that still cries out in me to be said? To make something whole of *us*, after all, of what we were and what we strove for. Or is that too neat for life and death? The ragged ends of something incomplete and flawed, rather, a more likely ending. Closer to something we might dare to call our *truth*. The questions left unasked and unanswered.

66

It's a bright clear Saturday morning. I'll write to Ann today. She doesn't specify how serious or trivial her illness might be, and I am left to think the worst. My wife and I are sitting in the garden reading the papers and drinking our morning coffee under the apple tree. Our son and his family were up on the weekend and we're both feeling needed and reassured. The day is very still. There is not a breath of wind. Sitting under the leafless apple tree in the sun it is warm, a feeling of spring, the jonquils already out, their perfume heavy in the air. There is the noise of traffic along the nearby main road and the squabbling of the wattlebirds in the flowering gum, chasing the parrots away, then getting chased away themselves by the bigger birds, whose name I forget. The traffic noise too, it has increased greatly since we came here to live nearly twenty years ago. The Council put a set of traffic lights in, so now we get heavily loaded trucks and cars accelerating up the hill. It's become a drag race out there.

Our lives are a series of days.

Our neighbour, Harold, passed away. He was ninety-four. We'll go to his funeral.

→

I am suddenly awake. My bladder is on fire. My dream vanishes. Another day. I'll have to get up and take a piss. The air in my room is cold. There's no sign of the dawn around the rim of the curtains. I look at my watch. It's six o'clock. I've done well. I've slept for nearly seven hours straight. I get up and put on a t-shirt and my old grey dressing-gown. I don't put on the light in case it wakes my wife. On the way to the bathroom I turn up the dial on the heaters. After I've taken a piss I go into the kitchen and put the jug on. My wife calls, 'Are you making tea?'

I say, 'Did I wake you?'

'I was already awake.'

We have separate bedrooms these days. We both snore and have different sleeping habits. I pour two cups of tea and spread margarine thinly on two corn biscuits and I carry the tea into her room—sugar in mine but no milk, a little dash of the thin milk in hers. She moves her book aside to make room for the tea and biscuits and I set them on the bedside table. Her book is Hilary Mantel's *Bring Up the Bodies*. I say, 'How's it going?'

'It has improved.'

'As good as the first one?'

She hesitates, looking thoughtfully at the cover of the book. 'Yes,' she says at last. 'It is.'

I say, 'Did you sleep okay?'

'I had a beautiful sleep,' she says. 'What about you?'

'I had nearly seven hours straight.' This is a boast.

She pushes a pillow behind her back.

I bite into the biscuit and take a drink of tea. We sit in silence a while. Then I say, 'Now I must write the book about Martin.'

To celebrate the life of my dear friend Martin Bloch, a brave good man who never told his story, dead now so many years, but not dead to me. To find the broken fragments of his story and put them into an order that will redeem him from the silence. It is not, after all, what we find beyond Lukács's empty horizon, whether grace or damnation, that consoles us, but the search itself. So long as the horizon remains empty, we go on. To go on is everything. That is our salvation. And the deeper we look within ourselves the less we understand.

After breakfast I go into my study and open my emails. There are no more shocks. Only the demand in me that I write the letter now and don't put it off any longer. There are not another forty-three years to wait. Did I ever speak to Ann about Martin? I can't remember. They're linked now, the two of them, in these rearrangements of my memory. They've both returned to me, almost on the same day. It won't be possible for me to rest until I follow Martin's broken trail. His story appears to me like one of the fragmentary Roman wall paintings I stood and gazed at in Pompeii—a part of a figure here, then a gap, then another part of some other figure doing something else over there, then more gaps, the connections missing. I was in Melbourne when he died but I didn't attend his funeral. That lapse will need explaining. Birte never understood why I stayed away. I'm not sure she forgave me. When she asked me why, I told her, 'Martin and I had an understanding about these things.' She scoffed at this. 'What do you mean? What sort of understanding?' I was unable to explain what I meant. I believed Martin would have understood. I was young then. Now, in my eightieth year, I would go to his funeral. I would go for Birte's sake and for my own. And if I were leaving Paris now and meeting my wife again, I would write to Ann at once and not impose on her what must have been a painful and inexplicably cruel silence. If I had my time over I'd do many things differently.

I think of Ann and how we lay under the stars that night at the farewell party for her and Phil. We have all known such uncanny moments of remembering. But who can know the unconscious trigger of time and death and the connection of images long buried in the vast echoing vaults of the mind? Places lost long ago to consciousness. The great French novelist Marguerite Yourcenar, in her first novel, *Alexis*, said of this opacity, *If it is difficult to live, it is even more difficult to explain one's life.* And perhaps it isn't explanation that is needed, after all, but merely to remember. Did Ann spend a lifetime of devotion and study on the work of Yourcenar?

I turn my head to the right and see my pastel drawing of the fighting man, the ochre of his muscular body against the dark miasma that is threatening to engulf him from below. It is a portrait of myself as a young man. Suddenly I know what I must say to Ann. Hanging beside my drawing is Ed's portrait of his mother, the richly overworked green background of that picture always putting me in mind of the deeply satisfying green background in Dürer's portrait of Michael Wolgemut in Berlin's Gemäldegalerie. Phil was right: Ed was a fine artist. He did several drawings of Lena, catching exactly the strength of her skull and her jaw, seeing in her a strange, elusive and determined woman, seeing her beauty, seeing her inner struggle. These attributes were there in his wonderful little sketches. I regret that I've lost track of the little sketch of her he gave me. He said he would paint her portrait in oils but he never did. Over the years I've grown to love his portrait of his mother as greatly as Lena loved it, and to see in it some of the quality that might have been in an oil portrait of Lena if he had made one. Ed's portrait of his mother has become part of the aesthetic of my existence, a cherished relic from those days. On the bookshelves at the level of Ed's mother's portrait, and to the right of it, is the copy of Thomas Mann's *Doctor Faustus* given me by Martin.

My past is collected in this room, just as it is collected in the strange diffusion of memory and imagination from which I am drawing the substance of this book. Like certain unwelcome memories—which I would be content to discard if only they would agree to being discarded—these material relics from my past can't be denied their place in the story if I am to locate some part of my own and Lena's truth within it. A more telling relic than any of these hangs beside the small window in our sitting room: the narrow tonal impression in oil of a view into a room through a partly open door that I've already spoken about. The accumulation of planes and shadows and the receding zones of reflected light suggesting a swirl in the air among the indeterminate shadows, a suggestion of someone's passing, impossible to catch again or to pin down, but undeniably there. It is a successful painting of silence and absence. It was painted by Lena towards the end of her life. She came to our town on my sixtieth birthday and presented it to me. She had wrapped it in newspaper and tied it with string. The three of us stood at the kitchen table, Lena, myself and my wife. Lena said, 'It's what you've been waiting for from me all these years.' I took the parcel from her. 'It's what I've been waiting for from myself,' she said. At sixty she was an old woman. She and my wife, friends by then, stood and watched while I unwrapped it. I took the paper off and stood the picture on the table before me. I said, 'It's a self-portrait.' Lena and I looked at each other and I saw how happy she was that I had understood at once. For she had described in her painting not the essence but the passage of love.

Looking at Ed's portrait of his mother now—a portrait of a very definite presence—I find myself remembering Lena's delight with Ed and the way they played together, children in the cruelty of their innocence. With him she at last began to find her answer to the terrible conundrum that had tormented her for years. She saw Ed then with greater clarity than I saw him, without the misery of my prejudices and my failures. She saw the tides and the wild energy in the man below the glint and glitter of his facetious make-believe. In Ed she witnessed the quality of freedom she longed for—not a liberation from authority, as I had often thought, but a liberation from the compulsion to perform her duty. A liberation from the burden of her conscience, the severe legacy of her class, her school, and above all, her mother and her home, a mother whom she had loved and whom even in death she could not bear to disappoint. In Ed, Lena caught sight of a way out of her bind.

I'm sitting here looking at Ann's email address on the screen. I shall tell her of the great joy I have had from writing during my long life. I shall remind her that she saved my life and set me securely on my path. I shall tell her it was all worthwhile. I will tell her how important she has always been in my life. And I shall remind her of our great happiness as we stood together on that bridge in Paris, the snow falling softly around us in the silence, the astonishing moment of our happiness, a happiness that was never given the chance to erode into routine but which remains in my memory as a moment of perfection. Without you, I shall say, I would not have done any of it. I shall remind her of our moment in the fairy story when the evil wizard's spell is lifted and the lovers are restored to their former selves.

I type *Dear Ann*, then delete it and retype *Dearest Ann*, then correct that to *My dear Ann*, and then *My dearest Ann*. How else are we to address the past, except to frame it as our legend? That past which is us, that legend which is ours and which sustains us.

My dearest Ann,
If it is difficult to live, it is even more difficult to explain one's life . . .

Acknowledgements

I would like to express my heartfelt thanks to my publisher, Annette Barlow, and the team at Allen & Unwin.

All of Alex Miller's novels have been critically acclaimed and have won or been shortlisted in all of the major Australian literary awards. He is twice winner of Australia's premier literary prize, the Miles Franklin Literary Award, and is an overall winner of the Commonwealth Writers' Prize for *The Ancestor Game*. In 2015, *The Simplest Words*, Alex Miller's first collection of stories, memoir, commentary and poetry, was published to great acclaim.

Alex Miller is published internationally and his works have been widely translated. He lives in Victoria.

www.alexmiller.com.au